Jul
in   with RTÉ for   years
un   ...tion of her first novel, *Mary, Mary*, in 1998. Such was the
suc   of the novel, both critically and commercially, that she became a
ful   me writer. Her subsequent novels, *The Courtship Gift* (1999), *Eager To Please* (2000), *The Guilty Heart* (2003), *The Hourglass* (2005) and *I Saw You* (2008) were all published internationally and translated into many languages. Her novella *The Smoking Room* (2004) was part of the Open Door series. She adapted *The Guilty Heart* for a five-part radio series for RTÉ and has written two plays, *The Sweet Smell of Cigarette Smoke* and *The Serpent Beguiled Me*, both for RTÉ radio. She is married and lives in Dun Laoghaire, Co. Dublin.

Praise for *Mary, Mary*

'A beautifully written and harrowing first novel.' *Joyce Carol Oates*

'Julie Parsons takes the psychological suspense thriller to places it rarely dares to go in *Mary, Mary*, a first novel of astonishing emotional impact.' *The New York Times*

'An admirable, beautifully conceived work of a dark, compelling and original new voice.' *Sunday Independent*

Praise for *The Courtship Gift*

'*The Courtship Gift* superbly reinforces what has become obvious about Parsons' talent: that she is one of those rare authors who can successfully combine psychological insight, literary style and heart stopping suspense. Haunting, evocative and compelling!' *Jeffrey Deaver, author of* The Devil's Teardrop

'A mesmeric portrait of obsession and evil.' *Sunday Telegraph*

'A skilful, high-quality suspense thriller in the Ruth Rendell mode.' *The Times*

'A web of love, betrayal, deviancy and murder are interwoven in this slick, psychological thriller with its Pandora's box of shocking twists and turns.' *RTÉ Guide*

'Parsons is a truly talented writer and this novel has real impact.' *Irish News*

Praise for *Eager to Please*

'Brilliant. A star in the making.' *Minette Walters*

'A classy, riveting psychological suspense by a writer who deserves to be with the big names in crime fiction.' *The Bookseller*

'Parsons refreshes the palate with her elegant and imaginative style.' *The Times*

'Masterful ... the ending as bittersweet as it is satisfying.' *Sunday Times*

Praise for *The Guilty Heart*

'It is a remarkable book quite outside the usual run and ambitions of crime fiction.' *Sunday Telegraph*

'Parsons handles each character, each scene with characteristic tact and skill ... engaging ... poetic.' *The Irish Times*

'A mesmerising tale of obsessive love, harrowing loss and perverse appetites ... skilful and compelling characterisation and evocative descriptions.' *Irish Independent*

Praise for *The Hourglass*

'Another great accomplishment, even more deftly written ... it has a gripping, underlying menace that makes it a spell-binding read.' *Irish Independent*

'Here what lingers [is] the subtle atmosphere of threat the writer so deftly creates.' *The Irish Times*

'This is a dark, deeply disturbing read.' *The Examiner*

Praise for *I Saw You*

'Genuinely shocking, and definitely one for connoisseurs of crime fiction.' *Irish Independent*

'Tense filled pages and a spine-tingling story will keep you reading until the very end.' *RTÉ Guide*

'Here is a relentlessly dark psychological novel.' *Elle*

The Therapy House

The Therapy House

Julie Parsons

NEW ISLAND

THE THERAPY HOUSE
First published in 2017 by
New Island Books
16 Priory Office Park
Stillorgan
Co. Dublin
Ireland

www.newisland.ie

Print ISBN: 978-1-84840-577-6
Epub ISBN: 978-1-84840-578-3
Mobi ISBN: 978-1-84840-579-0

British Library Cataloguing Data.
A CIP catalogue record for this book is available from the British Library.

Typeset by JVR Creative India
Cover Design by Anna Morrison
Printed by POLAND, PUP Intokar, www.introkar.com

New Island received financial assistance from The Arts Council (*An Chomhairle Ealaíon*), 70 Merrion Square, Dublin 2, Ireland.

To us

The Beginning

It was a Sunday, the day Judge John Hegarty died.

Sunday, 7th July, 2013, to be precise. It was hot. Later the temperature would get up to twenty-six degrees, but even at nine in the morning, when the judge opened the heavy curtains in his bedroom, the sun was shining from a cloudless sky and he could already feel its warmth.

The judge needed to urinate. He stood at the toilet. He waited. The urine was a pathetic dribble with a faint colouring of blood. It was painful. His brother, Liam, younger by eight years, had told him to go to the doctor. He had ignored his advice.

He finished, flushed the toilet and turned to the basin to wash his hands. He scrutinised himself in the mirror above. He didn't look bad for a man in his late seventies. He'd lost his hair, but so had most. He hadn't put on much weight, unlike many. He still had his teeth, well, the ones that were visible. His mind was clear, about some things at least. He could, if asked, quote chapters, verbatim, from his old law books. He could still remember judgments he'd written. And of course he could recall testimonies, almost word for word, from the most important trials he'd conducted.

He assumed he had prostate cancer. After all, most men succumb to it sooner or later. But he had no intention of subjecting himself to the indignities of the rectal examination. He didn't want some overpaid urologist half his age poking and prodding, and not just his rectum and his penis. He knew the kinds of questions he would be asked, and he had no intention of answering them. No one's business how he was leading the final phase of his life. He could look after himself, for the time being at least.

He dressed carefully, as was his habit. Everything clean today; yesterday's clothes dropped into the linen basket. Mrs Maguire would deal with his washing on Monday. A white vest, and over it a navy blue linen shirt. He put on his favourite cream cotton trousers, a pair of light grey socks and his new Camper runners. They gave his sagging arches support, but without the ugly bulkiness of so many of the cheaper brands. He looked at himself in the pier glass in the bedroom and tightened his plaited leather belt one more notch. He'd lost weight. Who could eat in this weather? And he would not eat this morning. He was old-fashioned that way. Like his grandmother whose house he now owned. No food before Mass. Nothing in his stomach before Holy Communion. He could hear the church bell calling. He didn't want to be late.

He walked downstairs. The walls were lined with paintings. Liam had a good eye. In this regard the judge had taken his advice. He had bought prudently, Irish artists, twentieth century. They had all increased in value, even if they had taken a bit of a knock in the crash. He stopped for a moment to straighten a large abstract by Felim Egan. He had moved it to cover the space left when he sold the small Jack Yeats. A cash buyer. No questions asked. The money would solve the problem which had arisen recently. An indiscretion from his past. The judge wasn't too concerned. He had learned through the years that money solved most problems.

Ferdie, his black poodle, was waiting by the front door. The judge picked up his lead and clicked it onto the dog's collar. He checked the time on the grandfather clock's decorated face. The clock ticked slowly, steadily. He took his straw hat from the hall table, checked his pockets for keys, wallet, phone, glasses. Picked up his silver-topped cane and together, he and the dog walked out into the sunshine.

He'd gone to this same church when he was a boy, when he used to stay with his grandmother at weekends and during the summer holidays. Since he'd come back to live here again he'd been a daily communicant. The dog would wait outside, his lead slipped over the railings. The judge would go to his usual pew, five rows from the front.

He'd genuflect before the altar. He'd sit, kneel, stand. He'd pray, receive the host, and leave the church, blessed, sanctified, forgiven.

Breakfast then in his favourite café and wine bar in the row of shops just down the road. Anthony, the owner, would smile and wave him to his table at the back. A large cappuccino and a pain au chocolat. A bowl of water for Ferdie. The judge would eat and drink with pleasure. He would read the Sunday papers. He would watch the other customers come and go. They would nod and smile and he would nod and smile in return. He would hear the whispers.

'You know who he is, don't you? Senior counsel, Special Criminal Court, Supreme Court, retired now of course. Wonderful man.'

Before he left the wine bar, he'd buy a bottle of sherry. Today the judge chose Manzanilla. His neighbour, Gwen Gibbon and their mutual friend, Samuel Dudgeon, were coming for an early evening drink. Gwen loved her sherry. Samuel would take whatever was put in front of him. He and the judge would play backgammon. Samuel would win. Samuel always won. But the judge didn't mind. They would bet as they played. Small amounts. Samuel would pile up his winnings and put them in his pocket. The judge didn't mind that either.

They strolled then, the judge and Ferdie, along the sea front. The judge was tired. He had a nagging pain in his side. He turned for home. He would lie down and doze. It was quiet today. The house next door had recently been sold. Builders had moved in. During the week it was noisy. His sleep was disturbed, Ferdie was upset. But on Sundays peace was restored. He would lie down, dream and remember. He would enjoy. And later on the bell would ring. He would get up and walk downstairs. He would open the front door. And his life would come to an end.

Eventually Michael McLoughlin got the house for way below its asking price. The estate agent had said there were lots of other people interested and there were lots of people at the Saturday viewings. But even he could see that most weren't that bothered. They clustered in groups admiring the white marble fireplaces and elaborate cornices. But he spotted them tut-tutting over the lack of a decent kitchen, the rising damp in the basement and the spreading water marks on the attic ceilings. And weighing up how much it would cost to take down the plasterboard partitions which had divided up the large Victorian rooms, making the house feel institutional.

And there were some who came just to wander around, stopping to sit in the low chairs, their eyes blank, their bodies relaxed, their gestures unconscious. *The Therapy House* was the name on the brass plate fixed to the wall beside the black-painted front door. The same group of therapists and analysts had practiced here for years. And for years and years the depressed, the paranoid, the lonely, the heartbroken had come to them for help and healing. And now they came to say goodbye.

When finally McLoughlin got the keys, after all the months of wrangling and negotiating, as the cherry tree in the neat front garden flowered, lost its flowers, got its leaves, got its fruit, he stood in the hall listening to the house. Creaks, clicks, gentle sighs, a fly buzzing against a window, a tap dripping somewhere upstairs and the low hum of memories. All those stories. Loss, rejection, anger, hurt. Tears flowing. Voices raised. And then the gentle balm of understanding. The salve of acceptance and self-knowledge.

He looked around. He liked the feeling of the house. It was calm and warm. It was peaceful and protective. It would be a good place to live. The row of Victorian houses, the green in front, scattered with wooden benches and a small grove of silver birches at either end.

A project, that was what he needed now he was retired. Something practical. He'd restore the old house. It would be an investment as well as a home. And when he got too old for it, he'd move into the basement and rent out the rest.

He closed the front door and walked down the front steps. He turned and looked back. The sun glinted off the glass, a large bay window, with a smaller one beside it on the top floor and another at hall level. It was so hot today. Strange to feel the heat after the long cold winter which had lasted well into May, so that nothing had grown. Even the large lawn around his old house in Stepaside had been lifeless. When he got out the mower to give it a final cut before the *For Sale* sign went up, he barely filled one plastic sack with grass. Selling one house, buying another, he'd expected it to be a nightmare but it wasn't too bad. His neighbour with the riding school had been only too happy to swallow up his garden. A residential equestrian centre, that was what she wanted now. His house would be perfect. She paid the price up front. Cash. There must be money in horses, he thought. All those stallion fees, tax free. And as for this house, he'd spotted it in *The Irish Times* property section. He'd cut out the photograph and phoned the agent immediately. He'd offered low. They'd held out for more, but he was a cash buyer too. And these were straitened times.

He jiggled the keys in his hand. He locked the doors, the black painted one at the top of the granite steps, and the smaller red one, tucked in at the side, leading to the basement. He pulled the front gate to. It squeaked loudly and the latch clanged as he slotted it into place. He checked his watch. Just time to get to the airport, to catch the flight to Venice. He put his bag into the car boot. Turned for one last look at the house. Then drove away.

That trip to Venice. His first time. No one ever told him it could rain so much. St Mark's Square flooded, his feet wet, tiptoeing across the raised wooden walkways. In pursuit of an errant husband and his girlfriend. McLoughlin followed them around from four star hotel to swanky café to restaurant, leaning over canal bridges to watch them cuddling in a gondola. One good thing: everyone in Venice had a camera or a phone. Click, click, snap, snap. A thousand photos of the canals, the bridges, the squares, the pigeons. Nothing suspicious as he caught them in action. Hugging and kissing as they drank their cocktails.

McLoughlin could understand the attraction of the younger woman. The aggrieved wife was well into her fifties. Giving birth to five children had thickened her waist, dragged down her ample breasts, padded her large bottom. Worrying about the kids and her husband's expanding property business had carved deep lines across her forehead and around her mouth and eyes. Anger and resentment had given her voice an embittered tone.

'The bastard,' she said to McLoughlin when they met to discuss the job. 'The fucking bastard. She's not the first. But she's the youngest. I've had it, up to here.' And she drew a line above her thinning hair. 'I want out. Now. Before he goes bust. He's going bust, I know he is. I can still read a balance sheet. So I want what's mine before it all goes down the Swanee.'

But, Venice, well, McLoughlin was bored. After day one he'd got all the evidence he needed. But the wife had paid him to stay for the duration. Three days and four nights. There was more rain. The husband and his girlfriend disappeared into their hotel. McLoughlin brooded as he hung around outside. If only he'd known about the wet he'd have brought his wellies. He contemplated buying a pair but the damage to his shoes was already done and he was offended by the price the street traders were asking. That was another thing. No one had told him about the rip-off factor. Sure, the city was beautiful. Sure, it was unique. Sure, it was all those things. But it was also unbelievably expensive.

He wandered aimlessly, ducking into doorways to avoid the heaviest of the showers. He couldn't get a hang of the place. There was no logic, no rhyme or reason to its layout. Narrow streets and walkways twisted and turned back upon themselves. Slivers of canal appeared and disappeared and little bridges suddenly reared up in front of him with awkward flights of steps and stairs. Not a good place to be wheelchair-bound, he thought sourly as he rounded a corner and found himself in a square, with a large church, beautiful against the grey sky. He was tempted to go in, but there was a queue, a crowd of American teenagers, all iPhones and gleaming white teeth, so he kept going.

The rain had stopped and now it was hot. Sweat dripped down his back. He crossed a small canal, little more than a ditch, the stone of the bridge, ornate and carved. The streets here were narrow. High brick walls with greenery hanging over them. Metal gates which gave intriguing glimpses of courtyards, washing drying, a child's scooter, a cat sleeping in a patch of sunlight. And then another church. He looked down at his guidebook, and found its name. San Simeone Piccolo, a large green-coloured dome, copper he presumed, stone steps up to a portico supported by what the book described as Corinthian columns. He picked his way slowly towards the tall wooden doors, past the other tourists who were lounging in the shade cast by the building. But the doors were closed tight.

He turned around. The Grand Canal was in front of him, busy with boats of all sizes jostling for position at the landing stages. And on the other side, a low modern building, wide concrete steps leading up to it. Another glance at the guidebook confirmed it was the railway station, Stazione di Venezia, Santa Lucia. He moved down towards the water, looking for the bridge, turned to his right and crossed. He stood still, jostled and shoved by people with wheelie bags. Then he took a deep breath, slowly climbed the steps and pushed through the smudged glass doors.

That trip to Venice. His first time. He stood in the railway station and looked up at the departures board. Saw the name he wanted. Bassano del Grappa. A name he'd heard years ago, told to him by an old friend in Special Branch, who had a friend in Interpol.

'Bassano del Grappa,' Dominic Hayes had said, 'that's where James Reynolds is. My friend says the Italian police have him spotted.'

James Reynolds. A Thursday morning, 1975. A routine delivery of cash to a suburban post office. Children's allowance day. The security van had made the drop and gone. No problem. But there was a car parked on the double yellow lines by the traffic lights. Sergeant Joe McLoughlin walked towards it. A shotgun blast. He died on the spot.

James Reynolds. That was his name. The man who killed his father. All those headlines. For weeks after the funeral. After they'd sat at home and mourned him. After they were supposed to have moved on. But they hadn't. No trial. No recompense. No justice. Because James Reynolds was gone.

Bassano del Grappa, the name on the departures board. A small town at the foot of the Alps. Tourists in the summer, commerce in the winter. McLoughlin had got out his old school atlas. Found Venice, on the Adriatic, surrounded by water on all sides, then let his eyes move northwards from the green of the Veneto lowlands to the dull ochre of the higher ground closer to the Alps. And saw there, an inch and a half away, the name of the town. Would he go? Would he look for him? Would he have the nerve? Would he be brave? But somehow he never did. He put it off. He waited. For the right time.

A train leaving in five minutes. A sudden clutch in his stomach, and sweat again, this time cold across his forehead. He shovelled euros into the ticket machine, found the platform, climbed aboard and sank into his seat.

The flat countryside rolled past. Villages with their red-tiled roofs and gardens filled with tomato plants, lettuces, fig trees, the fruit not yet ripe, and vines, no sign of the luscious purple bunches of grapes that would soon festoon them. Flowers too, swags of bougainvillea, and fields with sunflowers, their yellow faces turning towards the sky. And in the distance, mountains dark grey topped with snow. The Italian Alps, he reckoned.

When the train stopped he got off and headed into the town. It was damp and gloomy. He walked along a street with a row of trees, their branches pruned into odd umbrella shapes. 'Il Viale dei Martiri', the sign said. Screwed into each tree trunk was a small framed photograph. Young men, named, and the same date. 26.9.1944. He walked slowly, looking at the pictures, then turned away, down a steep hill, through a series of small squares, towards the river which rushed through in spate. 'Il Fiume Brenta', the sign by the wooden covered bridge which crossed it. A strange structure, McLoughlin thought as he stopped to look at the pictures displayed on huge billboards. A ruined bridge, a ruined town. Destroyed, he read, many times, but most recently during the Second World War. Hard to believe, he thought, that it could now look so pretty, quiet and friendly. All that violence, all that destruction, but somehow so quickly forgotten. Like the Troubles at home. In the past now; another country. And again the clutch in his stomach, the sweat on his forehead.

Phone calls made regularly every year. Spoke to the superintendent in charge of the investigation.

'We don't forget our own, Mick. Your father, one of us. We'll find the fucker sooner or later. Problem is,' and there'd be a sigh, a pause, 'we don't have enough evidence. We couldn't extradite him, we certainly couldn't convict him. But,' again the pause, and the voice now suddenly cheerful, 'don't you be worrying Mick. We'll get him. Sooner or later.'

He stood on the bridge. It was crowded, thronged. He scanned the faces of the passers-by. He recognised no one. He was hungry, his stomach rumbling, a long time since the cappuccino and pastry he'd had for breakfast, standing at the counter of a café just off Piazza San Marco. Now he felt light headed, out of sorts. Not sure what he was doing here.

At the far side of the bridge was a bar, built so it was part of the embankment which dropped steeply to the river below. He peered in through the window. It looked fine, quiet, empty. He was served by a white-haired man with a brown leather apron. A glass of local beer, dark bread with a plate of salame, sausage and cheese which tasted smoked. He ate quickly. And noticed a black arrow stencilled on the wall, pointing down narrow stairs and the words 'Museo degli Alpini' neatly printed beside it. He stood, wiping his mouth, and gestured to the waiter and pointed to the sign.

'*Sì, sì signore. Il museo, molto interessante, sì,*' the waiter nodded encouragingly.

Downstairs was *molto interessante*. If you were interested in war, which McLoughlin was. If you were especially interested in the awfulness that men could visit upon each other. Which McLoughlin especially was. The history of the Alpine Regiment was displayed in grainy black and white photos stuck haphazardly on the walls. McLoughlin leaned forward to get a better view. There were bodies hanging from trees along a road. *I partizani*, the caption read. McLoughlin recognised the place. He had seen it this morning. The trees, the photos, the names. And beside these photos more of *gli Alpini* with their comrades, German soldiers, on the Russian front.

He worked his way around the small room. Below the windows the river slithered like a huge green snake, light reflected from its surface playing across the ceiling. Uniforms, faded khaki trousers and shirts, belts and holsters, guns, bayonets, grenades were displayed on the walls. A series of tableaux of wartime scenes. Models of nurses tending the wounded in a field hospital, and soldiers in a trench. And music too. Songs sung by strong male voices. He stopped to listen. He couldn't make out the words, but the sentiments were clearly expressed. We're all in it together. We're fighting for faith and fatherland and in the end we'll beat the buggers.

'*Interessante, no?*' The waiter from upstairs. He stood in the doorway, a duster in his hand.

'*Sì*, yes, very interesting,' McLoughlin pointed to the photographs of the soldiers in Russia. His guidebook Italian was exhausted. 'The Italian soldiers. They fight with the Germans?'

'Yes, allies then.' The man shrugged. 'Then we support Mussolini. But some people, no. The partisans, they hide in the mountains around the town and the Germans, they capture them, bring them down and they kill them, leave them hanging from the trees. Leave them there as a warning.' He pointed towards the photo. Then to another board. 'And some people are even more brave. See, look.'

McLoughlin moved closer. A photograph of a young man, handsome, strong, wearing the distinctive peaked Alpine hat with its feather, and beneath the picture a certificate from Yad Vashem. Benedetto a Beni, it said, had been honoured as one of the righteous of the nations for his bravery in saving persecuted Jews during the Holocaust period.

'Thank you,' he smiled at the man, 'it's very good for me to see all this. I come from Ireland. We didn't take part in the Second World War. We were, what was called neutral.'

'Yes,' the man nodded, 'I think you Irish. Your voice, you know.' The man turned towards the stairs. 'Come up. I give you special drink.'

The lights turned off automatically as they left the basement. Upstairs the sun had come out and the rain had stopped. The barman fiddled with a number of bottles.

'Here,' he pushed one forward. 'This, grappa. Very special. It has flavour. Fruit flavour. You try?'

'Very strong, *forte, fortissimo*,' McLoughlin could see the words on the sheet music on the old piano at home.

'Sì, *fortissimo*, but we drink only little. Not like you Irish and your whiskey.' He poured a measure into a small glass. McLoughlin picked it up gingerly.

'Taste. You like. My friend, my Irish friend, he like.' The barman smiled encouragingly. McLoughlin sipped. It was smooth on his tongue.

He nodded, 'It's a bit like the drink we make at home.'

'Poo-cheen.' The barman pronounced it carefully. 'Very nice. Jimmy, my friend, sometimes his friends bring him some.' The man topped up his glass. 'You know Jimmy?'

McLoughlin shook his head. He sipped again. He felt suddenly sick.

'Look, here,' The barman pulled a photo out from behind the row of bottles. 'His friends come here last summer. Very important people. They bring peace to Ireland.'

He slid the picture across the counter. McLoughlin leaned forward. He reached into his breast pocket and fumbled with his glasses. He hated wearing them, tried to forget he needed them, tried to pretend he could read without them. But now he put them on. The faces were familiar. He knew who they were. Everyone knew who they were and what they had done. Some had called them freedom fighters; others called them criminals. Now they were respected. Politicians. Leaders of the peace process.

A third man stood between them in the photograph. Not a household name like the others. Known only to those who could not forget. And now, here he was, in this pretty little town, north of Venice, below the Alps, by the river.

McLoughlin took off his glasses. He gestured to the photo, pointing at Reynolds.

'Jimmy?' he asked.

'Ahh,' the man nodded and smiled 'Jimmy, *sì*, Jimmy, *molto gentile*. He has the bar, the bar Irlandese. The Shamrock Bar.' He pronounced the words carefully.

The Shamrock Bar. McLoughlin had seen it advertised on the website where he booked his flight. Pints of Guinness and glasses of whiskey. Pool tables and darts. Live music every weekend. A photograph, a good-looking blonde woman standing in the doorway. The caption identified her. Monica Di Spina Reynolds. And a statement in English. 'My husband is Irish and I am Italian. We are very happy to welcome everyone. We offer Irish hospitality with Italian style and service. *Céad míle fáilte agus buon giorno.*'

He had written down the address in his notebook. Now he reached in his pocket and pulled it out, flicking through the pages.

'Shamrock Bar, Via del Fiume. Is that near here?'

'*Sì, vicino*,' the man pointed. 'Next turn, *a destra*.'

McLoughlin picked up his glass, and drained it. He paid his bill. He fumbled with the coins, his hands not quite steady. He stepped out into the street. Next turn, *a destra*, to the right, and the sign, the big green shamrock hanging over the footpath. He walked towards it and stopped outside the window. It was decorated with tricolours, thatched cottages, hurleys and girls with long red ringlets and Irish dancing costumes painted splashily across the glass.

The door to the bar stood open. He hesitated conscious that his heart had begun to race. He stepped away and rocked back and forth on the edge of the pavement. The street was noisy, traffic backed up. A woman approached. Small and blonde, dressed in jeans and a crisp white shirt. She smiled and gestured.

'*Buon giorno, signore, caffè? Una birra?*'

He noticed the logo above her right breast. The bright green shamrock embroidered above the name.

'*Per favore.*' She ushered him in. His footsteps were loud on the wooden floor. She ducked beneath the countertop. Dark mahogany, like the shelves behind. Decorated with old stout bottles and a jumble of bric-a-brac. Half-burnt candles in brass candlesticks, hardback books with faded covers, an assortment of mugs, biscuit tins, Jacob's Fig Rolls and Mikado, postcards showing typical Irish scenes, donkeys on a bog with two red-haired children, mountains misty and blue, jaunting cars by the lakes of Killarney. And framed, in pride of place, those three familiar faces.

McLoughlin stared at the photo. It had been taken here. They were leaning against the bar, pints of Guinness in their hands. All smiling. A happy scene. Old friends meeting up again. He couldn't take his eyes from the picture. His face felt stiff, fixed, immobile. The blonde woman was watching him.

'*Irlandese?* You from Ireland?

'Yes, Irish,' he nodded.

'You know these people?' she pointed. 'Old friends of my husband.' She reached up and tapped the glass with a long red nail.

He looked away.

She picked up a cloth and wiped the counter top.

'You like a cup of tea? We have Lyons Green Label or maybe you like Barry's? I put on the kettle.' She flicked a switch on the wall. 'My husband, he always say. First thing when you go in an Irish house they put on the kettle.'

'Your husband?' At last he was able to speak although his throat was tight and his mouth was dry.

'Yes, here,' she touched the glass on the photo. She busied herself with the tea. Gave it to him in a Belleek mug, pretty with its scattering of shamrocks. Offered him milk in a jug with the same pattern and sugar in a matching bowl. Put some biscuits on a plate. And chatted away, in English with a slight Dublin accent. About her husband, Jimmy, how they met in Spain, in Barcelona when he was teaching English and she was working in a bar. Summer job. How he had come back to Bassano with her. How they had a son, grown up, away at university in Rome.

'And do you ever go to Dublin?' he asked.

She shook her head. 'My husband's family, they all gone now. Jimmy likes it here. He says life in Bassano is better than Dublin.' She paused and shrugged. 'And since things got so bad in Ireland. No more Celtic Tiger, so,' she shrugged again. 'And Jimmy gets visitors. From time to time old friends come to see him. He catches up with what he calls the gossip.' She smiled as she took his mug and wiped down the counter. 'You like more tea? Or maybe something a bit stronger. We have whiskey here.' She stood on tiptoe to reach for a bottle of Jameson.

'No, really, that's fine. I have to go. A train,' he took his phone from his pocket and checked the time. 'I'll be late. Thanks.' He jingled money in his palm but she brushed it away.

'No, no charge. Not for a Dubliner like you.'

'A Dubliner?' He looked at her

'Of course, your accent. I know your accent. You sound like some of Jimmy's mates.' She pulled a rueful face, 'Not like the others. They speak with that accent from Belfast.'

He let her chatter on for a few more minutes, until he could bear it no longer. He looked again at his phone. Said goodbye and turned away. Pushed through the glass door into the fresh air. Outside he stopped for a moment and breathed in. It was hot now. He took off his jacket, slung it over his shoulder and turned abruptly. And found himself face to face. James Reynolds. Smaller than he seemed in the photos. Older now. His hair which had been black and curly was grey and thinning.

The stubble on his cheeks and chin was grey too. But he still looked fit and strong. Broad shoulders in a tight denim shirt. No beer belly pushing over his belt buckle. And when he looked at McLoughlin his gaze was thoughtful and wary.

Or was it? Did he even look at him? Did he even see him? Notice him? Their encounter lasted for no more than a few seconds. Just long enough for McLoughlin to say '*scusi*', as he brushed past. And for Reynolds to nod, step aside and turn to go into the bar. What happened after that McLoughlin didn't know. He didn't stop. He didn't look back. He didn't turn and grab him by the throat. Pin him to the wall. Spit on him. Punch him. Headbutt him. Kick him in the balls. Break his arm. Drag him to the ground. Stamp on his face. Smash in his wind pipe. Kick his head until his eyes rolled back into their sockets. He didn't do any of that. He just walked away.

Bassano del Grappa. The perfect opportunity. Serendipity had brought him here. And what had he done? He'd bottled it. He'd walked away, tears of shame blinding his eyes.

Samuel Dudgeon crossed the green slowly. He was going to the judge's house. He had arthritis in his hips, his knees and his spine. It hurt to walk. It hurt to do everything. He was wearing his heavy tweed coat. He cast a deep black shadow on the grass. He stopped to look at it. A hat, a coat, a bag, and the outline of a man.

He was cold. He was always cold. He knew it was hot today because the people he passed as he walked through the town were all wearing, well, they were wearing virtually nothing. Young women in shorts and tiny little tops which barely covered their breasts and stomachs. Young men with huge naked arms and legs, decorated with strange shapes. Coloured spirals up and down and around their biceps and thighs.

They looked at him. They laughed at him. Sometimes they shouted at him. He didn't respond. He just pulled his coat more tightly around his small, shrivelled frame and clutched his shopping bag. The coat was too big. It hung off his shoulders and the sleeves trailed over his gloved hands. Well, it would be too big, wouldn't it? It had belonged to the judge, but the judge had decided it was time to get a new one, and he had given it to Samuel.

'Here,' the judge said, one cold winter's day when they were sitting in front of the fire in the upstairs drawing room, 'here, Sam, you have this.'

And he dropped the coat on the floor where it lay, like a body, headless but with arms outstretched.

Today the judge had invited him to come for a drink. Sunday, early evening. Glasses of sherry. The backgammon board would be set up. There would be crackers and cheese, and perhaps a bowl of olives. The judge liked olives. Gwen Gibbon would be sitting as usual on the sofa. She would sip her sherry delicately and wipe her mouth on the small embroidered handkerchief she kept tucked up the left sleeve of her blouse.

The judge would throw the dice to see who would go first. Not that it mattered. Samuel knew the dice would favour him. And even if they didn't he could read the board so well he was at least two throws ahead every time. The judge would shout and roar, with pleasure or disappointment. He would bet, using the doubling cube. Samuel would bet too. He would watch the judge. He was still handsome. Not quite the way he had been when Samuel first met him, but the years had been kind to him. They had not been kind to Samuel.

He reached the house. The judge had given him keys. He let himself in to the basement. Inside it was cool and dark. He was early. It would be a while before he was expected upstairs to drink sherry and play backgammon.

He walked along the corridor to the kitchen. There was that familiar smell. Damp and decay. Upstairs the house was elegant and beautiful, filled with light. Down here it was dark and cold, the way it had always been.

Samuel stood in the doorway. Barred windows looked out into the judge's back garden. A tap dripped into a large white sink, stained with a green smear from the water. Beside it was a coal-fired range. The slates on the floor were cracked and dirty. Cobwebs hung in swags from the ceiling.

He moved towards the pine dresser which stood on the other side of the sink. Its shelves were bare, its drawers and small cupboards were open, emptied. He reached behind and pulled out a rectangular package. He placed it carefully on the square kitchen table whose surface was pitted by woodworm. He picked up his shopping bag. Inside were his tools. A chisel, a hammer, a screwdriver. He pulled the paper from the package. A woman's face looked up at him from behind glass. He turned the painting over. The judge had told him. *Take it out of its frame. Careful, mind, don't do any damage. It's worth a lot of money.* Samuel turned it around in his hands. The woman was young and beautiful. She was wearing a pale blue hat which was decorated with cherries. Her expression was solemn. *Worth a lot,* the judge had said. *Money, worth money.*

Samuel turned it over again and examined the frame. It was old and the joints were loose. They had been well made. The woodwork teacher in the prison where Samuel had spent so many years would have approved. He was a perfectionist. Samuel took off his gloves and picked up the chisel. It would be easy to prise the frame apart. And to do it without touching the pretty young woman with the pale blue hat. The judge would be pleased. He would pay him well.

He began to sing as he worked. A song he remembered from his childhood in England. The washer woman who came every Monday, she sang it. Her name was Nellie and she was from Ireland. She taught him the words.

Oh Mary, this London's a wonderful sight
With the people all working by day and by night.

He couldn't remember all of it now. Just snatches here and there.

Ladies. Peaches and cream. Sip. Lip. Mountains of Mourne. Sweep. Sea.

He concentrated carefully on what he was doing. His hands were bent and twisted. They didn't work as well as they used to. He had to be careful. He leaned over the painting. Time passed. He hummed the song. Outside in the garden a blackbird sang. And then he heard another sound. He lifted his head. A voice from upstairs. Calling out. He put down his chisel.

A voice from upstairs calling out. He moved quietly towards the steep stairs which led to the hall floor. He took one step, then another, then another. He stopped. He listened. The judge's voice.

Help me, help me, help me. Please

And another. Loud and threatening. Frightening.

Shut the fuck up. Who the fuck do you think you are, you fucking shit?

And a bang, loud, echoing through the house, so Samuel turned away. Moved backwards, slowly, carefully, then dropped to his knees. Crawled under the table. Hands over his head, heart banging under his ribs, his mouth dry, sweat beginning to run down his face.

The dog was barking, barking, yelping. Then there was silence. It seemed to last forever. Then footsteps on the stairs above. Running down. How far would he come? Samuel curled into a ball. Above him the front door closed, slammed shut. Then silence again.

He waited. He crawled from beneath the table. He put on his leather gloves. It didn't do to be without them for too long. His fingers would turn white with cold. He picked up his hammer and moved slowly towards the steep stairs again. Up and up, step by careful step. He walked out into the hall. Silence here, just the tick of the grandfather clock by the coat stand. He felt in his pocket for his keys. He locked the front door, the Chubb heavy in his hand. Then he turned. Up, up, up. Sunlight shining through the bay window in the drawing room, as he stood in the doorway. Sunlight falling across the body on the floor.

Samuel took a couple of steps closer. The judge must have been kneeling. He had fallen forward on his face. His hands were fastened behind his back, his feet too, tied together with plastic. Samuel tried to squat but his knees and hips said no. He dropped his hammer and reached out. He pressed his index finger against the judge's neck. There was no pulse. He stood and walked away from the judge and sat down on the sofa. He could hear the dog whining. He must be in the bathroom, he thought. Best to leave him there. Samuel didn't like dogs. His mother had a Pekinese when he was a child. It snuffled and waddled. And it bit.

He looked around. The room was just about the way it always was. But now the pale green carpet was stained and spattered with blood. The two chairs, covered with the same flowered material as the sofa, stood on either side of the fireplace. The grand piano was in the bay of the window. A vase filled with roses and peonies from the judge's garden decorated it. And above the mantelpiece hung the painting, the man in uniform, peaked cap, dull green tunic, Sam Browne belt slung diagonally across. Gun in its holster, gloved hands clasped. The man's eyes seemed to scan the room, to rest on his son's body, the gaping wound in his neck.

Samuel stood. He walked across to the portrait. He looked up at him. His name was Daniel Hegarty. He was famous. He was brave. He was a killer.

'Look,' he said. 'Look at your son'. And he smiled and saluted.

He moved back towards the judge. And saw the gun beside him. He recognised it. The famous gun. The same as the one in the portrait. Usually it was kept in the mahogany cabinet which stood against the wall by the door. With the peaked cap and the ammunition belt, the cigarette lighter, the pair of binoculars, the black fountain pen, the wallet, the leather-bound notebook, the pocket watch, the missal, the jet rosary beads. All had belonged to the man in the portrait. All had been admired, venerated. Relics, they were, holy relics.

Samuel bent down and picked up the gun. The judge always kept it clean. Never allowed anyone else to touch it. The cabinet was open and the drawer below too. Samuel reached into it and took out the special cloth which the judge used to polish the gun. Now Samuel shined it and put it back where it belonged. He polished the key to the cabinet, the lock, the glass. He rubbed carefully, then returned the cloth to the drawer. He closed it, locked it. He would put the key in the desk downstairs. That was where it should be.

He looked around. Nothing else out of place, but there were two glasses on the small table by the sofa. He walked over and picked them up. Smelt whiskey. Saw a cup and saucer on the floor. Picked that up too. Walked out of the room, looked into the judge's bedroom next door. Noticed a plate and cup by the unmade bed. Gathered them up. Walked downstairs. Checked the dining room. Remains of lunch still on the table. A soup bowl and spoon, a piece of toast, half eaten, a packet of cheddar cheese. He moved into the kitchen. The sink was full of dirty dishes. A loaf of bread on the countertop, crumbs everywhere. A pound of butter flowing from its wrapper in the heat. And on the floor a selection of bottles, beer, wine, and the remains of a takeaway in its carton, dumped.

It wouldn't do, Samuel thought. Not fair on Mrs Maguire. He took off his leather gloves. He put on Mrs Maguire's yellow rubber ones. He filled the sink with warm water. He washed and dried. He went to the hall cupboard and took out the hoover. As he pressed the button and the machine burst into a loud roar he heard the dog upstairs howling. That dog, he thought, he's always hated that sound.

He cleaned and polished. Upstairs and down. Then he was tired. He took off the rubber gloves. He put on his leather ones. He put his foot on the lever of the pedal bin in the kitchen. He took out the liner. He dropped the rubber gloves into it, then tied the top in a knot. Left it by the kitchen door.

The light was draining from the summer sky. Soon it would be dark. He needed to rest. He walked slowly back upstairs. The dog heard him and barked again, loudly, frantically. Samuel stopped outside the bathroom door. He wouldn't let him out. He peered in through the door to the drawing room. He saw his hammer where he had left it, beside the judge's body. He picked it up. The judge's eyes were open. They looked up at him. Samuel hefted the hammer in his right hand. He lifted it high. He brought it down. It smashed through the skin, the bones of the judge's face. He lifted it again. And again he let it drop. Now the judge's eyes were no longer looking at him and his handsome face was no longer handsome.

Samuel backed away, the hammer in his hand. He looked down at his shoes. They were spattered with blood. He knelt, untied the laces and slipped them off. Drops of blood, too, on the turn-ups of his trousers. He closed the shutters, then picked up the shoes. He hurried out and up the stairs up to the small attic. It was locked as always. No one went there except for the judge. It was forbidden. Now Samuel used his keys to open the door. The single bed was neatly made, a white sheet stretched tightly. He took off his trousers, folding them carefully, and lay back, covering himself with his coat. Beneath his head he could feel the hard outline of the judge's laptop, hidden under the pillow. Above him on the wall hung a large crucifix. Christ writhed in agony. The judge, too, had suffered here in this small attic room. He had suffered for his sins, his many, many sins. Samuel had heard him cry out. Samuel had seen the marks of pain on his clothes. Samuel had taken them home and washed them, used bleach, hung them out in the sun to dry.

And now that was all over. Samuel closed his eyes. He sighed deeply. It was all over now.

The plane from Venice landed at around 11 p.m.

McLoughlin watched the errant husband and the girl hurrying into the arrivals area. He watched them separate before they went through customs. She looked tearful. He looked hassled. He saw the aggrieved wife waiting at the barrier. Her husband greeted her effusively. A big bear hug, a sloppy kiss that just missed her mouth, and a large plastic bag thrust into her hand. As they turned, heading for the exit, she looked back. McLoughlin smiled and nodded. She didn't respond. He held up his phone. She raised an eyebrow. He'd call her tomorrow. Arrange to send her the evidence.

He went outside to wait for the shuttle bus to the car park. It was warm here too. Not as warm as Italy but a lot warmer than usual. Above the airport lights the moon hung in the dark sky. He felt unaccountably lonely. As the bus appeared, slowed and stopped, he clambered on board and stood leaning against the window. He found his car and got into it. He was unable to move. He couldn't get James Reynolds' face out of his mind's eye. He stared at his hands on the wheel. The skin across his knuckles was unmarked. It should be bruised and bleeding, he thought. Torn from the impact, festering. His shirt front should be spattered with Reynolds' blood.

He started up the engine and put the car into gear. He moved slowly towards the barrier. He turned out onto the road and headed for the M50. And then remembered. He didn't live high up above the city any longer. Now he lived down by the sea. In the old house. Three stories above garden, as the estate agents put it. A waste skip parked outside. The builders at work. He sighed and put his foot on the accelerator. Hardly any traffic at this time of night and before he knew it he was turning off the motorway, his back to the mountains and dropping down towards the coast. He pressed the button on the door. The windows slid open and he breathed deeply. Salt air filled his lungs. He felt calmer as he drove slowly through the town, quiet and peaceful, the sea just over the railings, the moon's silver reflecting in the dark water.

He turned inland and drove the quarter mile to Victoria Square. He parked outside his house. Stood for a moment looking around before taking his bag from the boot and bumping it up the steps to the front door. The houses on both sides were dark. No lights visible from the street. An old area. In the bad times families had moved out. The houses had been converted into flats and bedsits. Junkies had moved in. The desperate and poverty-stricken has stayed on. But recently, during the boom when property was gold dust, the square had become valuable again. When he'd driven through, trying to get a feel for the place before the contracts were signed, he could see the changes. Elegant gardens with clipped box hedges and paving. Front doors painted subtle shades of mauve and pink. Young families, SUVs with child seats, and scooters and small bikes propped against railings. Well-dressed men with children in buggies. One guy washing his car. He'd stopped to have a chat. The guy was friendly enough, but he could see it on his face when he mentioned he was interested in the house. Indifference, really. That was it. Touched perhaps with a taint of disapproval. Big houses like these, they were for families. And he saw himself through the younger man's eyes. Old, alone, childless. It brought the reality home. It was too late for so many things; to have children, to have a good relationship with a woman, to have all those supports and comforts which so many people take for granted. Even his friends were few and far between. Now that he was retired, all that easy camaraderie had gone. What was there left?

He fumbled in his pocket for the set of keys. He unlocked the door and let himself in. Dumped the case and his jacket in the hall and headed for the tiny kitchenette at the back. Pulled open the plastic duty free bag, undid the extra-large bottle of Powers Gold Label and poured a generous helping into a mug left on the draining board. Took a swig. Felt the warmth spread through his body. Opened the back door. The fresh night air poured in. There was a strong scent of jasmine. The neighbouring garden, he'd noticed, beautifully kept, close-clipped lawn, herbaceous border stuffed with colour. The old man, his straw hat tipped over his eyes as he moved carefully along the gravel path. And the dog, a black poodle at his feet, barking loudly when he noticed McLoughlin peering over the wall. So the man shook his index finger.

'Quiet, Ferdie, quiet.'

The dog took no notice, his bark with a slight growl of menace. The man turned to McLoughlin.

'Ignore him,' he said, 'worse than his bite. Hope you don't mind. Neighbours on the other side, both deaf. And not a problem when the house, your house now, was the therapists or whatever they were. Didn't pay much attention to anyone here really.'

And McLoughlin smiled and reassured him. He wouldn't notice it either. He liked dogs. A long time since he'd had one, but he'd an aunt who'd had poodles.

'Clever creatures, aren't they?' he said.

And the man nodded and agreed.

'Very clever. Don't deserve the lap-dog reputation. Hunting dogs originally. Here Ferdie,' and he clicked his fingers and the dog sat, and when he clicked his fingers again he held up his paw.

'Good boy,' the man patted the dog's curly head. Then looked up. Supreme Court judge, John Hegarty. Retired a few years ago. Ill health, the official reason. Ill health, could mean anything. Word in legal circles and that included the guards too, was that he was losing his marbles.

But whatever about his marbles he knew his garden inside out. Whenever McLoughlin looked out the back windows he saw him. He walked with a stick but he was well able to weed, using one of those kneelers, with arm rests. Popping up and down to root out a dandelion or a dock. Inspecting his plants carefully. Dahlias seemed to be a speciality. McLoughlin recognised the plants, in weathered terracotta pots. Not flowering yet, but their foliage already lush. The aunt was mad about them, the one with the poodles. His father's oldest sister, Aunt Bea, unmarried, some mystery about that, living in what had been the family home, a former council house not far from here. Of course she was long dead, and the house long sold, but McLoughlin remembered well the Sundays when his father wasn't working and they'd go and visit Aunt Bea and sit in her little kitchen drinking tea and eating her cherry buns. Delicious they were, and he'd go out into her neat little garden and play with Dooley, the poodle. Throwing a well-chewed tennis ball until inevitably he'd knock over a pot and Aunt Bea would appear in the doorway and summon him. A slap across the back of his head followed by a handful of wine gums.

Now he stood on the top step, the mug of whiskey in his hand. He felt calmer, not so distraught. Tomorrow was Monday. First thing he'd email the photos to the aggrieved wife. He wasn't mad about the private work but it paid well. Minus, of course, the agency's 10 per cent commission. The matrimonial was simple and straightforward. Maybe he'd try a bit of insurance fraud next. That might be more challenging. And tomorrow he'd give Dominic Hayes a call. He'd tell him about Reynolds, see what he had to say.

He stepped back inside, drained the last drops from the mug and rinsed it out. It was depressing, this little cupboard of a kitchen. No room to put anything. A tiny Belling hot plate, no worktops, a miserable-sized sink. He couldn't wait for it all to be ripped out. The large room next door, the dining room when the houses were first built, was to be his new kitchen. He'd pored over the plans, putting it all together. Braved IKEA to get his huge pot drawers and cupboards. Gone to his favourite electrical shop to buy the hob, double oven, fridge freezer. Chosen a black granite worktop. A black limestone floor for the work area and Iroko wood for the rest. He'd feel better then when it was all done, when he could cook and eat, and order had been restored.

He walked through the house, turning off lights, and went upstairs to the room at the back where he was sleeping on a mattress. Once it had been used for meditation. There was still a strong smell of incense.

He opened the sash window up high, then stripped off his clothes. He settled himself, pulling the duvet up to his waist. He closed his eyes. It was quiet now. He sighed and turned over. His breathing slowed and calmed. He slept.

Woke suddenly. His heart was thumping, something wet on his face. He lifted a hand to wipe it and was certain, for a moment, that it was blood. But it was tears, streaming down his cheeks. How long since he had last cried? He lay back on his pillow, taking long deep breaths. Then he sank into sleep once more. Until he woke again. This time slowly, stirring uneasily, something banging away in his head. A sound, repetitive, irritating. He rolled over. A shaft of light caught his eyes so he put his hand up to cover them. Checked his phone. Six a.m. As bright as mid-day now.

He pulled himself up off the floor. Awkward, difficult, he'd have to see about getting something a bit more comfortable. He reached out to the windowsill for support and kneeled, looking into the garden. Just about to pull over the shutters but there was that sound. He stuck his head through the open window and listened. A dog barking. Christ, was he going to have to put up with this every morning? He listened again. Maybe it wasn't that bad. If he closed the window he probably wouldn't hear it. He didn't want to get into a row with the old man. Not about the dog. He grabbed hold of the edge of the window and gave it a tug. It dropped down with a bang, so the glass rattled. Sash cords gone. Something else to be added to the list, the endless list. Maybe the project wasn't such a good idea. He could have bought an apartment, brand new, walk-in condition, all mod cons.

He closed the shutters and lay back on his mattress. He'd doze until eight and then he'd start the day. But sleep wouldn't come. He tossed and turned. Dust rose from the floorboards beneath him. It made him sneeze and his eyes prickled and burned. Eventually he pulled himself upright and opened the shutters again. Light poured in. He stood, pulled on a pair of underpants and stepped out onto the landing. He looked around, then turned towards the room at the front. Once it had been large and spacious with high ceilings spanning the house. Now a plasterboard partition cut it in two. He padded in his bare feet across the threadbare carpet and pushed open the door to the second room. This was bigger, with the bay window giving more light. Yoga classes had been held here, so he had been told. The teacher was well known. He had a feeling that Janey might have come here for weekend workshops. She'd loved all that kind of thing. He remembered how happy they'd been when they first got married. But somewhere along the way it had all gone wrong. The miscarriages hadn't helped. Every year, year after year, the same sequence. Hope, excitement, a future to be anticipated. And then the fear. Sudden pain, bleeding, a frantic phone call. Go to bed, he'd say, I'll be home soon. But sometimes he wouldn't make it in time. She'd already have gone to hospital. She'd be hooked up to the machines. And they'd watch for the foetal heartbeat. And then he'd go back to work again.

He sighed. No point in dragging it all up. He hadn't seen her for years. He didn't even know where she was living now. Or what she was doing. Or who she was with.

He stood with his feet together, then bent forward. He rested his fingertips on the floor, then stretched his legs back into a downward facing dog. He'd learned yoga too. Part of his pre-retirement course. It was much more difficult than it looked. Some of the other lads had sneered, but they were silenced by how much it took out of them. Dog, plank, pigeon, triangle, the warrior poses, the sun salutations.

He worked his way through a simple sequence. As he stretched and moved from pose to pose his breathing deepened. He could feel sweat prickling his armpits and his forehead and the back of his neck was damp. He sank down, his legs and arms stretched out, then rolled over onto his back. And in the silence he heard the sound again. Muffled, faint, but unmistakeable. The bloody dog was still barking.

He pulled on a T-shirt and jeans and shoved his feet into sandals, then went downstairs and out onto the footpath. He looked up at his neighbour's house. He ran up the steps to the front door and rang the bell, then peered through the glass panel beside it. A polished floor, a rug, a large vase of flowers on a table. He waited for a few minutes. All he could hear was the dog barking.

He returned to his own house and walked through to the back door, down the steps and into the garden. Again he scanned his neighbour's windows. Nothing here either, but the sound of barking was louder now. He moved along the wall between the two gardens. On his side thick ivy had cloaked the granite. A dense mass of leaves and twisted tendrils as thick as his fist. Nettles here too, and he winced as he brushed against them. He turned to the wall and stood with his hands on the top. He lifted one leg to try and get purchase and felt something. Wooden, not stone like the rest of it. He pulled at the ivy, dragging it away and revealed a door, old and rotten and as he shoved it with his shoulder it gave way. He stumbled through, cursing softly as he lost his footing and slipped and fell, catching himself on the thorns of a rose. Shit, he'd made a mess. Crashed into a row of pretty bedding plants. He moved his feet off the flower bed and straightened up. Felt suddenly an intruder. Hoped no one was watching. Wasn't sure how he would explain his presence. But now he was here he'd better go and apologise. Maybe tell the judge he was a former garda. Remind him of the trials they'd both taken part in. A few he remembered in particular. When Hegarty was on the bench in the Special Criminal Court.

He moved quickly through the garden towards the house. A birdbath with a stone bird sipping the water was placed in the middle of the lawn, and a bronze sundial was framed by a clipped box hedge. And there were the same wooden steps, like his, leading towards a door. He took a deep breath and climbed them. A French window led into what was obviously the dining room. He could see a long mahogany table and a matching sideboard. Paintings hanging on the walls.

He leaned forward. He would knock, softly at first, hoping that the judge might be up and about. But as he touched the door it swung open. He took a step and called out.

'Hallo? Anyone home?'

He waited. No human sound, just the dog, his yap more high-pitched.

'Hallo, it's just me, your neighbour.' McLoughlin moved slowly into the room. He stood by the table. He dropped a hand to stroke its shiny surface. Again he called out.

'Hallo?' This time a question in his voice. But the only answer was coming from the dog, somewhere above.

McLoughlin walked through the dining room and into the hall. He turned towards the stairs. He called again. But again all he heard was the insistent yapping. He moved towards the sound. The stairs curled up ahead. A Persian-style runner covered them and the walls were hung, like the dining room, with paintings. Light poured from a skylight.

He reached the second landing. More doors, all closed. The noise was still coming from above. Another set of stairs, one door opening into a bedroom, and another shut tight. He opened it and the dog rushed out. Yapping, jumping, his short tail wagging furiously. McLoughlin opened the door further. A small bathroom, a strong smell, the floor filthy and awash with urine. He closed it quickly and turned back. The dog had disappeared but he could hear him still. Whining now, a fretful, anxious sound. Jumping up, his claws scrabbling against the door to the big room at the front of the house, hitting the round crystal handle so it swung open and he disappeared into the darkness inside.

'Here, come here Ferdie,' McLoughlin stood waiting on the threshold as the dog appeared again. He bent down and held out his hand. The dog rushed towards him. McLoughlin clicked his fingers and the dog sat. He clicked his fingers again and the dog put up his paw. McLoughlin reached out. It felt wet and sticky. All that mess in the bathroom. He put his hand in his pocket for a handkerchief and wiped his fingers. And saw. The handkerchief was covered in red streaks. He made a lunge for the dog's collar but the dog jumped away, twisting, turning, yapping as he darted back. McLoughlin followed him. The room was dark, shafts of sunlight coming from around the edges of the closed shutters. One shone across a chair, overturned on the floor. McLoughlin stretched out his hand, reaching his fingertips across the raised flock of the wall paper. He felt the smooth metal, the light switch. He pressed down. Instantly the darkness disappeared and he saw, beside the chair, a man, lying, legs together, a bloody mess where his head should have been, and a dark spatter across the pale green carpet. And the dog, now whining, nudging the man with his nose, then running off, red paw prints decorating the floor, then running back again, sniffing the man's head, whining, then running away, twisting in a circle, and everywhere those red, sticky prints.

McLoughlin reached out for Ferdie, grabbing a handful of his curly coat. The dog yelped in pain and tried to twist away but McLoughlin lifted him up, holding him tightly. As Ferdie's head turned, he sank his teeth into McLoughlin's hand, just below his thumb.

'Fuck,' McLoughlin shouted and nearly dropped the dog, but he clung on, bundling him out of the room, up the stairs and half threw him back into the bathroom, closing the door tightly. He looked down at himself. His white T-shirt was smeared with red. Blood dripped from the sickle-shaped wound in his hand. He wanted to go and wash it, but first things first. He wrapped the handkerchief clumsily around it, and ran back, towards the room at the front of the house.

Upstairs, in the attic room Samuel sat up. The dog was barking, more loudly. He could hear another sound. A voice, shouting. A voice he didn't recognise. He stood and pulled on his trousers. He shoved his feet into his shoes. The blood was dried now. He laced them tightly, then stood and put on his coat. He picked up the hammer, and pulled the laptop from beneath the pillow He opened the door and stepped quietly out onto the attic landing. He looked down. He couldn't see anyone below.

Then a man, holding the dog. The dog struggling, twisting and turning. The man shouting in pain. Throwing the dog into the bathroom. Turning away. Running into the judge's drawing room.

Samuel moved then. As quickly as he could. Down the stairs. Tiptoeing. Holding the hammer, the laptop, his coat pulled around him. Down to the kitchen, picking up the bin liner, then into the dining room. The door to the garden standing open. Closing it behind him.

Then remembering. The judge always said, *I'm giving you keys, Sam, but make sure to lock up*. Locking up now. Then quickly, down the steps. Opening the door to the basement. Locking it behind him. Rushing into the kitchen. The painting, the chisel, the screwdriver, the hammer, the laptop. All in his shopping bag. Hurry, hurry, hurry. Out through the door to the front garden. Stopping to lock it. Keep everything safe. Then up the path to the road. And hurry, hurry, hurry. Hurry home.

McLoughlin circled the man on the floor. It was the judge, no doubt about that. His hands were fastened behind his back with plastic ties. His feet too were locked together. McLoughlin knelt down to get a better view. Something like an entrance wound through the nape of his neck. There wasn't much left of his face. Blood, bone and brain tissue on the carpet. He could see that rigor mortis had set in.

He stood up and backed away, conscious that he was disturbing what was now a crime scene. He felt in his pocket for his phone. As he pressed the numbers 999, it occurred to him that he'd never used them before. A first time for everything, he thought, as he heard the voice say:

'Which service please?'

The guard was going from house to house. Gwen Gibbon sat on the wooden bench in her small front garden and watched. He had taken off his cap and his shirt sleeves were rolled up to his elbows. A handsome young man, tall and fair, with a clipboard in one hand, and a pen in the other. Looking at him as he walked briskly up the steps to the front doors, she marvelled at the size of people these days. She remembered when she was a child living here in this same square, in this same house, must be back in the 1920s. So many of the people she would see in the streets of the town were small, undernourished, their legs bowed with rickets, teeth missing, hair shaved, signs of ringworm on their skinny white arms. But that was a long time ago. People didn't look like that now.

The word in the square was that the judge had been murdered on Sunday evening. The same evening that she and Samuel Dudgeon had been invited for sherry. She'd left home just after six. She'd walked across the grass but as she stepped onto the road she had tripped and fallen. Landed smack down on her knees, her head too, hitting the hard surface. She had cried. Couldn't get up. Had lain, prone, shocked. And that nice lady, Elizabeth Fannin, one of the therapists from the house next door to the judge, had passed by, had stopped, knelt beside her, helped her to sit. Tried to staunch the flow of blood from her knees, her hands, her forehead. And said,

'I'll take you to hospital. I have my car here.'

Gwen had protested. She was fine. She just needed to rest. But Elizabeth Fannin overruled her protests. She had driven her to A&E, stayed with her for hours until she was seen by a doctor, who checked that she wasn't concussed, patched up her wounds, and sent her home.

Now Gwen shifted awkwardly on the bench's wooden slats. She should have got a cushion from the sofa. She was thin, even thinner than usual. She seemed to have lost her appetite. The heat of course, it was so hot these days. Unnaturally hot, although down in the basement where she lived it was cool, a chill which no amount of sun could banish. Back in the old days, the days when the children in the town had rickets and ringworm, Gwen and her father and mother, and her older brother William, had lived upstairs. Hall floor and first floor. Large, spacious rooms, warm and comfortable. A maid slept in the tiny box room at the back, beside the kitchen. There was a grand piano in the drawing room. And on days like this when the sun shone and the sky was cloudless Mummy would put a table in the back garden and they'd have tea there, the big silver pot, sandwiches with their crusts cut off, a jam sponge and a large bowl filled with strawberries, a jug of cream and sugar for sprinkling.

Gwen's mouth watered as she thought about it. Of course strawberries tasted of something then, not like the insipid pink mush that she had bought in the supermarket the other day. Cheap they were, on special offer, piled up on the stand by the entrance, a large sign in luminous pink. *2 for 1.* So she fumbled in her purse for her last few cents and splashed out. And regretted it when she poured them from their plastic punnet into a bowl. Half of them were mouldy and the other half were about to be. She tried to pull the green stalk from one and it squished between her fingers. Pale juice dribbled down her wrist. And when she lifted her arm and licked, there was no taste at all.

Gwen closed her eyes. She didn't sleep much. Death, it seemed, was hovering, waiting to snatch her away. A cold breath against her cheek. So she would sit up, her heart pounding with a sudden choking fear. Then she would chide herself, *Silly old thing, you really are a silly old thing. Beginning to show all of your ninety-one years.*

Ninety-one years a Christian, that was what Mummy would have said. But Mummy was long gone. Lying in the family grave in Dean's Grange cemetery with her husband, Thomas, who had died many years earlier. Gwen hadn't visited the grave for a couple of months. It was too difficult. She would have to walk into the town to get the bus. Then get off at the crossroads and walk to the graveyard's large wrought iron gate. The last time she went the judge had taken her. He had ordered a taxi and insisted on paying. She had gone to the Protestant section to put a big bunch of yellow chrysanthemums on her parents' grave. The judge had turned in the opposite direction towards the monument to his father and the other men who had died in the struggle for Irish freedom. Laid a wreath of laurel with a green, white and orange ribbon that flapped in the cold breeze, whipping across the rows of headstones.

Yesterday Gwen had stood outside the judge's house and watched his coffin being manoeuvred down the steps and into the hearse. Hard to believe that the man she had known since he was a boy, when he would come to their house and her mother would teach him the piano, was inside that dark wooden box.

A small crowd had gathered. Gwen knew most of them to see. Hardly any now to speak to. None of the old neighbours were still in the square. Gwen was the last of them. The house where she had lived all her life had been sold many times, most recently a couple of years ago. The new owner, a young woman with bright lipstick and very high heels, had paid her a visit. Told her she wanted her out. She was going to renovate the basement. Turn it into two apartments. Rent them for many multiples, yes that was the what she said, many multiples of what Gwen was paying.

'You can't evict me,' Gwen had stood. Tried to hide her trembling hands. 'I'm a sitting tenant. My tenure is protected.'

The young woman had shrugged. Picked up her large leather bag with its clanking gold handle. Fiddled with her phone.

'We'll see about that,' she had replied. Left Gwen with her stomach in a knot. Her legs shaking. She had asked Samuel Dudgeon for advice. After all, he was a solicitor. But he shook his head. Said he wasn't sure about Irish law, and anyway what did he know about anything? Now, after his years in prison. He suggested she speak to the judge. Of course, the judge, the obvious person. And the judge had reassured her. They sat in his beautiful drawing room, the portrait, the piano, the pale green carpet. The judge had given her tea in a porcelain cup and reassured her.

'No one can touch you. You're safe,' he had said and handed her his clean white handkerchief as tears fell down her pale cheeks.

And then the housing crash had come. The young woman had vanished. Life had returned to normal. However, Gwen didn't like what she was reading in *The Irish Times*. There was talk of prices rising. She prayed. 'Dear God, protect my home. Keep me safe until I am ready to come to you.'

She had stood outside the judge's house in the warm evening sun. Her knees were aching. She felt unsteady. Someone had started the rosary. Gwen bowed her head. The rosary wasn't her prayer although she knew the words.

Hail Mary, full of grace, the Lord is with thee. Blessed art thou amongst women and blessed is the fruit of thy womb, Jesus.

The voices droned softly. Gwen looked around. She clutched the small bouquet she had picked from her garden. Alchemilla mollis, green and frothy, a few marigolds, and some cornflowers. And she added into the bouquet some of the sweet pea that the nice young man had given her. The handsome young man, tall and slim with short black hair and eyes as blue as the sky behind his round gold-rimmed glasses. The friendly young man who'd stopped and chatted, one day a couple of weeks ago, then come back with the flowers. Thrust his nose into them, and said, 'Smell, they're amazing.' While his friend, the chubby boy with the bright red hair, had hawked and spat phlegm on the footpath. And the handsome young man had chided him, told him off, told him to say sorry to the nice lady.

She stepped forward and pushed through the crowd. The crime scene tape was still in place. She held out the flowers. A policewoman, her fair hair scraped up into a ponytail, took them. She smiled her thanks. She bent down and placed them beside the gate. Gwen stepped back and stood in the crowd, listening to the rosary as the judge was carried down the steps and taken away. And she wondered, if she hadn't fallen, if she hadn't gone to hospital, would he still be alive?

Now her front gate clanked. She looked up. The shadow of the tall guard, his uniform neat, fell across her.

'Excuse me, do you mind if I ask you a few questions?' He smiled.

'Of course not. Here,' she patted the bench. 'Sit here. I'd be delighted, if I can be of any help. You're hot, can I get you a drink?' Gwen got her to feet.

'No, really, I'm fine,' he tried to protest. But she disappeared inside, and came back with a glass of water.

'Here,' she held it out. 'With a slice of mint, I hope you like it.'

He smiled again, took the glass and swallowed its contents in one go. She watched his Adam's Apple jerking rhythmically as he drank. She could smell his sweat. It had been many years since she had smelt a young man. He smelt alive. Not like me, she thought, her body cold and dry.

The guard handed her the empty glass.

'Thank you, that was just what I needed. Now,' he picked up his pen, 'can I ask your name?'

He took her details. Name, age, marital status. He asked if she lived alone. She did, she said, for many years.

'And how long have you been here?' he looked at her.

'Forever, actually. I was born upstairs,' and she pointed, 'in the big bedroom on the second floor.'

'Born there, not in hospital?' he sounded surprised.

'Oh yes, everyone then, in those days, they were all born at home. It was the way it was done.'

'And was it safe?' he seemed interested. 'My wife, you see, she's having a baby in a few months' time. She wants a home birth, but I'm not sure about it.'

'Safe,' she pondered the question. 'Well, I suppose nowadays you'd say it wasn't. Sometimes babies died. Sometimes mothers died too. But mostly it was all right. The doctor came for me. The doctor didn't always come, but I was early. Sudden, unexpected.'

Her mother's waters had broken as she was walking the pier, a Sunday afternoon in summer, the sky and sea blue, and the town alive with visitors. Her father had called a horse-drawn cab from the stand along by the front and they had got home quickly. He had sent the maid for the doctor. By the time he arrived the baby was just about ready to come. There was blood, a lot of blood. Gwen still used some of the old bed linen, and some of it still had a faint brown stain.

'Now,' she sat up straight. 'You're not here for my stories. You're here because John Hegarty is dead. So, how can I help you?'

'You knew him, did you?' The young man's eyes were the dark blue of the Delphiniums her mother used to grow.

'Oh yes, I like to think we were friends.' She peered at him over her glasses. 'He was a generous man. Loved to entertain.'

And she told him. The day the judge died. She and Samuel Dudgeon, another friend, had been invited for a drink.

'Sherry it would have been. John knew I liked sherry.'

'And,' the guard's hand flew over the page. His hand, smooth, without wrinkles or age spots. His joints mobile and flexible. She clasped her hands together and tried to hide them in the folds of her skirt. They were ugly, red, the knuckles swollen and misshapen. 'The other person, Samuel did you say?'

'Yes, that's right. Samuel Dudgeon,' she spelt out his surname. 'He's English, actually. He's been living here for the last few years. He plays backgammon with the judge.'

'Backgammon?' the guard looked up.

'You know, the board game. Dice, red and white counters. Not my thing but the judge and Samuel, they love it, well,' she paused, 'they loved it, I suppose I should say. Anyway I didn't get there, unfortunately.' And she explained. The fall, the bleeding, Elizabeth Fannin picking her up, the trip to hospital, the endless waiting. She pushed out her leg and lifted her skirt, just a little so he could see the dressing below the knee. He bent over to get a better look.

'It's very bruised. It must have hurt.' His voice was concerned.

She nodded. 'It did hurt, but a lot of fuss about nothing. Not the end of the world.'

'And that,' he pointed his pen towards her forehead and another big bruise. 'I was going to ask. Did that happen at the same time?'

She nodded again. 'Silly me, I'm a silly old thing. I'm supposed to use my stick, but such a nuisance.'

He asked her again. What time had she crossed the square? Where exactly had she fallen? How long had she been there before the other lady came along. Took Elizabeth's name. Asked for her address but Gwen didn't know it.

'And as you were there on the grass, did you notice anything. Anything unusual? Out of the ordinary?'

She shook her head. 'Nothing, but I wasn't in a fit state to be a Miss Marple if you know what I mean.'

He wrote it all down, then asked her if she had an address or phone number for the other person, 'Mr…' He consulted his notes.

'Dudgeon, Mr Dudgeon.' She smiled at him. 'An address, not as such, but I do know where he lives.' And she explained that he had got housing from the council. A little complex just past the church and the shops. It was for single people, men mostly. 'It was the judge actually. He helped Samuel get the flat.'

She frowned. She hadn't approved. The judge had what they called 'pull'. Political connections. Her father had drummed it into her. His disapproval of that way of doing business. Years ago, before he had died he had said, 'Nowadays it's all about who you know,' his mouth turning down in despair.

The guard stood, thanked her. Said she should remember to use her stick. 'It's the same with my gran. She hated it. But she fell too, a few times. Last time she broke her hip.'

Gwen got to her feet, slowly, stumbling a little. 'Gosh, poor thing. I hope she's all right now.'

'She's in a nursing home. She's not happy, but,' he shrugged and walked towards the front gate. He put on his cap, turned back and saluted her, 'Thanks very much Miss Gibbon. You've been a great help.'

'So, tell me, the judge. What's the story?'

They were in Dominic Hayes' spacious sitting room four stories above the town. A new apartment in one of the blocks across from the DART station. Steel and smoked glass from the outside, inside bright and clean and easy to keep. A view right over the harbour, and Howth Head like a brooding crocodile in the distance.

Dom's wife was standing at the huge window which opened onto a wide balcony. She was pressing her hands against the glass and moving in tiny steps from side to side. From behind she looked perfectly fine. A woman in her late fifties, still slim, her figure neat, her hair in tightly permed curls, wearing a knee-length skirt and a white blouse, with fluffy pink slippers on her feet. From the front she looked almost all right, except that there was a blankness in her expression, an inability to make eye contact. Now she stayed at the window, her hands pressed to the glass as she inched from left to right.

McLoughlin sipped his coffee. It was surprisingly good. Produced from the swanky machine installed in Dom's shiny new kitchen. 'Mmm, that's delicious.' He drank again. 'Cost much? The machine?'

'Came with the place. I bought the show apartment. Fully fitted, fully furnished. Didn't have to do a thing.' Dom settled himself into the large leather sofa. It squeaked gently beneath his bulk.

'Great, lucky you. I'm beginning to wish I'd gone for a new build. All this renovation, refurbishment as they call it. Costs a fortune and one hassle after another.' McLoughlin stretched his legs. His back was sore. Sleeping on the mattress wasn't good for it.

'Well, it was the easiest option really,' Dom shifted uneasily, 'the way Joanne is, you know? I couldn't cope in the old house. Too many stairs, couldn't get her up and down. Much better here. All one level and we've three toilets. And a walk-in shower. Fantastic.' He lifted his mug.

At the sound of his voice Joanne turned. Her face crumpled, anxiously, then relaxed. She began to sing, softly, a sweet musical tone. McLoughlin recognised the tune.

Oh Mary, this London's a wonderful sight

'Good girl, Joanne,' Dom's voice was warm and comforting as he joined in.

With the people all working by day and by night,

McLoughlin put down his mug and took up the song:

They don't grow potatoes and barley and wheat,
But there's gangs of them digging for gold in the street

And the three of them singing together:

At least when I asked them that's what I was told
So I just took a hand with the digging for gold

Dom put up his hand to silence him as Joanne finished the verse by herself, her voice stronger now:

But for all that I found there I might as well be
Where the mountains of Mourne sweep down to the sea.

'Yay girl, go girl,' Dom stood up, clapping loudly. McLoughlin joined in and Joanne smiled and bowed as the doorbell rang once, twice, three times.

'Come on,' Dom took her by the hand. 'Your chariot awaits. Here,' he knelt and eased off her slippers, lifting each foot as she swayed and grabbed hold of him to balance. 'Shoes, now what did we do with your shoes?'

'These they?' McLoughlin reached down for the pair of red sandals by his chair.

'Just the job,' Dom carefully strapped each one in turn around his wife's thin ankles. 'Now,' he clambered to his feet, red in the face, breathing heavily. 'Now, say goodbye to Mick.'

Joanne nodded and smiled. McLoughlin stood up. He leaned over and kissed her cheek. Her skin was soft and smooth. She smelt of lavender.

'Come on now, love, your friends are downstairs.' Dom took her by the hand. 'Won't be a minute. It's the minibus. The Alzheimer's Society. Fantastic service. She loves it. Don't you sweetheart?' He put his face close to Joanne's and she smiled again, a mechanical grimace. 'Help yourself to more coffee, I'll be back in a minute and then you can bring me up to speed on all the other business.'

McLoughlin heard the door slam behind them and the faint whine of the lift. He walked to the window. He looked down. Below, parked at the curb, was a blue minibus. McLoughlin watched as Dom handed Joanne over to a large woman wearing a nurse's uniform. He watched as she was strapped into a seat, and the door slid closed. The bus moved off into the traffic.

He turned away and looked around. Love, a funny old thing really. Everyone used to think that Dom Hayes was one of the hard men. As tough as they came. Rumour was that he'd grown up in an orphanage. He'd clawed his way out of all that. Got himself an education. Got into the guards. Made a good life for himself and his wife and their four kids. Worked all the hours of the day. Up along the border when the Troubles were at their height. Saw friends die. Never spoke about it. And now, when he could have had a bit of fun, an easy retirement, golf, travel, a couple of security consultancies to bring in a few more bob, this had happened. Poor sweet Joanne. McLoughlin remembered. She was always a bit absent-minded, Dom had lots of funny stories about how she'd put her purse in the fridge, how she'd have her head in a book and forget to turn off the gas under the stew. How she'd lose her car keys and her house keys and phone him in a panic. But then the forgetfulness became something else, much more serious, much more profound.

The apartment's front door banged open and slammed shut.

'Now, where were we?' Dom's voice was loud and cheerful. 'Would you like a drink? I've a nice bottle of red open. I always have a glass when Joanne goes off. You'll join me, won't you?'

They sat in companionable silence. McLoughlin sipped his wine. It was good. Italian.

'So?' Dom looked at him over the rim of his glass.

'So, a mess. When the lads arrived I was covered in blood, running around the house like a madman, trying to find the keys to the front door.' McLoughlin shifted from side to side.

'Blood? Whose?'

'Good question,' McLoughlin held up his hand. The bandage was white and clean. 'Bloody dog bit me, so there was my blood, and the rest came from the poor unfortunate judge. The dog had spread it around the house.'

'Hmm, so much for the integrity of the crime scene.' Dom smirked.

The integrity of the crime scene. One way or another he felt like an idiot. The guards from Dun Laoghaire banging on the door and he couldn't open it. Until he spotted the bowl on the hall table, behind the vase of flowers, and the large bunch of keys in it.

'Hold on, I'm coming,' shouting at the top of his voice as he fumbled with the lock and the door burst open and before he could explain anything they had him in cuffs.

'For God's sake, it's not me,' he was shouting, 'upstairs, look upstairs, front room and for fuck's sake don't let the dog out of the bathroom.'

They made him strip and put on a white suit. Everything from top to bottom, his clothes and shoes, all in an evidence bag. They brought in a dog handler who put the poodle into a cage and carted him out to the van. And eventually they took off his cuffs and let him sit down on a chair in the kitchen.

'Wait, here,' the uniformed guard said. 'She'll want to question you.'

'She?' His hand was really sore. He held it up. 'Look, can I give this a wash? The dog, you know? It'll probably go septic.'

'Let him, his hand,' a woman wearing jeans and a white shirt, her feet in bright pink runners, hurried into the room. Her hair was scooped back in a loose ponytail. Her face was bare of makeup. She looked familiar but he wasn't sure he knew her name. She helped him to his feet and led him to the sink. 'You OK?' She turned on the tap and held his hand under the stream of water. It stung and he winced.

'Ouch,' he said loudly.

'Ouch is it?' She smiled broadly. 'You poor wee man. Here,' she called over her shoulder. 'Here, Harris, back here, you've a patient.'

Johnny Harris, the best forensic pathologist in the business. McLoughlin had known him for more years than he cared to count. Harris took his hand. He turned it around, into the light.

'You don't need stitches but you'll need a tetanus shot and a course of antibiotics. I'll call A&E. They'll look after you.' Harris patted him on the shoulder. 'You're looking a bit green. Are you OK?'

'Not really,' McLoughlin could feel his knees beginning to sag. He slumped down on the chair again. 'An awful mess up there. Poor guy. An awful mess.'

'Tell me,' the woman sat down beside him. 'I'm Min Sweeney, I don't think we've met before. I've heard about you of course.'

'Of course,' Harris joined in, 'everyone's heard of Mick McLoughlin.'

'Yeah, yeah,' McLoughlin waved his good hand. He looked at the woman again. He knew who she was. 'Inspector Sweeney, isn't it?'

She nodded and turned to Johnny Harris. 'Anything to say about,' she jerked her head towards the stairs.

'Well, I'll need to have a closer look but pretty obvious how he died,' Harris put his hand on her shoulder. 'Rigor's set in so it's been at least four hours. I'll know more when I open him up.'

Min nodded. 'OK, well the crime scene guys haven't finished, so it'll be a while longer. Anyone know anything about the family? We better get a liaison officer on the job. Declan,' she shouted loudly in the direction of the stairs. 'And now, you my friend,' she looked at McLoughlin, 'perhaps you can tell me what you were doing here.'

He explained. The dog, the barking, how he rang the bell, then tried to climb over the wall, falling through the rotten door into the garden, and then,

'So, the back door was open, was it?' She was taking notes.

'Open, I didn't realise at first. It looked like it was closed. It wasn't ajar, but when I touched it, well it was definitely open.' McLoughlin could feel the cold glass beneath his fingertips.

'And what then? Did you go upstairs right away?' she looked at him, her pen poised over her notebook.

He nodded. 'Yeah, it was the dog you see. Frantic, he sounded. It did occur to me that something wasn't quite right. But I thought, I suppose if I thought anything, old man, walked with a stick, a fall maybe?'

'But first thing you did was to let the dog out? Why was that?'

Why was that? He tried to answer. 'It was the noise. I didn't think there'd be anything like,' he paused, 'I mean if I'd thought there'd be blood or something I wouldn't have, but I don't know. It didn't occur to me.'

She smiled at him. A reassuring smile. 'And did you hear anything else? It looks like he was shot, so did you hear anything?'

He shook his head. 'No, nothing, it was late when I got home. Around midnight. I went to bed pretty much immediately. Slept through until about six. I didn't hear anything'

'OK,' she stood up. 'I'll need a proper signed statement from you. Tomorrow, come in tomorrow and if there's anything else—'

'Yeah,' he cut across her, 'of course if I remember anything else.'

'And we'll want access to your garden and house if that's OK,'

'Sure' he nodded. 'Anything I can do, of course.'

She turned to go, then turned back. 'And tell me, did you know him?'

'Not really. I've only had the house a short while. We had a chat or two over the wall. I recognised him of course. He was always in the garden. Him and the bloody dog.' The wound on his hand was beginning to throb.

'And visitors, family, see anything?'

He shook his head. 'As I said, I've only had the house a couple of weeks and I was away for part of that. I don't know any of the neighbours really. Seems a quiet place, not much going on.'

'Not much going on?' Dom raised his eyebrows as he reached for the bottle of wine and topped up his glass. 'Not sure I'd agree with that statement.'

'Yeah?' McLoughlin held out his glass for a refill. This was probably a bad idea but his hand was hurting. He'd gone to hospital and got the tetanus injection. They cleaned it, bandaged it. But the painkillers had worn off and he was still feeling something, shock, upset, fear. When he closed his eyes he could see the shaft of light edging around the shutters and falling across the chair. And the way the room looked when he switched on the ceiling chandelier. The dark pool of congealed blood, what was left of the judge's face. The quiet elegance around him. The large sofa and chairs covered in flowered material, the grand piano in the bay of the window, the white marble fireplace with its shiny brass tongs and poker. The portrait above it, a handsome young man in military uniform, whose gaze seemed to rest on the body. Daniel Hegarty, the judge's father. One of the greats of the War of Independence. Fearless, they said.

'Don't you remember? Good few years ago now. Your girl Sweeney, she was involved.' Dom sipped his wine. Silence for a moment. 'It was a terrible thing. That little boy.' Dom sighed. 'Sweeney was the one. Not long after her husband died. Do you remember him?'

'Andy Carolan? I didn't know him well. He was on the way up I know that. Brain haemorrhage wasn't it?'

'He was watching TV. She found him in the morning. Twin boys, seven or eight or something.' Dom shifted and the leather beneath him creaked. 'Sweeney did a great job. Got the guy who killed the kid. Must have left quite a mark on the place.'

'Yeah, I suppose. There's a wooden bench on the green with a plaque and his name on it.'

There was silence for a moment. They both had memories. Things they'd seen. People they'd met. Crimes that had shocked them.

'This is good,' Dom leaned back and closed his eyes. 'Quiet is good.'

'How long will she be gone?' McLoughlin looked over at him.

'Until four. Eleven to four Monday to Friday. It's a lifesaver.' Dom's eyes were still closed. 'She's pretty good really, but the nights are bad.

She wakes all the time and wanders around. I have to get up with her. She could do anything.'

'And the family? Do they help?'

'They try but you know, they've kids of their own and jobs and lives. They love her and they'll mind her if I'm really stuck, but,' he opened his eyes and sat up.

'Listen,' McLoughlin leaned forward, 'I wanted to ask you.'

'Ah,' Dom smiled and slapped his hand on his thigh, 'I was wondering.'

'I've just come back from Venice,' McLoughlin shifted in his seat.

'Venice, you lucky fucker. One of the places I wanted to take Joanne.' Dom lifted his glass, 'What brought you there?'

'Oh a bit of nothing really. A straying husband, his current girlfriend, a very pissed-off wife, you know the sort of thing,' McLoughlin sat back and crossed his legs. 'Nothing important. But don't you remember? Years ago. What you told me. About James Reynolds.'

'James Reynolds?'

'Yeah, remember, your friend in Interpol, the French guy, the rugby fanatic.' McLoughlin could feel anxiety knotting his stomach. 'He came over and stayed with you for those international matches, France and Ireland, the eighties.'

'Yeah, that's right, Stephane something or other, good guy, great drinker,' Dom smiled and for a moment looked like the man he once was. 'He had a thing about the Provos. Knew more about them than I did. Knew all about what they were up to outside Ireland. Before the days of the war on terror. Public enemy number one. Attacks on British soldiers in Germany. Remember when they killed those two Australian tourists in the Netherlands? '

'Yeah,' McLoughlin's voice rose a notch. 'You told me, that he told you, the Italian police had found Reynolds in a place called Bassano del Grappa. A little town north of Venice.'

'That's right,' Dom sat up straight. 'Problem was we couldn't put together a case for extradition. No evidence.' Dom leaned forward. He suddenly looked younger. 'We heard he'd gone to Holland, then the

Basque country. ETA, you know? A bit of an escape route, Amsterdam, Bordeaux, Biarritz, Bilbao. All the Bs. We'd heard that Reynolds had got as far as Bilbao, but not much officially after that.' Dom sat back and took a long swallow from his glass. 'And then Stephane told me about, Bassano, what was it?

'Bassano del Grappa, and you can add another B to that list.' McLoughlin sipped his wine. He could do with something stronger really. 'Barcelona, that's where he met his wife, so she said.'

'His wife?' Dom looked at him. 'You got close. How did you manage that?'

And McLoughlin told him. How he'd always remembered the name of the town and where it was. How he'd wanted to go, but.

'I have to be honest. I chickened out, time and again. I told myself I'd go next year, next year, next year. And then.'

He was offered the job in Venice. He couldn't avoid it any longer. He'd found the bar. He'd spoken to the wife. He'd met Reynolds outside in the street. Stood so close to him he could see the pores in his skin, the broken veins in his cheeks, smell the cigarette smoke on his clothes. Stood so close and did nothing. How he'd walked away in tears.

Silence in the room. The faint sound of traffic below, the DART rumbling into its tunnel. Dom stirred on the sofa. He lifted his glass and drained it.

'There's a difference between people like you and people like Reynolds and the rest of them.' His voice was soft.

'Yeah, there is,' McLoughlin could feel his hands shaking. 'They get away with it. Look at the peace process, how well they've done since then.'

'Christ,' Dom raised his glass, 'the fucking peace process. How did they swing that one?'

'Well, at least they're not killing the way they used to.' McLoughlin put his glass down, carefully so it wouldn't spill.

'You think so? You wait. It's not over yet.' Silence. A seagull shrieking loudly, swooping down past the balcony. 'Anyway, it's good to see you. Glad you've moved into the town. It's a nice place to live. Not perfect, mind you. But pretty close.'

He emptied the bottle into McLoughlin's glass, then got up and walked into the kitchen. McLoughlin could hear the sound of cupboards opening and closing, then the dull pop as a cork was pulled.

'Here,' Dom padded back into the sitting room. 'This deserves another. Now,' he settled himself back on the sofa. 'James Reynolds. So he's alive and well and living in Italy. What do you want to do about him?'

'Well,' McLoughlin sat up straight. His back was at him again. 'I spoke to Tom Donnelly in headquarters.'

'You did? You managed to get him off the golf course?' Dom shifted on the sofa.

'Just about. I left a load of messages and eventually,' McLoughlin raised his eyes to heaven.

'And?'

'What you'd expect. The case is still open. They regularly review all the evidence, but, with nothing new,' McLoughlin could feel his jaw tighten, tension creeping up the side of his face.

'The two other guys, the ones with him, they were caught, weren't they?'

McLoughlin nodded. 'Yeah, Reynolds was in the car. He shot my father through the window, then he took off, without them,' he paused. 'Conor McNally and Eamon Ryan, they were picked up a few minutes later.'

'Without the money I seem to remember, isn't that right?'

'Yeah, they threw the bags into the back seat before Reynolds left. So,' he took a long swallow from his glass and topped it up from the bottle on the floor by the sofa. 'They both got hefty prison sentences. Didn't give up anything in interrogation, kept their mouths shut.'

'Well,' Dom reached over and pulled a laptop from the coffee table. He opened it up, his hands moving swiftly, easily, across the keyboard. 'Here, have a look.' He turned it towards McLoughlin.

'What is it? I don't have my glasses. Can't see a fucking thing without them.' He pushed it back. 'Read it to me, will you?'

'OK, here goes,' Dom's fingers stroked the touch pad. 'Here we are. *An Phobhlacht*, the online version.' He scrolled and clicked.

'Here, I have it. *Comhbhrón*. You know what that is? You still have your Irish?'

'Sure,' McLoughlin smiled, 'fourteen years of the Christian brothers, I still have the Irish. *Comhbhrón*, condolences. So, who do we have?'

Dom began to read. 'Ryan, Eamon, Deepest sympathy is extended to the family of Eamon Ryan on the tragic passing of their husband, son and father. From everyone in Waterford, South East.'

'And when was that?' McLoughlin looked at him.

'June, 2012. Last year.' Dom hands grasped both sides of the computer protectively.

'How do you know it's him? There must be loads of Eamon Ryans.'

'I saw it and I wondered.' Dom shifted on the seat. 'I asked around. It's him all right. Lung cancer. He was diagnosed when he was in prison. He'd chemo, radiotherapy, the works. They let him out. He was never going to recover.'

'And the other one, McNally? What happened to him?' McLoughlin drank some more. The wine was beginning to give him a headache but somehow he couldn't stop.

'He's dead too. He died inside. Got into a fight. Stab wound to the chest.' Dom looked at him. 'I'm surprised you don't know all this. Were you not curious?'

McLoughlin got up, walked around the room, then took his seat again.

'I met Eamon Ryan. He wrote to my mother, said he wanted to see her. She wouldn't go. I went in her place.'

A small man. Pinched face. Grey skin, grey hair. Bad teeth, nicotine stained. Tattoos on his forearms, the usual, the tricolour, Bobby Sands, and *Tiocfaidh ár lá*. Our day will come. They sat facing each other. McLoughlin waited for him to speak.

'I wanted to meet your mam. I wanted to tell her I was sorry for what happened.' His voice was low, his accent from Wexford, Waterford, perhaps.

'Too late for that,' McLoughlin remembered he had said to him. 'Too fucking late for all that.'

'I know,' Ryan looked down at his hands, 'I know that now. It wasn't meant to happen that way. It was just about the money. It wasn't about,' and he paused, then coughed.

'So will you make a statement? Will you name the man who murdered my father? Will you do that at least?'

Ryan shook his head. 'I can't,' his voice was barely audible. 'It's not our way.'

'But if you did, who knows. Could have an affect on your sentence.' McLoughlin watched him. Ryan's face was scored with deep lines around his mouth and eyes. 'And if you got out, there'd be witness protection. We'd look after you.'

Ryan didn't answer. He looked down at his hands. He coughed again. A dreadful sound, from deep in his lungs. Then he stood.

'Tell your mam what I said. I'm sorry about your father. It wasn't about him. It was only about the money.'

Silence for a moment. Dom refilled their glasses.

'So, both of the guys who were on the raid with Reynolds are dead. I wonder about the other witnesses. No one in the post office saw anything.' Dom sipped.

'And from what I remember no one in the street at the time saw anything much either. They'd all had the knock at the door.' McLoughlin smiled.

'The knock at the door, you can't beat it.' Dom swirled the wine in his glass. 'And, what was the name of the guy who was with your father? His partner, on the day?'

'Dermot Sorohan, do you not remember?'

'Oh yeah. Sorohan. He never went back to work, did he? Died a year or so later. Was it suicide?'

McLoughlin shrugged. 'Car crash. Hit a tree. Four in the morning, not wearing his seat belt.' They sat for a moment in silence. Then Dom nodded towards the balcony.

'You never know. Now that McNally and Ryan are dead, and peace has come upon us, Reynolds might make an appearance. You see,' he pointed to the large telescope beside the patio table and chairs. 'I spend a lot of time out there. Come and have a look.'

He stood and walked over to the sliding door. He pulled it back. A warm breeze drifted into the room carrying the sounds of the street. McLoughlin joined him. He bent and looked through the eye piece. He could see nothing. He fiddled with the focus. Suddenly the ferry port appeared in his gaze. The high speed boat had just arrived from Holyhead. People were streaming through the gates. He could see them clearly, their faces, their features. He watched, men and women greeting each other. Kisses and hugs exchanged. An older woman in tears as she bent down to embrace a small girl. She turned in his direction and for a moment it seemed that she could see him. He stood up abruptly, suddenly embarrassed. He rubbed his eyes.

'So,' Dom sat down on one of the chairs. 'This is the way it is. Middle of the night it's the Plough and the North Star above it and Arcturus to the east and Regulus to the west. But during the day you'd be amazed what you see coming through.' He waved towards the crowds on the footpath. 'Fellas I arrested years ago when they were barely out of short pants. They'll be bringing in drugs, guns, women, you name it. They use the boat. The security's not nearly as tight as the airport. So,' he looked up at McLoughlin, a broad grin on his face. 'Your man, Reynolds. I'll add him to my list. And when I'm sitting here, whiling away my time, my sweetheart in her rocking chair, singing her old songs, I'll keep an eye out for him.' He stood up. 'It's funny isn't it? Joanne can't remember anything and I can't forget anything. I have all the names and faces in here.' He tapped his forehead. 'So, if I see him, I'll let you know.'

It was much later when McLoughlin left Dom's apartment. Joanne had been delivered home. Dom had sat her down on a large bean bag in front of the DVD player. He had put on her favourite programme. *Peppa Pig.* McLoughlin watched, fascinated as the little pink pig jumped and cavorted and splashed in muddy puddles. After a while Joanne fell asleep.

McLoughlin yawned. He was worn out too.

Dom looked over at him. 'Bed's what you need. A bit of peace and quiet. Your hand,' he pointed, 'must be sore.'

McLoughlin nodded and stood. He wasn't completely steady. They walked together to the lift. Joanne woke and sat up. McLoughlin waved to her and blew kisses. She waved back. As they stopped to say their goodbyes McLoughlin saw a small room through an open door. A bed with a lacy canopy, a bright pink duvet and a pile of pillows, also covered in pink flowery material. A high-backed chair like a throne decorated with a small crown. A dressing table with an ornate gilt mirror and a set of silver hair brushes.

'Nice,' he whistled softly.

'Yes, it is, isn't it?' Dom leaned against the door jamb. 'Joanne doesn't want to sleep with me anymore. I think I frighten her.' He shifted his bulk and tucked his shirt in more securely. His belly loomed over his belt. 'So when we moved here we sat down and looked at her favourite books and I got it fitted out like this.' He stepped into the room. 'We never had a girl. Four boys, one after the other. We never had the chance to get in touch with our inner princess. So.' He smoothed down the duvet. 'She's happy here, and that's good enough for me.'

They waited for the lift together. The doors opened. McLoughlin stepped in.

'Just one thing.' Dom reached towards him. 'One thing, about your neighbour's death.'

'Yeah?' McLoughlin put his finger on the doors open button.

'This place. Everyone knows everyone else. The local intelligence is phenomenal. You can be sure whoever killed the judge, well someone knows, but people around here are good at keeping secrets.'

It was hot outside. The sun was still riding high in the sky. McLoughlin walked through the town. Away from the seafront it was quiet. The main street was run down and neglected. For Sale and To Let signs hung from every second shopfront. He glanced from left to right. The side streets gave vistas of Victorian houses. Some were offices, most parcelled-up into flats. The spire of the Mariners' Church towered over their slate roofs. No longer a place of worship. Not for years. The Maritime Museum, now. He remembered his father telling him, when he was a young man, the town was a Protestant town. Polite people who kept to themselves, went to church on Sundays, didn't play games or go to dances on the Sabbath.

'We didn't mix with them,' he'd said. 'The girls were gorgeous. But not for us.'

Not like that anymore, McLoughlin thought. Hardly any trace of those days. There was still a Protestant church by the park, Christ Church, said the name on the noticeboard outside. The royal crowns on some of the post boxes could still be seen, but painted green now, not imperial red. The Victoria fountain on the seafront had recently been restored after years of vandalism and neglect. And some of the street names harked back to the past. Like Victoria Square, where he lived now.

He turned off the main road and walked across the green. He stopped by the bench under one of the silver birches. He bent down to read the small metal plaque screwed to the back.

We remember Owen Cassidy who played here. We remember him always with love. Mummy and Daddy

He sat down. He looked across to the row of houses. Owen had lived in number 26. It was at the far end, closer to the main road. They had found his body under the summer house in the garden next door. He had lain there undisturbed for years, where his neighbour, Chris, had buried him. There had been calls for the house to be demolished, the garden to be concreted over. But time had passed. No one talked about it. People moved on. That's the way it's done.

His head was really throbbing. He shouldn't have let Dom open that last bottle. He stood and began to walk across the grass. The crime scene tape outside the judge's house fluttered gently in the evening breeze. He looked up at the bay window on the first floor. Hard to believe what had happened there. Even though he had seen the judge dead, seen the blood, seen his face.

He moved past the waste skip parked at the curb. The guards had searched it. Dumped everything out, and hadn't done a great job about putting it all back again. Rubble, old plaster, rotting wood in a haphazard pile on the footpath. He stopped and looked at it. The builders could deal with it tomorrow.

He walked up the steps and went inside. The house was quiet. He picked his way carefully through the piles of timber and bags of cement, toolboxes and ladders, up the stairs to his room. He pulled the shutters together and sank down on the mattress. He lay on his back, staring up at the ceiling, then rolled over on his side and wrapped his arms around himself. It was the way he had always slept. As a child and as a man. As he would sleep now.

The builders were ripping the plaster off the walls in the hall. McLoughlin could hear the thump and crash of the sledgehammers and smell the dust as it rose through the house. He got up. He felt bad. That last bloody bottle of wine. He'd learned from bitter experience that he shouldn't drink so much. But it was always so tempting. And besides, he'd been doing Dom a favour. Poor guy. He was on his own a lot. Joanne and *Peppa Pig* were no substitute for a bit of adult company, no matter how much he loved her.

McLoughlin stood on the landing. The builder's name was Ian. He was a nice guy. Young and handsome. He could hear him singing down there. Good to know that someone was happy. He'd been delighted to get the job. His price was at least ten thousand less than McLoughlin had estimated. One of the few good things about the recession.

He turned away and climbed the small staircase that led to the box room and the tiny bathroom at the top of the house. You couldn't really call it a bathroom. It was more like a cupboard, a toilet with a basin and somehow a shower head squeezed under the eaves. He was reluctant to use it. The lino was lifting from the floorboards and there was mould on the stick-on panelling on the walls. When the house was finished his study would be up here. The box room and bathroom knocked together, a new window which would give him a great view over the houses and gardens behind, perhaps a glimpse of the sea.

He turned on the shower and stood beneath its dribble of water. Hardly worth it really. He turned off the tap and began to dry himself. And saw through the small window the crime scene lads in their white overalls working their way, step by careful step, through the garden next door. And among them the woman with her hair in the blonde ponytail, dressed like the others, but unmistakeable. Something about her demeanour. Her face bright and animated. They were all laughing now. As she swung around and looked up he drew back, self conscious, the towel sagging around his middle. Not that she could see him from down there in the garden.

'Mick, are you up there?' He could hear his name being called. He opened the bathroom door.

'Mick?' the builder came up the stairs two at a time, a hammer in his hand, his dark hair streaked with plaster dust, a face mask swinging around his neck. 'Sorry Mick, but you've a visitor.'

The woman who was standing in the hall was tall and thin. Her hair, dark with grey streaks, was cut short. He noticed that her skin was sallow and her eyes were brown. She was, in contrast, brightly dressed, loose red trousers and a red blouse, the sleeves rolled up. He noticed her heavy amber necklace and the rings on her fingers. Silver, studded with turquoise and something that looked like amethyst.

'Sorry,' he moved towards her, tucking his shirt into his waistband, smoothing his wet hair back from his forehead. 'Sorry about the dust.' He opened the door and ushered her outside. Warm again today. The sky an improbable blue.

'No, really I should be apologising. You're in the middle of all that.' She gestured to the house. 'Not fun.'

'Well,' he shrugged. 'I have to keep reminding myself. It's a process. All things must pass.'

'All things must pass away,' she smiled. 'Are you a George person?'

'Not really,' he smiled too, 'I used to be a Paul person, but he's become an awful softie. Not the same without John. They needed each other.'

'Yin and yang, maybe?'

'Or chalk and cheese, perhaps,' he laughed. 'Now, we've got that out of the way, what can I do for you? You're not here I hope to complain about the noise and the extra traffic and all the general mayhem.'

She shook her head and explained. 'My name is Elizabeth Fannin. I was one of the therapists, you know?' She reached over and ran her index finger across the brass plate. His eyes followed her hand. He saw her name and a row of letters. 'I worked from here for the last, well, must have been thirty years. Very sad to leave, but,' she shrugged, 'all things must pass.' She paused. He watched her face. Heavily lined, around her mouth, beneath her eyes, across her forehead. But somehow when she was talking the lines weren't so noticeable. 'Anyway, I was wondering. Your basement. Do you have any plans for it in the immediate future?'

'I don't know. I haven't thought about it that much. So far I've just been using it to store all my stuff.' He looked down into the front garden. It had become a dump. A pile of rubble waiting to be emptied into the skip. 'My immediate concern is the house itself.' He gestured. 'I suppose I will eventually tackle it but—'

'Well,' she cut across him. 'I was wondering if I could rent it back from you. You see, I've a few clients, they're all older people. In their seventies and one lady who's eighty-five. I've been seeing them here, in fact there, for quite some time,' and she pointed to the windows below. 'Most have some level of dementia. Not enough to disable them completely but enough to make them sensitive to change. Little differences are very disorientating. Windows in different places. Shadows, lights, new furniture, pictures on the wall, that sort of thing.'

McLoughlin remembered his mother. When she moved into a new room in the nursing home it had taken her weeks to adjust.

'We all had to leave when the house went up for sale. I've a new place, it's nice. It's in a practice in Monkstown. However, my older clients, they're finding it a real challenge and so am I.' She paused. 'It's hard, it's all very confusing. Fear of the future. Memory lapses. A sense of unreality. One constant. Death looming. So,' she looked at him.

'So, well, in principle I've no problem. But, the noise, the racket from up here, won't that be difficult? And then there's,' and he pointed towards the crime scene tape.

She shook her head. 'That's not really a problem for them, or me. You'd be doing us all a huge favour.'

'OK, well, let's have a look, shall we?' He began to move down the steps towards the basement. She followed him.

'It's a kind of a mess, really,' he paused, 'but if you like…'

He pushed the small side gate open and they picked their way through to the little door. He fumbled with his keys.

'Here,' he stepped aside and she moved past him. He reached for the light. The corridor stretched ahead.

'Here,' he pointed to the room at the front. 'I've a load of stuff stored here.'

'That's OK,' she called over her shoulder. 'This is what I'm interested in.'

She disappeared from sight. He heard her voice.

'Come in. It's fine.'

He peered through the door. She was standing in the middle of the room. She was smiling.

'I can put my desk back. And my pictures. And everything they're used to. It'll be great.'

'Are you sure about that?' The noise from upstairs was muted, but he could still hear the thumps, the bangs, the crashes.

'Yeah, I often work in the evenings. It'll be great,' she said again and smiled at him. He could feel he was smiling too.

'Well, OK, you can have it. We can sort out a fair rent, given all,' he pointed at the ceiling, 'but, if I decide I want it back.'

'That's fine,' she cut across him, 'I'll have to deal with the move eventually, but it would give me a bit more time. To be honest, I know that a couple of them won't be coming to me for much longer. But there's one man in particular, it would mean a lot to be able to see him here.' She held out her hand. 'Can we shake on it?' Her grasp was firm and cool.

He smiled. 'OK, we'll give it a go. Let me know when you want to start and I'll get the front cleared up.'

'No, no, don't worry about it. I'll take care of everything. I have a few willing helpers I can call upon.'

They walked together to the door. He stopped to lock up.

'I'll get a key cut. You can pick it up any time.'

She nodded and smiled. 'No need, actually I still have my old one. Oops,' she put her hands up to her face, 'think I should have handed it back, but well,' she shrugged. 'Anyway, thank you very much. I really appreciate this. If you give me your bank details I'll set up a standing order. Or,' she paused, 'would you prefer cash?'

'Cash? Why not?'

They walked together to the gate. She turned away, then looked back and waved. She set off across the green, a distinctive figure, her red clothes, her confident stride, her grey head erect. He watched her until she disappeared behind the grove of birch trees. He hoped he'd done the right thing. But it might be good karma. A blessing on this house, and all that. He turned to go back inside and heard his name being called. Min Sweeney was hurrying down the next-door steps.

'Mick, hold on a minute.'

She had changed out of the white overalls. She was wearing a short black skirt and a beige blouse. He noticed that her legs were bare and her sandals were leather with a wedge heel. She stopped by the gate. A large satchel was hanging over her shoulder and she was holding a blue folder in her hand. She waved it towards him.

'Your statement. There's just a couple of things I'd like you to clarify.'

'Yeah? Clarify? What?' He was unaccountably defensive. It was an unfamiliar feeling.

'It won't take a minute. Just a couple of questions.'

'Yeah, OK, if you insist,' he smiled. 'Look, I'm just about to make some coffee, would you like a cup?'

They sat, perched on fold-up garden chairs in what he referred to as the yoga room. He'd found an empty cardboard box, turned it upside down and made a makeshift table. Large mugs of coffee steamed gently. He laid out a few bits and pieces brought back from his Italian trip. Fat green olives, salami sliced thinly. There was silence as they ate.

'Yum,' she wiped her mouth on a tissue. 'Is this what's it's like, being retired?'

He shrugged. 'Sometimes, and sometimes it's just a bowl of porridge and a cup of tea. Depends on the mood.'

'Well, glad to know I've caught you when your mood is good.' She smiled at him as she reached for more salami.

'I'll give you some to take home. I've more than I can eat. Now,' he put down his mug. 'You wanted to ask me about my statement. What can I do for you?'

She went through it, line by line. What time had he rung the doorbell? What did he see when he looked through the glass panel into the hall? Why had he decided to climb over the wall? Was that the first time he became aware of the connecting door? What did he see when he walked up the steps to the judge's house? How did he know the door was open? What did he touch when he went into the house? What did he hear? Which rooms did he go into? And on and on and on.

'You see,' she said, 'there's a couple of things. Did you close the door to the steps behind you when you came in?'

He paused. He couldn't quite remember. He'd put his hand out to open it and it was open already. He'd stepped into the house slowly.

'I felt embarrassed really. I was intruding. I almost felt as if I was breaking in. I remember I stopped. I called out. The dog was going crazy. Then of course I felt worse. So I don't think I did close the door. I was more intent on finding the dog, and apologising to the judge. That was my priority.'

'Yeah, that's what's in your statement, but I wanted to check because when the guys got there, the back door was closed. In fact it was locked.' She looked down at the typed pages.

'Locked? I certainly didn't lock it.' He put his mug on the box. It wobbled. He picked it up again. 'Where was the key? Was it in the door?'

She shook her head. 'No, it wasn't. Eventually we found it in the kitchen, in one of the drawers, along with a load of other keys, bits and pieces of stuff, a small screwdriver, some string, some plastic bags full of coins. You know that kind of a drawer.'

'Yeah, there's always one isn't there?'

She nodded and smiled, 'Of course we don't know if that was the key which was used to lock the door. Or a spare key.' She paused, looked down at the notes again, then back up at him.

'So,' he spoke slowly, 'so what you're saying is that whoever killed the judge was still in the house?'

'Whoever killed the judge, perhaps, or someone else, we can't be absolutely certain who, but,' she paused again, 'if you didn't lock the door…'

McLoughlin smiled, 'Well that's a surprise.'

'So, did you, hear, see, anything else?'

He closed his eyes. He was trying to think back. He opened his eyes and shook his head. 'I honestly can't say I heard or saw anything. I was so taken up with the dog and the barking and then the blood and then when I saw your man on the floor all I could think about was calling you guys. So I don't know. Anything could have been going on downstairs or even upstairs for that matter. I only went as far as the little bathroom but if his house is like this one, there's another floor above it. So,' he shrugged, 'that's it really, although,' he made a face, 'bit of an eejit, really, to think …' he stopped.

'Well,' she smiled and reached out and patted him on the knee. He felt for an instant like one of her sons, 'Can't change any of that. What happened, happened.' She tapped the blue folder. 'Did you notice a computer, a laptop?'

Again he shook his head.

'Apparently he had one, but there's no sign of it. And another thing. Can you tell me, did you notice, the kitchen, was it tidy?'

'I wasn't in the kitchen. I went straight from the dining room, straight up the stairs towards the barking. It was only after I let the dog out that I went into the front room. I didn't go into any of the other rooms. Just the dining room, the small bathroom and then the big room where the judge's body was.' He could see it again. Hear the sound of the dog, feel the sticky blood on his hands. See the man on the floor, the bloody mess on the carpet. He looked away and around his room. Same marble fireplace, same elaborate cornice, same ceiling rose. 'The tidy kitchen? The significance?'

'Well,' she paused. 'One of the people we've spoken to so far is a lady called Mrs Maguire, Mags Maguire. She's the judge's cleaner, or more like a housekeeper. Cooks for him. Does his shopping. Generally keeps the place in order. We brought her into the house to have a look around, in case something was missing. And the first thing she said was that someone had done the washing-up. She was amazed. She only works Monday to Friday and she said that when she goes in on Monday morning the place is always in an awful state. Apparently the judge wasn't good at the domestic stuff. She'd leave him food to be heated up and he could just about do that, but he'd never clean up after himself. She thought maybe his daughter had been to see him. Because the place was so spick and span. But the daughter was away. In Paris for the weekend. Only just got back. So it's a bit of a mystery.'

Mrs Maguire had noticed that the washing up was done. She stood in the kitchen doorway, a small plump figure, her shopping bag dropped by her feet. She walked slowly across the lino to the sink. She ran her finger over the stainless steel.

'Look at that', she said, 'it's dry. Look.'

She opened cupboards and drawers.

'Look,' she pointed. 'All put away. He might wash a cup if he wanted tea, but that'd be all.' She moved towards the pedal bin in the corner. She put her small foot on the lever.

'Look,' she pointed again. 'See? The bin's empty. There's a new liner in it too.'

'Is that not the way you left it?'

'Yeah, I left a clean plastic bag, but that was Friday. There's no way it would still be clean on Monday. No way.'

She walked out of the kitchen into the dining room and then into the small sitting room in the front of the house. She looked around, rubbing the carpet with her shoe. Then she moved back into the hall and opened the cupboard tucked in below the stairs. She pulled out the vacuum cleaner.

'Now this, this isn't right either.' The flex trailed out in a pile behind her. 'I'd never leave it like this. Look,' she put her foot on one of the buttons on the front of the machine. As she pressed down, the flex shot in, coiling itself neatly.

'And why did she look for the Hoover?' McLoughlin shifted on the garden chair.

'I asked her. She said you can always tell if a carpet's been hoovered. Specially with the dog. Terrible shedder, she said.'

'But the dog is black? Would you notice?' McLoughlin raised his eyebrows.

'Well,' Min smiled and shrugged, 'I probably wouldn't, but my standards aren't be that high. Whereas, Mrs Maguire now, she's a pro. If she said the carpet had been hoovered I'd believe her.'

'So, you checked the black bin outside of course.'

'Of course. And it was empty. Emptied on Friday around here. So whatever was in the kitchen bin didn't go into it.'

McLoughlin sipped his coffee. 'So, how you doing, on suspects?'

'Suspects, Jesus,' Min pushed a loose strand of hair away from her face, 'where do you start? Fifty years, mostly criminal law. First as a barrister, prosecuting.'

'Not always,' McLoughlin butted in, 'I seem to remember he was pretty good at defending too.'

'Well, yeah, but then you remember, when he moved to the bench. Special Criminal Court in the eighties and nineties. Paramilitary trials and then a lot of gangland. A heavy sentencer. A reputation for it.' Min reached for another piece of salami. 'What were you doing in Italy? Holiday?'

'No, unfortunately,' McLoughlin's mouth turned down, 'a bit of work. Naughty husband with young girlfriend and an angry wife.'

'Ah, you're into that are you? I was wondering. This,' she looked around, 'must be costing a packet.'

'Not as much as you'd think. The builder was desperate for the job. Shaved his price to the bone. It's an investment too. When the market goes back up, if I decide to sell I'll make a few bob.' He paused. 'But the way it is, when you retire, you have to do something. I've never been a great one for the hobbies. Work, now that was my hobby.'

'What about the sailing? I seem to remember you were into boats.'

McLoughlin shrugged. 'Used to be. Had my own boat once. When I get all this finished, maybe.'

'Well,' she sucked on another olive, 'I'm surprised you haven't taken up the law. There's a crowd of former members down in the Law Library.'

'God, yeah, are they not happy with their pensions? All the young barristers devilling hate them. My niece, Constance, my sister's daughter, she's trying to get by on the scraps from the table.' McLoughlin leaned back, crossing his legs. 'Those old guys, they should get out completely, leave it all behind.'

'Like you?' Min smiled at him.

'Like me, look at me,' he spread his arms wide. 'A man is murdered in the house next door. I find the body. But am I interfering? Am I making suggestions? Am I trying to do your job for you?'

'Wish you would,' Min stood up, smoothing down her skirt. 'Wish you fucking would.' She picked up her bag.

'Hang on a minute. Don't go just yet.' McLoughlin felt suddenly alone, useless. 'Have you established time of death? Any of the neighbours hear the shot?'

'Can't be definitive about time of death. The weather's so warm, it's hard to tell. And so far no one's sure about hearing anything. Everyone watching something, listening to something, talking to someone. All very busy.'

'Door to door, anything come up?'

'Yeah, actually. There's an old lady across the square. Apparently she and a friend had a date with the judge on Sunday. Sherry and backgammon, if you please, at six. But she fell on her way over the road and ended up in hospital.'

'And the friend, did she go?'

'It's a he actually. And he wasn't very well, it seems. Had a bad headache. He didn't go either.' Min shifted from foot to foot, her bag heavy on her shoulder.

'Bad luck, bad fucking luck for the judge.' McLoughlin looked at her.

She nodded. 'Bad luck all right. Oh,' she paused, 'one other thing I suppose I can tell you.'

'You can?' McLoughlin stood too, picking up the dishes.

'Yeah, we found the murder weapon.' She shifted her bag on her shoulder.

'You did? What was it?'

'The Webley revolver .45. Daniel Hegarty's gun.'

'Where was it?'

'Where it always was. In the cabinet in the judge's sitting room.'

'Cabinet? What cabinet was that?'

'Oh for God's sake, Michael, don't tell me you didn't notice. The mahogany cabinet with the glass doors. His father's cap and belt and gloves all nicely displayed.' She smiled at him. 'And his gun. His Webley revolver. It was there along with all the other stuff. We checked. It had been fired.'

'But,' McLoughlin spoke slowly, 'surely it wouldn't have been loaded.'

'No, it probably wasn't. But the drawer, in the bottom of the cabinet. One of those old boxes of Winchester bullets. Four of them left. And all that old cleaning stuff. The little bottle of Hoppes oil and the bronze brush, I'm sure you remember them.' She looked at her phone and shifted her bag again. 'The judge kept the gun in working order, for some strange, or maybe sentimental, reason.'

'And was the drawer locked?'

'It was, same key as the key to the cabinet. We found it in the desk in the front room downstairs. Or at least Mrs Maguire found it. She said it was always there. No one was allowed touch it.' She moved towards the door.

McLoughlin put up his hand. 'So, fingerprints? Yeah?'

She shook her head. 'Nothing, everything clean as a whistle. We don't have the ballistics report yet, but so far, it looks like the judge was killed by his father's gun. Single shot to the back of the neck.'

'Not by the blows to his head?'

'Mick, did you not notice?' She began to move towards the door.

'Notice?' He followed her.

'The pattern of blood spatter. The fine mist on the carpet. Caused by the gunshot wound. If he'd still been alive when he suffered the blows to his head the blood would have covered the walls.' She smiled, turned away, waved her hand. 'See you.'

After she'd gone McLoughlin walked down the steps into his garden. The grass was long and neglected. The flower beds on either side were overgrown. Nettles, dandelion, dock, all flourishing. He stopped by the remains of a green house, panes of glass broken and missing, then walked towards the sycamores which hung over the end wall. His gate stood open, hanging off its hinges. He pushed through. The lane here was shaded, dirty. An abandoned washing machine and fridge. A smell of urine and a pile of empty Dutch Gold beer cans. He turned to his left. The gate to the judge's house was made of metal. He pushed. It stood firm, bolted from the inside. He stepped back and scanned the ground. No rain for days. He squatted down. No footprints here, just a pile of dried leaves.

Killed by his father's gun. Daniel Hegarty, a teenager when he joined Michael Collins' men. His exploits, the stuff of legend. Daring escapes, ambushing the British army, knocking off spies and informers as they slept beside their wives. Falling out with Collins after the Treaty was signed. Going on the run. More daring exploits during the Civil War, more killing. But it all came good in the end. Dan Hegarty, hero of the War of Independence, hard man of the Civil War, rewarded by his grateful country with a series of good jobs. Running the electricity service, the bus and train company, on the boards of banks, building societies, hospitals, universities. Respected and admired by all. And his eldest son, John Hegarty, retired Supreme Court Judge. Respected and admired by all. Dan Hegarty died in his bed in his early nineties. A state funeral. Guard of honour, the 'Last Post' played over his grave. And his son? Shot in the back of his head. Hands and feet tied behind him. An execution. That was how it seemed. Killed with his father's gun. Now, why was that?

They knocked at Samuel's door just as he was finishing the washing-up. He took his time. He wiped down the countertop and hung the tea towel on the back of a chair to dry. He took off his rubber gloves and put on his leather ones. He checked himself in the mirror in the hall. He straightened his tie, and turned towards the front door. He could see two figures through the frosted glass panel. He took a deep breath, put out one hand and twisted the lock.

It was a man and a woman who had climbed the stairs to Samuel's flat. Hurried along the second floor walkway to his door. Number 28, the brass numbers, shiny. She seemed to be in charge. She introduced herself. Samuel didn't catch the name. He was nervous, his stomach churning. They pushed past him through the front door. At least everything was tidy. Neat and tidy. They wouldn't be able to fault him for that.

'You don't mind if we sit, do you?' The woman smiled at him. She fanned herself with her hand. 'It's hot today, isn't it?'

She sat on one of his small armchairs. The man, who was tall and muscular, lounged against the wall.

The woman waved a hand towards the other small chair. 'Sit, do, sorry we've made ourselves at home.'

Samuel said nothing. He had learned in these circumstances it was best to say nothing. He slid into the chair and looked down at his shoes. Wiped with a damp cloth to remove the spots of the judge's blood, then rubbed with black polish and shined. Wearing different trousers today. The old ones ripped to pieces and dumped in a bin behind a restaurant down by the seafront.

Now he kept his gaze averted. It was best not to look directly at these people. They could see things in his eyes, he knew that.

The women opened her notebook. 'We know from what Miss Gibbon has told us, you know Miss Gibbon, don't you?'

'Miss Gibbon?' For a moment he wasn't sure.

'Her name is Gwen, I think.' The woman looked down at her notes, then up at him again. He glanced in her direction, just for a moment. Her eyes were very blue, like hard blue stones. They reminded him of a doll, one his mother had when he was a small boy. He put his hands up to his eyes and covered them.

'You're wearing gloves. Are you not too hot, a day like today? And you've a sweater on too. Are you feeling all right? Do you need something?' Her voice sounded concerned, but he didn't believe her. He moved his hands to the top of his head, clasped them tightly and tried to disappear.

'Look, Mr Dudgeon, sorry, perhaps we should start again.' She cleared her throat. 'My name is Min Sweeney. Detective Inspector Min Sweeney. This is my colleague Garda Declan Murphy. OK?'

He didn't reply. He wrapped his arms tightly around his body.

'We've come to talk to you about last Sunday. We understand that you and Miss Gibbon were due to visit the late judge, John Hegarty, at about six o'clock that evening. Miss Gibbon didn't go because she fell. Did you go to the judge's house? You see,' she paused. He felt her hand on his arm. He shrank back. He didn't like strangers touching him. 'You see, we think the judge died sometime in the early evening. So it's very important, if you were there. For whatever reason. If you could tell us, if you saw anything, at all.'

He could hear her voice. On and on. See anything. Hear anything. Know anything. Where was he? What was he doing at that time? He was cold, very cold. He could feel the life draining from him. He kept his eyes closed tightly. He couldn't open them now. He wasn't sure what he would see.

'Look, Mr Dudgeon, please. If you don't answer my questions, I'm afraid we will have to take you to the station.' She made as if to stand. He could hear her shoes on the lino on the floor.

He moved then. Hands down, head up, eyes open, feet braced.

'I didn't go to the judge's house. I had a migraine. I couldn't go out. I get nauseous. I get photophobia when I get a headache like that.' He looked at her, quickly, then looked away. She was sitting forward in her chair. Her blue eyes stared.

'Did you contact the judge or Miss Gibbon to say you wouldn't be going?' She tapped her pen on her knee.

He shook his head. His mouth was dry. He swallowed.

'I was in too much pain. I have pills, so I took them. I went to bed. I closed the curtains. Eventually I went to sleep. I didn't wake up until the next morning.' He lay down. His head was bursting with pain. He pressed the ice to his left temple. And eventually he slept.

The woman nodded and smiled. 'Good, that's good. Thank you for telling us.'

She'd go now. He knew she'd go. But she didn't move. She wanted more. Had anyone seen him that day? Did he speak to anyone that day? How long had he lived here? Where was he from? How well did he know the judge? Did he work for him? What kind of work did he do? He remembered. What to do when you're being questioned. Tell them only as much as they want. Don't volunteer information. So he answered her questions. He had lived in this little flat for four years. He was from England, Ashford, a small town in Kent. He met the judge through Miss Gibbon. They shared a passion for backgammon. They played regularly. He didn't know whether anyone had seen him that day. He was in such pain. He had gone to bed. He had slept.

'And,' again the look, the eyes like the eyes of his mother's doll. Adalina, she was called. She lay on his mother's pillow and stared up at him. 'We understand, again from Miss Gibbon, that the judge was instrumental in you getting this apartment. Is that right?'

He nodded. 'He helped me with the application process. I wasn't sure what to do. He was very kind.'

'Kind? Indeed he was.' She stood up. She looked around. 'You were lucky. You've a lovely place.' He could feel the hard blue stare. It bit through the walls, through the floor, into the small space beneath the boards in the cupboard where he kept the dustpan and brush. Where the painting lay, wrapped in a blanket. With the judge's laptop, stuffed full of secrets. And the hammer. He'd washed it with bleach and scrubbed it but he could still see the blood from the judge's head. He closed his eyes for a moment. He lifted his hands.

'Your gloves. Why the gloves?' Curiosity perhaps, just plain human curiosity.

'I have a condition. Reynaud's syndrome it's called. I get very cold. My hands turn white. My fingers are useless.' He tried to keep his voice neutral. Tell her nothing she doesn't ask.

'Oh yes, I've heard of that. So you wear the gloves all the time, do you?' She picked up her bag.

He nodded. 'They're like a second skin to me now.' Soft, smooth, the leather cleaving to what lay beneath.

'OK, just one more thing. We understand you have keys to the judge's house.'

He nodded. He put his hand in his trouser pocket and pulled them out.

'If you don't mind I'll take them.' She reached towards him. He held them by their ring. They swung gently to and fro.

'Thanks. We'll leave it at that, for the time being.' She reached in her bag and pulled out a card. She put it on the narrow mantelpiece. 'We will want to take your fingerprints and swab for your DNA and if you think of anything, anything at all, please call.' She held out her hand. She took his. She squeezed. Gently at first, then her grip tightened. He could feel her skin through the leather, against his. He felt sick.

He closed the door behind them and locked it. Fingerprints, swabs, he felt sick when he thought about it. He pressed his face to the frosted glass panel. They had gone. He stepped backwards into the hall. The floorboard gave beneath his weight. He opened the cupboard. He looked down. He'd copied the judge's keys. He'd put them with his other treasures. Hidden away. Nothing here to show what lay beneath. Nothing at all.

The pile of flowers on the footpath outside the judge's house was growing. It had begun slowly. A small bunch left by one of the old ladies from across the square. McLoughlin recognised marigolds, cornflowers and sweet pea. And every time McLoughlin went through his gate he noticed more. Lots of lilies, the big pink ones called Regale, their scent rising in the warm air. His mother had hated them, hated their cloying smell.

The guard on duty had become an unofficial flower arranger. Taking the bouquets and placing them carefully, then, McLoughlin noticed, standing back to assess the overall look and moving some of them around. Putting the smaller bunches to the front and arranging the lilies so they draped gracefully against the railings.

McLoughlin bent down to look more closely at the cards shoved into the bouquets. There was no doubting the esteem in which the judge was held. Expressions of shock and horror at the manner of his death from some; sadness and affectionate memories from others. As he straightened a car pulled up to the kerb. He watched the passengers get out. Three men and a woman. Judge Hegarty's children. The oldest, Ciarán, was a well-known cancer specialist. Media happy, McLoughlin thought, always on the news: this was wrong and that was wrong and there should be more of this and more of that. The others: one a barrister, following in his father's footsteps. The third son, a property developer, probably bankrupt now like the rest. And the judge's daughter, equally well known, a journalist with a column in one of the tabloids. He'd spoken to her often, when he was still working. She'd got hold of his mobile number and she'd ring to ask for updates. He didn't like that. It was an intrusion. But she had a way with her. Somehow she always made him laugh and sometimes he gave her a quote. An innocuous, harmless piece of information transformed by a strange kind of alchemy into a striking headline.

As she passed him by he caught her eye. He smiled.

'I'm so sorry,' he held out his hand, 'so very sorry.'

She nodded and swallowed. He could see she was on the verge of tears.

'Thanks,' her face was pale, her eyes red-rimmed. 'Are you?'

She stopped, looking up at the uniformed guard.

'No,' he shook his head, 'retired now. As it happens.'

'Oh of course,' she smiled. 'It was you, wasn't it? Who found him.'

'Yeah, that's right. I'm very sorry,' he repeated his words, unsure now what to say. 'If I can do anything, at all. You have my number.'

'Yes,' she nodded again, and he saw the family resemblance. A handsome lot, the Hegartys. The portrait on the wall upstairs. Dan in his prime. McLoughlin could see his bearing in his grandchildren.

He watched as they walked up the steps and through the front door. The guard closed it firmly behind them. A small knot of people had gathered. Young mothers with kids in buggies, a jogger in shorts and a damp T-shirt, and three photographers, cameras with huge lenses all pointed at the windows. As another car approached, slowed, stopped, and a voice called out his name.

'Hey, Michael,' Johnny Harris, unmistakeable, the characteristic booming volume. 'Fancy a drink?'

They sat in the yacht club bar. It was empty. Sunlight played across the low mahogany tables. The windows, wide open, looked out onto the deck, thronged at weekends with sailors, but deserted now save for a large fat seagull. A faint tinkle of rigging banging against masts drifted into the large, high-ceilinged room. McLoughlin leaned back into the deep, tweed-covered armchair. It creaked beneath him.

'This is nice,' he sipped his coffee.

'Yes,' Harris raised his cup. 'Very civilised.'

There was silence for a moment. Just the sound of the club burgee flapping gently in the light breeze and the far off clatter of cutlery as the tables in the dining room next door were laid for lunch.

'So?' McLoughlin looked across at Harris. 'The post-mortem. Tell me all.'

There was no doubt how the Judge had died. A bullet fired at close range into the nape of his neck. Exited through his neck. Death was instantaneous. Spinal cord severed. But it hadn't caused the damage to his face.

'It wasn't the bullet that did that. Although, the Webley .45, as you know, is the largest calibre. Developed by the British Army in the 1880s, designed to stop a chappie with a spear or a bow and arrow at a hundred yards.' Harris sipped his coffee.

'Yeah, knock-down power, all the energy goes into the body.' McLoughlin lifted the small biscuit from his saucer and began to strip off the cellophane. He'd had no breakfast. The big Polish labourer had taken a sledgehammer to the kitchenette this morning. There'd be precious little cooking done from now on. 'So the shot killed him, but didn't do the rest?'

'No, the angle was wrong. It smashed through the vertebrae. But the face, that was something like a hammer.' Harris reached across and snatched the biscuit from his fingers.

'Hey,' McLoughlin's expression was one of mock outrage. 'Eat your own.' He leaned over and slid the other biscuit from Harris' saucer. He rested it in his palm for a moment. 'It was done after death of course, obvious from the blood spatter, or lack of it.'

'Congratulations. You haven't forgotten everything.' Harris bit down on the biscuit.

'Not everything. Just most things.' McLoughlin began to strip away the wrapper. 'But why? Doesn't make sense, does it?'

'Well, disfigurement, dishonouring,' Harris shifted. 'You'd often see it, but usually associated with a sex crime.' He paused. He munched.

'I heard about the Webley. In the glass cabinet, and the ammunition in the drawer.'

'You did, did you? Aren't you the clever one?' Harris' mouth was full of biscuit. 'Mmm, nice. Do you want another?' He waved his hand in the direction of the barman who was polishing a row of wine glasses. McLoughlin shook his head, patting his stomach.

'Watching my weight, all part of the new leaf I've turned over, since I moved down to the town.' He picked up his cup and swirled the remaining coffee around. The barman appeared. He bent down. He placed a handful of biscuits on the table between them.

'Anything else, sir?' His accent was Eastern European.

'Thanks, no,' Harris shook his head as he helped himself.

'So, interesting, isn't it?' McLoughlin sat back on the sofa and crossed his legs. 'The gun, the Webley, pride of place with all the other Hegarty memorabilia. I'm surprised, actually, that he still had it. I'd have thought he'd have handed it up in '72 when the gun amnesty came in.'

'Well,' Harris licked his fingers, 'if you were a Hegarty, you wouldn't think something as pedestrian as the gun amnesty applied to you. That was for ordinary folk, with ordinary guns, ordinary guns used in ordinary crimes. Not the Webley. Not part of the shrine to the blessed Daniel. Someone took that gun and used it on his son. An act of defiance. Almost an act of sacrilege. A despoilment, a blasphemy.' Harris crunched down on a biscuit, scattering crumbs across his shirt.

'Kind of nasty,' McLoughlin placed his cup neatly on its saucer.

'Not as nasty as,' Harris paused, 'as the rest of what was done to him. Means there'll be no open coffin at the wake. There'll be no public viewing, and those things matter to a lot of people.' Harris sat back.

'A hammer, eh? Sweeney didn't mention anything about that. I did notice the lads going through the skip outside. I wondered what they were looking for. They made an awful mess. My guys were pissed off having to put it all back again.'

'Sweeney eh?' Harris grinned at him. 'Chats with the lovely Inspector Sweeney is it?

'Not chats, an interview, about my statement. Very particular she was, very careful.'

'Well she would be, wouldn't she? A lot of people watching. She won't want to put a foot wrong.' Harris finished his biscuit and wiped his fingers with a paper napkin.

'And the ties around the judge's wrists and ankles? How long do you think he'd been like that?'

'Well,' Harris's hand reached out, his fingers twitching, withdrawing, then seizing a biscuit, like a blackbird pulling a worm from a lawn, 'can't be definitive. But a good few hours. There were deep lesions from the plastic. Not nice.' He paused. He looked down at the table.

'And?' McLoughlin leaned towards him. 'Come on, what else? I know you really want to tell me.'

Harris munched. 'I shouldn't, I know I shouldn't, but,' another long pause, 'he'd been beaten, pretty badly. Marks on his back, kidneys, heavy bruising on his groin.' He paused, swallowed. 'And some other very nasty stuff.'

'Yeah?'

'Yeah, he'd been gagged. Bruising inside his mouth and remains of fabric stuck between his teeth. Cigarette burns on his stomach and on the backs of his hands. Horrible.' He swallowed again, 'And other marks, some of them not new, on his shoulderblades and above. Healed scars.'

'Any ideas?'

Harris shrugged. 'Not really. Could be,' he paused, 'well a number of things. Not sure at the moment.'

They sat in silence. McLoughlin could see the judge, toppled forward, fragments of brain and shards of bone on the carpet and his hands and feet tied together. Harris sighed. He picked up his coffee and finished it. He wiped his mouth carefully with a paper napkin, crumpled it up into a ball and dropped it on the table. 'And now, that'll teach me. I feel sick.'

'Fresh air, that's what you need,' McLoughlin stood up. 'Come on outside, I want to show you a boat.'

They walked along the terrace and down the steps towards the marina pontoon. It was hot, even at the water's edge, sunlight bouncing off the sea, and sparking from the chrome fittings on the yachts tied up alongside. McLoughlin could feel sweat pooling in the small of his back.

'Lucky to be alive, aren't we, on a day like this,' he stopped.

'Yeah, we sure are,' Harris breathed in deeply. 'Smells good down here. All that salt. Positive ions, aren't they?'

They moved slowly along the wooden walkway.

'There, look,' McLoughlin waved his arm towards a medium sized cruiser. They both turned and gazed at her.

'Nice, very nice,' Harris nodded approvingly. 'Roller rigging, very handy, plenty of room in the cockpit, in case you might find someone to share your bunk.'

'I should be so lucky,' McLoughlin smiled, 'and you? Any love in your life?'

Harris shrugged. 'Not so you'd notice. My last young man didn't go the distance. Bright lights, big city beckoned. I heard he'd fetched up in Milan.' He sighed. 'A boat now. There's fidelity. Seaworthy like this one. You could go places in her. Condition looks good, any idea of a price?'

'Asking is somewhere around twenty grand, but,' McLoughlin paused and ran a hand appreciatively along the boat's railing, 'not many people with cash these days, so I reckon I could knock them down closer to fifteen. What do you think?'

'Sleep on it, don't make any hasty decisions, plenty more boats around and you've a lot on your plate already with the house.' Harris walked towards the boat's bow, peered down towards the waterline, then walked back. 'Good nick, looks to me. But let it sit for a while. Don't make an offer just yet.'

They moved back towards the clubhouse. A group of young teenagers, boys and girls, were dragging their small dinghys up the slip.

'Lovely for kids, isn't it?' McLoughlin stopped to watch.

Harris nodded. 'It is, right enough. I don't expect I'll see any of them on my slab any day soon.' He glanced down at his watch. 'Which reminds me, I'd better go back. Two more drug killings last night. It's going to be a long old day.'

McLoughlin walked with him to the car park. Harris fiddled with his keys. 'One other thing about John Hegarty.'

'Yeah?' McLoughlin put his hand up to shade his eyes against the sun.

'He had prostate cancer.' Harris opened the door. 'Advanced. He must have been in pain. It had begun to spread.'

'Wasn't he having treatment? His son, Ciarán, isn't he a consultant?' McLoughlin could feel drops of sweat on his forehead.

'Well that's the funny thing. I checked with his GP. I know him as it happens. A couple of years behind me in Trinity. He said the judge wouldn't have his PSA checked. Didn't want to know. Same about his cholesterol. As it happens that was all fine. His heart was that of a man years younger.' He drummed with his fingers on the car roof. 'His prostate now, he'd have been dead within the year.' He waved one hand in a farewell salute as he slammed the door.

McLoughlin watched him pull away from the curb, the characteristic two toots on the horn. He began to walk back to the house, along the seafront. Bright sunshine, a perfect summer's day, but he couldn't get the sight of the judge out of his mind's eye. It brought him back to that day, all those years ago. He was still in training. Just up from Templemore for a stint in the city centre. Word had come over the radio into the Bridewell. A guard had been shot in Dundrum. A terrible silence fell over the station. He knew what his father's movements had been.

His body was brought to the morgue in Store Street. The superintendent asked him if he would do the identification. He couldn't. He was scared of what he would see. They sent a car for his mother. She did it. She was the brave one. He was the coward. They never talked about it. All through those dreadful days of mourning. When the coffin came home with the lid closed and the house was filled with relatives and neighbours and guards from every station around the country. He sat up that night, sat in his father's favourite chair, candles lighting, the coffin closed. He sat, the bottle of whiskey beside him. He drank.

And the next morning when the undertaker's men wheeled the coffin from the house to the hearse, McLoughlin put his hand on the polished wood and whispered, 'Bye Da, see you soon,' the same words he had said three days before, as his father had left for work. 'Bye Da, see you soon.'

He was tired by the time he got back to Victoria Square. He was looking forward to his afternoon nap. But even from outside the house he could hear the banging. He sat down on the Cassidy bench. He'd wait here for a while.

'Hey Mick, how's it going?' Ian appeared on the top step, holding steady a wheelbarrow filled to overflowing. He paused, waved, then pushed it down the ramp and into the skip. A cloud of dust rose up. Ian coughed.

'Where's your mask?' McLoughlin called out.

The builder shrugged. 'Fucking thing, too hot for this weather.'

'You'll clean up the mess, won't you?' McLoughlin gestured at the heap the guards had left behind. Ian grinned, then waved again and turned, dragging the wheel barrow behind him. He disappeared into the house.

McLoughlin swung himself around so his feet were up on the seat and leaned his head on the armrest. He began to drift off, then stirred. A shadow had fallen across his face. He squinted one eye open.

'Hi, sorry, am I waking you?' Elizabeth Fannin was standing beside him. He hadn't heard her footsteps on the grass.

'No, not at all. Here,' he swung his legs down and patted the wooden seat. 'Set a spell, as they used to say in,' he paused, 'that TV programme, from way back.'

'*The Beverly Hill Billies*,' she laughed. 'You and me, we seem to have the same taste.'

She sat beside him. Her shirt and trousers today were the saffron of a Buddhist monk's robe. She closed her eyes and lifted her face towards the sun.

'I can't get over the weather,' her voice was soft and gentle. 'After last summer, dreadful the whole thing, everyone miserable. But this year,' she breathed deeply and he could see her amber necklace rise and fall.

'Yes, it's amazing. Every morning when I wake up, it's just fantastic, and then you start worrying.'

'Will it be the last beautiful day?' She opened her eyes and half turned to him. 'We're a terrible lot aren't we? Always waiting for disaster, anticipating what's to come.'

'We should be living in the now.' He stretched out his legs on the grass. 'Mindfulness, the new buzz word.'

'Whatever,' she closed her eyes again, 'just enjoy it while it lasts, that's what I say.'

They sat in silence. McLoughlin looked towards the judge's house. He twisted on the seat. He could feel his jaw tensing, his fists clenching. And Elizabeth must have felt it too. She opened her eyes and turned towards him. Her expression was full of concern.

'What's wrong?' She reached out, her hand resting on the back of his.

He shrugged. He felt close to tears.

'What is it? Tell me.' She took his hand and squeezed it.

The tears were coming now. A slow, steady drip and a deep, rasping sob. 'Michael, what is it?' She pulled a tissue from her pocket. She turned his face towards her and gently wiped the tears away. He swallowed hard. He tried to speak.

'Shh,' she said, 'there's no rush. Whenever you feel like it.'

They sat in silence. He was conscious of her body. He could feel her thigh almost, but not quite, touching his.

'It's just,' he swallowed hard. 'I'm thinking about my father.'

'Your father? Oh yes,' she smiled at him. 'I remember when he was killed.'

'You do? And how did you know that I was, that he was…' his voice trailed away.

'Oh, you know. You can't keep secrets here. Everyone knows something about everyone.' She stroked his hand. Her rings shone in the sunlight. 'So, tell me about him.'

McLoughlin stood outside the church gates. The bell tolled a single note. The hearse had just arrived, escorted by police motorcycles followed by a number of long black cars. The family gathered in a knot. Judge Hegarty's three sons, daughter, daughters-in-law, grandchildren and a scattering of older men and women. All wore expensive black. A crowd milled around. McLoughlin recognised a number of the faces. The Ministers for Justice and Health, a few TDs, two army officers, aide-de-camps to the President and the Taoiseach, the official gold braid aguillettes on their shoulders. Up and down the footpath on either side and across the road the curious had gathered. Press photographers and TV crews poised for the dramatic moments of celebrity grief. A cameraman having a last pull on his cigarette. As the back of the hearse opened, all sprang into action.

The priest appeared at the church door. He blessed the coffin and turned. The undertakers hoisted it onto their shoulders. The family followed. All began to walk slowly inside. McLoughlin waited until they disappeared from view, then moved forward. He found a place at the back, squeezed between two tall men in suits. Silence fell as the funeral party processed up the aisle. The organist was playing 'Jesu Joy of Man Desiring'. At the altar five more priests waited. A moment of stillness, then the mass began.

McLoughlin shifted awkwardly from side to side. Around him people muttered the words, made the familiar gestures, knelt, stood, knelt again. A soloist sang hymns in Irish. The gospel readings and the prayers for the faithful were said by the Hegarty grandchildren, good looking like their parents, their voices strong and confident, their

82

accents ranging somewhere between middle-class Dublin and the intonations of Hollywood. The parish priest, a tall handsome man, grey haired, spoke in glowing terms of the judge's service. To the church, the parish, his wife and children and last but not least, to the State. An older priest, stooped and bent, came forward to the altar. McLoughlin recognised him. He was a bishop, one of those criticised for their lack of vigilance in the child abuse scandals. There had been calls for his resignation, but he had toughed it out, ignoring his accusers with a mixture of arrogance and clerical self-confidence, until eventually he had to go. He was also a Hegarty. McLoughlin hadn't made the connection before. Not an uncle, but perhaps some kind of cousin, once removed or second, perhaps? Despite his physical frailty the priest's voice was strong as he said the prayer for peace. McLoughlin turned to the man on his right and shook his hand. All around clasps were proffered and exchanged. He leaned back against the wall and watched the communion rite performed. The host was held up and blessed, wine poured and drunk. The familiar words echoed around the church. The last supper, Christ and his disciples breaking bread together. The prophecy of suffering and death, and the promise of redemption. The magic and mystery of the bread and wine becoming body and blood.

The communion lay-servers took their places halfway down the aisle. McLoughlin watched the queues form. He didn't receive any longer. Last time had been at his mother's funeral a couple of years ago. It would have been churlish to refuse. She'd have given him a look if he'd hung back, the look that said, don't let me down. Don't be like your sister. Clare, the rebel, who'd vanished to London as soon as she graduated from UCD with a degree in social science. Who'd lived in student squats, eventually marrying a guy from Glasgow, when she became pregnant with her daughter. She came home, reluctantly, when their mother died. She didn't take part in the mass, ill at ease with the rites and rituals. She had sat with her head bowed, her hands tightly clasped in her lap. Rejected his handshake, and left as soon as possible afterwards. Never phoned or emailed. Gone from his life.

Now he stood watching the queue shuffling forward. The soloist was singing 'Che farò senza Euridice'. He leaned back against the wall, closed his eyes and let the music wash over him It was a tear-jerker, no doubt about that. In his mind's eye it was Elizabeth Fannin he could see. Walking slowly towards the house, her saffron clothes glowing in the afternoon sun. The warmth of her touch as she comforted him. The sympathy and understanding in her voice as they talked about his father's death. The way her smile transformed her face.

He opened his eyes. People were still moving from their pews into the aisle, and filtering then, back to their seats. There were faces he recognised, the garda commissioner in uniform and behind him Min Sweeney, looking tense and anxious. He felt a pang of sympathy for her. No arrests, no dramatic dawn raids on suspects' houses. Nothing to satisfy the media or the commissioner. He watched Min settling herself. He'd call her after this was over. Maybe she'd like to chat, shoot the breeze.

He looked away and back towards the shuffling queue. It was nearly at an end now, a huddle of people waiting to sit down. Among them two familiar figures. The men from the photographs in James Reynolds' bar. McLoughlin felt his stomach churn, a bang in his heart and the hairs rise up on the back of his neck. He wanted to leave, to get out and breathe some fresh air, but the crowd pressed in around him and now there was silence as the soloist ended. A sudden burst of coughing, throats being cleared and movement at the top of the church as a man, dressed in a black suit, took his place at the pulpit. McLoughlin recognised him. Liam Hegarty, John's younger brother, a businessman of note. Started life as an accountant, then moved into high finance. A collector of contemporary Irish art. Hugely respected, solid investments, not like the fly-by-nights of the boom. McLoughlin had come across him years before when his house had been ransacked and burgled, his wife and children threatened.

Liam Hegarty cleared his throat. He began to speak. He came before this congregation, a broken man. Not only had his beloved and revered elder brother died, but the manner of his death diminished us all. John Hegarty was possessed with rare integrity. He had given up much to serve the people. He had put the pursuit of justice before the pursuit of personal happiness, personal satisfaction. His community owed him their gratitude.

McLoughlin listened as Liam Hegarty spelled out the nature of his brother's brilliance, his goodness, his worth and value. His voice echoed through the church. McLoughlin glanced around. All were spellbound by the oratory, the power of the words. Liam Hegarty was, he realised, placing his brother in the pantheon of those who had lived and died for Ireland, the men who were executed in Kilmainham, shot during the Civil War, who died in Derry on Bloody Sunday.

'Something is wrong,' Hegarty said, 'something is very wrong with our world when a man like my brother can die like this. It is up to all of us, every single member of the community, to ask ourselves why did this happen? And to make a solemn promise. We will not tolerate this kind of lawlessness, this kind of cruelty. In this, our republic we will not allow this kind of obscenity to exist any longer.'

His voice rose, then fell and he was silent. Applause echoed around the church and the congregation stood as one. The parish priest moved towards the coffin. He raised his hand in final blessing. The younger priest by his side swung the thurible vigorously and a cloud of incense-laden smoke drifted up to heaven. The male members of the Hegarty family stepped forward. They lifted the coffin onto their shoulders. They walked slowly down the aisle and out into the sunshine. McLoughlin waited for the family to pass, then began to push through the crowd.

Outside it was the usual post-funeral mass scene. There was an air of excitement, of a ritual having been enacted. The family stood by the hearse. People crowded around. McLoughlin watched. The men he had recognised in the photograph that day in Bassano del Grappa approached. The tallest of the two put his arm around Ciarán Hegarty's shoulder. He bent his head and shook his hand, whispering in his ear. The other man embraced Róisín Hegarty. She smiled up at him, her expression grateful. The two of them then moved slowly from the church towards the road. The crowd parted, people reaching out to slap their backs, offering support and admiration.

McLoughlin could stand it no longer. He followed them quickly as they walked towards their car, parked by the row of small shops.

'Hey,' his voice was loud in his ears, 'hey, you.'

He broke into a jog. Ahead of him the two men seemed not to have heard. He shouted again, louder this time, his voice bordering on hysteria.

'Don't walk away from me. Look me in the face.'

He skirted around, standing between them and their car. He could see they didn't have a clue who he was. He shouted again.

'Remember the 31st of August 1975? Remember Garda Joe McLoughlin? Remember how he died?'

They both stopped and turned towards him. McLoughlin could feel their power, their sense of authority. These were men who knew how to lead, to dominate, to control, to kill, to get their own way regardless of the damage they caused.

The taller of the two looked him up and down. He began to speak, slowly and deliberately.

'Friend, keep calm.' He raised his arms. 'Whatever you're talking about, this isn't the place to do it. Respect, friend, respect for the family.'

Beside him the other man smiled. He turned away and jerked his head. Immediately a third man appeared. He was large, well built, his expression blank as he placed himself in front of McLoughlin. A solid wall of body.

'You can't get away with this,' McLoughlin's voice was loud, angry. 'James Reynolds. I know where he is. I've seen him. I know you've seen him too. Come back. Face me. Speak to me. '

The stocky, heavily built man moved closer. He crossed his arms over his torso, his legs spread wide. Behind him the other two were getting into their car. McLoughlin could just about see them, over the bodyguard's shoulder. He could hear the doors slamming.

'Come back you bastards. Come back and face me.' The bodyguard was moving away now, step by careful step, leaving McLoughlin standing on the footpath, alone, and with again that sense of weakness, of helplessness, of paralysis. The car drove off. He stared after it, then shouted again, waving his fist. Conscious now that people were looking at him. Cameramen rushed forward. A TV reporter shoved a microphone in his face, and the crowd milled across the road, threatening to engulf him, as Min Sweeney appeared, taking him by the arm and pulling him away.

'Don't look back. Don't look at any of them. Keep walking.' Her arm through his, her pace brisk, so he almost tripped as he tried to keep up, as she half-dragged him down the road and away from them all.

They sat in the Eagle House bar. Min had pushed him into a dark corner, far from the blare of the TV. She put a glass of whiskey on the table, and two large cups of coffee.

'Drink,' she said. 'And then tell me for God's sake what was going on out there.'

His hand when he lifted the glass wasn't quite steady. But the whiskey helped. It burned as it slid down his oesophagus and a warm glow spread through his body, soothing him.

'Well,' he began. He told her. His trip to Venice. How he'd gone to Bassano del Grappa.

'Where?' she poured milk into one of the cups and stirred in a sachet of sugar.

'North of Venice, towards the mountains. An hour or so by train.'

'And?' She glanced at her watch.

He told her then about James Reynolds, about going to the little museum, his conversation with the waiter, finding the Shamrock Bar, the woman who served him tea, and finally the encounter with Reynolds outside.

'And I couldn't get over it,' his hand still wasn't quite steady as he lifted the glass. 'I saw him, I was so close to him. He looked at me. He didn't know me. That man who almost destroyed me and my family and he looked through me. Like I was any old tourist visiting any old picturesque town in Italy. Just any old tourist looking for a pizza and a glass of red wine. And I did nothing. I said nothing. I walked away. And I haven't been able to get him out of my head since.'

She sipped her coffee. 'I take it you knew he was there.'

He shrugged. 'I'd heard, years ago, he'd been there. I didn't know if he still was, but the website, you know,' he sighed heavily, then drank some more.

'Well,' she sipped her coffee, holding the large cup with both her hands. 'There's nothing you can do now, Mick. You have to accept that it's over.'

'Why?' He looked at her. 'It's not over for me, or any of the other people they killed. It goes on and on. And you know something? The more time passes, the worse it gets.'

He hadn't thought of it like that before, not really, not so clearly. But it was true. When it happened it was terrible. But so were lots of other killings. Time passed and the pain seemed to lessen. He was in that active part of his life. The job, his marriage, his future. It was all bright and intense. And there was still a belief that someone would be punished for his father's death. But there was no punishment. Those who were responsible for the killings stopped being pariahs. Now they were peacemakers. And he had watched, incredulous.

'The aftermath to war,' Min shifted in her seat. She crossed her legs. She was wearing a black suit today. Her hair was pulled back into a sleek roll. Her heels were high, shiny black leather. 'It's messy and nasty. Justice isn't done. That town, didn't you say, they fought on both sides? Imagine what it was like there after the ceasefire. Imagine who had to shake hands with whom so life could go on.'

He shook his head. He drank his whiskey. 'I can't accept it. I know what you're saying. But I can't accept it.' He got up and walked over to the bar. He gestured to the barman and lifted his glass. He turned towards Min. 'Another coffee?'

'Look,' she pointed towards the TV. It was the lunchtime news. He saw the church, the coffin, the family, the dignitaries, the crowds spilling outside. He saw himself, the confrontation. The tall man was interviewed outside Dáil Éireann. His words were soothing. Unfortunate, bad timing, not the place. If he wants to meet me, no problem. Terrible things happened. Communities suffered. Oppression, discrimination, time to move forward, time to heal. We have all suffered the loss of loved ones, but bitterness serves no one.

'You've done me a favour,' Min raised her cup. 'If you hadn't had your little set-to, they'd have been door-stepping me, looking for a suspect, looking for answers.'

'And do you have any?' McLoughlin sat down again.

Min shook her head. 'To be honest we haven't a clue. The house is full of fingerprints. Fucking useless. It'll take us weeks to get through them. And DNA too.'

'CCTV?'

'From the main street, nothing in the square. Also fucking useless.'

'Anything online?'

'There's a desktop computer in the study. Emails, mostly to do with some academic research. Family stuff, photos, the usual. His google history was what you'd call unremarkable. Bought himself a few books, nothing much.'

'Getting anywhere with suspects?'

She smiled grimly and shook her head. 'You'd have known a lot of them, wouldn't you?'

'Indeed I would. It was a bad time, nasty stuff.'

'O'Leary, he was the one.' She fiddled with her cup.

'The one indeed. The first to really organise his boys into a gang. The first to turn it from a hobby into an enterprise. I never thought we'd get a conviction. Had to be the special court. The only way to get a bastard like Brian O'Leary. And,' he leaned back in his seat and folded his arms, 'he was a savage. That stuff done to the judge, apart from his face, that's the kind of thing O'Leary would have relished.'

'What stuff?' She looked at him. 'What do you know?'

'Oh, just, nothing really.' He smiled.

'Fucking Harris, can't keep his fucking mouth shut.' She picked up her bag. 'The face I'll give you, after all you saw it. But the rest of it, I'm warning you, Mick. Keep it to yourself. We've too many guys making a few bob on the side. Selling information, the new way to top-up your wages and curry favours.'

McLoughlin reached out and patted her hand. 'Calm down, would you? I know what side I'm on. Yours, and only yours.'

'Yeah, well,' she stood up, 'doesn't solve my problem. O'Leary's in prison, and who's going to care enough about the judge to kill him?'

McLoughlin smiled. 'Who knows? Hate, love, jealousy, the workings of the human heart. A mystery, always a mystery.'

'Yeah,' she checked her phone, 'a mystery I need to solve. I've a briefing this afternoon. I'd better get back to the office and get my ducks in a row.' She stood. 'You want a lift anywhere?'

He shook his head. 'Thanks, no. I'll just sit here and finish my drink, and ponder.'

She moved towards the door, then turned back. 'Good luck with the pondering. Let me know if you come up with anything. And,' she paused and fiddled with her phone which had begun to beep loudly, 'in relation to Reynolds. I seem to remember that Tom Donnelly from Harcourt Square, he was involved in the investigation. Why don't you give him a call? You never know what's been going on.'

'Been there, done that,' he smiled up at her.

'And?'

'What you'd expect. Investigation still open, any information gratefully received.'

She nodded and shrugged. He watched her walk away. He didn't envy her. She'd drawn the short straw with this one. Murders usually solved themselves. Gangland? Well it was pretty obvious. Just join up a few dots. Domestic? Similarly obvious. Drunken row? Drinking buddy. Eastern Europeans? Other Eastern Europeans. But the judge? He ran over the possibilities. He felt bad. He was his neighbour. He should have known something was wrong. And how could he not have realised that there was someone in the house when he went in? He drained his glass. Time to go.

He walked back towards the church. All was quiet now. He was hungry. It was lunchtime. If his timing was right Ian and his lads would have stopped for their break. He'd make himself a sandwich. He'd sit in the wreckage of the house and imagine how it would be in a few months' time.

He walked across the green. Another beautiful day. The grass beneath his feet turning brown, scuffed and lifeless. The skip outside the gate was full. They'd cleaned up the mess on the footpath. He paused, looked at it, then carried on up the steps. Fumbling in his jeans for the keys, as he heard an excited bark and saw the little black dog sitting on the judge's front step. Jumping up to scratch the door, his curly tail wagging overtime as he whined. Then, as he noticed McLoughlin, he scurried down, rushed towards him, his small body thrashing from side to side. He lay at McLoughlin's feet, and rolled over, his mouth opening and his long pink tongue lolling. Then jumped up again, and sat, one paw held out and his ears pricked up.

'Well Ferdie, what brings you here?' McLoughlin bent down. He patted the dog's head. He looked into his large brown eyes, opened the door and stood back. The dog ran in.

'This way,' McLoughlin called and the dog followed him up the stairs. He found a bowl and filled it with water from the bathroom. The dog drank, greedily. Then lay down and closed his eyes. A shudder ran through his body. His chest heaved. His breathing slowed. He slept. How far had he travelled? McLoughlin wondered. The homing instinct, a powerful emotion. Wanting to get back to where you come from. Wanting to belong. It wasn't only dogs who had it.

Today would be an Elizabeth Fannin day. Samuel liked Elizabeth Fannin days. Or he used to. For a while they had been difficult. When the 'For Sale' sign went up on the house she had told him she would have to move. He didn't like that. He couldn't find her new place. She had given him the address and told him which bus to take and where to get off. But he couldn't figure it out. His sense of direction had deserted him. He had got lost many times. Confused, frightened, wandering around on his own.

But now, the relief. She told him she'd got her old room back. And so today it was an Elizabeth Fannin day, and it was going to be just like old times.

Except it wasn't quite like that. The house was the same although there was a lot of rubbish outside and a large skip filled with wood and concrete and plaster and all kinds of other stuff. Samuel had something in his bag. He wanted to get rid of it. He'd been carrying it around for days now, trying to find a hiding place. He'd cleaned it thoroughly. But he didn't like having it with him. It reminded him. The sound of the hammer as it crashed into the judge's skull. The sight of the blood bursting from beneath the skin, the eyes, falling out of their sockets. The tiny drops of blood on his shoes and his trousers. It made him feel sick. Although he knew he'd been right to do it. The judge needed to be punished.

Samuel peered into the skip. It was full of nooks and crannies. It looked good. But there were men working in the house still, going in and out with wheelbarrows, the roar and thunder as they emptied their loads. He'd wait until later, when it would be quiet again, and he could take the hammer from his bag. And he'd never have to look at it again. Ever.

Now he walked to the little red door. He pressed the little white bell. He waited. The door opened. Elizabeth smiled.

'Come in,' she said. She took him by the hand. She led him down the corridor. It was cool and dark. She opened the door. She stood back. He walked inside. He looked around. Two windows in front of him, barred. Elizabeth's chair. His chair. The pictures on the white walls. He knew them well. The lemon tree with its yellow fruit hanging low. Another one with big red flowers. And his favourite, the blue mountains and the white cottages with the stack of turf.

He took a step forward, and felt his feet on the rug, red and blue and orange and black. He knew it well. He'd looked at the pattern so many times. It was worn in spots and he liked that about it. It felt the way he felt. Worn in spots.

Elizabeth waved him towards his usual place.

'Now,' she said, 'is this better?'

He nodded and smiled. He sat down. His breath came out in a long sigh. She sat too.

'Now,' her voice was soft and comforting, 'tell me Samuel, how have you been?'

The lorry pulled up outside the house promptly at 7.30 in the morning. The driver jumped from the cab. He hitched the skip to the long metal arms which hung down from the back. Then he got into the cab and put the hoist in gear. The skip began to lift from the ground. It hung suspended in mid-air. It rose higher. And the load shifted. Masonry, plaster, stone, suddenly tumbling from the skip so that it tilted, almost upending. A pile of rubble on the ground as the driver increased the pressure and the engine revved and rumbled and the skip levelled out and moved, slowly, onto the lorry.

The driver got out of the cab. He looked at the heap. He bent down and picked something up. A hammer, a wooden handle smooth to the touch. He shook it to see if the metal head was loose. Amazing the things that people threw away. Good tools were always worth keeping. He swung up into the cab and dropped the hammer on the seat beside him. He released the handbrake and drove away from the house. Good to get an early start. It was hot already, sunlight pouring through the windscreen. If the day stayed like this he'd get home early and take the kids to the beach for a swim. He leaned into his seat and began to hum. Such a lovely day.

Another lovely day. McLoughlin had been woken early by sun streaming around the shutters and the bang and clatter of the truck picking up the skip. He'd heard the sound of falling debris but by the time he got himself out of bed and down the stairs the truck had gone, leaving behind a large pile of rubble. He stood on the top step staring at it, then with a sigh of resignation he grabbed a wheelbarrow and a shovel and set to work cleaning it up. There'd be another skip coming later and there was no point leaving the mess for Ian to sort. He'd already done enough cleaning up after the guards.

He worked away, getting some kind of satisfaction from the restoring of order. The dog followed him onto the footpath. He stopped at the gate to Hegarty's house, sniffed around, lifted his leg, sniffed again. McLoughlin watched him. He looked dejected, suddenly sad, his curly little tail drooping, his ears flopping forward, the expression in his brown eyes downcast. McLoughlin leaned down and patted his head. He was overwhelmed by a sense of sadness, a sense of loss.

'There's a good fella, there's a good boy', his voice was soft and gentle. The dog looked at him and lifted his paw. McLoughlin took it and gave it a formal shake. He'd never had a dog. His mother hadn't liked them. Or any other animals. And Janey had been a cat person. But now as he watched the little black poodle, he felt a warmth which surprised him. He'd better, he supposed, contact Hegarty's daughter. She'd probably want the dog. Or maybe, he thought as he pushed the wheelbarrow out of the way of the steps and picked up the shovel, maybe he wouldn't. Maybe he'd wait for someone to come looking for him. In the meantime he could stay here.

He stood for a moment and looked up and down the terrace. Front doors were opening. Cars starting up and driving off slowly. People going to work. He pushed the wheelbarrow filled with rubble out of the way. He was hungry. The builders would be here soon. He went back into the house and made himself coffee, spreading butter and honey thickly on a piece of brown bread. He called the dog, and together they walked down the steps and into the back garden. He sat on a rickety garden chair. Ferdie ran up and down investigating the overgrown greenery. McLoughlin watched him with interest. He was surprised he wasn't trying to get over the wall but he showed no inclination. He ran and panted and sniffed and every now and then would rush towards McLoughlin and sit before him, his eyes fixed on the piece of bread in his hand. Then rush away, ferreting through the overgrown grass and shrubs. And rush back again, this time with a balding tennis ball which he dropped at McLoughlin's feet and stood, waiting, panting with excitement.

'Go on, make his day,' Ian stood at the top of the steps. McLoughlin got up and threw the ball in a high arc. Ferdie stood on his hind legs, balancing and watching as it flew, waiting, then running beneath it, leaping up and catching it in his mouth.

'Woo hoo!' Ian cheered and clapped, as the dog ran to McLoughlin, dropping the ball at his feet, stepping back a couple of paces and waiting.

'Look what you've started,' McLoughlin bent down to retrieve it. He juggled it in his hands. 'I'll be at this all day now.'

'And what better way to spend your retirement,' Ian waved as he ducked back inside.

'OK, one more for luck,' McLoughlin lifted the ball and threw it again, this time towards the house. It bounced crookedly and slammed against one of the basement windows. He cringed, waiting for the sound of breaking glass but the ball glanced off and the dog seized it and this time ran away, lying with it trapped between his front paws. The window opened and a voice called out,

'Having fun?' Elizabeth Fannin's face appearing as he walked towards her.

'Sorry,' he stopped, smiling, 'you're here early.'

She held up a pile of papers and waved a pen at them.

He beckoned, 'Come on out, lovely sunshine, come and enjoy it.'

There was another garden chair folded up against the wall and he opened it, placing it beside his. He sat down again as she appeared. Once again she was wearing loose linen trousers and a shirt. This time they were deep purple, the colour of the Morning Glory he had grown one summer up a wigwam of bamboo canes in his garden in Stepaside. He made a mental note. Next year he'd have them here.

He patted the chair beside him. 'I won't say it.'

'Set a spell,' she butted in, and smiled. And again the world was a brighter, happier place. She sat on the chair. It wobbled beneath her and she kicked off her leather sandals and braced her feet.

'Not sure how reliable these are.' She shifted and the chair wobbled again. 'We bought them years ago. One of my colleagues was very keen on eating his lunch outside. It must have been during those good summers back then, 2005, 2006, can't remember which, but we went through a phase of having picnics. That particular guy, Tony was his name, he was a very good gardener and he kept it all beautifully. It was lovely,' and she smiled again and leaned back, closing her eyes.

McLoughlin felt a surge of jealousy. He chided himself, don't be ridiculous, but somehow just hearing her mention another man, another relationship, spoiled the moment. He looked over, taking the opportunity to examine her face properly. She must be in her fifties, he reckoned. She must have been very beautiful when she was young, when her skin was smooth and unlined, when her hair was dark. He looked at her hands, loosely clasped in her lap and her feet strong and tanned, her toes splayed out, her body relaxed. She was still beautiful, he decided, and not just when she smiled.

As if aware of his gaze, she opened her eyes and straightened up. She fanned herself with her hand. 'It's hot out here. The basement is always a lot cooler.'

'Yes, cooler, probably downright cold.'

She shrugged. 'It's OK, I don't mind. I bring a shawl for the evenings.'

McLoughlin turned slightly towards her. 'Can I ask you, if I'm not being too nosy.'

'What?' she looked anxious.

'Your clothes,' he gestured towards her trousers, 'always the same design and the colours, beautiful colours, strong, powerful, not a pastel in sight.'

'Aah, you've noticed,' she sat up straight.

'Yeah, is there a reason?

'Actually there is, kind of,' she fiddled with the top button of her shirt. McLoughlin noticed that it was made of something like mother of pearl.

'So? Tell? If you want to. If I'm not being too nosy,' he smiled.

'Well, the reason for the colours, well,' she paused and looked away, 'it'll sound ridiculous to you I'm sure, but years ago when I was a student I was a disciple of the guru, the Bhagwan. Do you know anything about him?'

'The guy the Beatles went off to visit?'

She smiled. 'He was the Guru Maharishi, all beads and sitars. Mine was the Bhagwan. We were orange people. Remember now?'

A vague memory. 'Not the Hare Krishnas?'

'No, they were into chanting and selling magazines and incense on Grafton Street. I don't know what we believed really, but we all had to wear orange, although it wasn't just orange. There was a spectrum of colours from orange, through red, to crimson, and purple was OK too. I still like the colours and so in the summer, I wear them. They're sort of positive, life affirming, they make me feel good.'

They sat in silence for a moment. Ferdie had given up on the ball and was lying quietly, snoring under the lilac.

'You were a bit of a rebel?' McLoughlin stirred. The chair wasn't comfortable. But he didn't want to move in case she would take it as a cue and get up and go inside.

'Yep, I was the classic. It started with the guru. I ran away to London when I was very young. I lived in what was called an ashram, a kind of a commune,' she shuddered. 'God when I think of it. Someone had squatted a big house in Ladbroke Grove. A floating population. Lots of dope, lots of brown rice and lots of beautiful young men being waited on hand and foot by stupid young women.'

'Really? Weren't you all feminists then?' He turned and looked at her again.

'Far from it I'm afraid. I realised after a few weeks that it was just another con,' she smiled. 'When I think of it. The pill seemed such a good idea to begin with, but then, rather than giving us power it took our power away. And all those so-called communes. There was nothing communal about them. At the top was always a man, and us poor orangey girls were way down the pecking order. Cooking the food, rolling the joints, providing the comfort.' She sat up straight in the chair and it wobbled dangerously from side to side. 'But, going to London was great once I escaped from the clutches of the guru.'

'Yeah? I didn't do it. I was destined for the Guards and after my father was killed, well, I couldn't leave my mother.' He looked down at his hands. 'My sister, Clare, she was the rebel, the runaway. She did a version of what you're describing. But I think her squat was more political. Socialist Workers, all that kind of thing.'

'Well I'm afraid I was a bit of a Clare.' She paused and looked away. 'I didn't have any scruples. I don't think I gave a thought about my poor parents. It was all fun, fun, fun.' Her expression was suddenly sad. Her mouth drooped and her shoulders sloped. She crossed her legs, wrapping them tightly around each other. He wanted to reach out and touch her hand, but he wasn't sure if he could do that. The silence this time was uneasy. Even the dog seemed to sense it. He got up and came over, nuzzling his curly head against McLoughlin's knee. He reached down and scratched behind his ears and the dog whined softly.

'You've a friend there.' Elizabeth leaned over and patted him too. 'I thought he'd gone to the family.'

'He turned up yesterday, outside the house. He must have figured how to get here, clever boy. So I thought I'd just bring him in. Actually,' he paused and stroked the dog's neck, 'I like him. He's fun. I'll wait until someone realises he's gone missing and comes for him.' He pulled Ferdie's face towards his. 'Won't I little fella? Won't I?'

Elizabeth uncurled her legs and straightened herself up. Colour had come back to her face. 'I remember when the judge got the dog. We were all amazed. He didn't seem the poodle type.'

'No? You knew him?' For some reason he was surprised.

'Yes of course. I remember when he moved in. His wife had died. He'd retired. We were all pleased to have him in the house. It had got very rundown. Lots of different tenants, people coming and going. It wasn't great really, so,' she paused, and smiled, 'it was a bit of a relief to have the judge in residence. He was very sociable. He had a party, invited all of us and pretty much everyone from the square. It was a great night. Food, drink, there was music too. He was a very good pianist. He could play the lot, Chopin to Scott Joplin.'

The piano. McLoughlin could see it. In the bay of the drawing room window. The dark wood gleaming in the daylight. The judge lying on the floor.

She shifted in the seat and again it wobbled and she braced her feet on the grass. 'I remember an extraordinary moment. His children were there and his grandchildren too, and they all started to sing with him. 'She Moved through the Fair'. It was incredible, moving.' She paused, looked away. Her face clouded, her expression changed. 'I just can't understand what happened. To think of him up there,' she gestured to the windows above, 'he must have been so frightened.' She stopped and looked away. Again he felt suddenly annoyed by her feelings for the judge. Stop it, he chided himself, just stop. Just move the conversation away to something else.

'So, you were here in this house longer than he was next door. Is that right?' He was pleased. He'd changed the subject.

She didn't answer immediately. A robin hopped, springy-legged along the weedy concrete path. It stopped and looked up at her, its head to one side. She shifted again and folded her arms across her body. 'Oh yes, oh years longer. This group of therapists, well they've been here for, I don't know, forty years or so?'

'So before you got involved?'

'Oh yes, ages before,' she sat back in her chair. 'It's a good story, if you're interested.'

'Fire away.' He smiled at her. 'This house. Now I'm living here I sometimes feel it has a life of its own.'

She began to speak. The house had belonged to a doctor. His name was Ben Bradish. Ben had joined the British Army during the Second World War. He had been appalled by the number of men who had suffered what they called then shell shock.

'Post-traumatic stress disorder, PTSD really,' she explained. 'But it wasn't recognised then. A lot of men ended up in hospital. Loony bins, that's what they called them.' She looked down at her hands and in what McLoughlin had begun to recognise as a habitual gesture, she twisted the rings on her fingers. 'Cruel but accurate. Terrible places. Dumps for the incurables. They were locked in, prescribed huge amounts of medication, given shock treatment too.'

She explained. Bradish had worked in a number of such hospitals in England after the war. When he came home he had hoped to get a job in Dublin.

'But all the good jobs had gone to the guys who stayed put,' she shrugged, 'understandable really. So Ben had to take whatever he could and he ended up working outside Dublin.' She paused. 'Shocking it was, truly shocking. People treated worse than animals. Filthy conditions, inhuman. And Ben, well, Ben was a pioneer. He started reading, thinking, studying and he became convinced that the answer lay with Freud. He went back to London and trained with some of the great therapists of the post-war era and then he returned to Dublin and started the Therapy House, here in his family home.'

She looked up, looked away. 'He was before his time really. People were suspicious. The medical establishment closed ranks. They tried to get him struck off, disbarred from practising, but Ben, he just stuck to his guns.' She smiled. 'He was one of a kind. A rebel in other ways too,' she said. 'A genuine believer in what they used to call free love. Another commune.'

'Here? In this house? My house?' He couldn't keep the surprise out of his voice.

She nodded. 'Yeah, it didn't last. They'd high ideals, but you know, human nature?' She laughed. 'Of course we therapists don't really believe in human nature, not in that determinist, essential kind of way. But there are certain patterns, characteristics.'

'Like, for example? Jealousy? Resentment? Ambition? Greed? All round nastiness?'

'Yeah, you could say, things like that,' she looked away. 'Anyway, the commune bit of it fell apart, but the therapy bit grew from strength to strength.'

'So he never settled down, got married or anything like that?'

'No,' she shook her head. 'I think it was what happened to him in the war. He was very damaged. I think he always thought that he was about to die.'

'The guy who sold me the house, his name was Bradish.' McLoughlin shifted. His back was acting up.

'That was Jack. Ben had four children, all with different mothers. He left Jack the house. Jack hung onto it for as long as he could, but eventually decided to sell. We thought we could raise the money ourselves to buy the place, but in the end we went our separate ways. It's sad really. Ben was a great teacher and leader. I learnt a lot from him. He was a wonderful man. I miss him still.'

They sat in silence. McLoughlin looked around the garden. He could see that it once had form and structure. At the far end, in the old greenhouse, a luscious climber clung to life, twining itself through and around some kind of trellis.

'What's that?' He pointed.

'Oh, that,' she got up and began to walk through the long grass. She pushed the door open. 'Look, grapes.' He followed. There, nestled among the large leaves were bunches of small green fruit.

'Are they?' He reached up to pick some.

'Don't,' she batted his hand away. 'Leave them. They're not ripe yet. Ben planted the vine. He was very proud of his grapes. He tried to make wine once but it didn't work. But we'd have grapes, often, lovely, lovely grapes.'

Again that feeling of jealousy, of her intimacy with others. They stood side by side in the ruined greenhouse. It was warm, even with half the panes of glass missing. He'd restore it. He'd keep the vine. And maybe sometime he and she would sit in the garden and eat the grapes together.

A shout then, someone calling out.

'Mick, hey Mick, you there?' Ian stood on the top step.

Elizabeth pushed past him. 'Better go. Work to do.' She walked quickly away, towards the house.

'Mick, hey, come on, someone to see you,' Ian's voice was insistent.

'OK, OK,' McLoughlin followed her. He waited until she had disappeared from sight. Then he looked up. A man was standing beside Ian at the back door. Soberly dressed in a dark suit. Calling out to him in a voice he recognised from the judge's funeral.

'Michael McLoughlin, hallo.'

They stood in the judge's upstairs sitting room. Liam Hegarty had unlatched the shutters and pushed them back. Sunlight flooded in. McLoughlin looked around. His gaze moved from the dark stain on the pale green carpet to the sofa and three armchairs, pushed awkwardly against the wall, the grand piano in the bay by the window, to the mahogany cabinet, its doors smeared with black powder and finally to the portrait above the fireplace, the glass also smeared and dirty.

McLoughlin walked slowly towards it. The man in the picture fixed him with his steady gaze. His eyes were very blue. His hair beneath the peaked cap was dark brown with a slight wave. His expression was stern but there was a hint of a smile on his full mouth. His uniform was smart, his leather belt shiny.

Hegarty stood beside him. 'It's good isn't it?'

McLoughlin nodded. 'Very nice.' He took a few steps back. 'It's a Keating?'

'Yes. I remember Seán Keating coming to the house once. The picture had been damaged. See, there.' He pointed to a small blemish below the chin. 'My mother was moving it and it fell. The glass broke and a piece sliced into the canvas. So Keating came and took it away, patched it up, brought it back. You wouldn't notice really,' he paused, 'of course it could have an impact on its value, but John would never have sold it and whoever in the family gets it now, I doubt if it'll be going under the hammer.'

'Worth a few bob though,' McLoughlin regretted the words as soon as he said them. Not the time or place. But Hegarty didn't seem bothered. He shrugged, stepped back a couple of paces and folded his arms, his head to one side.

'Well,' he paused and McLoughlin remembered, of course, Hegarty's view of the painting wouldn't be just personal. He probably had a few Keatings in his own collection. 'Hard to know whether the value would be based purely on its status as a painting. It also has, what you could call, its iconic status. It's been used so many times. Posters, book covers, there was talk of it being on one of the new euro notes. It's been on stamps, and every time Easter comes round, well. And, of course, with all these centenaries, 1913, 1916, 1920s, and onwards. I'd say it'll get quite an outing.'

Hegarty moved closer again. He reached up, one long thin finger, gently pushing the gilt frame a fraction to the left. 'There, that's better.' He turned and looked around. 'What a mess. I'll have to get Mrs Maguire in. She'll sort the place out.' He gestured to the chairs. 'Why don't we sit down?'

McLoughlin shrugged. 'Sure, if you're comfortable here. If you don't mind.' He waved towards the mark on the floor.

'No, it's OK.' Hegarty moved to the sofa and took his place. McLoughlin sat on one of the armchairs. It was large and soft and his back instantly began to complain. He fumbled for a cushion and pushed it into the space behind him. He smiled apologetically. 'The back, you know? I was a bit too free and easy with a shovel this morning and it's punishing me now.'

Liam Hegarty smiled. 'Backs, we all have backs these days. Everyone has their favourite cure, their miracle worker. Physiotherapists, osteopaths, chiropractors, massage, ach.' He threw his hands up in the air. 'John, now, John had an operation a few years ago. Some kind of disc fusion, something like that. It was a great success. I think he was half in love with the surgeon. A very smart young woman. It was she who suggested he got the dog. Said the exercise would be good.'

'You've come for him, I take it.' McLoughlin felt a sudden pang of something.

'The dog? No,' Liam looked away, 'no, that's not why I'm here. As I said, I wanted to ask you something. I wanted your opinion.'

There was silence for a moment. Liam Hegarty took off his glasses. He pulled a handkerchief from his trouser pocket. He polished them, holding them up to the light to check for smudges, then replaced them on the bridge of his nose. He blinked a couple of times. Then cleared his throat.

'I remember you from when we had that terrible robbery. I liked you, the way you treated us, the way you treated the whole thing. I liked your manner. You were efficient. You were thorough. You were also very kind to my daughter.'

McLoughlin remembered. She was fifteen when it happened. The raiders had climbed in through her bedroom window. She woke to see a man in a mask beside her. He'd grabbed her, put his hand over her mouth, walked her into her parents' room. She said she could smell smoke from his hand. And the tang of cheese and onion crisps, and something else, she wasn't sure what. The men had tied them all up, her and her two younger sisters. Tied up her mother. Beaten Liam until he had given them the combination to the safe. They had loaded the best of the paintings into their van, taken passports, lots of jewellery, and taken the oldest daughter with them. Insurance policy, one of them said. They released her six hours later. Dumped her on the side of the road, fifty miles away, in her pyjamas, the middle of winter.

'She spoke to you about it. She wouldn't speak to me or her mother. She never told us what they did. But we knew they did something bad.' He looked away. 'You didn't catch them. They were pros.'

'No, we never caught them. At the time we assumed there was a paramilitary element. But maybe not, maybe they were just gangland. They were very organised.' He remembered the daughter well. Her name was Sorcha. He'd seen her death notice in the paper years after and wondered what had happened. Wondered if it might have been suicide. But it was a heart attack, apparently.

'I got some of the paintings back. There was a Jack Yeats, a little beauty. It surfaced in London and a couple of Louis le Brocquys. They knew which ones to pick. But I didn't care about the paintings. You can replace them. But Sorcha,' his voice tailed off.

'She died,' McLoughlin leaned forward.

'Yes, I don't know, afterwards,' Hegarty paused, 'she seemed OK. We sort of got back to normal. But she got sick. We didn't understand what was going on. She lost a lot of weight. We thought it was just a diet, a teenage thing. But it was more than that. She pretty much starved herself to death. Eventually her heart gave out.' He sighed, his shoulders sagged. 'We did everything we could to save her, but somehow we couldn't.'

'I'm sorry. I remember her well. She was very brave.' There was one man in the back of the van with her. He didn't take off his mask. He held her down, the hand over her mouth as he raped her, more than once. She described his body. He had an appendix scar. He had a scattering of moles across his stomach. And he smelt of smoke and cheese and onion crisps, and that other smell. She couldn't put her finger on it. A sort of menthol, she thought, peppermint maybe.

'Anyway,' Hegarty straightened up. 'That's not why I'm here. I'm here because of John's death.'

McLoughlin looked at him. Hegarty was staring at the floor. Then he stood and walked over to the dark stain.

'We'll never get this out. The carpet's ruined. I never liked the colour. I thought John should have got the boards sanded and got a nice rug. Something Persian or Turkish, like the ones in the hall and on the stairs.' He rubbed the carpet with the toe of his shoe. 'But he said no, the floor wasn't in good condition. Better to cover it up.' He moved to the mahogany cabinet. 'The guards insisted on taking all my grandfather's things. For forensic examination they said. You'd know all about that.' His hands were smeared with the black fingerprint powder. He pulled out his handkerchief and wiped himself clean. 'The gun, you know about the gun?' He turned back towards McLoughlin.

McLoughlin nodded.

'And you know, of course, about the other injuries. You saw them. The violence done to his head, his face?'

McLoughlin nodded again.

'And you know that whoever killed him was here in the house for some time. Both before and, we understand, afterwards.'

'Yes, of course I know and I also know, much to my shame and sorrow, that he was in the house when I was here. I keep on trying to figure out how,' he slapped his knee in emphasis, 'how it was that I didn't hear him going down the stairs and out the back door. But I suppose, my attention was focused...' and he pointed towards the blood stain.

Hegarty didn't respond immediately. He pushed the glass doors and they closed. He walked around the room, stopping to look out the windows for a moment, then moved to the piano. He bent down and touched the keys, then lifted his hands. Again his fingers were darkened with the fingerprint powder. Again the handkerchief came out of his pocket.

'He was a fantastic pianist, you know. He could have been a professional. His teachers in the Academy wanted him to take it up full time.' He touched the keys again. The sounds rang out. Scales, up and down, up and down. 'But our father was against it. And what the Da wanted, the Da got. He wanted John to be a barrister. He wanted John to be a judge.' And John loved his father and wanted to please him.' Hegarty closed the piano lid with a bang. He walked back to the sofa and sat down.

'This isn't easy to say. I'm not sure I'm doing the right thing telling you. But I've talked it over with my wife. Do you remember her?'

McLoughlin nodded. Her name was Sally-Anne. She was small and blonde and had been very pretty. A rosebud mouth and round blue eyes. But tough. She'd tried to stand up to the raiders that night. One of them had punched her in the face.

'Sally-Anne said I should talk to you. She said you'd know what to do.'

'Sally-Anne, of course. I didn't see her at the funeral.'

Liam Hegarty shook his head. He looked at his hands. 'Sorcha's death hit her very hard. She doesn't go out really, these days. She said she'd be more use helping with the reception afterwards. She likes doing things like that.' He sighed again, and took off his glasses. Again he polished them with his handkerchief and replaced them on the bridge of his nose.

'There's no easy way to say this. John was homosexual. I always knew it. Our mother knew it too. Da probably had some idea but of course we never spoke of it.' His words came out in a rush. 'John went to college. Did brilliantly. Went to the bar, did brilliantly. Got married to Miriam, lovely girl, good wife, great mother. They had the four children. John was mad about them. He was a fantastic father, gave them everything. But, there was this thing. It was part of him. It wouldn't be denied.' He stopped. Silence. A dog barking outside. McLoughlin recognised Ferdie's plaintive tone.

'So,' McLoughlin spoke slowly, 'so, are you saying that you think your brother's death might have had something to do with his sexuality, is that what you think?'

Hegarty looked at him. He shrugged. He looked away. 'I just don't know. But it was John's one secret. Everything else about his life was public. He was well known. He was liked, respected. He was part of the establishment.' He pointed to the portrait. 'Our father was a national hero. One of the greats. For years to come Dan Hegarty will be revered. The stuff of legend. There are songs, ballads about him. That's a heavy burden to carry.' He crossed and uncrossed his legs. He shifted on the soft cushions. 'There's something else and it's part of why we thought I should speak to you.'

McLoughlin staightened. He wanted to get up and stretch, unlock the kink in his lower back. A bit of yoga would help. A few dog poses.

'You remember the robbery?'

'Of course. I remember it well.'

'They took the paintings and they took everything from the safe.'

'Yes, I remember.' The safe was buried in the floor in a large walk-in wardrobe. Underneath a rack of shoes. Imelda Marcos jokes were made. Poor taste at the best of times, but Sally-Anne Hegarty obviously loved her Manolos, her Jimmy Choos.

'I told you about the jewellery and our passports. I didn't tell you about the cash. Close to seventy thousand pounds. Money from sales of paintings. Undeclared.'

'Seventy thousand pounds. What would that be now? A hundred thousand euros? Probably more?' McLoughlin could see the embarrasment on Hegarty's face. 'Ah, no, you didn't tell us that.'

'But it wasn't just the money. There was an envelope. Photographs. Pictures of John taken in a club in London, years ago, the sixties. He'd been blackmailed. He told me about it. I dealt with it. My older brother, my hero, better than me at everything. School, college, sport, you name it. The one thing I could do. I could fix things. I had access to cash and I paid up. I got the photos back, negatives too.' Hegarty's eyes were fixed on his shoes.

'Who had them?'

Hegarty looked up. 'A little thug, an Irish guy would you believe. A roofer by trade, but a handy little sideline in extortion. He'd a mate who worked in the club. Opportunists really. So,' Hegarty fiddled with the tissue, 'I brought in my own muscle. Got the photos back. I kept them in the safe.' He put his head in his hands. His shoulders shook. 'Why I didn't get rid of them immediately, I don't know. I just shoved them in there. Sally-Anne told me to burn them. I was going to. And then.' He looked up. His eyes behind his glasses were red rimmed.

McLoughlin stood. The pain in his back was intense. He walked to the window and looked out. Ferdie was running around on the green. A small boy was holding up a ball. Ferdie waited, ears pricked. The boy threw it and Ferdie ran. McLoughlin turned and stood with his back pressed against the wall.

'Did anyone ever use the photos?'

'No, never. For a while I expected something to happen, but time passed. I tried not to think about. I tried not to think about it so hard that somehow it was as if it had never happened.'

'And your brother, did you tell him?' McLoughlin shifted from foot to foot.

'Eventually. It took me a while.' Hegarty got up. 'I put it off for a long time. I felt so bad that I'd messed up, but eventually I had to tell him.'

'And, how did he take it?'

Hegarty shrugged. 'With his characteristic cool. One of these days, he said, someone will knock at the door. And we'll handle it, the way we handle everything.' He walked towards the stain on the carpet. He looked down.

'And did that ever happen?'

Hegarty shrugged again. 'Not as far as I know, but, John's face, the guards told me what was done. It was destroyed. They advised me not to look at him. Our doctor identified his body,' Hegarty paused, 'It wasn't an ordinary killing. There was something else going on.'

McLoughlin took a deep breath. 'I take it you haven't told the Guards about this.'

Hegarty shook his head. 'I know you're going to tell me I should, but I just can't. Not yet. I might be wrong. It might be someone with an axe to grind, a grudge. I know that's what the Guards think. And maybe they're right.' He walked towards McLoughlin. He held out his hand. He put it on McLoughlin's shoulder. 'We need help. I know you helped Sorcha. I know she talked to you. I often wanted to get in touch with you when she was so sick. But the doctors took over. She spent months in hospital. They'd feed her up, back to normal weight, but as soon as she came home she'd stop eating. I always thought it was the shame that killed her. She just wanted to disappear.'

'And your brother?' McLoughlin looked at him. 'Was he ashamed?'

'Ashamed? Yes. I know for a fact that for years he wasn't, how would I put it, active. But I also know that after Miriam died and he moved out here, I think he wanted a last fling. He was getting old. He was ill. He knew it and I knew it too. I also knew there were things going on. I don't know exactly what, where or with whom. But that's what I want you to find out. And maybe, the photos, I have a feeling…' Hegarty looked away. His face was pale and drawn. 'I heard through an art dealer I know, my brother sold a painting recently. A Jack Yeats. He'd bought it years ago. He loved it. According to my friend, it was a cash sale. Untraceable. So,' he looked up, his face pale and tense, 'I know you've been doing some private work. I want you to find the photos. Find out what's been going on.'

McLoughlin walked across the grass and sat down on the Cassidy bench. Ferdie had given up playing with the little boy. He was lying on his side in the sun, deeply asleep, his ribs beneath his black curly coat, moving up and down.

McLoughlin moved and the dog woke. He got up and came over, nuzzling McLoughlin's knee with his head. Shame and its corrosive effects, McLoughlin knew all about it. He remembered his friend, Peter Dunne. They'd gone through Templemore together, then found themselves, a few years later, working together in Dublin. He remembered when they found Peter. Fished him out of the sea off Killiney. It had been all the talk in the station. Talk and jokes, snide innuendo. Peter hadn't been well. He was very thin and pale, an unusual sore on his nose. He was the walking dead. Another funeral with a closed coffin. A quiet affair. No guard of honour. No ceremonial folding of the flag. Just the family and a couple of friends. Devastated. Shattered. Broken.

Lunchtime, Ian and the lads appearing in the sunshine. They sprawled around him on the grass, eating, laughing, joking. Offered McLoughlin cheese sandwiches and a can of Coke. After a while McLoughlin got up. He and Ferdie walked back across the road. Hegarty had given him the keys to the house.

'Stay here if you like,' he had said. 'All that mess in your place. Stay here.'

He stood outside the gate and looked up at the windows. Hegarty had told him. His father, Dan Hegarty, had lived there as a boy. His mother was a widow. They had a room in the basement. She worked for the family who owned the house. She cleaned, too, for the neighbours, and others around the town. After independence and the Civil War was over, when there was peace, Dan bought it. He got it for a song. The landlord was leaving. He didn't like the new Ireland. Dan gave it to his mother. She moved from the basement to the hall floor and became a landlady herself.

'May was a tough old bird,' Hegarty said. 'She brought Dan up on her own. No one helped. She put her trust in God and her son. And they both stood by her.'

'I didn't realise,' McLoughlin said. ' I didn't know your father was from Victoria Square.'

'Yes,' Hegarty nodded. 'There was a suggestion that the name be changed. Get rid of the old imperial reminder. But Da blocked it. We have to remember our past, he always said. Have to remember where we come from. Otherwise we won't know where we're heading.'

'But your father, he didn't go into politics. Did he not want power? To be at the heart of it all?'

'No,' Liam Hegarty shook his head, 'no way. As far as he was concerned the real power was to be found in making money. No money in politics he always said.'

McLoughlin let himself into the house. He walked from room to room. Hegarty was right. The forensic team had left the place in a mess. He stood in the hall, Ferdie beside him. He whined softly and scratched at the small door beneath the stairs.

'What is it boy?' McLoughlin pulled at the handle and it opened. He peered in as the dog moved quickly, his claws rattling on the wooden steps. McLoughlin fumbled for a light switch. A steep staircase led down into the gloom. He followed the dog, leaning against the wall for support. He was in a kitchen, unchanged for years. A solid-fuel range against one wall, a rectangular white sink with one tap against the other. An old-fashioned dresser, emptied of its china. The floor was stone flags. A large square table stood beneath a light bulb, hanging from the ceiling, without a shade. The barred window, looking out on the garden, was dirty. Cobwebs hung everywhere.

'Ferdie,' McLoughlin called. The dog appeared. He whined, then disappeared from sight.

'Come on Ferdie,' McLoughlin walked towards a half-open door. He pushed and it squeaked and groaned and stuck on the flags. McLoughlin pushed again. He reached for a switch. Again a single bulb, this time with a faded pink shade. The room was dominated by an iron bedstead. The guards had flung off the bedclothes, revealing a lumpy old mattress. There was another small bed pushed beneath the window. Against the inner wall was a small wooden dressing table. Its drawers were pulled open. McLoughlin moved closer. Women's underwear trailed out. He looked more closely. The clothes were worn, faded, the elastic stretched and loose. Stitched into the back of a corset was a small piece of pale pink satin and embroidered on it was the name, *Madame Nora*.

On the top of the dressing table was an assortment of makeup. An old-fashioned powder puff and a large box of loose powder. A selection of lipsticks. He picked one up. It was new and shiny. Maybelline was the brand name etched into the silver top.

Suddenly Ferdie began to bark. Something shot from beneath the bed, a long narrow shape with a tail which slithered along the stone floor.

McLoughlin's heart raced and he could feel his toes in their sandals curling up in horror. He rushed out into the kitchen. He hated rats. A nightmare, recurring. Rats on his chest, rats on his face, rats eating him alive. He struggled towards the stairs, taking them two at a time, the dog at his heels. As he reached the top, he slammed the basement door behind him. He stood in the hall, his heart racing, his palms wet, waiting until his breathing slowed. The grandfather clock ticked, ticked, ticked. He turned to look at the painting on the wall beside him. A large abstract, hanging crookedly. Blocks of glowing colour. Red, yellow, orange, cream. The paint was thickly applied, rich and textured. He gazed at it, and felt calm return. He turned towards the door, the keys in his hand. He looked down at them.

He had told Liam Hegarty he couldn't help him. He wouldn't help him.

'You should be speaking to the guards, not me. Inspector Sweeney, she'll deal with all this in a sensitive manner.'

Hegarty shook his head. 'I don't want that. With respect I know what the gardaí are like. The word would be out. It'd be all over the papers.' He paused. 'Look, I know who you are. I know what happened to your family.' Silence for a moment. 'I know what happened outside the church the other day.' Another pause. 'I can understand your feelings. So...'

'So?'

'So. I want something from you and I can give you something that I know you want.' Again the glasses, polished with the handkerchief. 'My family has many connections. If you do what I'm asking I will put you in touch with someone who can help you.'

'Help me?'

Liam Hegarty nodded. 'Help you get the evidence you need to convict the man who killed your father.'

McLoughlin looked at him. Hegarty looked away.

'Are you serious?'

'I wouldn't be saying it if I couldn't.' Hegarty moved towards the door. McLoughlin followed him.

'And you've never thought to come forward before?' McLoughlin could feel his voice rising. Hegarty turned and faced him.

'I'll leave it with you. It's a good offer, the best you're likely to get.'

McLoughlin checked the lock on the front door. He moved from the hall, into the dining room. He opened the door to the garden. Ferdie trotted through. McLoughlin followed him, closing the door and locking it. He walked down the steps. He turned and looked back up the house. He moved towards the wooden gate in the wall and pushed it open.

'Come on Ferdie,' he called, 'time to go home.'

The Middle

McLoughlin and the dog walked along the path by the railway line. He'd phoned Dom, said he'd buy a bottle and come for a drink. Said he had a problem he needed to share. Dom was waiting, hovering at the lift door, the TV remote in his hand.

'Look, the six o'clock news, you'll want to see this,' he paused and looked down at the dog. 'Who's your four-legged friend?'

'Meet Ferdie, belonged to Judge Hegarty. I seem to have acquired him. Here,' he thrust a bottle wrapped in tissue paper into Dom's hand, 'is it OK if?' he gestured to the dog.

'Sure, quick, take a seat.'

He sat on the sofa, Ferdie pressing against his leg. A TV reporter, a young woman, was standing on a stretch of bog. In the background a large yellow digger was at work. The reporter explained. During the years of the troubles a number of people, men and women, had been taken by the Provisional IRA. It was presumed they had been tortured and killed. Their bodies had never been found. They had come to be known as the Disappeared. Now pressure had been put on the leadership of Sinn Féin to return their remains to their families. McLoughlin settled back against the cushions. The man from the photographs in Bassano, and the same man from the judge's funeral, was interviewed outside Dáil Éireann. His tone was calm, his manner conciliatory

'Sinn Féin is ready to help in whatever way we can to find these people, so their loved ones can give them a proper funeral. We acknowledge that mistakes have been made in the past.' He paused, looked away, looked down at the ground, then raised his eyes to meet those of the interviewer. 'The situation was different then. Things were done on both sides which, with hindsight should not have been done. Many people suffered. But now is not the time to dwell on the past. Now is the time to look to the future.'

The report cut back again to the digger and a group of men with long-handled shovels. The voiceover explained. The summer's dry weather had caused the bog to shrink. A body had been found. It was not, as first thought, an ancient body. This man had died in the more recent past. Now a team headed by a forensic anthropologist had come to assist.

McLoughlin could hear the sound of the cork being pulled from a bottle and wine being poured. The dog slumped to the floor and rolled over on his side. Dom approached the sofa, a large glass in each hand. He sniffed from one.

'Mm, nice. Slightly spicy tang. Where did you get it?'

'Do you know that fancy off-licence near the church? It was a favourite of the judge's.' McLoughlin reached out his hand for his glass as Dom sat down. 'Ferdie practically dragged me through the door. He's on speaking terms with all the shopkeepers from here to Dalkey.' He took a sip. Dom settled back into the sofa's leather cushions. 'Cheers.' He raised his glass. McLoughlin held out his and they clinked gently, a soft chiming sound.

'It's funny, you know, going out with a dog.' McLoughlin looked over to where Ferdie was lying, head on his paws now, eyes closed. 'People are friendly in a way they're not when you're on your own. There's a whole community of doggie people, just dying to have a chat.' He took another swallow. 'And of course they all want to talk about the judge too. He was a popular man around here.'

'Not universally popular though, someone didn't like him.' Dom picked up a bowl of peanuts and passed them over.

'Well,' McLoughlin paused, helping himself, 'you're right about that.' He crunched loudly. He looked around the large bright room. 'Where's Joanne?'

'Respite, a week on my own. They take her in to the nursing home a couple of times a year.' Dom let out his breath in a long sigh, and settled back. 'This is nice. A good bottle and a bit of peace and quiet.' He lifted the glass and drank again.

'So.' McLoughlin shifted. His back was still sore. He needed more exercise. Swimming would be good. He'd been meaning to join the local gym since he moved to the town. It had a twenty-metre pool. He'd prefer it bigger but it was such a long time since he'd swum that twenty metres would be plenty.

'So. The Disappeared. The poor fuckers.' Dom opened his eyes. 'Do you think,' he paused, 'they'd have brought in a priest before they got the bullet in the back of the head?'

McLoughlin shrugged. 'Good question.'

They sat in silence. The sounds of the street drifted in through the open glass doors. McLoughlin got up. He walked out onto the balcony. The town below was busy. People rushing for the DART, rushing for the bus, rushing home after a day's work. A fresh breeze from the sea. He could smell the salt.

'Hey,' Dom was sitting up straight, pointing at the screen. 'It's all go this evening.'

McLoughlin joined him on the sofa. He saw the outside of his house, the crime scene tape fluttering next door, the cars coming and going, the forensic team in their white suits. Then Min Sweeney standing at the garda station, phone in one hand, notebook in the other, as the reporter shoved his microphone in front of her mouth. He heard her voice.

'All I can say at this time,' she paused. She looked tired and drawn. 'All I can say is that we've made an arrest. We're questioning a suspect. He can be held for twenty-four hours and if we feel it's necessary we'll apply to hold him for a further twenty-four hours. For operational reasons, that's all I can say. Thank you.'

There were more pictures then. A young man being taken from a house, bundled into a car, driven away, and the crime reporter, his face alight with excitement, his voice high pitched. McLoughlin recognised the street. The large corporation estate just a couple of miles away from the centre of the town. The camera swung towards a van parked outside. The logo read 'Plumbers on Call'.

'I heard something,' Dom said, 'there was a bit of talk locally. The guy I buy my paper from. A great man for the chat, ears and eyes open all the time.'

'Yeah?' McLoughlin sipped his wine.

'There've been a load of robberies recently. Pensioners. Targeted, they reckon. Plumbers now, plenty of access.' Dom stood. He picked up the bottle and refilled his glass. 'Will you have a bite to eat?' He moved towards the kitchen.

McLoughlin hesitated. 'Don't want to put you to any bother.'

'It's no trouble at all.' Dom opened his large stainless steel fridge. 'I've a lovely piece of steak here. Fillet. Joanne doesn't really eat much these days. And eating alone is no fun,' he pulled some onions from a bag, 'so please, join me.'

The steak, when it was cooked, was worth waiting for. Dom had also made fried onions and chips, delicate little strips of potato, crisp and tasty. They sat at the table and ate in silence. Ferdie hovered.

'Here.' Dom threw him a piece of meat with an edging of fat.

'Shouldn't do that really.' McLoughlin put down his knife and fork. 'Give him bad habits.'

'Ach, why not?' Dom leaned down and patted the dog's head. 'He's a nice lad, isn't he? You've forgiven him the bite, I take it.'

'We so don't discuss it,' McLoughlin laughed. He sat back and pushed his plate away. 'That was really good. Thanks.'

'No problem. Any time,' Dom stood up, 'and now I'll open another bottle.'

They sat, glasses in hand, as the sun left the sky. The TV flickered in the corner, but Dom had turned the sound down. The dog sprawled at McLoughlin's feet, occasionally twitching in his sleep, his little tail thumping.

'I had a dog once,' Dom stirred. He'd been dozing for a while, his head slumped forward, but his hand still grasping the stem of his glass. 'When I was a lad.'

'Yeah?'

'Yeah, I was fostered. They moved me around from place to place. But one family, they lived just off the canal by Portobello. They were great. They had a dog. His name was Alfie, a clever little thing. Didn't look like much, but tricks, he could fetch and carry and find and hunt and sit and lie down. And swim too. You've no idea. All day he'd swim in the canal. I was mad about him.' McLoughlin could see the smile on Dom's face.

'What happened to you? Why were you fostered?'

Dom sat up straight.

McLoughlin turned towards him. 'You don't have to.'

'It's fine,' Dom's voice had a slight slur, 'sure it's grand. No one ever asks me. But I'm fine talking about it.'

And he told him. Mother not married. Sent to a mother and baby home. Baby put up for adoption. But the first family, some kind of problem, the mother got sick, they couldn't cope, so the child, a toddler by now, was sent back.

'I was in a kind of limbo. Too old to be adopted. People only want babies. I spent a lot of time in children's homes, and every now and then I'd go off and stay with a family for a while. The ones with the dog, they were the best of them.' Dom rubbed his face with the palm of his hand 'They made sure I went to school. They really looked after me. They stood by me and gave me a future. Lovely people. And the dog, well he was the icing on the cake.' He drank some more of his wine, then stood up. 'My back, it's at me now. Interesting, the Hegarty family, if you read any of the biographies, of which there's quite a few, there's a bit of a suggestion that Ma Hegarty might not have been married.'

'Really?' McLoughlin couldn't keep the surprise out of his voice. 'Are you sure about that?'

Dom walked stiffly over to the glass door and leaned against it. 'Not sure, not for certain, but the books all skate over Da Hegarty. Suggestion he might have died working in England, or he might have been in the States. He's what they call, a shadowy figure.'

McLoughlin sipped some more. 'Of course it would have been a terrible slur back then. Nobody'd give a fuck about it now.'

'Not now, but then,' Dom walked slowly back to the sofa, 'then, being illegitimate was no joke.'

Silence for a while. Then Dom spoke.

'That stuff about the plumber. That won't go anywhere. She must be desperate to come up with a suspect.'

'Yeah. It wasn't a robbery gone wrong. The shooting, and the use of the hammer. Still,' McLoughlin straightened up, 'throw a stone in the pond and watch the ripples. You never know.'

Silence again. An ambulance siren cut through the quiet.

'Hegarty, Dan that is. The term charismatic is over-used, but he was charismatic.' Dom lifted his glass.

'Yeah?'

'Yeah, the family, the dog family. They had what they called a proud "Old IRA" tradition. Guns hidden in the attic, grannies carrying them to the GPO in 1916. They had a photo of Hegarty, framed, in their little parlour. We all thought he was the man.' Dom stretched his arms up, over his head. 'I was a supporter. I remember Bloody Sunday. If someone had given me a gun I'd have gone over the border and taken out a few Brits.'

'Yeah, well,' McLoughlin reached for the bottle and topped up both their glasses. 'You wouldn't have been alone. We all felt like that.' He sipped. 'But the Provos wrecked it, for me anyway, when they started planting bombs and killing the way they did, well...' his voice trailed off.

'I hung on for a while.' Dom spoke slowly, deliberately. 'My generation of guards, a few years ahead of yours, we weren't so certain about the Provos.' Dom rubbed his face again. 'There was that whole way of thinking. How we were taught our history, we couldn't help but admire the hard men, the tough guys. We all hated the Unionists. The B Specials with their guns, the RUC beating the civil rights marchers, the discrimination, housing.'

'Yeah?'

'Yeah, I wanted to believe, people like Hegarty and the others, they were noble, different, idealistic. But,' he shrugged, 'feathering their nests, they were. And all that shit that went on up North. After a while you had to ask yourself, what was it all about?'

They sat in silence. It was dark now.

'You know.' McLoughlin bent over and rubbed the sleeping dog's flank. 'That town, Bassano del Grappa, the place where I saw James Reynolds, there's a mountain above it, Monte Grappa, it's become a monument to the fallen of the First and Second World Wars. It's a sacred place. Thousands of graves, thousands of people come to pay their respects. Families go there, have picnics, bring their children and grandchildren. Remember their dead.' McLoughlin put down his glass. 'And then there's those poor fuckers, the Disappeared. Disappeared into the bog, into the sand, into the sea. No funeral. No respect. No monument. Nothing.'

There was silence. The fridge clicked on, a comforting background hum. McLoughlin drained his glass. He put it down on the floor. Dom lifted the bottle and held it out. McLoughlin shook his head.

'Listen, there's something...' He got up and moved towards the windows.

Dom looked up at him. 'At last, the something, what is it?'

McLoughlin walked around the room. Outside the lights were beginning to sparkle. He could see the long row on the pier, and further out across the bay, the lights on the road to Howth. 'I've been asked to do something, something which I know, is not only unethical, but potentially illegal.'

'Asked? Should I ask by whom?'

McLoughlin stopped and leaned against the glass. It was still warm. 'The whom doesn't matter so much. It's more the why and the what if.'

Dom shifted again. He stretched out his legs. 'Well I suppose the real question is what do you get out of it. If, as you say, it's unethical and possibly, probably illegal, why would you even think about it?'

'Well,' McLoughlin moved again, this time towards the sliding doors, 'that's it. It has the potential to give me something that really matters. To me, that is. Really matters to me.'

Dom refilled his glass. He lay back against the cushions. 'Something that really matters to you.' He drank. 'And that something I take it has to do with your father.' He tilted his head back.

McLoughlin opened the doors and stepped outside. It was cool up here now. He looked down. The footpaths below were deserted. He stretched his arms out along the railings. He felt a hand on his shoulder. He turned towards Dom.

'You know I spoke to Tom Donnelly. But.' McLoughlin shrugged.

'Yeah,' Dom stood beside him. He looked out towards the sea. 'Yeah, that great big but.' He sipped from his glass. 'I'm not sure what I can say to you, Mick. But the one thing I know is this. You owe nothing to no one. You served your time. You did your bit. You're on your own now. You know that. I know that. So, whatever it takes. My advice, for what it's worth: whatever it takes.'

It was late when McLoughlin left Dom's apartment. He had initially refused, then accepted a glass of brandy. And another one. Knew he shouldn't have and could feel how unsteady he was as the lift door opened and he and Ferdie pushed through the heavy street door, turned away from the apartment towards the traffic lights. The dog stood by his side as they waited for the green man to shine. And then, suddenly, Ferdie took off, rushing across the road, his nose down, his tail up. Rushing ahead, disappearing into patches of darkness, then reappearing in the lights from the shops and cafés along the seafront. McLoughlin cupped his hands around his mouth and called, repeatedly. But the dog ignored him and soon he could barely see him. He waited for the screech of brakes or the yelp of injury, but all was quiet. He crossed the road towards the park which ran along the seafront. No one around, just the murmuring of the waves as they slipped over the shingle at the base of the wall.

He called again and whistled, but the dog had disappeared from sight. He walked on, towards a little grove of trees, much darker here, no street or house lights to brighten anything up. Just the sudden flare of a cigarette lighter cutting through the night. A face illuminated as someone bent into the flame, then pulled back. A scattering of benches among the shrubs and the outline of the building which used to be a public toilet, but now as far as McLoughlin knew, was closed and virtually derelict.

And suddenly the dog at his feet. His tail wagging excitedly as he jumped up, his pink tongue lolling from his mouth, his claws scraping against McLoughlin's knee. Then stepping back and turning and rushing off into the shadows. And a figure appearing. A man, with another man behind him. And another and another and another, more and more men, standing facing McLoughlin. He couldn't see their features, just the outlines of their bodies. Some were tall, some small. Some slim, some well-built. The dog yapping as he sniffed their shoes, his tail wagging with delight, his little body wriggling, as he rubbed himself against their legs. And one man standing apart from the others.

'Ferdie,' McLoughlin clicked his fingers. The dog did not respond. He sat, leaning against the man's knee, then he lay down, his head on his paws.

The man bent to pat him, then straightened. He took a step closer. Beside him another man lit up. And McLoughlin could see now. A strong face. High cheekbones, a long nose. Dark hair. Slicked back. A silver earring in one ear.

'Nice to see Ferdie again.' The man bent down again and scratched the dog behind the ears. 'We've missed him.' He looked up at McLoughlin. His face was blank, expressionless. 'You looking after him? You a friend of the judge's?'

'A neighbour. I bought the house next door.' McLoughlin felt tense, anxious. He was conscious that his voice was slurring just a little bit.

'A neighbour.' The man stood straight. 'Of course, the house next door, the one with the builders.' He looked around at the others. 'The judge told us about them, didn't he?' He sniggered.

Behind him the others were coming closer. Five, six, seven. Standing shoulder to shoulder.

'What was it he told us about you?' The man put his head on one side, his index finger to his top lip. 'Let me see if I can remember.' Beside and behind him the other men copied his actions. Head to one side, finger to top lip. 'Ah yes, now I remember. Former cop, straight as a die. Dull, oh so dull.' He dropped his hand to his belt. There was silence for a moment. 'So, Mr Plod, time for you to go I do believe. Unless, of course,' he held his arms out wide, embracing the man beside him, small, plump, bald, a grin on his round face, 'I can interest you in a bit of, what will we call it?' His fingertips slid down the man's abdomen and rested on his thigh. 'You'd like that, Mr Plod, wouldn't you? And as for Davy here, well Davy, what would you think?' He pressed his lips to Davy's ear and whispered. Davy smirked, then giggled.

'The dog,' McLoughlin held out his hand, 'I'll take the dog.'

'You will, will you?' The man pulled away and looked down at Ferdie who was still pressed against his leg. 'What will it be Ferdie, fun, fun, fun with us, or bor-ing.'

McLoughlin stepped back. He clicked his fingers. Ferdie didn't respond. 'Go, little fella, go. Fly away, little guy. Bye bye, little bloke.' The man lifted Davy's hand and twined his fingers through it and kissed him hard on his mouth. Then rested his head on Davy's fleshy shoulder, just for a moment. There was silence. McLoughlin shifted uneasily. The man lifted his head. He waved his arms and took a step forward. As behind him and around him the others too, their bodies moving together, their hands moving as one, stepped in his direction.

'Go, little fella. Fly away, little guy. Bye bye, little bloke.' Their voices, chanting the words, their voices low and soft to begin with, then louder and louder as they moved towards him. Out of the darkness, into the glow of the street lights. He saw their faces, their expressions cold and unforgiving. Advancing towards him, a phalanx of men. Reaching out, their arms extended, their fists balled, stamping their feet and chanting, 'Go, little fella, go. Fly away, little guy, bye bye, little bloke.' So he found himself walking backwards, pushed away by the force of their presence. Until he stumbled off the footpath onto the road, one ankle twisting beneath him and a cry of pain, as he sank down on it.

The men stopped for a moment, then began to retreat, chanting still, until once again they were swallowed up by the darkness beneath the trees. And all was quiet again. Just occasionally the hint of laughter, an indrawn breath, a sigh, as McLoughlin stood up, wincing and began to limp, slowly, away.

It had been Gwen's idea, to go to the cemetery at Dean's Grange. She had persuaded Samuel. It would be interesting. They would take the bus and then they would walk the rest of the way. It wouldn't be too far, she'd promised.

'But the last time you went, the judge took you, didn't he?' Samuel remembered the day. He had been doing some jobs in the house. A taxi had been called. The judge had stood on the top step. He was wearing his favourite Panama hat, his blue blazer, his linen trousers. A large pink rose in his buttonhole. The dog sat beside him, panting gently, then sprang up as the taxi slowed to a stop and the driver got out.

'Where to boss?' The driver leant against the car, a shiny black Mercedes. He swung his keys around in his muscled hand.

'A minute, Damien, if you don't mind,' the judge had pointed towards the green. Gwen was approaching. She was dressed for the occasion. A long print skirt with a white blouse. A straw hat with a wide brim, a black ribbon trailing from it, and a bouquet of yellow flowers cradled in her arms. Samuel moved from the shelter of the front door out onto the step. He watched the judge and the dog as they got into the taxi, and the way the driver held the door open for Gwen. Then took his place behind the wheel and slowly pulled away from the curb.

Today they took the bus. Got off at the stop by the library. Gwen scanned the road, like a child. Look left, look right, look left again, then grabbed Samuel by the arm and tugged him across. They reached the other side of the road. Samuel could see the high grey wall of the graveyard ahead. It looked so far away.

'The taxi, the judge always got the same taxi, didn't he? That driver, what was his name?'

Gwen could see that Samuel's resolve was slackening. She tightened her grip and began to walk with deliberation. 'His name was Damien. He and the judge seemed to know each other well. They had quite a conversation.'

It was hot. She wanted to stop and rest, but she didn't dare risk it. Besides, the flowers in Samuel's bag would wilt if she didn't get them into water soon.

'Yes, quite a conversation. The judge was very interested to know.' Samuel's arm was heavy so she dropped it and took hold of his hand. The leather of his gloves was cool to the touch. 'Who was where, and what was what. In prison, out of prison, gosh,' she licked her lips. There was a bottle of water in Samuel's bag too. Meant for the flowers but she would have a swallow first.

'Clients, I suppose, of the judge's. Would that be right?' Samuel wanted to know more.

Gwen shrugged. 'Possibly, probably, or perhaps people he'd sent down, isn't that the expression?'

Sent down. The words sent a small chill along Samuel's spine. He too had been sent down. The courtroom had been crowded. Most of the people from whom he had stolen were there. They had trusted him and he had taken their money. He had got away with it for years. Robbing Peter to pay Paul, that had been his strategy. Always just ahead of the pack.

They reached the cemetery's high wrought-iron gates. Samuel stopped. The bag was suddenly too heavy for him. The café was open. He peered through the windows. A plump blonde woman was arranging cupcakes on a plate. His mouth watered. But Gwen had the bit between her teeth.

'After, we'll go in after. Come on, it's not far now.' She tugged his sleeve and together they walked along the wide path. Old graves on either side. Tall headstones, some in the shape of Celtic crosses, intricate carving, spirals swirling. Most were abandoned, untended, but every now and then a sudden bright flash of colour. Geraniums in a tub, red and shocking pink. A vase stuffed with yellow roses. Plastic flowers, purple and white.

Samuel's pace had slowed right down. He needed to rest.

'Look, here,' Gwen had moved ahead. She was standing, one foot on the marble rim of a grave, her head up close to the stone. 'Here, Samuel, here they are, your grandparents.'

She turned and beckoned. Then took the bag from him, pulling out the flowers, a large jam jar and a litre bottle of water. She busied herself, arranging long spears of gladioli with feathery bunches of cosmos. She lifted the bottle high and took a sip. Water dribbled down her chin and she wiped it away with the back of her hand, then tipped the rest into the jar.

'Now,' she stood back. 'What do you think?' She reached out and took hold of his sleeve. Samuel moved forward. The writing on the stone was faded and blurred. He put his face up close. He read out loud.

In Loving Memory Richard James Lane, called Home, 9th July 1921.
And underneath it in smaller lettering.
And his wife Elsie, died 10th October, 1927.
And underneath again.
And their daughter Cecily Elizabeth Lane, died 6th May, 1947.

'Now,' Gwen patted him on the back. 'See? You do have a family. Your grandfather and grandmother, Richard and Elsie, and your mother, Cecily. All here together.'

But Samuel felt nothing. He could feel Gwen looking at him. He knew she wanted emotion. Tears, anger, excitement, melancholy. Instead there was nothing.

'I'm hungry,' his voice had a plaintive quality. 'Hungry, do you hear? I want something to eat.'

'OK,' Gwen stepped away. Her heart was behaving oddly. It seemed to be skipping beats, jumping, racing, then almost stopping. 'You go to the café. My parents,' she pointed to another grave, an irregular piece of stone with a small brass plaque screwed to it. 'Just a minute with them and I'll join you.'

The café was almost empty. A woman with a small girl was at a table near the door. There was a strong smell of coffee and baking. Samuel stood at the counter. There was a choice. Lemon drizzle cake. Fruit scones with jam and cream. Chocolate cake too. He ordered a piece of everything and a pot of tea, and sat down by the window. He could see Gwen. She was bending over the grave and now she straightened and began to walk slowly towards him. He bit into his scone. It was delicious. Its taste reminded him of something. Perhaps it was those Monday mornings when Nellie the washerwoman came, singing 'The Mountains of Mourne', with scones bundled in a tea towel in her basket. She would set them on top of the Aga to warm. Then serve them with butter, melting, her home-made blackberry jam and a dollop of whipped cream.

Gwen sat down. Her face was pale and her hands not quite steady. She sipped her tea. Samuel held up the plate of cakes. She shook her head. Around them the café was filling up. Groups of people, some wearing black, others carrying flowers. Samuel munched. He was surprised by his appetite. He closed his eyes and breathed in. He opened his eyes. Nellie sat on the other side of the table. She smiled and opened her arms. He wanted to get up and crawl onto her lap. He wanted to bury his head in her soft bosom. He wanted to hear her voice as she sang her old songs. He reached across the table to take her hand. And saw another hand, a black leather claw, lying flat by the sugar bowl. He stared at it, then tried to poke it, to push it away. But now there were two hands, both the same. They moved, as he moved. They stopped as he stopped. And when he tried to hold up his hands to look at them, the black leather claws moved too. He leaned forward in his chair and whimpered.

'Samuel, what is it?'

The woman on the other side of the table spoke to him. He lifted his eyes to look at her. Nellie had gone. He looked around. He half stood and peered out the window. Where was she? How had she gone so quickly? He pushed the table.

'Samuel, what's wrong?'

The woman with the pale thin face, the white hair, the white blouse, the print shawl around her shoulders, half stood too. Samuel was beginning to panic. He couldn't let Nellie go. He grabbed his bag and headed for the door pushing through the queue which had formed at the counter.

'Samuel,' he heard the voice behind him. Who was she? Was she Mummy? Mummy didn't like him sitting on Nellie's knee, eating Nellie's scones, singing along with Nellie's old Irish songs. He opened the door and stepped outside. He began to run.

Gwen watched Samuel. She was surprised he could move so quickly. He cut an ungainly figure. The heavy tweed coat, the wide brimmed hat, the gloved hands, the shopping bag banging against his knee. He turned abruptly and disappeared behind a dense row of cypress trees. She pushed a stray lock of hair back and slowly began to follow. She found him not far away. He was sitting on a stone seat. She could hear him humming. She sat beside him. He turned. He smiled.

'Look,' he pointed towards a new grave. Earth was piled high and the clods of clay were covered with wreaths of flowers, their colours fading.

'Look,' Samuel repeated the word and again he pointed. A small wooden cross had been placed at the foot of the grave. On it was a polished brass plate. Gwen leaned forward. She read out loud.

'John Hegarty, 1933 – 2013. RIP.'

Beside it was a large black granite monument. At its base someone had placed a laurel wreath, the Irish colours, green, white and orange, twisted through it. The lettering on the grave was in Irish. Ó h-Éigeartaigh, it said. And the names beneath it Domhnall, Máire. Daniel Hegarty. Gwen could see him in her mind's eye. Tall and handsome as he strode around the square. Didn't have much time for her and her kind.

They sat in the sun. Samuel's head drooped. His eyes were closed but he could see. Beneath the earth piled high, the fading flowers, the judge's face. Smashed, destroyed, ruined. The judge's eyes were open. They stared up at the coffin lid. Samuel whimpered.

Eventually Gwen got to her feet.

'Time to go home,' she reached down and took hold of Samuel's arm. They walked slowly towards the high gates.

That day, when she had come here with the judge, Damien had parked the taxi close to the Hegarty monument. He had carried her bouquet of flowers and waited while she tidied her parents' grave. Then he had taken her arm and helped her back towards the judge. She could see him standing, in the distance, leaning on his stick, his head bowed as if in prayer. But he was not alone. A man was with him, his head bowed too, his mouth close to the judge's ear. And the judge looked smaller, diminished somehow.

Damien had dropped her arm and hurried on ahead. The man turned towards him. Gwen was too far away to hear what they were saying. But she could see their expressions. Damien stepped close to the judge. His manner was protective. He put his arm around him and began to guide him down the path towards the car. The other man turned away and broke into a brisk trot. Gwen had heard stories about robberies, muggings, assaults here among the dead. Her hands began to shake. Damien opened the car door. He pushed the judge inside. He gestured to Gwen to get in too. The judge was pale, sweat beading his forehead. Damien sat into the driver's seat. The locks on the doors clicked into place. He looked into his rear-view mirror.

'Yous all right back there?'

The judge leaned against the headrest. He closed his eyes.

'Martin fucking Millar.' Damien put the car in gear. They moved slowly through the gates and out onto the road. 'Martin fucking Millar,' he repeated the words. 'Who the fuck does he think he is?'

'Are you all right, Sam?' Gwen put her arm around his shoulders.

'I'm fine, Gwen, just a bit tired. Time to go home I think.' He smiled at her and together they walked slowly towards the bus stop.

McLoughlin sat on the front steps. What exactly had he seen last night as he stood in the darkness with the dog? A group of men, together. A group of men who knew each other very well. Who knew the judge, well. A group of men, alike, but unlike him.

He reached for the mug of coffee at his side. Behind him in the house he could hear the usual hammering and crashing and every now and then the screech of a saw. The new wood for his kitchen had arrived first thing this morning. It was stacked high in the hall. He could smell its tangy scent as he squeezed past. A bit of a relief to feel that they were making progress, that it wasn't just destruction, that soon his new home would be taking shape.

He hadn't slept well. His ankle was still sore. Not sprained, just twisted enough so he winced when he put weight on it. He felt something else, was it embarrassment, shame, anger at the way they had chased him away? An outsider, an untouchable. For once the boot on the other foot, he thought.

Now he watched the comings and goings in the square. And saw Elizabeth Fannin wearing the saffron yellow today. Her head held high, her stride loose and long, her leather satchel hanging from her shoulder, as she walked towards him.

'Hello,' he heard her call and she waved. 'Another lovely day.'

His phone rang. He glanced at the screen. It was Constance, his niece.

'Hi Constance, what can I do for you?' He watched Elizabeth until she disappeared from view. Sorry to have missed the opportunity for a conversation.

Constance was coming to the District Court in the town. It wouldn't take long. Could she drop around afterwards and see his new house? Would there be the chance of a cup of coffee? He remembered he wanted to give her his mother's jewellery box. It was somewhere in the front room, in the basement, with all his other possessions. He pulled himself upright and, taking care of his ankle, hobbled downstairs. Quiet here, cool, the light dim, Elizabeth's door shut firmly. He found what he was looking for and returned to his seat in the sun and waited.

He hadn't seen Constance for a while. She was looking very grown-up in her smart black suit, her laptop bag in one hand, her iPhone in the other.

'Here, sit down, have a look at this and I'll make you coffee.'

He handed her the jewellery box and went back into the house. When he returned a few minutes later, holding a mug and a plate of chocolate biscuits, she had emptied its contents onto her lap. A silver locket, some mismatched earrings, an array of bracelets and a gold ring, set with a small piece of jade.

She took a swallow of coffee and picked up the ring. 'This is unusual.'

'Put it on,' McLoughlin took it from her. 'Or here, let me.'

'Right or left?' She held out both hands.

McLoughlin screwed up his eyes. 'Well I think Mammy wore it here.' He touched the ring finger on her right hand. 'I seem to remember that one of her old aunts gave it to her. It was,' he paused, 'I think it was Auntie Maeve, and there was a bit of a scandal attached to it.' He slipped the ring over her knuckle.

Constance held it up and scrutinised it. 'Nice, lovely, I love it. Thanks Uncle,' and she leaned over and kissed him on the cheek. And he realised. How long it had been since anyone had touched him like that. He pulled away quickly, but not too quickly. He picked up his coffee cup.

'Yes, a bit of a scandal,' he sipped.

'Tell, do tell.' Constance was sorting through the rest of the jewellery.

'I don't know all the details.' She was, he could see, very pretty. White-blonde hair cut in a neat bob. From her father, he reckoned. Like the rest of her features. High cheekbones, a small chin with a dimple, and a neat rosebud of a mouth. Nothing like Clare, who shared with him and their mother a square jaw and a broad face. 'But word in the family was that the ring came from a boyfriend who'd gone to India to work in the colonial service.'

'Oh God,' Constance's wrists jingled as she slipped more and more bracelets onto them. 'A colonial oppressor, who'd have thought.'

'Yes, what they used to call a castle catholic.' McLoughlin reached down and picked up the locket. He prised it open. 'Look, here.' He held it out.

Two photographs. Faded now and dulled. A young man and woman. Both wearing hats. Their features indistinct.

'Ah,' she took it from him, 'how sweet. Young.' She snapped it shut. 'What happened? They didn't marry?'

'No,' he leaned back against the steps. 'He died. Something like cholera or yellow fever. She stayed at home and looked after the old folks. Anyway, we don't have much in the way of family stuff. So take it, take it all.'

They sat in the sun. She talked about her work. It was tough making ends meet.

'So, today, what was it? Something interesting?'

She shook her head. 'Parking fines. The guy I was representing. Ridiculous. All he has to do is pay them when he gets a ticket. Or,' she paused, 'even better, pay for the bloody parking. Hey, look who's that?' She pointed. The dog was walking slowly across the grass. He stopped at the gate. He was panting, his mouth open, his tongue flopping.

'Well what do you know?' McLoughlin straightened up. 'You've decided to come back, have you?' He held out his hand. The dog walked carefully up the steps. He pressed himself against McLoughlin's legs and whined.

'I'd say he's thirsty,' Constance reached out and stroked his ears. 'The judge's dog, I take it.'

'How did you know?' McLoughlin got up.

'A bit of chat about the judge, down at the court. Someone had figured that I was related to you. They seemed to think I'd have the inside story.' She lifted her hand to push back her fringe and the bracelets jingled. 'The dog was mentioned. Apparently the judge and the dog were a familiar sight around the town. Is he here to stay?'

McLoughlin nudged Ferdie with his foot. 'I doubt it. He's not the most loyal of four-legged friends. But for the time being,' he leaned forward and patted his head, 'we're stuck with each other, aren't we, little fella?' He moved towards the door. 'I'd better get him some water.'

'You do that,' Constance looked at her phone. 'Reckon I've another few minutes before the next lot of unfortunates are lined up. Meanwhile I'll just sit here in the sun. It's a lovely place you've got, Uncle Michael. '

Ferdie slurped from the bowl. McLoughlin watched him, and wondered. The man with the earring, under the trees. Who was he?

Constance's eyes were closed. 'Peaceful here,' she murmured. 'I could get used to this.' Then she sighed and looked around. 'Better go.' She pulled the bracelets from her wrists. 'Doesn't do to jangle too much in court.'

'But you enjoy it.' McLoughlin stood.

'Yeah, I do, it's kind of fun.' She held out the jewellery. 'You sure about this? About me having them all?'

'Of course,' McLoughlin handed her the box. 'Take this too. Your grandmother would be delighted to know that her bits and pieces are going to a good home. Here, let me.' He packed the jewellery away and turned the tiny key in the lock. 'Here,' he handed it to her. 'Will it fit in the bag with your computer or will I get you something else?'

They walked across the green and down to the main street, Ferdie running ahead, then stopping and looking back. McLoughlin carried a shopping bag containing the jewellery box. Constance's pace was brisk. He was hard pressed to keep up with her. He remembered from somewhere that her father had been a runner. They'd only met once or twice. Alexander was his name, Alexander Cameron. Clare and he had separated when Constance was a young teenager. McLoughlin had never really known what had happened between them.

'Constance,' he put his hand on her arm.

'Yeah,' she looked down at her phone. 'Shit.'

'What is it?' McLoughlin stopped.

'Oh nothing really. Just the eejit with the parking fines. He says he won't pay up.' She shook her head. 'He'd want to be careful. He could wind up inside if he doesn't do what he's told. Some people,' she sighed and smiled. Again a look of her mother. She held the phone to her ear. Silence for a minute, then she spoke, a detached tone to her voice. 'Hi, Martin, I got your message. Listen, I'll be with you in a couple of minutes. We should talk about this. OK?' Pause. 'I'll see you soon.' She turned. She reached up and kissed McLoughlin on both cheeks.

'Bye, Uncle Michael. Thanks.' She bent down and rubbed Ferdie between the ears. 'And bye to you too.' She turned away. He handed her the shopping bag. He watched her hurry up the road. He remembered when his life had been like hers. Full of urgency. Full of meaning. Always another crisis to be handled. He sighed. And his phone rang. He looked down at the screen.

'Hi Johnny, how are you?'

McLoughlin leaned on the gallery rail and looked down.
Harris was bending over a stainless steel table. A small group of students clustered around what must have once been a human being, living and breathing. Now it looked more like a piece of dried-up old leather. A torso and two arms, legs missing, but the shape of the skull, the skin stretched tight, unmistakeable. Scraps of clothing too. A belt with a rusted buckle and fragments of a shirt, the kind with press fasteners down the front, rusted too.

Harris was in full flight. McLoughlin listened intently. He was explaining the effect of bog water on skin, its preservative quality, its particular properties. Natural mummification was how he described it. Harris gently stroked the dead man's leathery cheek. He bent closer to examine his right ear.

'One gold stud.' He touched the lobe. He turned the head. 'Left ear, the lobe split.' He paused and looked around at the rapt faces. 'Now, we'd better open Patrick Brady up and see what we can find.'

McLoughlin watched. He'd lost count of how many post-mortems he'd attended. He never quite got used to them. There was always that moment when nausea threatened, when dizziness hovered, when revulsion tapped him on the shoulder. He'd never actually vomited or fainted or had to leave the room. There were little tricks he'd use. He'd look away, find a spot on the floor and stare at it. He'd put his hands in his pockets and hold onto a coin or his wallet or handkerchief, rubbing the fabric between finger and thumb, distracting himself from what was in sight. There had been a few occasions, however, when his strategies failed. One in particular, he couldn't forget. The case of Mary Mitchell.

Years ago. She'd been tortured, murdered. Burnt with cigarettes, raped, then beaten over the head, died of a bleed to the brain. He remembered her. And her mother. And her mother's grief.

Now he watched as Harris turned the body and pointed out the place where the bullet had entered. Just above the nape of the neck. His gloved fingers crept along the line of the jaw bone. Stopped.

'Ah,' he paused, 'a break here. Fracture of the mandible.'

He picked up a small saw. He flicked the switch. He began to slice neatly through the bony plates of the skull. A terrible sound. McLoughlin could feel the hairs standing up on his arms. Harris removed a circular piece from the top of the dead man's head. He placed it in a steel dish. Then he put both hands inside Patrick Brady's head and pulled out his brain. It would be weighed and measured.

'Now, look at this,' Harris had a long tweezers in one hand. 'Got it.' He held up a bullet. 'Perfect.' He dropped it in another dish and began to slice through the leathery skin, pulling it back to expose the dead man's rib cage and abdomen.

'Here, look, seventh and tenth ribs fractured.' He touched them with his gloved finger. McLoughlin leaned forward to get a better view.

'And now, let's take a gander at the internal organs.'

McLoughlin watched as Harris's hands disappeared inside the body. There was hardly any smell, just the faintest odour of stagnant water. Out came the heart, kidneys, liver, pancreas, spleen, all measured, weighed, their condition noted. Harris cut through the stomach wall and emptied out its contents. He pushed up his glasses and bent down to get a better look.

'Hard to know,' he glanced up at the gallery, 'last meal of a condemned man. A few pints? Steak and chips? A cheese sandwich?'

The atmosphere in the room suddenly changed. McLoughlin sat down. He put his face in his hands. He was trembling. He could see it. Patrick Brady, beaten, jaw broken, ribs broken, the gold stud pulled away. Was he kneeling now? Was he blindfolded? Was his killer behind him or in front? How many other men were there too? Where was 'there'? A house, the TV on, the smell of rashers frying and toast burning? A barn or a shed? Cold and damp? Breeze blocks and stone, a cement floor? His knees hurting as they pressed into the concrete. Or maybe he was killed outside. In a field. Beside the sea. In daytime or at night. Looking up, his last glimpse of the sky, blue and beautiful or dark, the stars pinpoints of light. Perhaps a full moon, its silvery sheen the last he ever saw. Patrick Brady, destined to be forgotten.

They sat in Harris's office. It was, McLoughlin noticed, meticulously tidy. Nothing on the desk but an Apple laptop and a silver Parker pen. Everything filed away in brightly painted cabinets. It looked like an ad from a high-spec office furniture catalogue. Harris was busying himself with the coffee. He placed a full plunger pot on a tray. Two large white mugs, a jug of milk, a few sachets of sugar, and a plate of chocolate biscuits.

'I like them, what are they?' he looked back over his shoulder.

McLoughlin held up the packet. Leibniz chocolate thins. 'My current favourites. I gave some to my niece this morning. I thought we could finish them off.'

Harris put the tray down on a small side table. He poured coffee, gestured to the milk and sugar. He picked up a biscuit and bit into it. They sat in silence. McLoughlin could still see the body, or what was left of it, on the table.

'Patrick Brady,' he swallowed some coffee.

'Ah Patrick Brady, poor bloke.' Harris swivelled in his chair.

'What happens now?' McLoughlin reached for another biscuit then withdrew his hand. He could feel his stomach pushing over the top of his waist band. It was a sensation he didn't like.

'Well,' Harris poured more coffee, 'when we've confirmed his identification he'll be returned to his family and they can give him a decent burial. Unfortunately,' he lifted his mug and wrapped both hands around it, 'unfortunately his mother and father are both dead. But I've met his siblings. They'll do right by him I'm sure.'

'And the bullet? The evidence? The beating?'

'Ah,' Harris sat up straight. 'Now that's where it all gets a bit vague.' He put his hand in his pocket and pulled out a small plastic bag. He dropped it on the desk. It fell with a soft thud. 'We're not actually supposed to go digging around for things like that. The rules of the Commission.'

'The Independent Commission for the Location of Victims' Remains,' McLoughlin swirled the coffee round in his mug. It was good stuff.

'Well done, top of the class,' Harris smiled at him as he pushed the small bag towards McLoughlin with the tip of his finger. 'The ICLVR. Nice people, good people. All they want is the body so the family can have what's known these days as closure.' He picked up a biscuit and began to nibble the chocolate rim. 'It's a handy concept, closure. God forbid we might want to find anyone responsible. Or we might want justice not only done, but seen to be done.' He paused and swallowed. 'You know all about that, don't you?'

McLoughlin nodded. Harris looked over at him.

'Your trip to Venice, you didn't tell me. How did it go?'

McLoughlin shrugged and sipped some coffee. 'It was hot, it was wet, it was crowded, it was expensive.'

'And?' Harris lifted his mug. 'A little bird tells me you went up country.'

'I'm impressed,' McLoughlin smiled and bowed, 'what little bird would that be?'

Harris shrugged. 'Well let's just say, you know what the guards are like, fucking useless at keeping secrets.' He finished off his biscuit with a flourish. 'So James Reynolds, I presume?

McLoughlin nodded. 'You presume right.'

'You get anywhere with him? He didn't make a dying declaration into your phone before you strangled him with your bare hands?'

McLoughlin looked away. So close he could see the pores in his skin, the broken veins in his cheeks, smell the cigarette smoke from his clothes.

'But something's happened, hasn't it? Something's changed.' Harris took a sip of his coffee. McLoughlin looked at him, then looked away again. Harris put down his mug. 'OK, don't tell me, I don't need to know.'

McLoughlin nodded. He swallowed. His throat felt tight. He took a breath, 'The forensics from my father, the shot from the gun and all that, do you still have it?'

Harris swung from side to side. 'We do. We have everything. Post-mortem reports, blood samples all that stuff.' He paused. 'You know, in the cases of the disappeared,' he mimed the inverted commas with the index fingers of both hands, 'we're only supposed to make the formal identification, but,' he shrugged, 'old habits die hard.' He swung again this time tipping backwards in the chair. 'You open him up, you might as well go the whole hog.' He swung forward again, the chair creaking and groaning. 'So, this little bit of evidence.' He tapped the bullet in the plastic bag. 'I suppose I'll just file it away, somewhere it won't get lost. Along with all that stuff from your father's case.' He looked up at McLoughlin and smiled, a cheerless grin. 'And you never know. Sometime in the future. Attitudes change. Priorities change. And if someone comes looking for that little piece of lead, I'll still have it.' He picked up the bag and opened the desk's top drawer. He dropped it inside and pushed it shut again. 'You know, I'm sorry in some ways he's been found. At least when he was in the bog he was at peace. He couldn't be used for propaganda.'

'Yeah, I suppose so.' McLoughlin drained his coffee. 'Interesting companions down there in the dark. None of them came to a good end. Weren't they all sacrificed? I went to the exhibition once in the National Museum. Ropes around their necks. Cuts to their bodies. Broken bones, ribs. Sounds a bit like poor Patrick Brady.' McLoughlin stood up. He was conscious that he had left Ferdie in the car. He didn't like to think of the poor dog. He'd be thirsty now.

'So why was he sacrificed?' Harris looked up at him. 'The archaeologists say the bog bodies were kings who outlived their usefulness. Their magic wasn't working anymore so they were done away with. But you know,' Harris stood too, 'it's all completely speculative. We've no evidence about those times, thousands of years ago. Those blokes in the bog, they were never meant to be dug up. They weren't like the Egyptian kings, mummified, ready to take their place in the next world. It was pure chance that the bog bodies survived. Who's to say they weren't just gangsters, murderers, rapists, thieves. Chased out of their miserable little villages. Hunted to death, then their bodies dumped, the way Patrick Brady's body was dumped. A handy place, easy digging in the bog, not like most of the stony soil. Handy, wet, soggy. Get rid of them. Out of sight. And out of mind.' He shoved his hands in the pockets of his baggy corduroy trousers. 'Death, pointless, as always.'

Silence for a moment.

'What's up, Michael?' Johnny's voice was warm and sympathetic.

'I wanted to ask you.' McLoughlin paused. 'It's kind of awkward.'

'Well, you know how best to deal with awkward, among friends that is. Cut to the chase as they say in all my favourite TV series.'

McLoughlin took a deep breath. He told him. The evening with Dominic Hayes, leaving the apartment, and the dog, running on ahead, running towards the grove of trees, the men coming forward. The way they responded to the dog. The way they responded to him. When he'd finished he looked away. There was silence. It seemed to last forever.

'So,' Harris swung back in his chair. 'Cutting to the chase. You're asking me, what exactly?'

'Well, exactly as you put it. I'm asking if you might know the man with the earring. The man who seemed to know the dog so well.' McLoughlin could feel his palms sweating, his heart racing. He didn't like having this conversation with his old friend.

'And why, exactly do you want to know this?' Harris steepled his fingers. His expression was severe. His customary smile had vanished.

'I can't tell you Johnny. Not now, not yet. I'm asking you to trust me. I've been presented with an opportunity to make something right. Something that really matters. Not just to me, but to many people.' McLoughlin got to his feet.

'The man with the earring. The man in the trees. The man who knew the dog so well. The man who,' Harris stopped. 'I'll tell you what

144

I'll do. I'll make a few phone calls. I'll help you if I can.' He pushed back his chair and stood. 'We've been friends for a long time. I've never doubted your integrity. I hope I won't have cause to doubt it now.' He put out his hand and rested it on McLoughlin's shoulder. 'You go home, I'll call you later.'

It was later. No phone call. McLoughlin sat at the top of the wooden steps, his back against the kitchen door, a glass of white wine in his hand. Coming up to five o'clock in the afternoon and the shadows cast by the tall sycamores across the end of the garden were crisp and black. He watched Ferdie running up and down the rough patch of lawn. He was chasing a butterfly, a Peacock, its beautiful iridescent eyes on show. From where McLoughlin was sitting he could see the judge's garden next door. Huge red and orange poppies fell out of their beds across the paths. The judge's roses too were flowering. Albertine in a pale pink swathe across the far wall, and dotted around the garden splashes of white, yellow and a deep red.

He stood up to get a better look at the flowers, then walked down the steps and over to the door between the two gardens. He stepped through. He could smell the evening scent. It was from the stock which trailed along the edge of the beds.

The door to the dining room opened. A voice called out. He turned around. A woman was standing on the top step. She was small and plump, her hair, iron grey, cut short. A flowery apron was wrapped around her ample waist. She was holding a duster in her hand and shaking it vigorously.

'Hey, you.' She waved the duster towards him, and picked up the mop at her side.

'Sorry, I'm sorry,' he turned to face her. 'I live next door. I'm Michael McLoughlin.' He took a few steps, away from the flowers as Ferdie appeared. When he saw the woman his tail began to wag and he gave voice to his repertoire of whines.

'Ferdie, there's a good boy,' the woman came down, carefully, one step at a time. She held out her hand and the dog rubbed his head against her legs, wriggling with pleasure.

'What's he doing here?' she straightened and rested for a moment on the mop. 'I thought Róisín had him.'

'He showed up a few days ago. He seems happy enough.' He smiled and held out his hand. 'You must be Mrs Maguire. Liam told me about you. He said you'd sort the house out.'

'Right,' she grimaced and shook her head, 'the state of the place. I've cleaned everything, did the beds up lovely.' She paused to gather breath. 'And the poor man, poor Mr John, Lord have mercy on him, the blood all over his lovely carpet.' She picked up the mop and with her large hands reddened by years of work, started to wring it out on the grass. 'That lovely man, not a bother on him and then this.'

'Here, let me do that.' McLoughlin took it from her. He wrapped his hands around the soggy wet head and squeezed hard, watching the dirty water flow.

'Now, look at you,' she reached out and took the mop from him, 'you'll have to come into the house and have a bit of wash. I've the kettle on and Mr Liam left me a gorgeous tin of biscuits. Will we open it?' And she squinted up at him, a broad grin on her round face.

They sat on tall wooden stools at the kitchen counter. Mrs Maguire poured tea. She offered him milk, which he took and sugar which he declined. He sipped. The tea was hot and strong.

'That's good.' He scrutinised the biscuits, his hand hovering. 'What do you recommend?'

She put her head on one side, looking for a moment like the plump child she once must have been. She pursed her lips.

'Well,' her hand closed over a Mikado, 'I love the jam and the coconut.' It disappeared in one gulp into her mouth and she reached again, and again.

'Go on,' she nodded towards the tin, 'you'd want to get a move on. Every man for himself.'

She talked as she ate. She knew the Hegartys, seed, breed and generation. Knew them inside out.

'My ma, you see, she worked for old Mrs Hegarty. The Hegartys needed a maid so my ma came here. Too many kids in her house, she was oldest, so she left home first. The Hegartys were very good to her. Mrs Hegarty, well, she was tough. She'd very high standards. You'd never have had your tea in the kitchen like this when she was alive. Tea was always at the big table. The silver pot and all the other stuff. She taught my mammy how to run a house.' Mrs Maguire paused and munched, her hand automatically heading towards the tin.

'So,' McLoughlin reached over her and grabbed a lemon puff, 'so who lived here? Dan was an only child wasn't he?'

'Yeah,' Mrs Maguire nodded, 'yeah, the one and only. The apple of his mammy's eye. When he was a kid they lived in the basement. His da was dead and Mrs Hegarty went out charring for people. But then Dan did very well for himself. He bought her the house and she started taking in lodgers. That was when my mam came here.' She looked around her. 'Mammy got married when she was eighteen. And she and my da, Billy was his name, they lived here then for a few years until they got their own place. I was born here. In the attic. Up there was where Mammy and Daddy lived. And me too.'

McLoughlin sat and listened. Mrs Maguire, 'Mags, call me Mags,' she said, as she warmed to her subject. Dan got married and moved to Rathgar. Eventually she'd gone to work for him and his growing family. She was the same age as her mother had been. And the same age as John. She lived in and looked after them all. John and Liam and their sisters. While they were at school she was busy, picking up after them, washing and scrubbing and cooking. But she didn't seem to resent it. As she talked about them her expression softened. John, McLoughlin could see, was her favourite. She described him lovingly. He was tall, he was strong, he was handsome, he was clever.

'He was a lovely lad.' She looked away. Tears filled her bright blue eyes. She smiled and McLoughlin could see the prettiness in her. 'God love him. We were all so proud. I remember his gran, when he graduated, she went along to the college to see it.' Her hand hovered over the biscuit tin. McLoughlin picked up the pot and refreshed their cups. 'It was Trinity College he went to. He got the special thing from the Archbishop.'

'The dispensation, he got the dispensation?'

'Yes,' she nodded vigorously, 'he got that, so he could go to a Protestant university. Old Mrs Hegarty was so proud. She told all the neighbours. 'Cause the neighbours, well a lot of them, not now, but then, a lot of them were Protestants,' her fingers closed over a chocolate digestive, 'all around here was Protestant, they all went to the Mariners, the big church, you know, down by the sea. And they were all very, very snooty, terrible snobs and Mrs Hegarty, well she didn't like them. And she always said they didn't approve of her Dan and, I can tell you,' and she pointed her index finger, smeared now with chocolate, 'God help anyone who didn't approve of her Dan.' She popped the last of the biscuit in her mouth and chewed vigorously. McLoughlin picked up his cup and sipped his tea.

'So the Hegartys had this house for years?' He raised his cup in emphasis.

Mrs Maguire nodded. 'Years and years. In fact Mrs Hegarty outlived most of the neighbours.'

'The Protestant neighbours?'

'The Protestant neighbours. That's right. Hardly any of them left now.' She wiped the corners of her mouth with a tissue extracted from the pocket of her apron.

'So who lived in my house? Did you know them?'

'Oh yes, of course, well,' Mrs Maguire paused, 'it was set out in flats, your house, some of them more like bedsits, rooms really.'

'Really? Even then? I thought there would have been just one family, owner occupied.' McLoughlin picked up his cup and swirled the tea around.

'Oh no,' Mrs Maguire shifted her weight on the stool, 'Mammy told me, an awful state a lot of them houses were. But they always had the brasses on the front door nice and shiny. Old Mrs Hegarty now, she was a one for the polish. She knew all about elbow grease. She'd worked in a lot of the houses round here. Your house too, I remember Mammy telling me. She did for the people in your house. That would have been when Dan was a young lad.'

'So,' McLoughlin swayed on the stool. It wasn't very stable. He put one foot down to steady himself. 'So Mr Hegarty, Dan's father, he was dead, you said.'

Mrs Maguire nodded. 'Dead, years ago. She was a widow woman. And it was terrible in them days. No pension, no nothing.'

'No family to help her?'

'Not that I know of. She was from somewhere out in the west, Mayo I think, up the side of a mountain, Mammy said. Anyway in those days no one had any spare cash. No hand-outs in them days.'

No hand-outs in them days. A woman on her own. The photo in the polished silver frame on the mantelpiece in the front room. A big woman, solid. A strong face, almost masculine. McLoughlin leaned closer. Dan had inherited her nose, aquiline, and he'd passed it on to his children and their children too.

He followed Mrs Maguire around the house as she pointed out particular treasures. A large silver platter given to John by the Bar Council. Engraved with all their names. A cabinet filled with trophies. Swimming, athletics, tennis even, from John's student days.

'Terrible amount of polishing, all that silver.' She leaned forward and inspected the gloss on a large cup. 'They look lovely, though, they do.'

Everything lovingly cared for, a strong smell of Pledge rising from the mahogany furniture. But upstairs, despite the scrubbing, the bloodstain was still clearly visible. Mrs Maguire stood and stared down. 'I tried everything, but it won't budge.'

'Yes, I'm afraid the carpet's ruined.' McLoughlin moved towards the piano, stepping over the hoover. 'This is lovely though, isn't it? I hear the judge was a great pianist.'

Mrs Maguire nodded. 'Very musical. His father too. That piano now,' and she pointed, 'it came from the people who used to live in your house. Mammy told me. One winter, after their da died. They'd no money for fuel. 'There was talk of it going in the fire. So Mrs Hegarty swapped it for a few bags of coal.' She walked slowly towards it. McLoughlin noticed she was limping, favouring her right leg. 'It's lovely having a piano in the house. I always wanted my kids to learn but they weren't bothered.' She took the duster from her pocket and wiped away a few specks from the piano's shiny lid.

'So when the judge moved back here?' McLoughlin sat down on the stool.

'He asked me if I'd come and keep the place clean. I'd stopped working really. I had the pension. But Mr John needed someone. He said I could be my own boss. Come in every day and tidy up. Do a bit of shopping. Cook his dinner. But no weekends. I made that clear. I don't work weekends. He didn't mind.' She walked around the room, dusting as she went. 'His wife had died, see? He'd been living in Ballsbridge, but he told me he wanted to come back here. He said to me, "Mags, this house is home to me."' She flicked the cloth over a small portrait by the door. 'That's Miriam. She was a beauty but she was cold. I didn't like her.'

'So it suited both of you, the arrangement?' McLoughlin could see his face reflected in the polished wood.

'Ah yeah, it was grand. Bit of extra money, and sure what else would I be doing?' She was fluffing up the cushions on the sofa, moving them around, then standing back to see how they looked. 'I'd get the bus down to the town every day. Into the shopping centre. Bit of a gossip. Then I'd come here for a couple of hours.'

He asked her then, about her observations of the house. Was it really so obvious that it had been cleaned?

'Oh yes,' her expression was certain. 'Now, don't get me wrong. I loved Mr John. I really did. But he was an awful man for the mess. Weekends he'd always have takeaways and stuff. And there'd be bottles, beer and wine.' She looked up at McLoughlin, and he could read it in her face. Shouldn't have said that. Shouldn't have mentioned any of that.

'Well,' he paused, and he could see her waiting for his response, 'isn't it great he had you to look after him?'

They walked back down through the house. McLoughlin carried the hoover. Mrs Maguire stopped for breath every few steps. When they reached the hall she pointed to the cupboard under the stairs and he opened it and pushed the hoover inside.

'The basement,' he gestured to the other door beside it. 'The stairs, I'd say they're steep. Do you find them a bit of a struggle?'

'The basement? Sure there's nothing down there. I'd never go near the basement. Not part of my job.'

She turned away. He looked at her. She was tired. He could hear the rasp of her breath in her chest. A lifetime of smoking, he thought, although he couldn't smell it. Just the all-pervasive scent of the lavender polish.

'Tell me Mags,' he took her by the elbow, 'his friends, did you know any of them?'

She didn't reply.

'Legal types, big shots, I suppose they'd be.'

She began to limp towards the kitchen, the duster in her hand. She bent down to wipe the skirting board.

'Here, let me.' He tried to take the cloth but she pushed him away.

'None of my business, the judge's friends.' Her voice was brusque. She straightened up.

'No, of course not,' he held the kitchen door open, 'but you would wonder, you couldn't help but wonder, what happened to the judge.'

She began to limp towards the kitchen. Then stopped. She was close to tears again.

'I don't know what to do,' her voice was quiet, 'I should have told the guards, that nice lady, but I couldn't. I don't want to get anyone in trouble.' She put her hands over her face and began to sob. McLoughlin put his arm around her shoulder.

'You can tell me,' he said, 'I was a guard once. Tell me and I'll know whether you need to tell anyone else.'

It was Vince, her grandson, that was the problem. He was always in trouble. He stole her TV once and sold it to pay for his drugs. His own father, her son and his wife had died from AIDS. She tried to look after Vince but it was no good. He'd called in to see her on the Friday before the judge was killed. He wanted money. He said he was in trouble. She said she had none. He swore at her, said she'd be sorry that she hadn't helped him. He'd have to do something, he said. After he left, slamming the door so hard it nearly fell off its hinges, she'd gone out to visit her friend Rita, who lived down the road. They went to bingo. When she came back someone had broken in through the kitchen window, taken her savings from the tea caddy in the cupboard. The place was a state, everything thrown everywhere. Except the keys to the judge's house. They were on the hook by the door where she kept them.

'He knew where I worked. He knew I had keys. Maybe he took them, got them copied. He could do that. He was clever like that.' She was sobbing now, her whole body shaking. 'Maybe he went to the judge, tried to get money from him. And then,' she couldn't finish her sentence. She gasped for breath, then carried on. 'I went looking for him. No one knows where he is. What'll I do? I know he's bad but he's, you know, he's...'

McLoughlin reached over and put his arms around her. He pulled her close.

'Look,' he rubbed her back, 'I know the detective in charge of the investigation. Would you like me to give her a call and tell her what you told me? They'll want to talk to Vince. He might have wanted to do a bit of thieving, but I don't think he'd have done anything more than that.' He moved away. He fished in his pocket and brought out a clean tissue. He wiped the tears from her face. 'And you don't either, do you?'

She didn't answer him. She looked down.

'Will I call her?' He took out his phone. She nodded. 'Get it over with?' She nodded again, the breath coming out of her body in shudders. He took her by the hand and led her into the dining room. He sat her down at the shiny mahogany table. He flicked through the numbers until he found Min's. He pressed the call button.

It was late by the time he got home. He had brought Mrs Maguire down to the station. They had sat in the canteen, drinking strong tea while

Min questioned her. She had given Min her grandson's address, his phone number, told her all about him.

'That's Vince Maguire, isn't it?' Min had opened up her lap top.

'Yes, I 'spose you know him.' Mrs Maguire's expression was resigned.

'Since he was a little fella.' Min smiled at her. 'His father, well that was sad. Your son?'

Mrs Maguire nodded. 'His anniversary, his fifteenth, is coming up soon. We'll have a mass for him. We always do.'

Min reached out and squeezed Mrs Maguire's hand. 'I knew Tommy, and Philomena, his wife, too. They had another son, didn't they? Where's he?'

'That's Eddie. He's in Australia. Went to school. Did his Leaving Cert and then he emigrated. He's doing great. I wanted Vince to go out to him, but he couldn't get a visa. He'd been in too much trouble.' Her eyes filled with tears again. 'You won't tell him, will you? That it was me.'

'Well, as it happens Mrs Maguire, you don't need to worry about Vince.' Min fiddled with a biro, twirling it between her fingers. 'We've already checked him out. His name came up a few times. He has an alibi for the whole of that weekend. As you probably know he's been out on temporary release for the last few months. He was arrested on the Friday night, in town. Threatening behaviour and assault. Breached the conditions of his licence, so,' she shrugged, 'he's back inside and you don't need to worry about him any longer. He definitely wasn't involved in the judge's death.' Min smiled at Mags. She gathered together her files and pushed back her chair.

'Min, just a minute.' McLoughlin stood too. 'The plumber, any luck?'

She stood. She shook her head. She looked worn out. 'Nothing, nothing at all.' She smiled, a wan smile. 'Actually, now I have you here. Perhaps a couple of things.' She looked at Mrs Maguire, 'Would you mind, would it be all right if you took a seat in the hall for a minute. I just need to have a quick word with Mr McLoughlin and then he'll take you home. Won't you Mick? Make sure Mrs Maguire is OK?'

They sat again in the canteen.

'So?'

'I've been thinking about Brian O'Leary.'

'Yes?'

'You knew him well, didn't you?'

McLoughlin pondered. Did he? He remembered him of course. Vividly. There had been times years ago when every waking and some sleeping moments were taken up with thinking about Brian O'Leary. The first of the really organised Dublin criminals. The first to take drugs seriously, to work out how to make big money.

'I remember …' McLoughlin drained the last of the tea from the polystyrene cup, '…his mother, I remember her really well. She was an extraordinary woman.'

'Yes?' Min looked impatient. This wasn't what she wanted.

'Did you ever meet her?'

Min shrugged. 'Not sure.'

McLoughlin smiled. 'Not the right answer. If you'd met her you'd remember. Boy you'd remember.'

All those pro-life marches, back in the eighties. When the pro-life movement was stoking the fires, priming the political parties to amend the constitution to guarantee the right to life of the unborn. O'Connell Street overflowing with protesters, shouting and praying. Waving placards, grainy black and white photos of dead babies and scraps of foetus. Enough to chill the blood. And Cáit, Bean Uí Laoghaire, a mountain of a woman, her red hair streeling down her back, her rosary beads entwined through her large white fingers, leading the pack.

'She was an Irish speaker, a devout Catholic. She had every TD in her constituency cowed into submission.' McLoughlin picked at the plastic cup.

'And her son? How did he fit in?' Min was scanning her phone.

'They were devoted to each other. I remember when he was a kid, when he first got into trouble. Small acts of thievery. Sweets, cigarettes, alcohol. He was picked up with pockets full of contraband. Brought into the station. She arrived. Not alone. Even then he had the best legal advice. His arse didn't touch the seat in the interview room.'

'And now, what do you think about him now?'

'Well,' he clasped his hands, then unclasped them. The dog bite still hurt. 'I think he's in prison, he's been there for years and he's years left on his sentence. But,' he inspected the dressing. It looked dirty. He should change it when he got home. 'From what I can gather he's still running his own show. We might have put Brian away, but we haven't cleaned out the nest. Ask anyone. They'll tell you. Nothing moves in this town without Brian O'Leary's say so. Prison or no prison.'

'So,' she put down the phone and looked at him. 'You think, then it's possible, the judge?'

McLoughlin nodded. 'It's possible. One other thing to remember about Brian. He's vain. If he was involved he'd want people to know. He likes to leave his mark. There was one kid I remember who fell out of favour. When we found his body, he'd been branded. A picture of O'Leary right across his stomach.' He swallowed hard. 'A nasty bastard.'

'Makes me wonder. The disfigurement of the judge's face, there must have been a reason for that.'

'Or no reason at all. Purely for the fun of it. '

'O'Leary's trial, the last one?'

'Had to be the Special Criminal Court. Too much intimidation of jury members for an ordinary court. And even then we had to increase security on the judges. And after he'd gone to prison there was a spate of killings. Young men. All had been stabbed, mutilated. Ears hacked off, eyes gouged out. Just letting everyone know. He might be in prison, but nothing else would be different.' He remembered. He'd gone to Portlaoise to question him. O'Leary had sat stock-still throughout the session, his eyes fixed on a crack in the wall and said nothing. Then as he was going back to his cell he'd turned towards McLoughlin and giggled. Hitched up his trousers and winked. '*Slán abhaile*,' he'd said.

He got to his feet. 'If you need anything else let me know.' He turned to go. 'I'd better get Mrs Maguire home.'

Home to the corporation estate at the top of the hill. Where his Aunt Bea had lived with her poodle and her dahlias. Where his father had grown up. He helped Mrs Maguire from the car. She winced as she swung her legs onto the ground. Her limp was even more pronounced now. She clung to his arm as he walked with her to her front door.

'I'm waiting. For the new hip.' She rooted around in her bag and pulled out her bunch of keys.

'Will you be all right here, on your own?' He couldn't help but feel worried for her.

She nodded. 'I didn't know about Vince. No one told me he was back in prison. He didn't phone.'

'Well, maybe he felt bad about taking your money.' McLoughlin took the keys from her and opened the door. He helped her inside.

'Just a minute,' she held onto his wrist, 'I knew it would come back to me.' A triumphant smile on her plump face.

'Yes?'

'The name of the people who used to live in your house. The ones with the piano.'

'Yes?' McLoughlin fiddled with his keys.

'Lane, that was it. Their name was Lane.' She smiled at him and patted him on the arm, then turned away.

McLoughlin walked down the narrow path and got into his car. He sat and looked at the house. He watched her lights turn on, shining faintly through the net curtains. He watched them turn off and then come on upstairs. He sat in the car until the upstairs lights, too, turned off. He checked his phone. A missed call and a message from Johnny Harris. A name, Derek Green, and a phone number.

Call him now. He'll see you tonight.

Almost dark, but still warm, heat radiating up from the footpath as he walked quickly from the square, where he'd left his car, the dog trotting at his heels, towards the address the man called Derek Green had given him on the phone. He stopped off at the wine shop and bought a bottle of the Sicilian red. He tucked the bottle, wrapped in tissue paper, under one arm.

It wasn't far to Derek Green's apartment. McLoughlin had walked past the high gates many times. From the street the apartments were barely visible. A long drive with mature trees and shrubs and behind them red-tiled roofs. The name 'Ballyroan' was cut into the imposing granite gateposts. Once there must have been a house of that name with a large garden. But like so many of the old houses around here, it had been bought, demolished and the land built on. High density, that was what the council wanted. High density, that was how the developers made their money.

McLoughlin pressed the buttons on the intercom beside the gate. He noticed the small camera lens. He smiled into it, hoping he looked friendly and unthreatening. He waited. The lock on the gate buzzed loudly and clicked. He pushed and it opened. He moved through. It clanged shut behind him. He turned away and began to walk along the path towards the apartment blocks behind the trees. Light from tall lamps cut through the twilight. House 2, bell 5, Derek Green had said.

They walked on, Ferdie keeping to McLoughlin's heels. House 2 was set back from the path. Three wide steps led up to the front door. More buzzing, more waiting. Good security, McLoughlin noticed. Cameras everywhere and heavy external and internal doors. A small lift which creaked and clanked. Another camera. He wondered if they were just for show or if they were actively monitored. You never knew these days.

Number 5 had no name below its bell. But McLoughlin noticed the small ceramic scroll to the right of the door. He reached out to touch it, just as the door opened. The man standing in front of him smiled. 'The mezuzah.' He too touched the scroll, then put his fingers to his lips.

'Come in,' he stepped aside. McLoughlin walked ahead into a large room which smelt strongly of cigarette smoke. It was dark, just one small lamp turned on. The walls were painted white. A striking abstract hung over a gas fire, modern, polished metal and stone. The furniture was also modern, a chrome and leather sofa and two chairs and a couple of steel and glass tables which McLoughlin recognised as copies of Eileen Grey's work.

'Nice,' he gestured towards them, 'where did you get them? The job on my house, it's nearly finished and I'm in the market for some new stuff.'

Green hooked his thumbs in his belt. He was thin, McLoughlin noticed, angular, his face in the lamp light, all planes and sharpness. Black hair slicked back against his skull, dark brown eyes, a fleshy mouth, his lips full and curved. Stubble showed on his chin and jaw.

'A shop in the city,' he moved towards the table.

'Expensive?' McLoughlin joined him and the two stood side by side looking down at the circle of glass and its simple but efficient steel frame.

'No,' Green shook his head, 'surprisingly cheap. They're probably knock-offs. I looked online and the ones from the licensed suppliers are four times the price I paid. Still,' he trailed one hand across the table's shiny surface. 'They do me, I like them. Now,' he turned away, 'enough of the small talk. Sit down, why don't you. But if you don't mind perhaps you'd put the dog on the balcony. Outside is where dogs belong.' He took a couple of steps towards the houseplants, reached behind and slid open the door. Ferdie, without being told, trotted after him. He lay down on the tiles, his head on his paws.

They sat, McLoughlin on the sofa, Green on the chair facing the huge flat-screen television. His usual seat, McLoughlin reckoned, the ashtray on the table beside him, a packet of cigarettes and a lighter along with the collection of TV and DVD remote controls and a pile of books. McLoughlin noticed the sophisticated sound system. Bose speakers and a small neat CD player and tuner on a shelf on the wall.

'I brought this,' McLoughlin proffered the bottle of wine.

'I don't drink,' Green didn't smile. 'It's the one bad habit I don't have.'

McLoughlin felt distinctly uneasy. He had been counting on the wine to loosen things up. He waited for Green to offer tea or coffee or even water but no offer was forthcoming. Green sat perfectly still. He lifted his head slightly and looked up at the ceiling, the tips of his fingers gently rubbing the chair's arms.

'Well,' McLoughlin shifted uneasily.

'Yes?' Green didn't look at him.

'I'm not sure what Dr Harris has told you.'

'Ah,' Green folded his hands together and crossed his legs. His feet were bare, brown and bony. 'The doctor. A brave man. One of the best.'

'Yes, he is. I've known him for years. His work is always first class. He's a good guy too.' McLoughlin crossed his legs and folded his arms. He was conscious of how awkward he felt without a glass in his hand.

'Good? Hmm,' Green put one finger to his lips. 'Depends what you mean by good. He has lapsed, he has fallen, he has been led astray and in his turn has led others along the same path. However,' he smiled, a sudden exuberant expression, 'I think I'll allow that he is, as you put it, a good man.'

'And what about John Hegarty?' McLoughlin could feel his name rippling through the room, 'was he a good man?'

Green didn't reply. He leaned his chin on his hand, looking at the polished parquet flooring.

'John was a sad man.' He lifted his chin from his hand and stared for the first time directly towards McLoughlin. 'He'd spent his whole life pretending. That's not a good way to live.'

'But perhaps it was the only way he could.' McLoughlin felt suddenly defensive on the judge's behalf.

'I disagree.' Green moved his hands back to the arms of the chair and began to drum rhythmically with his fingers. 'I disagree completely. Secrecy engenders dishonesty. It makes men lie and cheat and hurt people. John Hegarty lied to everyone. He cheated everyone. He hurt many people.'

'And you know this, do you?' McLoughlin moved uneasily. 'You know this for sure?'

'I know this, as you so quaintly put it, for sure,' Green mimicked his accent. 'I know this to be true because John Hegarty, the judge, hurt me. He hurt me badly.'

He got up. He stood with his back to the fireplace. He rocked on the balls of his feet. McLoughlin could see that not only was Derek Green thin but he was also extremely strong. The muscles in his thighs tensed inside his denim jeans and his biceps, visible beneath the short sleeves of his white T-shirt, bulged.

'Hurt me, he did, hurt me badly,' he repeated the words. 'When I was a teenager. When I met him first many years ago. Met him one night, one dark, dark night. He took me in his car. To a house he had. A big house, tall, dark, empty. Cold it was, cold and dark and empty. I fell in love with him. This man, this good man. I thought he would change my life. And he did. He changed my life. But not the way I wanted it changed.'

McLoughlin watched him. It was as if he was in a trance. His eyes were closed. He was swaying from side to side. Then his eyes flicked open.

'I fell in love. I was a teenager. I was trying to find someone to love me in the way I wanted to be loved. I thought John would be that man. He told me he loved me. He told me I was the most important person in his life. And then...' he moved away from the fireplace. He sat down. He picked up the packet of cigarettes. He pulled one out and lit it. A Zippo lighter, clicking the metal lid back and forth as he inhaled deeply, then let the smoke out, pouring down his nose, the click click of the lighter lid and one foot jiggling on the wooden floor.

'And then?' McLoughlin leaned forward. Green didn't reply. He sucked on the cigarette so the tip glowed red.

'And then,' he shrugged. 'He cast me aside. I thought he would love me forever but he cast me out. Into the darkness, into the night.' He leaned forward, the cigarette in his mouth. He folded his arms, one over the other, one hand rubbing backwards and forwards over a small tattoo McLoughlin could see on his inner left forearm. It reminded him, its bluish tone, its size, of something, he couldn't think what.

'But you met him again?'

Green pulled the cigarette from his mouth. The ash dropped on his thighs. He flicked it away and it fell on the floor, grey, worm-like.

'I met him again. I saw him one day walking along the pier with the dog. I didn't think he recognised me. He didn't look at me. But when I sat down on the bench, the one near the plaque to Samuel Beckett, he sat beside me. He said he'd like to meet me again. I told him where and when.' Green lifted the cigarette to his mouth. The smoke drifted from his lips. 'I told him there were friends here. People like us. People who understood, who wanted what we want, who would do what we did. I told him he'd be welcome.' He closed his eyes and leaned back in his chair. McLoughlin thought for a moment he could see a tear slide beneath Derek's eyelid. He continued to speak, his voice quiet so McLoughlin had to strain to hear what he was saying, 'I'd followed his career, his rise through the judiciary. Sometimes, just sometimes,' he sat up again and blinked his eyes open. He looked over McLoughlin's head. No tears now. A smile, a tight leer, 'I thought I might tell on him. Spill the beans, rain on his parade.'

'But you didn't?'

'I didn't. For years he'd stayed away from the scene. I didn't think anyone would believe me. And I was having a hard time of it anyway.' Green pulled out another cigarette and lit it from the glowing stub before crushing the first one in the ashtray. 'Hard times, hard times, not glad to be gay, not back then. Pink triangle territory really. Keep it hidden, keep it secret. Don't rock the boat. Don't tell anyone. *Oh Derek*,' and he mimicked a woman's voice, '*no girlfriends. Such a pity, mama wants grandchildren, that's what mama wants.* But,' and his voice slipped back to its usual register, 'mama's not going to get grandchildren. Poppa's going to get an awful land. Poppa doesn't like queers. Poppa has stories, terrible stories, men who tried to bugger him, men who would trade a blowjob for a scrap of bread, camp guards and soldiers who would make a pet of a boy. Keep a boy from the gas. Keep a boy from the whip. Keep a boy from the gallows.'

And McLoughlin realised then, the tattoo on Derek Green's pale inner arm. A number starting with a B. Crudely done, the line uneven, blurred.

'Your tattoo?' McLoughlin pointed.

'Oh at last. Top marks Mr McLoughlin. Top marks for observation. My father's number. Given to him in 1944 when he was fourteen, deported from Hungary to Auschwitz. The only thing I have of his now. He told me. You're no son of mine. He shut the door in my face. So I took his tattoo. If I'd been in the camp I'd have had a number. For most of my life I've been in the camp. The camp where John Hegarty belonged. He was a denier.'

'And is that why he's dead? Is that why someone shot him, and destroyed his face? To shame him? Is that what this is all about?' He stood up. His heart was pounding.

Green didn't answer. He put down the cigarette. He buried his face in his hands. He sobbed. McLoughlin waited.

'I don't know,' Green looked up at him. His face was wet. His eyes were red. 'I don't think so. But here,' he stood too. 'Something I want to show you.'

Samuel sat in his favourite chair. The backgammon set was on the small card table in front of him. He opened the wooden box. He began to put out the pieces in the pattern ordained for centuries. Two reds, five blacks, three blacks, five reds on one side of the board. And on the other side, the opposite. Two blacks, five reds, three reds, five blacks. His fingers touched the pieces gently as he lined them up. They clinked, one against the other. His father had given him this set when he graduated from university. An upper second, not the first his father had hoped for. He had seen the look of disappointment on his face, noted the slope to his shoulders.

'Well,' he had said, 'with a first you could have been an academic. Now I suppose you'll have to make do with a job. The firm will take you in. William Dudgeon and Son.'

But still he had given him the backgammon set. Made of mahogany, the interior of rosewood and boxwood. Thirty ebony and boxwood pieces with an ebony shaker. One of the few possessions which Samuel had managed to hold on to. Through the years, from house to house, from marriage to divorce, from freedom to imprisonment. He had brought the set with him when he was processed on his way into the gaol. When the contents of his supermarket plastic bag were checked and noted and put away. The officer had looked at the large rectangular box.

'Nice bit of work,' his fingers had run up and down the grain, 'but we can't keep it here.'

'Please,' Samuel had been close to tears.

'Get someone to take it. Wife? Mum? Sister? Brother? Friend?'

Samuel had shook his head. 'There's no one. Please. Please keep it.'

The officer had opened it then, admired the inlay, fingered the red and black pieces, looked over to his colleague, a large blonde woman whose curves were held in place by the stiff fabric of her uniform.

'What you say, Betty?'

She glanced at Samuel, must have seen his despair, his humiliation, his abject state. She looked at the box and shrugged.

'Why not. I'll put it away in the top of the cupboard.' She winked at Samuel. 'Don't you worry, it'll still be here for you when you get out.'

Now Samuel sat back in his chair. He picked up the two dice. They weren't made of wood like the rest of the set. He wasn't sure what had happened to the originals. These were hard plastic. Heavy, he weighed them in his palm. Heavy, the judge had weighed them in his palm. Shook them vigorously then threw them across the board. The judge never used the ebony shaker. He liked, he said, to feel the dice. He was sure, he said, that he could influence the throw with the shape of his hand. Samuel didn't agree. It didn't work that way. And it never worked that way for the judge. Samuel had sat in the big, beautiful sitting room, the portrait on the wall above the fireplace, the backgammon on a small table between them and watched how the judge would flounder, would fail, would lose on the throw of the dice.

Now he put them in the ebony cup. He shook them vigorously. He dumped them out on the board. Double sixes. He smiled. The judge sat on the other side of the table, his legs in their cream cotton trousers crossed, and he smiled. Or he tried to smile. His face was a mess. Sticky black blood coated his skin. One eye was missing, the other rolled around in its socket. His nose was smashed. Only his mouth was intact. His lips pulled open and Samuel saw the judge's teeth. They were bared in a grin. It was cheeky. Like the grin he had that night in the club in London. The big cheeky grin. The boy on his knee. The scared little boy, his body white, so white and his veins so blue showing through the translucent skin. His fingernails bitten to the quick, his bare feet, dirty. And the judge, although he wasn't a judge then, all those years ago. He was a barrister, ambitious, clever, good at his job. Sent to London to advise on a court case. A racehorse. Gone missing from a race meeting in England. Bred and trained in Ireland. Owned by an Englishman. Insured in Ireland. Missing in England. A complicated situation. Legal advice needed on Irish insurance law.

'We'll get the best,' his father had picked up the phone. 'It's worth a lot. The fees will be huge.'

The young barrister from Dublin. Handsome, clever, did the job. Won the case for them.

'Take him,' his father had said, 'take him out. Make sure he gets whatever he wants. We've done well out of him. There'll be a bonus for you this year.'

The young barrister, his suit of fine wool, his shirt of cotton, his tie of silk, with the boy on his knee, one hand grasping him around the waist, the other lifting high a glass of whiskey. And men behind him, beside him. A boy here, a boy there, a boy kneeling, a boy lying. And as the camera clicked, as the flash bulb popped, all mouths open, a loud cheer. And Samuel stood at the back. He watched for a moment. He had done his job.

Make sure he gets whatever he wants. Samuel could do that. He knew his way around. He wasn't his father's son for nothing. He bent down and whispered in the Irishman's ear. Handed him his card.

'I'll be back for you later. But if you need anything phone me.'

And the young barrister grinned and nodded. Drank his whiskey and stood up. His hand on the nape of the boy's neck as they moved towards the private rooms behind the curtain.

Now Samuel moved the backgammon pieces. Double sixes. You could do a lot with them. He picked up the dice and placed them in the ebony cup. He shook and shook and shook.

The barrister went back to Dublin. Samuel drove him to the airport. They shook hands. Samuel turned his hands over and looked at them. He expected to see blood. There had been blood everywhere. The low couch in the back room in the club had been soaked. The floor was wet. Sticky handprints on the wall. Blood on the barrister's white underwear.

'Sort it out,' his father had shouted. 'Use your fucking head. No one cares about the boy. A bit of city rubbish. '

Samuel watched the barrister walk away. Tall and slim, a black Homburg hat on his head, a Crombie coat and shoes shined to a high gloss by the night porter in his hotel. And tried not to think of the boy, the piece of city rubbish, swept down the drain.

Now Samuel dumped the dice on the board. A six and a four. Just what he needed.

'I've got you,' he smiled at the judge. 'You're stuck. You can't move. You're helpless.'

The judge's mouth stopped smiling. He tried to get up but he had no strength. He sank down. What was left of his head drooped. And Samuel sat upright. One gloved hand stroked the other. He giggled. He remembered the mound of earth in the graveyard. The pile of rotting flowers.

'You'd better go back where you belong. You're nothing now.' He clapped his hands. He looked down and when he looked up the judge had gone.

Samuel smiled. He piled the backgammon pieces into a tall tower. They tottered, swayed from side to side. Then toppled, red and black tumbling to the floor.

'Take it,' Derek Green said, 'take it and leave me alone.'

A sports bag, black leather, closed with a zip.

'Where did this come from?' McLoughlin weighed it in one hand.

'The judge, he asked me to keep it. He'd turn up from time to time and he'd get something from it.' Green had moved away into the small hall.

'Something? What?'

'I don't know. I didn't ask him.'

'And you didn't look?'

'Not while he was alive. When I heard he was dead I opened it. I'm sorry I did. Now,' he held the front door open, 'I want you to leave me alone. Get out and don't come back.'

His tears had dried. He was standing straight. His face had returned to its former expression of arrogance and contempt. McLoughlin called the dog. He heard the door slam behind them. He carried the bag home. He resisted opening it. He waited until he had shut the front door firmly. He stepped over the sacks of cement, the ladders, the electric drill, the tubs of tile adhesive and stacks of tiles. He sat down on the stairs, the bag beside him. He looked at it for a moment. Then grasped the zip and pulled.

He'd never seen a flagellant's whip before. A wooden handle, a bit like a child's skipping rope, but attached to it four knotted cords, with small wooden beads twisted into them. He'd hefted it in one hand, then held out his other palm and swung it gently. Even though the cords barely grazed the skin he flinched and cried out loud with the pain. It took him back, for a moment, to school, the Christian Brother, a big man, the leather raised above his shoulder, then whistling down. His hand red and swollen for hours afterwards.

But nothing as painful as the whip in the bag. He held it up to the light. Dried blood, clearly visible, was caught in the small knots and around the beads. It must have been used regularly, frequently. It must have left scars, marks on the body. What was it that Harris had said? Scars, old, healed. Not sure where they came from. Min would know, or at least suspect. She'd be looking for something like this. He flicked it again. And she'd be even more curious if she saw what else was in the bag. He put down the whip and lifted out a plastic sack. He pulled it open. Inside was a large amount of money. Fifty euro notes in bundles of a thousand euros. Fifty such bundles. And a phone. Turned off. When he held down the power button there was no response. He turned it round and looked at the small apertures on the top. He walked into the sitting room. His charger was plugged into a socket. He switched it on and attached the phone. He'd wait for it to power back up, to see what secrets it was hiding.

It was late now. He was exhausted. Even his mattress looked tempting. He lay down, covered himself up, wrapped his arms around his body and slept.

Woke, the sun in his eyes, the builder's radio on loud, and the usual crashing and banging. He got up. Found the kettle, found the tea bags. Made himself a cup. Dressed and walked out onto the front steps. Hot already. The sky blue and everything beautiful. And his name being called. Elizabeth Fannin was standing at the gate. Beside her a little girl, her dark hair a tumble of curls, wearing a bright pink dress, a choc ice in one hand and a doll in the other.

'Michael, hi, there's someone I'd like you to meet.' Elizabeth was smiling, her hand resting lightly on the child's head.

McLoughlin hurried down the steps. The little girl looked up at him. Her face was smeared with chocolate. He pulled out his handkerchief and offered it to her. She smiled, and shook her curls, twisting one bare leg around the other.

'Say hallo to Michael,' Elizabeth gave her a little push. McLoughlin held out his hand.

'Aren't you the lucky one?' He bent down. 'I love choc ices. Can I have a taste?'

'Go on, Leah, give Michael some,' Elizabeth's voice was cajoling, but the child would have none of it. She turned away, her face set, the toe of one sandal scraping over the granite path.

'It's all right,' McLoughlin was sympathetic. 'People like me are too old for ice creams. Makes us fat.'

The child looked up at him, squinting in the bright sun. 'Ask my granny. She'll get you one. She's lots of money in her bag. The ice cream man's over there.'

'Right, OK, granny,' McLoughlin grinned at Elizabeth, 'how about it? Ice creams all round?'

They sat, McLoughlin, Elizabeth, Leah and her doll, on the Cassidy bench. Ferdie crouched in front, waiting.

'So, you're a grandmother?' McLoughlin licked his choc ice.

'Yeah,' Elizabeth stroked Leah's curls.

'And a mother obviously?'

'That too, strangely enough,' she smiled at him. 'My daughter, Jess, Leah's mother, my one and only.'

Leah wriggled from the seat. The dog reached out and sniffed her sticky little hand.

'Ferdie, come here,' McLoughlin made a grab for his collar.

'It's all right, Leah's good with dogs. She loves them. She's a brave little thing. Intrepid really.' Elizabeth's face softened.

The girl and the dog began to run together across the grass.

'Funny,' McLoughlin shifted on the seat. Elizabeth's dark red trousers brushed against his jeans. 'Somehow I've never put you down as a mother, or a grandmother for that matter. Sorry,' he paused, 'sorry, that sounds ridiculous. How would I know?' He shook his head. He wiped his hands on his handkerchief and held it out to her. She took it, nodding her thanks. As she rubbed some of the ice cream from her fingers he noticed again her collection of silver rings. She held up her hand so they shone in the sun light.

'None of them for a wedding, I'm afraid. I had the child, but I never managed the other bit.'

He looked at her. She seemed wistful, sad, her face clouded.

'Anyway,' she smiled, 'you can't have everything.'

'Yeah, I know what you mean.' He sat back on the bench and folded his arms. 'I had the marriage, for as long as it lasted, but we didn't have children. That did for us really.'

'Oh I'm sorry, that must have been terrible. Childlessness, well...' her voice trailed away as the child and the dog came running back.

'Look Biddy, look at me,' and the little girl held up an old tennis ball. 'Look what I found.' And she flung it as hard as she could, up high in the air in a curving arc, so the dog jumped and ran after it.

'Biddy? She calls you Biddy? Not Granny?' McLoughlin turned towards Elizabeth as if to scrutinise her. 'You don't look like a Biddy to me.'

'No? I don't?' Elizabeth scooped the child up on her knee. 'What do you think Leah? Am I Biddy or am I Granny?'

The child put her arms around her neck and planted a kiss full on her mouth. 'You're my Biddy Biddy,' and she jumped down and began to skip away, singing loudly, 'Biddy, Biddy, Biddy, Biddy.'

Elizabeth smoothed her blouse. 'When Jess had Leah I was so delighted to be a grandmother, I would have been quite happy to be called Granny or anything. But I'd been called Biddy when I was a child. And Jess sometimes used the name, actually to annoy me, and somehow or another Leah got hold of it and it stuck. So now I'm Biddy, to her anyway.' She crossed her legs.

'She's a lovely little girl.' McLoughlin watched as she chased the dog across the grass. 'And she loves you, that's for sure.'

Elizabeth smiled again, 'I look after her a couple of days a week. It's the least I can do. Jess is having another baby soon. It's wonderful,' she paused and clasped and unclasped her hands, 'I'm delighted for them, but, life these days, it's hard.' She began to get up, uncrossing her legs, reaching down to her big brown satchel. 'I've a few things I need to leave in my room. I'm coming back this evening. So this is just a detour on the way to the playground in the park. Then home for an early dinner.'

'Where do you live?' McLoughlin suddenly realised he didn't know. He had a moment of anxiety. Somehow it hadn't occurred to him that Elizabeth had a life separate from Victoria Square.

'Not far away, walking distance actually. Adelaide Street, just up from the seafront. Do you know it?' She turned from him, waving to the little girl.

'Yeah, near the entrance to the Maritime Museum?'

'That's right. I grew up there. I inherited the house when my parents died. That was why I came back from London, when they were getting old and couldn't manage on their own.' She slung her bag over her shoulder. 'Come on Leah. I have to go inside.'

'No,' the child's mouth turned down, 'don't want to, want to stay here and play with the doggie.' She stamped her sandal on the grass.

'You go,' McLoughlin moved away from the bench, 'get what you need. I'll keep an eye on her.'

'You sure?' Elizabeth looked sceptical.

'Of course, go on, we'll play chasing,' he began to jog on the spot, and called out to the dog. 'Here Ferdie, come on boy.' Elizabeth turned away, hurrying across the road to the house. She disappeared through the side gate. And McLoughlin ran and chased the dog and the child, then all three collapsing in a heap on the ground beneath the trees.

The mobile phone, the judge's mobile phone. He stood and watched Elizabeth and Leah as they walked away across the green. The tall slim woman, her dark red clothes, and the child, hopping and skipping, her curls bouncing, her bright pink dress swirling out around her. And remembered, he had left the judge's mobile phone attached to the charger, beside his mattress.

He took the front steps two at a time, then up to his room, scrabbling around to find it. He sat down on the floor, and pressed the power button.

The screen brightened. *Enter PIN code*, he was instructed. The code, what could it be? He tried a few combinations. One, two, three, four? Didn't work. Two, four, six, eight? Again no joy. Three, six, nine, twelve? The same lack of response. There was a Chinese guy in the shopping centre. He'd be able to unlock it for him. Half an hour it would take, that was all.

Half an hour and ten euros, that was all. He sat on the wall outside the church. He looked at the phone. He pressed the power button and put in the new PIN. The screen brightened. He selected Contacts. Only one number stored. No name to identify it, just the letter X. He took a deep breath. He pressed the call button. It rang and rang and rang. Voicemail. The factory settings. He breathed out. A sort of relief. Wasn't sure he was able for whatever was to come.

Beside him the dog got to his feet, sniffing the breeze from the sea. McLoughlin got to his feet. He picked up the phone and as he turned away it began to ring. He looked down. The caller was identified as X. He pressed the button to answer.

'Hallo,' he tried to keep his voice as calm and neutral as possible.

'Who the fuck are you? Who the fuck is using this phone?' The voice was gruff, deep, aggressive.

'I could ask you the same question.'

'Yeah? You could? And what kind of an answer do you think you'd get?' The man on the line was breathing heavily.

'You tell me. Who are you?' McLoughlin moved away from the café, towards a bench on the footpath. He sat down, the dog jumping up beside him.

'You don't know. You don't know me. But you must have known our mutual friend.' The volume on the call was fading.

'It's why you knew him, that's what I want to know.' McLoughlin felt as if he was shouting now. He could hear the man breathing. And a noise in the background. Something familiar, but he couldn't put his finger on what it was.

'Well that, mate, is for me to know and you to find out.' The voice was suddenly loud. McLoughlin held the phone away from his ear. There was silence.

'Hallo? Hallo?' He stood up and moved around, holding the phone out, then looking at it again. The screen was blank. The connection lost.

'Shit,' McLoughlin swore out loud. He pressed the call button. He waited. Again straight to voicemail.

He took a deep breath. 'Listen,' he was trying to sound calm, reasonable, even friendly. 'Call me again, will you? I'd like to talk to you. I've a feeling we got off on the wrong footing. OK? Thanks.'

They walked home. He stopped at the corner shop, bought dry dog food, bread, butter, cheese and a few bottles of beer. He pulled the phone from his pocket. Silence. No further contact. He'd leave it for the time being. He'd try later.

Ian and the guys were gone by the time he reached the house. All was peace and quiet. At last it looked as if they were making progress. He hurried upstairs. The plaster had been stripped from the walls. The partitions which had divided the rooms on the top floor had been taken away. McLoughlin looked around. The original mouldings were visible now. The plasterwork was ornate, pretty, a decoration of leaves and small egg shapes. And ceiling roses of ornamental acanthus leaves, large with deep lobes. They'd moved his mattress from upstairs, down to the room at the front of the house. The plastering, rewiring all done, just waiting for the finishing touches.

He walked downstairs. The kitchen was really coming on. The countertop was in and the sink unit installed. McLoughlin opened the bag of dog food and poured some onto the cool stone floor. The dog ate greedily. He took out the bread and made a couple of sandwiches, and opened a beer. Together he and the dog went out and sat on the back steps. It was still light, still warm. He ate and drank. He looked at his watch. Tried not to look again at the phone. Got up. He'd start moving some of his stuff upstairs. Boxes of books which he could sort through. Kitchen equipment. Household things. Anything to keep his mind off the phone.

He finished eating, then went back into the house, and opened the front door. Walked down the steps and towards the basement. Let himself in. It was dark here, but he could see light showing from

Elizabeth's room at the end of the hall. He moved towards it. He could hear music playing softly, jazz. He cleared his throat loudly, and tapped on the door

'Hi, Elizabeth? Are you there? Are you busy?'

Her room was cool and the light was low. She was seated behind a desk made of pale wood, a pile of papers in front of her and a pen in her hand. There were two chairs, wooden frames, cushions of a deep turquoise on either side of the window, and a low leather couch pushed back against the opposite wall. The room was painted light grey. A multi-coloured rug brightened the floor. A number of large prints were hung on the walls. They were of trees and flowers. One was particularly striking, a lemon tree, its fruit hanging down.

'Nice,' he looked up at the picture.

'Yes,' she nodded, 'I really like it. You almost feel you can reach up and pick one. Squeeze it, really juicy or a nice chunky slice for a gin and tonic.'

'Now you're talking.' He could taste the sourness and the fizz on his tongue.

'I'd offer you one, except, I don't keep any drink here. Not really appropriate. Sit down.' She gestured to one of the chairs.

'Well,' he shrugged, 'thanks, if I'm not disturbing you.' He sat back and looked around. 'It's nice here, comfortable, secure.' He closed his eyes.

'You're tired. You've a lot on at the moment.' Her voice was soothing.

He opened his eyes and looked at her.

'The house and all that goes with it. Very stressful.'

He nodded. 'Yeah, I'm beginning to wonder why I got involved at all. It seemed like a great idea at the time. Buy a fixer-upper. Fix it up. Sell it, make a few bob, move on, but you need a certain type of personality for all that.' He shifted.

'And what type of personality is that?' She got up from behind the desk and came towards him, taking her place in the chair opposite. She crossed her legs. He noticed her feet were bare.

'Oh, organised, meticulous, a great one for lists. I used to be a great one for lists, but I've lost the touch.' He looked around again. 'Getting old I suppose. It's funny the way it hits you. You don't have the energy any longer.'

'Maybe not,' she shifted and folded her arms, 'but you have other qualities.'

'Like?'

'Sensitivity, empathy, understanding.'

He smiled. 'Perhaps. You now, I'd say you have all those qualities. I can imagine coming here, if I had something I wanted to get off my chest.'

She smiled, and shifted, twisting one ankle around the other.

'I went for counselling a couple of times, when I was still working. The guards provided it.' He looked over at the lemon tree.

'Did it help?'

He looked down at his hands. 'If I'm honest I don't think so. I was looking for something to kill pain. I found whiskey more effective.'

'Short term maybe,' she fiddled with the rings on her fingers, 'it does it short term, but pain is a sneaky little so and so. Always looking for breaches in the defence.'

He looked away. She sat still. Outside he could hear a car alarm screeching.

'Pain, yes, you're right. Persistent. One thing,' he leaned forward.

'Yes?'

'People who enjoy pain.' He could see the little whip, the knotted cords, the dried blood between the beads. 'I don't get it really.'

'No?'

He shook his head.

'Sometimes it's just about the ability to feel. To feel alive,' she moved again, her feet twisting on the rug.

'And what about punishment?'

'Well,' she paused, 'it can be using one pain to drive out another. One pain that's more bearable, maybe more controllable.' She looked down at her hands again. 'And maybe the after-effects make it worthwhile.' Silence for a moment. 'People who self-harm. Often they'll have a

176

ritual. They can anticipate the knife, the razorblade, the scissors. And afterwards they feel such relief. Clean, better, almost perfect.'

'I knew a girl once. A case I was involved in. She was raped,' he could see Sorcha's pinched, white face, 'she stopped eating and she died. I've often tried to imagine what she went through.'

'Yes, very hard. And what's hardest to imagine, to understand, how the pain of her starvation was easier to bear than the pain, the shame, the humiliation of the rape.' Elizabeth shifted in her chair. Silence again inside, the car alarm wailing outside. She looked away.

'Maybe, some evening, if you're not working,' he felt awkward, adolescent. He stopped.

'Yes?' she looked at him. And suddenly the shrill sound of a ring tone.

'Sorry,' he fumbled in his jeans. He pulled out his phone. He looked down. The screen was blank. But the sound still filled the room. He stood up. He felt in his shirt pocket. He pulled out the judge's phone. The caller ID was X.

'Sorry,' he turned away, 'sorry I have to take this.'

He hurried through the door, pulling it shut behind him. He pressed the answer button.

'Hullo,' he said.

The voice which answered was the same as earlier.

'Your friend, the judge,'

'My friend the judge?'

'He owes me money.'

'He's dead, you know,'

Pause.

'He still owes me money. We had an agreement. The conditions still stand. A thousand a week or—'

'Can you be more specific?'

Pause. A sigh, a sniff. A clearing of the throat. Then silence. McLoughlin stood, the phone in his hand. The door opened. Elizabeth came out. Her bag was over her shoulder and he noticed she was wearing her shoes.

'Sorry,' he held up the phone. 'Sorry about that. Rude of me I know. I hate when people, you know, just when you're in the middle of a conversation.'

'It's OK. I have to go anyway.' She walked towards him. She smiled. She had her keys in her hand. 'Better, you know,' she nodded towards the front door.

'Yeah, of course, sorry, of course.' He turned away. She followed him. He stepped outside. It was warm. Surprising to feel the heat at such a late hour. The sky beginning to pale and a crescent moon, hanging.

'Look at that? Isn't it incredible?' He turned back to her. She finished locking up.

'Yes, beautiful. Aren't we lucky to be alive?' She lifted her face towards the sky. He was aware of how close she was. He could smell her hair.

'You mentioned gin and tonic. I think I could just about rustle one up, if you fancy.'

She smiled again and took a step past him. 'Thanks, but, a bit late and I've an early start.' She opened the gate and moved towards the footpath.

'Oh,' he felt let down, 'that's a pity. Some other time?'

She didn't answer. She waved her hand as she walked away. And a small breeze shook the leaves of the birch trees.

It was silver-polishing day. Gwen Gibbon sat at the round table, in her small basement sitting room. All her pieces of silver were laid out. She held a stained cloth in one hand, the tin of Silvo polish in the other. She sang as she worked. Hymns were her favourites.

He who would valiant be,
'gainst all disaster,
let him in constancy,
follow the master

She selected the small round tea caddy. She pulled off the lid. One of her mother's favourites. Once it had contained Earl Grey, aromatic, pungent. Now it was empty. She smeared the polish over its surface, then picked up the cloth and rubbed vigorously. It shone in the morning light. Her hand hovered over the other objects. Which would she clean next? The teapot, the milk jug and sugar bowl? The salt cellar? The collection of spoons big and small? The magnifying glass with its silver rim? The commemorative silver salver, her grandfather's name engraved on it?

Alexander Gibbon,
on his appointment as Visiting Physician to the Royal City of
Dublin Hospital
with affectionate esteem from his colleagues.

As she began to wipe away the film of polish there was a loud bang from above. The ceiling light shuddered. Voices, shouting, swearing, a child crying loudly. She dropped the cloth and put her hands over her ears. She closed her eyes for a moment, her shoulders hunched. Then she straightened. Mustn't show weakness. These upstairs tenants were no better or worse than many she had endured through the years. They came. They went. They shouted and screamed. They threw things at each other. Their children fought and played. Their television sets, radios, CD players disturbed her dreams, kept her awake. Sometimes she befriended them. Sometimes she ignored them. Sometimes she was frightened by them. Not so much these days. The square was more benign now. It had gone through bad times. She had lain awake at night listening to footsteps tramping up the steps to the front door. The grass in the morning littered with used syringes, scraps of bloody cotton wool, spoons, burnt and blackened. And once a body. A huddle of what looked liked rags over in the corner underneath the trees. A young woman, stick thin, her jeans pulled down, a needle still hanging from the vein behind her knee. So, Gwen chided herself, a bit of banging and crashing upstairs wasn't that bad.

Kindness, now a bit of kindness went a long way. Like the nice young man who brought her the sweet pea. She'd seen him, tall and thin and very dark, with his gold-rimmed glasses and his friend, the fat boy with red hair and freckles, a few times walking around the square. He'd admired her flowers, the marigolds and the cornflowers. He'd said his granny had lovely sweet pea. He'd bring her some. The other boy had smirked and giggled and spat on the footpath, and his friend had turned on him, scolded him for his bad manners.

She hadn't expected he'd come back with the flowers. But he did. A big bunch, tied expertly with raffia in a bow. Not from a local garden she didn't think. And not from the supermarket either. They had the look of a florist. She sank her face into the blooms and breathed in their sweet scent.

'Thank you,' she said, and he touched his forehead with his index finger and bowed.

Now Gwen polished and sang.
We sow the fields and scatter
The good seed on the land
But it is fed and watered
By God's almighty hand

In years gone by a servant would have done this. A Mary, a Bridie, a Kate, instructed carefully by Gwen's mother. But servants were a thing of her past. Sometimes Samuel came to sit with her and keep her company. He wasn't much good at polishing. He wouldn't take off his gloves for long and he could be clumsy. He liked cleaning, though. His little flat was always spotless. He had been lucky to get it. The judge, of course, the judge had put in a word for him. She would never have asked the judge for that kind of help. One had one's pride. But Samuel and the judge were close in an odd kind of way. She didn't really understand it.

She remembered the first time they had met. It wasn't long after Samuel had come to Ireland. He was living in one of the bedsits in the detached house at the end of the square. Victoria House it was called.

It must have been a Sunday because they were walking back from church. It was cold and wet. She had invited Samuel for lunch. A bowl of soup in front of the fire. They had met the judge on the road. The dog had been running ahead. He was carrying his lead in his mouth and the judge was trying to catch him. The judge was getting annoyed. Samuel had stepped on the dog's lead, trapping him. Then reached down and took hold of the end. Held it out to the judge, his leather gloves muddy. And something happened between them. A look, something. The judge snatched the lead, didn't seem to notice that it was dirty. Didn't say thank you. Just jerked the dog away. Didn't say 'good afternoon, Miss Gibbon', the way he usually would. She had stopped and looked at him. Then looked at Samuel and said, 'I must apologise on Judge Hegarty's behalf. He's not usually like that.'

And saw the expression on Samuel's face. A mixture of emotions, she thought afterwards. Shock, surprise, fear, perhaps?

'Do you know the judge?' She asked him later, when they'd eaten and warmed up in front of the small fire.

'The judge? Is that what he is?' Samuel had put down his spoon.

'Yes, retired of course now.' She held out a plate with brown bread. 'Supreme Court judge, very well known.'

Now she held the silver salver to the light. They had lived, the Gibbon family, in a large house in Belgrave Square in Monkstown.

Thomas, her father, was the youngest boy. Went into the insurance business. No head for books. Not a university man. A disappointment to the family. He had died when she was fifteen. For years his death had been a mystery. No one spoke of it. She had watched her mother, how she struggled to manage. She taught the piano in the big room upstairs, every afternoon from two until six, a succession of girls and boys. While Gwen and William, her brother, did their homework in the kitchen behind. Cold in the winter. No heating. Chilblains on their hands and feet. Early to bed, hot water bottles and heavy eiderdowns. Gwen and her mother in one room, and William on the fold-up bed in the sitting room. And then the move, down to the basement. William would have saved them but William died in the war. And Gwen's job in the school was part-time, poorly paid.

'So, do you know the judge?' she asked him again. And again he didn't answer. But later that week he called to see her again. He was wearing a warm tweed coat. She thought she recognised it. Could have sworn that it belonged to the judge. And she began to see him, coming out of the judge's basement.

'I'm doing some jobs for him,' he said when she asked. 'I'm good with my hands. He wants to play backgammon with me. He thinks he can beat me.'

And he smiled, a sudden sweet smile. And she was pleased.

Now she sat at the table. She sang and she polished. Every three months the same ritual. Would she make it through to the next silver-polishing day? Even now, sitting down, she was breathless.

She put down her cloth. She screwed the top back on the polish tin. Who would take care of all her little pieces when she was gone? There were cousins somewhere. New Zealand, she thought. Or perhaps it was South Africa. But they would not be bothered with her things. Death would come soon she feared. Someone would find her, lying on her bed in her damp little room, her body stiff. That nice Elizabeth Fannin, perhaps. She would arrange her funeral. She would parcel up her few possessions. But soon she would forget her. And even poor benighted Samuel. Soon he would no more know her than the man in the moon.

She pushed herself to standing. She held onto the back of a chair. She eased herself to the small sofa. She sank down. She closed her eyes.

'Go away death,' her voice was but a whisper. 'Go away death. Not today, not yet. Don't take me yet.'

Three missed calls on the Judge's mobile phone and a text message overnight. *Won't wait for ever. I want the money.* And with it a photograph. He had looked at it. He had felt sick.

Now he sat in the judge's drawing room, the morning light glancing across the piano, the stain dark on the carpet. He waited for Liam Hegarty to arrive.

He heard the sound of the front door opening, the click of the lock, the heavy thud as the door was closed, then silence, the footsteps muffled by the stair runner. Was this what it was like for the judge that Sunday when he died? Did he sit here, in this lovely room, the piano, the painting, the cabinet, the carpet, the comfortable sofa and chairs? Waiting, anticipating? What was it? Pleasure or pain? Or were they one and the same thing?

The door opened. Liam Hegarty hurried in. He was red-faced, his jacket slung over one shoulder, the sleeves of his freshly ironed shirt rolled back.

'You said it was urgent.'

He listened in silence as McLoughlin spelled it out. The whip, the money, the phone, the threat.

'Did he actually say he had the photos?' Hegarty took a folded white handkerchief from his trouser pocket and wiped his forehead.

'Not to begin with, but he sent me this.' He pulled out the phone and handed it over. The judge's naked torso. His eyes closed. And a head pressed against his groin.

McLoughlin watched. Liam winced. His face turned pale, his large frame suddenly grew smaller.

'What will he do, do you think?' Liam's voice was uncertain.

'If we don't pay up, you mean?' McLoughlin reached over and took the phone back. 'I think it's pretty obvious. Wouldn't take a minute. Email the photos to the newspapers. Or put them up on the web. All out in the open then. However,' he paused, 'if he does that, then bang goes his steady income.'

'And bang goes my brother's reputation. All he stood for. All we stand for. What we, our family did, to make this country.' Hegarty moved towards the portrait. 'My father, he was a brave man. Ruthless, determined. He stood up for us. He stood up for the people. And what would happen if this,' he paused, 'this bullshit comes out? Everything would be tainted by it. And it wouldn't be fair. John had a weakness. So what? We all have weaknesses. But our family would be fucked.'

'So?'

'So, call him. Set up a meeting. You want the photographs.' Hegarty got up. He began to walk around the room.

'It's not going to work, you know,' McLoughlin watched him.

'Why?'

'Because he's copied them, scanned them, got them on his phone, the easiest thing in the world. You can't only have one photograph or one set of photographs now. You know that.' McLoughlin drummed on the sofa arm with his fingers.

'So what are you saying? That I should go on paying him indefinitely?'

'No, I'm not saying that. I'll do what I can, but,' he shrugged, 'what about your part of the deal? I'm still waiting.'

'Ah, that, you and all that.' Hegarty's forehead and nose were shiny with sweat. He took off his glasses. He began to clean them with the handkerchief.

'Yes, me and all that.' McLoughlin looked around. The room was peaceful. Apart from the marks on the carpet it was hard to imagine that anything out of the ordinary had happened here. He could hear the dog barking outside and a sudden rumble as a load of rubble was dumped into yet another skip. 'Your nephew, Ciarán, he's the one with the connections isn't he?'

Hegarty pushed his glasses back up his nose. He looked tired. 'Ciarán's a bullshitter. Got involved when he was in college. Says they're the future. Does a bit of fundraising now and then.'

'So? What does he know? Who does he know?'

'He knows nothing. He's no use to you. Spoilt rotten. Like all the rest of John's children. Had it far too easy. No, I've a cousin. A retired bishop. You might know of him. Declan Hegarty.'

The priest on the altar at communion. 'I know who he is.'

'He's who you want. I've spoken to him. He's reluctant, but he knows all about shame, vilification. He knows what happens when certain,' he paused, 'certain information gets out into the public domain. So,' he began to walk towards the sitting room door. McLoughlin got to his feet. He followed Hegarty down the stairs.

'So?' They stood together by the front door.

'So, when I hear that you have the photographs, then and only then, Declan will meet you.'

He held out his hand. McLoughlin took it. Hegarty's palm was damp.

'And just in case you think you don't need me and my say-so, I can guarantee that Bishop Hegarty would have no intention of speaking to the police, you, or anyone else, without it. OK?'

He pulled open the door and together they walked into the sunshine. Ferdie was waiting on the step. He stood up, his tail wagging.

'You still have the dog,' Hegarty looked down at him. 'Do you want me to take him? I could drop him over to Róisín.'

'No,' McLoughlin clicked his fingers and the dog lifted his paw. 'No, leave him with me. For the time being anyway.'

Hegarty began to move away, down the steps.

'Hold on,' McLoughlin called out to him. 'Just one thing.' He hurried down to join him by the gate. 'You didn't seem to have anything to say when I told you about, you know, what I found in the bag with the phone and the money.'

Hegarty looked down, fiddling with his keys. 'I don't think there's anything about my brother that could surprise me.' He began to walk towards his car. Then stopped and turned back. 'Declan, speak to Declan about it. He's a wise man. He'll fill you in.

'Yeah?' A sudden urgent beeping as a huge skip lorry pulled up and began to reverse into place.

'He was John's confidante. John spoke to him about pretty much everything.' He got into his car. McLoughlin watched him drive away, and the skip lorry move into his parking space. He watched as it manoeuvred then stopped, the driver swinging down from his cab to hitch the skip to the trailer. He nodded and smiled.

'Great day.'

McLoughlin smiled back, shutting the judge's gate to keep Ferdie in.

'Bet you're sick of all the dust and mess,' the driver began to fix a huge net over the pile of rubble, pushing pieces of wood, bits of brick into place, 'it's always hard on the neighbours.'

McLoughlin nodded.

'Think this'll be the last of them.' He stopped and pulled back a large tile, shoving a gloved hand out of sight as he burrowed down into the heap, then pulling it out again. 'Thought I saw something useful.' He turned away, taking off his gloves. 'You'd be amazed what people throw away. Perfectly good tools. I got a hammer last week. Screwdrivers, drills, saws, you could start a business with them.' He climbed into the cab. McLoughlin watched, as the skip rose from the ground, hung swinging gently, then settled into place. The driver saluted, and pulled out, accelerating away. As the phone in McLoughlin's pocket beeped. The judge's phone. He hunted for it. He pressed the call button. He waited.

'So, where will we meet and when?' McLoughlin sat in the sun. He sipped a coffee. The dog snoozed at his feet. The pier was crowded. He shifted on the wooden bench, and nudged the sports bag with his elbow.

'No rush,' the man chuckled. His tone was decidedly more pleasant than it had been. There was silence for a moment. He blew his nose, a loud honking sound. 'Hay fever, fucking hay fever. This time of year, it's the flowers. Fucking hanging baskets. My neighbours are all at it. There's a competition. They're all mad to win. It drives me crazy. I need some antihistamines.' Another pause, more nose blowing.

McLoughlin remembered what Sorcha Hegarty had told him. The man smelt of smoke, and cheese and onion crisps, and something else. A nasal spray, was that it? Peppermint perhaps? The kind of thing you put on a tissue and breathe into your nose. The evidence from the robbery. No fingerprints, he was certain about that. But DNA, he wondered. He was pretty sure they'd have kept Sorcha's pyjamas and her slippers. He could see her, small, slight, her head bowed as she sat in the interview room.

'You don't have to tell me what happened if you don't want to.' He had tried to reassure her. 'But if we're to catch the guys.'

She fiddled with her fingers, tearing a piece of skin from her cuticles. 'There are people who can help you. People you can talk to about it all.'

She didn't look at him. 'I know, those rape crisis places. I don't want to talk to anyone.' Tears slid down her cheeks. 'He hurt me, he really hurt me. It was disgusting.'

McLoughlin had seen the doctor's report.

'I don't want my parents to know. I couldn't look at them again if they knew. I just want to forget about it.' Sorcha stood. 'Can I go now?'

McLoughlin had watched her walk out of the garda station. It was the last time he had seen her.

'So, where will we meet?' He shifted the phone in his hand.

And he heard that sound, he'd heard before. What could it be? McLoughlin knew it, but couldn't place it.

'Somewhere nice. Somewhere in the sun. I like to get out of an evening. The judge and me, we'd meet for a coffee sometimes. Go for a little stroll. Not too far. Neither of us now, we're not in the bloom of youth, if you know what I mean.' Pause, more nose blowing, clearing of his throat. 'How about the pier, the bandstand maybe? How would that suit you?'

McLoughlin heard the town hall clock strike the half hour. 5.30. He stood, lifting the bag. The dog got to his feet too. They began to walk slowly towards the bandstand. It had recently been restored to its former Victorian glory. The local council had done a thorough job. It even had wi-fi and as McLoughlin approached he could see there was the usual crowd of teenagers lounging on the steps, phones and iPads in hand. He looked around. He pushed past the kids and stood in the middle of the stage. He took out the judge's phone. He waited.

A teenage girl, pretty, blonde with a stud in her bare navel and another in her nose, leaned down, holding a hand out to the dog. Ferdie sniffed it, a breeze from the sea blowing his ears back. The girl crooned endearments and he rubbed himself against her bare brown legs.

The judge's phone beeped. Twice. McLoughlin looked at the screen. He pressed the button. *U cld do with xercise end pier bring fone.*

Shit, the last thing he wanted was messing.

'Come on, Ferdie, time to go,' he clicked his fingers.

'Ah,' the girl looked up. Her makeup was expertly applied. 'Can he not stay here with me?' She smiled, showing perfect white teeth.

'Sorry, not today. We've a date, haven't we, Ferdie?' McLoughlin hurried down the steps and together they began to walk away. The dog looked up at him. He whined and licked his lips. It was even hotter now, the sun glancing off the paving, right into his eyes. McLoughlin was sweating. He could feel a damp patch in the small of his back and on his neck. Sweating, not sure if it was heat or anxiety. He gazed at the people on the pier. A row of rod fishermen stood near the edge, their lines trailing into the water. They were always here now. Mostly Chinese, sometimes Polish or other Eastern Europeans, Lithuanians, Latvians. Sometimes Roma gypsies too. He stopped for a moment to see what they were catching. He didn't recognise the fish. Pollock, maybe or mullet or some other variety. Most people would have thrown them back. The dog sniffed blood on the stones. A woman, wearing a long skirt, red and blue, her hair hidden under a scarf made from the same material, waved her hands at him.

'Go,' she said, 'you, dog, go away.'

'Sorry,' McLoughlin reached for Ferdie's collar. 'Sorry.' But Ferdie had found something interesting and edible. He buried his nose in a piece of old newspaper.

'Stop it, Ferdie, come on, drop it,' McLoughlin grabbed Ferdie by the collar. With the other hand he prised the newspaper from his mouth. A half-eaten fish head dropped to the ground. McLoughlin reached in his pocket for a handkerchief and wiped the dog's face. A noxious combination of blood and skin. 'Christ, you messy creature. Come on now.'

He dragged him away, conscious that a small crowd had gathered to watch.

'I should throw you in,' he said to Ferdie, who ignored him, and whined cheerfully. McLoughlin swung the judge's bag by the handle. It was heavy. He felt as if everyone could see what was in it. He climbed the narrow steps to the pier's upper level and stood, the wind ruffling his hair and blowing his shirt away from his body. A double beep. A text. *Time 4 coffee ur hands r filthy.*

McLoughlin looked around. Skateboarders, dog walkers, fishermen, the man who was always busking, a pile of coins in his guitar case. A couple entwined in an embrace, leaned against the sea wall. The phone beeped again. He read the message. *Wash ur fuckin hand coffee time 10 min our fave place dog knows way.*

He looked around again. The busker was singing 'Dirty Old Town', his voice plaintive. The embracing couple were now sitting on a bench, the girl on the boy's knee, her face buried in his neck. A woman with a large dog, a boxer, was standing, looking at the boats moored in the harbour, a takeaway coffee in one hand and a cigarette in the other.

McLoughlin hurried towards the steps which led to the water. He put down the bag. He knelt and dunked his hands in the cold sea. A wave washed up, soaking his sleeves. He stood, picked up the bag again and took the steps two at a time, back up to the pier. He began to jog, the dog leaping excitedly around him.

Away from the sea breeze it was hotter. McLoughlin's shirt was sticking to his back as he ran past the park, along by the railway line. The dog knows the way, the text had said. And the dog certainly seemed to know where he was going. He trotted briskly, barely stopping, not allowing himself to be distracted by tempting scents. He stopped outside the wine bar. Today there were people sitting at the small tables on the footpath. McLoughlin recognised them as locals. Retired couples, with time on their hands.

'Ferdie,' one of the women, grey hair flopping over her face, bent to greet him. 'How are you, sweetie?' She scratched him behind his ears and he wriggled with pleasure. McLoughlin noticed the diamond-encrusted bracelet on her wrist. She looked up. 'The poor judge. We do miss him. Any news?'

McLoughlin shook his head. 'Nothing as far as I know.' He clicked his fingers. 'Come on Ferdie.'

Inside it was dark and crowded. Anthony greeted them like long-losts. He ushered Ferdie to his usual spot behind the counter and waved McLoughlin to one of the high stools near the coffee machine.

'You'll have?' Anthony gestured to the selection of wines on offer.'Just an Americano, thanks.' McLoughlin looked around. Again faces he recognised. A few hidden by newspapers and one man slumped in the corner by the toilets. He looked as if he was asleep.

'Can I tempt you?' Anthony held up a bottle of Calvados. 'A little extra something?'

McLoughlin shook his head. 'No, thanks, still got a bit of work to do.' The machine hissed and gurgled, spitting steam and the phone in his pocket beeped. He pulled it out. He read the message. *Coffee outside now.* The noise of the machine. The hissing and gurgling. That was the sound he'd heard in the background to the calls.

He got up, his heart pounding. He gestured to the open door. 'Nice today. I'll have it here, if that's OK.'

'Sure thing. Take a seat. I'll be out to you in a tick.' Anthony smiled and flapped a tea towel at him. 'And a bowl of water for himself?'

McLoughlin nodded his thanks and eased himself off the stool. He could see his face reflected in the machine's stainless steel. He looked pale. He could see panic in his eyes. He clicked his fingers and Ferdie got to his feet. McLoughlin held the door open and the dog walked through. He slumped in a patch of shade behind a large pink hydrangea in a terracotta pot. McLoughlin sat down at a small round table, the judge's bag between his feet. He scanned the street. The sun had brought everyone out. Groups of children coming and going from the playground in the park. Joggers spilling out onto the road.

'Here we are, one Americano, and one bowl of water.' Anthony appeared at his side, a tray held high. He carefully placed the cup and saucer on the table, then bent down to the dog. McLoughlin held out a five euro note and Anthony took it and backed away. 'Much appreciated, and do let me know if you want anything else.' He turned towards the two women at the next table.

McLoughlin lifted his cup and took a sip and noticed a motorbike pulling up across the road. The driver dismounted. He was wearing leathers and a heavy helmet, the visor down. He walked towards the café, then paused as he put his foot up on the path. One hand disappeared inside his jacket.

McLoughlin's heart began to hammer. He replaced his cup on its saucer. It made a soft musical clink. The man pulled something out. It looked like a padded envelope. He walked towards him and stood by the small table. He looked down. He pushed up his visor. Only his eyes were visible.

'For you,' his voice was calm, his accent neutral. 'You have something for me, I think?'

McLoughlin fumbled beneath the table. He lifted up the bag.

'I'll take that,' the man stretched out and at the same time handed McLoughlin the padded envelope.

'Just a minute,' McLoughlin put the bag down, anchoring it with his foot. He tore open the envelope, and flicked through its contents.

'OK.' He lifted his foot. 'All yours.'

McLoughlin watched the bike as it turned and went back down the road in the direction from which it had come. He checked the time on his phone. Anthony was still chatting to the customers at the next table. McLoughlin raised his hand.

'I'll have a drop of the hard stuff if you're still offering.' He held out his cup.

'Of course, dear boy,' Anthony disappeared inside the café, then reappeared a few minutes later. McLoughlin sat in the sun. He sipped. He could feel the spirits in his throat, in his stomach. The envelope lay in front of him. He put one hand flat down on it. He could feel the stiffness of the photographs through the bubble wrap. He sipped again. His heart was thumping in an unnatural way. Ferdie stirred and sighed, and rolled over. Then his ears pricked up. McLoughlin could hear the roar of a motorbike. Coming back, speeding, going too fast. He watched it pass by. He watched it disappear out of sight. He checked his phone. Seven minutes, since the exchange, that was all. Seven minutes at approximately fifty kilometres per hour. He did the sums. Roughly six kilometres, three there, three back.

He drained his cup and stood. He put a handful of coins on the saucer. He picked up the envelope.

'Come on Ferdie, time to go.' The dog whined and got to his feet. He dipped his muzzle in the water and drank deeply. McLoughlin moved away from the table. Ferdie followed. He stood on the footpath. His nostrils flared in the evening air. He looked up.

The dog knew the way. McLoughlin bent down and stroked the soft curls on the Ferdie's head. He held the envelope in front of his wet nose. The dog sniffed, and looked up at him, then turned. McLoughlin followed, as the dog began to trot briskly down the road.

A nice evening for a walk, the sun beginning to dip behind Killiney Hill. Heat radiating from the footpath, but a breeze now from the sea. Sweet scents from the gardens as they walked past. Mock orange blossom, McLoughlin thought. Philadelphus, creamy white flowers with a touch of purple at their centre. A favourite of his mother's, he remembered.

They walked on. A small shop stood at the corner. The dog stopped at the door. McLoughlin went in. Rows of soft drinks and packets of biscuits. Tins of beans. Loaves of sliced white bread. An ice cream fridge. McLoughlin walked to the chill cabinet. He pulled out a small bottle of water. He moved towards the counter.

'I'll have a plastic bag too,' he said. The young man, Chinese, smiled and produced one from beside the cash register. He nodded towards Ferdie who was slumped down, on the doorstep, his chin on his front paws.

'He's a good dog. He won't come in. He knows his place.' He took the coins McLoughlin held out. 'You a nice boy, Ferdie, aren't you?'

'You know him?' McLoughlin fiddled with the bag, opening it up. He put the envelope into it, along with the bottle of water.

'Everyone knows Ferdie.' The young man smiled. 'The judge, he come here often. Always he buy chocolate. Fruit and nut, his favourite. He go to visit his friend, Mr Smith.'

'Mr Smith? Does he live near here?'

'Yes, not far, apartments for old people. Just down the road.' He pointed.

McLoughlin stepped into the sun. He looked at the judge's phone. No more messages. The screen was dark. Whoever had been watching him must have stopped. He wasn't sure who it had been. Too many people around. No one who stood out. He'd done a fair bit of surveillance in his time. He'd been good at it. He knew when to hang back, when to speed up, when to turn away, to cross a road, when to watch reflections in shop windows. Now he looked around. The street was quiet. Cars parked along the footpath. Dinner time, he reckoned. Families gathering. Children to be fed, bathed and put to bed. Stories to be read. Fears to be soothed.

He began to walk again, the dog running on ahead. Past large, detached houses set in their own gardens. Then rows of newer ones, smaller, pebble-dashed, terraced. Views of the sea down the side streets. He clicked his tongue, but Ferdie ignored him. He trotted along, his tail wagging, stopping every now and then to sniff and smell, to scratch at a clump of dandelions and grass growing out of a crack in the path. Then suddenly, without warning, he took off, crossing the road, heading towards the two-storied building set back behind a high brick wall. The dog ran in through the open gates. McLoughlin followed slowly. He stopped and looked around. A neat lawn was bounded by flower beds, bright with colour, orange and yellow. On one side was a small car park. Beside it a large waste bin and some plastic rubbish bags piled against it. He stood and looked at the building. He counted the front doors, each painted the same dark red. Ten on the ground floor, and above another ten, with a walkway in front. Hanging baskets swung gently in the breeze beside each.

He looked around, then moved slowly towards the stairwell. He began to climb the steps. Ferdie was sniffing around the bin. McLoughlin clicked his fingers but the dog ignored him. McLoughlin turned away. When he reached the top he looked down the walkway. Baskets hung beside every door, except for one. McLoughlin walked slowly towards it. A frosted glass pane, a doorbell and below it a flap for mail. He lifted it carefully. He bent down and peered through. A small narrow hall, a door to the right and a door at the end. Both stood open. He could hear a sound. Coughing and the guttural catch of phlegm being cleared from a throat. He took a deep breath. He pressed the bell. He heard it chime. He saw a figure approach. The door opened, just a crack, but McLoughlin was ready. He remembered the old days. The dawn raids, the battering ram breaking the lock, the shouting and roaring as the guards forced their way in. The importance of surprise.

The importance of surprise. The door opened just a crack, but he was inside the house before the man, tall and overweight, with a shock of white hair, knew what was happening. A complacent fucker. A bully. McLoughlin had him by the throat, forcing him to the floor, pulling up his T-shirt. The appendix scar and the scattering of moles across his fat white stomach. He kicked him hard in the testicles, then stood on his ankle, hearing it crunch beneath his foot. He grabbed him by the hair and dragged him into the small kitchen. A table and on it, the judge's bag and an open laptop. The man was trying to stand, bellowing with rage, gathering his strength. McLoughlin looked around. There was a small cast-iron saucepan on the cooker. He reached for it. Half-full of baked beans. And before the man could do anything McLoughlin had smashed one hand with it, then smashed one knee. And the man screaming now, in pain and fear.

'The hand is for Sorcha Hegarty, for what you did to her. The knee is for me.' McLoughlin was panting, breathless. 'Consider yourself lucky I've left the other untouched. But if I get a sniff, the slightest hint that those photographs are anywhere other than where they should be, I'll be back. And next time,' he rested the saucepan on the man's forehead, then pressed hard. He could smell the pale skin burning.

McLoughlin stood up. He looked down. Baked beans were scattered across the floor. He picked up the judge's bag. The money was still inside. He put the laptop in beside it, wrapped the saucepan in a tea towel and put it in too.

'You said you had a deal with the judge. But the judge is dead. All deals are off. Enjoy your dinner.'

He closed the door quietly behind him. The judge's bag in one hand, the plastic bag in the other, as he hurried away.

The photographs. McLoughlin sat on the floor in the front room, his back pressed against the wall, the bottle of whiskey open. He drank. He felt sick. The whiskey wasn't helping. But then, nothing would help.

He fanned the photos out. There were ten of them altogether. And the negatives. Black and white. Some close-ups, some wide shots. The judge as a young man, still immediately recognisable. There were other men, too, in some of the pictures. And there were the boys. They were young. McLoughlin guessed at their ages. Maybe between ten and fifteen. Maybe younger. In some of the pictures their faces were obscured by their actions. But their bodies were plainly on view. Small, white, thin. They reminded him of boys he'd seen when he was at school. Boys from the orphanage next door. They'd share their classrooms for a couple of years and then they'd disappear. They were all small and thin. Their heads were shaved. Their teeth were yellow. At break time they drank their milk and ate slices of white bread, smeared with margarine, as if they'd never eaten before. McLoughlin and his friends had despised them, stayed away from them, mocked them. Now, knowing everything about the industrial schools, he felt ashamed of the way he had behaved. Now he looked at these boys in the photographs and felt even more ashamed. Of how he had colluded with Liam Hegarty to keep this part of the judge's life a secret. To protect his reputation, his standing, his place in the world. Ends and means, that was it. Worth it in the long run. No matter how bad McLoughlin felt now, how bad he would feel in the future. He had to believe it would be worth it.

He poured more whiskey into his glass and drank. And coughed. And retched. He got up and walked down the corridor to the kitchen.

His new sink had been installed. It gleamed in the moonlight which angled through the large rectangular window. The sink unit was stainless steel. Custom-made to fit the space, and with a beautiful mixer tap. He turned it on and filled a glass with water. It was cold and clean. He drank again. And again. But he couldn't get the taste of vomit off his tongue, the stench from his nose. He drank and spat, then wiped his mouth with the back of his hand. He walked through the house. He picked up the pictures and put them together in a neat pile. Then he slotted them into the padded envelope. He looked at his watch. It was nearly time.

They walked in silence through the judge's house. Liam Hegarty opened the door to the upstairs sitting room. McLoughlin settled uneasily on the sofa. Hegarty stood beneath the chandelier. He smiled and held out his hand.

'You've got them?' He moved towards McLoughlin.

'I've got them.' McLoughlin sat still.

'Great, well done, fantastic.' Hegarty stood over him. 'I'll take them. And this time I'll get rid of them.' He smiled again, but now his smile was tense, a grimace.

'I don't know about that.' McLoughlin shifted.

'Really? Why not?' Hegarty's smile faltered and failed.

'Why do you think?' McLoughlin stood up. He shoved his hands in his jacket pocket, feeling the envelope.

'You've looked at them.' Hegarty glanced around the room.

McLoughlin nodded.

'And you didn't like what you saw.'

McLoughlin nodded again.

'Look,' Hegarty tried to smile, 'those pictures, it was a long time ago. Things were different then, you know?'

'In what way, different?' McLoughlin could taste the vomit in the back of his throat.

'You know,' Hegarty spread his hands wide. 'Look, sit down with me. Talk to me. Tell me what's up.' He sat on the sofa, crossed his legs, then patted the cushion beside him. 'Here. Come on.'

'Different? I'm interested in your definition of different.'

'Well,' Hegarty's face tightened, 'you know, so many things have changed, over the years. We never thought, well, you know, we never...' His voice died away.

McLoughlin said nothing.

'Look, all I'm trying to say, my brother's dead. And those, well, rent boys they were, that's what they were, rent boys. They got paid, they got something out of it, look at them.' Hegarty's voice was getting louder.

'I have looked at them. I'll tell you what I see. I see children, that's what I see.' McLoughlin was shouting now. The dog shifted, whined, cowered. 'And I see your brother. And I'm thinking, men like him, they never stop.'

Hegarty stood up. His face was white.

'And you,' McLoughlin moved closer to him. 'How can you defend him?'

'Because, because,' Hegarty looked away. He moved towards the mantelpiece. He picked up the framed photograph of his grandmother. 'She suffered a lot, you know, old May. She got pregnant. She was put out by the family. My grandfather married her, then he went to England. He died over there. So the money dried up. We were always taught, it was beaten into us. Family first, family last.'

He stood at the window looking out at the square.

'Look, I've told you. The bishop, he can help you, but he won't if you don't help me. Give me the photos, and he'll phone you in the morning. You'll get what you want.' He turned and looked at him. 'Something you've wanted, for how long? Nearly forty years?'

McLoughlin stood at the bay window. He watched Hegarty leave. A compromise. Hegarty would get the photos after McLoughlin had got what he wanted. He held the padded envelope between the tips of his thumb and first finger. He swung it backwards and forwards. It was unclean, dangerous. He felt as if the images would burn their way through the plastic and paper. He needed to put it somewhere, out of the way. He didn't want it in his house. It would pollute his safe haven. He turned away from the window. He began to walk down the stairs. Ferdie trotted behind him. McLoughlin opened the door to the basement. He reached through and felt for the light switch. He tugged it once.

'Go on, Ferdie, go on boy,' he pushed him ahead down the narrow steps. Down into the old kitchen. McLoughlin stood and looked around. Then moved towards the range. The oven door was open. He pushed aside a battered roasting dish, burnt black, and pushed the envelope deep inside. He closed the oven door, carefully, slipping the latch back in place. He stood and looked around, then moved into the bedroom. He switched on the light. The bed, eiderdown, pillows, the wardrobe, underwear strewn everywhere. A strong smell of damp and decay. The beauty, the quiet elegance of the floors above resting on this, McLoughlin thought, and he shivered and looked up at the ceiling. And felt rather than saw, cracks, shudders, shakes and turned, calling the dog, a note of panic in his voice as he hurried upstairs.

He stood outside the house. He could still see Smith, the scattering of moles across his fat white stomach, his mouth open, screaming. It had been easy. He was a sitting duck. A rapist, a blackmailer, a piece of shit. So why hadn't he been able to respond like that when he saw Reynolds in the street in Bassano? So close he could see the pores in his skin, the broken veins in his cheeks, smell the cigarette smoke on his clothes. Frozen, that's what it was. He was frozen by the weight of responsibility. For his father and his mother, his whole family. All that grief, his own grief, it should have made him crazy and vicious. Instead it had made him weak and helpless, as if his legs had been cut off at the knees.

He looked across the green. Moonlight silvering the trees and grass. A shadow moving slowly through the trees. A sharp bark from Ferdie and the shadow stopped, turned, the fox's narrow face suddenly visible. As she gazed at the man and the dog, the man's hand on the dog's collar, two more shadows appeared, smaller, rounder, pausing by their mother's side, and all three began to walk with measured pace, away.

Man and dog turned away too. Up the steps to McLoughlin's house, unlocking the door. Going inside, the lock clicking into place behind them. Lights on. Lights off. Silence, darkness.

Twenty-four hours, they'd agreed. McLoughlin would give him twenty-four hours. When he woke the next morning it was late. The house was strangely silent. The dog too, asleep at his feet. Beside him lay a tattered old lead. When McLoughlin had run down the stairs from Smith's flat, Ferdie had been waiting for him by the rubbish bins. The lead was in his mouth. McLoughlin had tried to pull it away but the dog wouldn't let it go. He'd carried it all the way home. Dragged it into the house.

McLoughlin lay back on his pillows. He was hungry, not as hungover as he'd thought he would be, although the whiskey bottle was empty, lying on its side where he'd kicked it as he was getting down onto the mattress.

He rolled himself to sitting. He stood up and opened the door. He walked into the kitchen. Sunshine again, glancing off the draining board. He filled a glass with water and drank it down. Opened the door to the garden so the dog could go out. Wandered back to the front room, grabbed a towel, then up the stairs to the tiny bathroom under the eaves. And realised it had gone. The Pole had taken his sledgehammer to it. The men sitting around on the garden chairs in the yoga room, having their morning brew, nodded and smiled.

'No shower?'

'Sorry,' Pavel lifted his mug, 'had to go. We put in new bathroom soon. There is toilet in basement, yes?'

'OK,' McLoughlin turned away. He'd have a quick wash in the kitchen then go out for breakfast. Best thing to do.

He sat outside the café looking out over the sea front. Coffee with hot milk, a pain au chocolat, *The Irish Times* unread beside him. He tore chunks from the pastry, dipping it in his large cup. Around him conversations ebbed and flowed. A succession of young women with buggies passed by on their way to the playground. He could hear the children's voices and see the heads of the more adventurous as they climbed to the top of the high slide and swung from the climbing ropes. And he recognised the child called Leah, Elizabeth Fannin's granddaughter, her dark curls swirling around her face as she hung upside down. He stood, and Ferdie stood too. He picked up the old lead. It trailed from his mouth. McLoughlin took it from him and clicked it onto his collar. Probably better with so many children around.

He walked towards the child. And saw Elizabeth sitting on the low wall, a book open on her lap, a coffee in a takeaway cup in her hand. And the child falling suddenly, a cry bursting from her mouth. Elizabeth jumped up, the book dropping to the ground, as she rushed to her.

'She all right?' He sat down beside them, closing the book and placing it carefully beside her bag.

Elizabeth nodded. 'Yes, a lot of tears, but I suspect an ice cream might dry them.' She kissed the top of the child's head. 'What do you think, Leah? Ice cream?'

The child nodded, still unable to speak, sobs racking her small body, her fingers twisting together.

'Tell you what,' McLoughlin stood. 'Why don't Ferdie and I go and get them? Would that be a good idea? Orders please, I'm taking orders.'

By the time he got back with three cones, strawberry, chocolate and vanilla as requested, calm had been restored. Leah was now on the swings, Elizabeth standing beside her, giving her the occasional push. At the sight of the ice cream, Leah put up her hands to be lifted off and together the three of them sat on the wall, intent on finishing the cones before they melted away.

McLoughlin turned around and looked out towards the bay. It was dotted with white sails. He must, he thought, get in touch with some of his sailing friends. See if he could get a place as crew in one of the regular evening races.

'Lucky, aren't we?' he nodded towards the sea, the pier, the walkers.

'Yes, we certainly are.' Elizabeth finished her ice cream and wiped her fingers on a piece of tissue. She bent over her granddaughter, dabbing her chin and cheeks. The child twisted away, and jumped down from the wall. She began to hop, one small foot planting squarely on the paving. Hopping, then skipping and humming, her voice tuneful. He watched her. He could see the judge and the boys, their faces turned towards the camera. Mute pleas for help in their pinched expressions.

His phone rang. He turned away from Elizabeth and looked down at the screen. Liam Hegarty. He pressed the answer button. He listened. The bishop would see him, this afternoon. He must get there before 4 p.m. After that the bishop would no longer be available. The bishop lived outside Mullingar in the midlands. Not easy to find the house. Hegarty would send him the GPS coordinates. And he would expect, Hegarty's voice was cold, he would expect McLoughlin then to cooperate.

'We'll see,' McLoughlin's voice was equally cold. He pressed the red button and put the phone away. 'Sorry, have to go, have to see a man about a dog,' and he smiled. He waved towards the child, who turned and held up her face to be kissed. He bent down and brushed her soft cheek. She smelt of soap and ice cream.

'You're honoured,' Elizabeth raised her eyebrows, 'she's not free with her favours, that one.'

He couldn't help but feel smug. He shrugged, in a self-deprecating way, and apologised for having to leave so quickly. He took Elizabeth's hand, the first time he realised, he had intentionally touched her. And said, 'I've been meaning to thank you.'

'For what?' She didn't pull away. He was glad of that.

'For being so kind, when I told you about my father.' He squeezed her fingers gently. 'I didn't mean to blurt it all out.'

She smiled. 'You don't need to thank me. I was just doing what any friend would do.'

'Well, as you know my house is a long way from being finished, but perhaps you might come and have dinner with me. I hear there's a couple of nice places in the area.'

He waited for the excuses but they didn't come. Her smile broadened.

'Thank you, that would be lovely.' She picked up her book and her bag. 'Actually I was talking to Jess about your house. Did I tell you that she was an archivist? She's done a bit of digging and she has a few titbits of information. You might find them interesting.'

'Great, well,' he began to move away. 'I'd better get going. Will I book us somewhere, Saturday night, would that be good?'

And she smiled and nodded and waved as the child called out and she turned away from him.

Bishop Declan Hegarty. He opened the door of his modern bungalow on the outskirts of Mullingar. A small man, bent over with some kind of scoliosis. But bright blue eyes, sharp and clear in his wrinkled face, his head bald, pink and freckled, a few strands of white hair slicked across it. He ushered McLoughlin inside, into the sitting room, modestly furnished, a shiny laminated floor, a small sofa, two armchairs, a large flat-screen TV and an oval coffee table. Above the gas fire a crucifix hung. At the far end, a large glass door looked out onto the fields behind. Horses grazing, the grass cropped short.

The bishop was dressed in grey trousers and a white shirt. Open necked. Navy blue slippers were on his feet and he shuffled awkwardly.

'Tea? You'll have tea?'

McLoughlin nodded. 'Thanks, yes, tea.'

The bishop gestured to him to sit. He turned away and moved out of sight. McLoughlin could hear the sound of a kettle, and the clatter of crockery. What was it Reynolds' wife had said to him, that day in Bassano del Grappa? Every time you go into an Irish house, first thing is to have the cup of tea.

He lowered himself onto the sofa and looked around. Not much to see. No books, no magazines, no newspapers. Nothing of a personal nature either. No photographs or pictures on the walls or the mantelpiece. Only the body of Christ, his eyes closed, his head twisted to one side, drops of blood on his breast, his hands, his feet.

The door opened. The bishop came in, a mug in each hand. He dumped them on the table, shuffled back to the kitchen and reappeared with a litre carton of milk and packet of chocolate digestive biscuits. He sank down into the chair. He gestured to the milk, and the biscuits.

'Help yourself,' his voice was hoarse. McLoughlin could hear the whistle of his breath. Emphysema. He knew the signs.

'I'm sure you don't take sugar, no one does these days.' The bishop fumbled with the biscuits, pulling at the packaging so it tore and they tumbled out on the table. He picked one up. 'My favourites. I'm not supposed to eat sweet things. Diabetes, you know. But...' he held it aloft and for a moment McLoughlin could see the host held high above the altar. The bishop bit on the biscuit, crumbs scattering across his shirt. He brushed them away, his fingers knotted and twisted. McLoughlin lifted the mug. The inside was stained brown. The tea was strong and bitter.

'Now,' the bishop swallowed. 'We have some business to attend to, I understand. Some sensitive business.'

He shifted in his chair. McLoughlin could see that he was in pain.

'You've come into the possession, I understand, of some photographs which show my second cousin, John Hegarty, engaged in immoral and illegal activities. You are, understandably, shocked and upset. You want to make these activities known. Despite the fact that John Hegarty is dead, that these photographs were taken many years ago, and to be honest, very little would be gained by their publication.'

One hand reached for a biscuit, then withdrew. McLoughlin put his mug down on the table. He began to stand.

'Hold on, hold on,' the bishop held up both his hands, palms out. 'Look, OK, let me start again.'

Again he reached for a biscuit.

'I knew John Hegarty very well. We went to the same school. Holy Ghost fathers. From the word go everyone could see he was special. School in those days was tough. Beatings were commonplace. But somehow John was never touched. Not by a cane or a leather. He was protected. There was a priest who had a soft spot for him. He was his pet. No one commented. No one said a word. And neither did John. He was always smiling, always happy.' He paused. He bit into the biscuit. He closed his eyes. He put his head back. He munched and swallowed. 'After school I didn't see much of John. I became a priest. He became a barrister. We were both busy. We were both ambitious. He was heading for the Supreme Court. I would have liked to think I was heading for a post in the Vatican. I got as far as the Bishop's Palace. Then my career stalled. The past was catching up. Allegations of abuse. Mistakes made. Children not listened to. I don't have to spell it out. It became a witch hunt. They tried to drive me into the wilderness. Well,' he opened his eyes. 'They succeeded.' He looked around the room. 'I don't even have a housekeeper.' He smiled. 'Tea all right?'

McLoughlin didn't reply.

'One day, years ago, I was a parish priest at that time, nice area, out near you. I got a phone call from John. He wanted to see me. He sounded in a bad way. He wanted to talk.'

He described it. How they sat together in the presbytery sitting room. They drank whiskey. And John told him everything. The trips to London, the adventures in Dublin.

'You see, he was getting married. He'd met Miriam. Her father and his father were friends. It wasn't exactly arranged, but it suited everyone. John was, well, he was an honourable man. He didn't want to go into the marriage with a stain on his conscience. So, we discussed it. He told me he intended to abstain from his activities. He wanted to be faithful to Miriam. To be a good husband. To be a father. He wanted the inside and the outside to match, if you know what I mean.'

McLoughlin knew what he meant. 'Why did he speak to you? Was he making his confession?'

'No, I offered the sacrament. He didn't want that. If he had I wouldn't be talking to you now. The seal of the confessional, well,' he picked up his mug and drank. Tea slopped onto his shirt. 'I suppose he came to me because he knew I'd know, how… ' He stopped. Outside a bird screeched. The bishop looked away, looked down at the floor.

McLoughlin cleared his throat and shifted awkwardly. 'So what did he want from you, if it wasn't absolution?'

The bishop put down his mug. 'He wanted to know that he could do it. That he could live that ordinary, everyday kind of life. He wanted to know how I did it.'

McLoughlin lifted the mug to his lips. He sipped gingerly.

'I told him I prayed for help. I put my trust in the Lord. And sometimes.' He paused. Again he looked away. 'Liam told me you found John's whip.'

McLoughlin nodded.

'John asked me about it. I told him I felt it had its,' he paused, 'uses.'

The bishop got up. He went into the kitchen. When he returned he was pulling a little trolley. He sat down, fumbling with the tubes which protruded from the top. He slipped them into his nose. He breathed deeply.

'I don't get many visitors. I'm not used to so much talk. It's tiring.' He breathed in and out, slowly, his chest heaving. 'So,' he paused again, 'he'd visit me regularly over the years. We'd pray together. I was part of his family. Whenever they needed a special mass they called on me. Christmas, Easter, parties, celebrations, I came to the house. When his oldest son got married, John asked me to officiate. When Miriam died, must be six years ago or so, I said the mass at her funeral.' He paused, then breathed in deeply. 'I thought he might need me afterwards, help him with his grief, counsel him, comfort him, but,' he shrugged, 'I didn't hear from him, not for quite a while. He moved back to the family home in Dun Laoghaire. And then.'

McLoughlin's back was sore. 'And then?'

'And then not long before he died,' the bishop looked away, looked down at the floor, 'Liam phoned. He said John wanted to talk. He said he'd bring him here. He sat there, where you are. He told me he'd started again. He said he was frightened.'

'Frightened?'

'Yes, frightened of the way he felt,' he paused, 'the intensity of his feelings. Frightened that nothing else mattered. The memory of his wife, his career, even his children, now they were as nothing to him. He sat where you're sitting and he cried.' He paused, leaned down and fiddled with the controls on the oxygen bottle. 'I could see he was in pain. But I could also sense his excitement. There was an anticipation of,' he stopped, looked down, then looked up again his eyes searching for McLoughlin's, 'ecstasy, yes, that's what it was, ecstasy. There was nothing more I could say. And that was the last time I saw him.'

Silence in the room. The bishop got to his feet. He pulled the tubes from his nose. He swayed and McLoughlin half rose. The bishop waved his help away. He shuffled out into the kitchen. This time when he returned he was carrying a bottle of whiskey and two small glasses. He flopped back into his chair.

'You'll join me?'

McLoughlin shook his head. 'Driving.'

The bishop shrugged and poured himself a large tot. He sipped it appreciatively. 'It was interesting, listening to John. I wondered if he was in love. But,' he swirled the whiskey in his glass, 'how would I know? How would I know how that kind of love would feel?' He drank some more, then pushed the oxygen tubes back into his nose. 'A mystery I'm afraid.'

'You never loved?'

'No, didn't want anything to get in the way of the job. The vocation. The calling. But now,' he paused, 'look at me. I have no one. Even God has forsaken me. When I pray there is nothing, no response, no answers. All my life God was there for me. But now...' he drank again, his Adam's apple jerking up and down. 'Do you have children?'

McLoughlin shook his head. 'Unfortunately, no.'

The bishop topped up his glass. 'I thought not. You have that empty look.' He held up one hand. 'I long sometimes to touch. Not in a sexual way. Desire has left me. But I long for the warmth of another human being. To hear their breathing. To touch their skin. To feel their life.' He swallowed the whiskey in his glass in one mouthful. Silence for a moment.

'Now, to business,' he paused. 'I can't get up again. You,' he pointed at McLoughlin, 'top of the stairs, room on your left. Top drawer of the desk. An envelope. Read what's written on it, and bring it down.'

Up the stairs, narrow, cramped, the banister rough beneath his palm. The room on the left, small and dark. Books in piles on the floor. A desk, cheap. Made of MDF, more books and cardboard files. McLoughlin did as he was told, found the envelope. Read what was written on it. Hurried back down the stairs. Handed it over.

The bishop tore it open, pulling a pair of reading glasses from his shirt pocket. He scanned the wad of pages. He peered up at McLoughlin then folded the pages together and stuffed them back into the envelope.

'You can have this. It will give you enough information to go the authorities and nail James Reynolds. And when I say nail, I don't mean it figuratively. Eamon Ryan's sworn statement, witnessed by me, his confessor, by his wife, Theresa and his son, Padraig, gives chapter and verse of the preparations for the robbery, the planning, who was involved, when and where. And it also spells out the fact that there was no reason for Reynolds to kill your father. Your father was unarmed. Reynolds could have driven away with the money. He could have left him alive. Eamon Ryan never got over seeing your father die. It was only his terror of being labelled an informer which prevented him from naming Reynolds. But as death beckoned his conscience could no longer contain his secrets. So,' he dropped the envelope on the table. His face was the colour of milk. His breathing was laboured. He waved his hands, his fingers twitching. 'Take it. Do with it what you want. If there is a trial I will give evidence. Eamon Ryan wanted Reynolds to get what he deserved.' He leaned back into the chair. 'Pour me some whiskey. And go.'

McLoughlin picked up the bottle. He poured. He picked up the envelope. It was heavy.

'Just one thing. Why you? Why did he tell you?'

The bishop smiled, a wan, pathetic grimace. 'I have history with the Ryan family.' He lifted his glass. McLoughlin waited. 'Eamon's older brother, Father Con Ryan, he wasn't a good man. He did some terrible things. At the time, well,' he paused and shifted uneasily in his chair. 'At the time, I didn't believe what I was being told by others. I chose to believe him. When there were complaints I ignored them. I moved him away, I moved him somewhere else. I'd always liked him. He had a certain charm.'

McLoughlin looked down at the envelope in his hands.

'When the truth of what happened came out, even though I could see how he had sinned, I also felt that I had been wrong. He was a weak man. I should have been stronger. You may remember, after he was arrested and charged he took his own life. He hanged himself in his cell. I went to see his family. I conducted the funeral mass. I believed then in God's infinite capacity to forgive.' He cupped the glass in his hands. He sipped from it.

'And now? What do you believe now?'

Bishop Hegarty closed his eyes. His head slumped forward.

'Go, just go.'

McLoughlin stood up. He turned away, then turned back.

'Just one more thing.'

'What?'

'Do you have any idea who killed the judge?'

The bishop lifted his head, lifted the glass. 'No,' his voice wasn't much more than a whisper. 'No, I don't.'

Samuel watched the boy on the skateboard. It was as if the board was screwed to his feet. His balance was miraculous. He could jump and land and spin and jump again. Samuel had no idea how he did it. There were a couple of signs at the gate. A bicycle with a red diagonal slash through it and another, a skateboard with the same kind of slash. But the boy never paid any heed. He would swish in, his phone to one ear, and stop at the foot of the stairs, then pick up the board and tuck it under his arm as he took the steps two at a time. He was Mr Smith's messenger boy. Coming and going at all times of the day and night, the soft rumble of his wheels as he flew down the walkway towards Mr Smith's front door. A nice-looking boy, his blond hair cut short at the back with a quiff at the front. Headphones in his ears, the white lead trailing down into his shirt pocket.

Samuel would watch him going into Mr Smith's flat, then see him leaving, a plastic bag with a couple of bottles of cider, or a six pack of lager. Too young for the off-licence. Mr Smith would follow him out and stand looking over the balcony wall, watching as he jumped onto the board and headed off down the road towards the town. A cigarette in one hand, the smoke trailing into the still air, the other hand scratching his stubble, rubbing his big belly, jingling the coin in his pocket. Then turning and seeing Samuel. Winking as he lumbered back inside.

There were always people visiting Mr Smith. He had lots of friends. Samuel couldn't imagine what that would be like. Samuel had never had lots of friends. Well, that wasn't strictly true. When he was up at Oxford he had friends. Clever young men from good families. Smart young men whose futures were mapped out. The way Samuel had thought his future was mapped out. He would work for his father and when his father died he would take over the firm. He would inherit the family home. The detached house in its own grounds. The accumulation of Dudgeon wealth and prosperity. He would marry. He would have children. A son to take over when he became too old and infirm to carry on. William Dudgeon and Son would become Samuel Dudgeon and Son. Life would go on as ordained. Father to son, father to son, down through the generations.

Samuel watched the boy on the skateboard. He smiled at Samuel as he passed him by. And for a moment Samuel could see himself through the boy's bright blue eyes. A crazy old man with a heavy tweed coat, a wide-brimmed hat, and black leather gloves.

Mr Smith liked lounging in his doorway, watching. He was there the day Samuel got the key to his flat. The judge had come with him. They'd got the taxi from the square with Samuel's suitcase and a few shopping bags. The judge had opened the door and the taxi driver had carried in the bags. The place was small. It was dirty, a strong smell of chip fat coming from the kitchen. But Samuel knew how to deal with that. Hot water and detergent. The judge had reached out to pat him on the shoulder but Samuel had shrunk back. So the judge had said goodbye. Said he'd see him in a couple of days. He had a few jobs for him to do.

And later the little door knocker clattered and banged. Mr Smith was there, the cigarette in his mouth, smoke trailing out into the still air, the sleeves of his sweater rolled up so Samuel could see the thick grey hairs on his fat forearms, his hands fat too, and a heavy gold bracelet hanging down over his left wrist. He walked in, looking here, there, everywhere.

'Needs a bit of work, but cosy enough,' he drew on his cigarette. 'If you need help, you know where I am.'

'Thank you. You're very kind.' Samuel tried to avoid his eye.

Mr Smith drew hard on his cigarette. 'Not a bad place to live. Only problem is the rubbish out there,' he waved his arm towards the door. 'Council are shite. People dump stuff and they never come and pick it up.' Smoke drifting from his mouth. 'Brit are you?'

Samuel hugged his arms around his small body. 'English, yes. I suppose I am.'

'Suppose?' Mr Smith perched on the arm of one of the small chairs. It tipped slightly. He braced his legs and straightened up.

'Yes, I suppose.' Samuel felt cold. Fear always made him cold. 'But my mother. She was from around here.'

'Is that right?' Mr Smith sat into the chair. He crossed his legs. 'And what was her name?'

'Her name was Cecily Lane. She was from Victoria Square.'

'Ah, Victoria Square. Where the judge lives. You know the judge?' and Mr Smith smiled and flicked his ash on the floor, 'of course you do, didn't he help you move in?'

Samuel said nothing. He didn't know what to say.

'So,' Mr Smith looked up at him, 'your mammy was from the square. That's nice. Married an Englishman did she?' He grimaced and make an ugly face. 'Fee, fi, fo, fum, I smell the blood of an Englishman, be he alive or be he dead, I'll grind his bones to make my bread.' And he laughed out loud. 'Love that, really love that. One of them children's stories.'

'Jack and the Beanstalk,' Samuel couldn't bring himself to look at the man seated in the chair opposite.

'That's the one.' Mr Smith shifted uncomfortably. It was obvious he was too big for the seat. He got slowly to his feet and threw his cigarette butt in the direction of the fireplace. It missed and lay smouldering on the linoleum. Mr Smith looked at it. 'Better pick that up before it makes a mark.' He turned to go. He stopped and looked at Samuel.

'The judge, he's a lovely man.' Mr Smith pulled the cigarette packet from the pocket of his tracksuit. 'I could tell you a few things about him.' He tapped the side of his nose. 'Between you and me.' He waved the packet at him. 'One of these days, call into me, I've a few things I could show you.'

The boy on the skateboard had swooshed in through the gate just as the ambulance was leaving with Mr Smith. The driver turned on the siren. It was so loud, Samuel put his hands over his ears. The boy stood, one foot on the ground, one on the board and watched them leave. Samuel watched them too. He had heard Mr Smith scream. He had waited, counted to a hundred, come out of his front door, stepped into Mr Smith's hall. Saw the blood on the floor. Heard Mr Smith, crying for help. Backed away. Stepped over the blood spatters. Shut his own front door. Heard the siren as the ambulance arrived. Heard the tramp of heavy feet as the paramedics bundled him out, manoeuvring him onto a stretcher and down the stairs. Only then as the siren shrieked its message of pain and fear did he come out again. He lifted one hand in salute.

'Bye bye, Mr Smith, bye bye.' Then he turned away and closed his door. And heard the soft rumble of the boy's wheels as he flew up and down and up and down the walkway.

It was late by the time McLoughlin got home. He drove slowly into the square. He parked the car outside the house. He got out, picking up the envelope the bishop had given him. The sky was bright with moon and star light. It was still warm. He walked up the steps to his front door and opened it. Ferdie was waiting, standing expectantly, his tail wagging. McLoughlin stood aside and the dog rushed out, pausing for a moment then racing down, crossing the road, disappearing into the trees. McLoughlin followed. He needed fresh air. He could still smell the stuffy dustiness of the bishop's miserable little house. He could almost feel sorry for him. Almost, but not quite.

He sat down on the Cassidy bench. He watched as Ferdie ran around, sniffing, smelling, enjoying his freedom. The dog ran to him, jumping up, gently butting him with his head. McLoughlin scratched him behind his ears, and the dog closed his eyes, whining softly. Then pulled away and set off once again. Asserting his territorial rights as he roamed the square from one end to the other.

McLoughlin leaned back, stretching his arms along the top of the bench. When he breathed in he could just about smell the sea. He sat now on the bench in the moonlight. He looked towards the judge's house. The photos in their padded envelope, tucked into the oven in the old range, pushed behind the roasting tray. Liam Hegarty would have to wait a bit longer. Until he'd gone through Ryan's statement. Until he was sure he'd got what he wanted.

He stood, clicking his fingers for the dog and began to walk towards the house. His legs were heavy, his step slow. He took hold of the iron railing and pulled himself upwards. The dog trotted behind.

McLoughlin opened the door and together, they went inside. He walked into the kitchen and cleaned his teeth, drank a glass of water, gave the dog some food, then hurried back into the room at the front of the house. Tonight even his mattress looked inviting. He lay down, fully clothed, the bishop's envelope beside him. He closed his eyes. He slept.

And woke, the sun in his eyes and his phone ringing, insistently. The sun in his eyes, the shutters left open last night. He fumbled beneath the duvet. He squinted at the screen. He pressed the answer button.

'Min, hi.'

'Mick, we need to talk.' Her tone was peremptory.

He pushed himself up onto one elbow. He rubbed his face.

'We do?'

'We do. This morning. As soon as possible.'

'Why?' He sat up.

'I think you know why. Suddenly, wherever I go I hear that you've got there first. I'm not happy about it. Get yourself down here as soon as possible.'

'OK,' he sighed. 'Give me half an hour. I'll see you then.'

They sat in one of the station's conference rooms. The air smelt stale. An oval table was between them, the veneer chipped, the surface marked. McLoughlin had had his fill of rooms like these. Once there would have been a couple of ashtrays and the room would have smelt of smoke. No smoke, not any longer, but the same feeling of oppressive airlessness. Min didn't offer refreshments, not even coffee from the machine in the public office. Her skin was pale and drawn. There were deep shadows beneath her eyes which were red-rimmed and bloodshot.

'Out of respect, Mick, I'm not cautioning you.' She folded her hands together and placed them on the table. 'Nor am I recording our conversation. But I expect you to treat me with the same kind of respect. I expect you to be honest with me. Do you understand?'

He nodded. 'Sure, of course.' He tried to smile, but she didn't respond. 'What do you want to know?'

'We're not stupid.' She moved back in her chair and crossed her legs. Jeans today, and runners. 'We're not fixed in our opinions. We're open to exploring any and all possibilities.'

'Of course, I know, I understand that.' He sat up straight. He was hungry. His stomach rumbled loudly.

'The question of the judge's sexuality. We do know about that.' Her expression was grim.

'You do. Of course you do.'

'Yes, we do. So I would have expected more from you.' She pushed a stray lock of hair back and into her bun.

'You would?'

'Your visit to Derek Green. He told me you'd been to see him.'

'He did?'

'Yes. He told me you seemed to think that the judge's murder had something to do with him being gay.' She shifted on her seat.

'He did?'

'For fuck's sake, Mick, will you stop being so fucking thick.' Her voice was loud, suddenly high pitched. 'What I don't understand is why you went to see Green. Why was that? If you had suspicions why didn't you come to me?'

He shrugged again. 'It was nothing really. A bit of gossip. When you're hanging around, walking the pier, when you're retired, and you're at a bit of a loose end, well, you hear things. His name came up a couple of times. I just thought I'd have a bit of a nose. Old habits really. I'd have told you if it had come to anything. Really I would.'

He paused, waited. Waited for her to mention the bag and its contents.

'What did you make of Green?' She sounded tired, worn out.

McLoughlin shrugged. 'I dunno. He wasn't friendly. He didn't say much. Look,' he spread his hands on the table. 'If I was you, if this was my case I wouldn't get too hung up on the judge's sexuality. If you think about it, how the judge was killed, and the disfigurement, all that, your theory about Brian O'Leary makes more sense. He's a mad fucker. Do anything to prove a point.'

She looked at him. He could see doubt across her face.

'Do you remember, the reason his trial was moved to the Special Criminal Court? Every single person picked for the jury had been threatened. And only one was brave enough to report the intimidation. Do you remember her?'

Min shook her head.

'A young mother. When she left the Four Courts after jury selection she'd gone to pick up her kids from school. One of O'Leary's boys had beaten her to it. She had twin daughters, aged six. When she got there they were sitting on the edge of the curb eating ice cream. They told her the ice cream van had come, and the nice man had given them the ice creams for free. He said if they were good, next time he'd come to their house. And, the little ones were so excited, he said he knew where they lived. And he knew that they slept in the bedroom at the back of the house. And that they both had the same pyjamas, with fairies all over them.' He could see the woman's face when she came into the station. Whiter than white. Her lips trembling. 'So,' he shrugged.

Min shifted on the hard chair. 'I went to see him yesterday. He didn't even do the "no comment" routine.' She mimed the inverted commas. 'Just stared at the ceiling and kept a smile on his face. We've checked around his boys. Nothing to connect any of them with the town, that day, or any day.' she paused, took a breath. 'Look, I want you to stay out of this. Get a hobby. Go to a cooking class, take up painting, go sailing, do something, just stay away from me.'

He smiled, and made as if to get up. 'Just one thing, Derek Green, did he tell you anything about,' he paused.

'About?'

'The judge and—'

'The judge and Derek's friends, is that what you're asking?'

He shrugged. 'Well...'

'Well, not really. All he said was that the judge didn't participate. He just liked to watch.'

McLoughlin smiled. 'Am I free to go?'

She stood. 'Just before you do. One other matter.'

'Yeah?' He had a horrible feeling he knew what it was.

'A man called Paul Smith was brought into St Michael's A&E a couple of days ago. He had a smashed hand and a smashed knee, broken ankle and a burn on his forehead. He was in a bad way. His grandson found him, called an ambulance.' She paused and looked at him. 'The hospital called us in. Mr Smith declined to make a complaint or a statement. Despite the injuries done to him, the pain he had suffered, he kept his mouth shut.' She drummed on the table. 'Our lads asked around. Came up with a description of a man and a dog, heading in the direction of Smith's apartment. Would you know anything about it?'

McLoughlin looked into the middle distance. Found a spot on the wall above her head. Then looked at her. Found her blue eyes and stared into them.

'Haven't a clue,' he smiled.

'I thought you'd say that.' Her expression was chilly. 'I'm warning you, Mick. I don't know what you're up to. I'm assuming that your involvement with Mr Smith has something to do with your new career in private investigation. I didn't realise that thug was part of the job spec. And,' Min got to her feet, 'if Mr Smith should decide to make a statement about the attack, I hope for your sake you have an alibi.'

He left the station. He was hungry. He wandered along the main street looking for something to eat. But nothing was tempting. He pulled out his phone. It was just coming up to eleven. He'd call Dom. Maybe if Joanne had gone off for the day he'd be in the mood for breakfast.

He sat on Dom's wide balcony. Scrambled egg with toast and coffee.

McLoughlin lifted his fork. 'Thanks, just what I needed.'

He ate in silence. Dom sat down beside him. He picked up the heavy envelope which McLoughlin had laid on the table. He pulled out the pages. 'You've read it?' Dom put on his glasses.

'I had a look.' McLoughlin lifted his mug and took a deep swallow. 'So?'

'I don't know, I thought I'd want to read it, but it makes me sick. I can't.' He paused. 'Would you? Fresh eyes, maybe?' He wiped his lips with a paper napkin. 'This is good, thanks.' He returned to the eggs, shovelling them into his mouth.

Dom spread the pages out on the table. He hummed as he read. Snatches of the 'Mountains of Mourne'. He had a pen and a piece of paper and he was making notes.

'Well,' Dom sat back and picked up his mug. He added two spoons of sugar and stirred it briskly. 'He's certainly thorough. The planning of the robbery. Who was involved. The safe house where they stayed. Their movements on the day. Where the gun came from. Everything. His comments about your James Reynolds are particularly damning. Rich boy playing at being a revolutionary. Posh boy slumming it.' Dom squinted up at the sky, and fanned himself with the sheaf of paper. 'Bloody hot today. What does it say?' He gestured towards the thermometer screwed to the railings.

McLoughlin leaned over to have a look. 'Twenty-four. What's that in real money?'

Dom looked at him. 'Double it and add twenty-eight, that'll get you close enough.'

'So, that's twenty-four and twenty-four, that forty-eight and twenty-eight, that's—'

'Seventy-six, you dopey eejit.' Dom batted him gently on the head with his napkin.

'Well, hot in any language.' McLoughlin finished off the egg and pushed the plate away. 'Thanks, just what the doctor ordered.'

'Come on,' Dom stood up, the pages in his hand. He pushed his chair back so it scraped across the tiles. 'We'll go in, have a look at your man's confession and you can explain to me how you managed to get it.'

Inside, the apartment was neat and tidy. A plastic washing basket filled with clothes, neatly folded, was on top of an ironing board. Dom walked slowly into the kitchen. He picked up the iron. He filled it with water, then plugged it in. He stood watching as it heated up, steam beginning to puff out.

'The bishop,' Dom put the washing basket on the floor. He bent down and pulled out a pile of pillow cases. He selected a pair decorated with pink princesses. He laid one on the board and began smooth it down. 'One of *the* Hegartys I assume.' McLoughlin watched him. The careful way he moved the iron. Backwards and forwards, up and down until the cloth was flat, even, all the wrinkles removed.

'Yep, one of *the* Hegartys.' He shifted in his seat. He felt sleepy now, tired after all the food. 'A miserable old man. Emphysema, depression I'd say too.'

'Drinking?' Dom raised his head. 'Not, I have to say, that I'm one to talk.' He nodded towards the pile of empties stashed in a wine box.

'Drinking, lots of whiskey, don't think he eats much. Doesn't have a housekeeper any longer. I wouldn't think cooking was high on the curriculum when he was in Maynooth.' He felt cold suddenly, as he thought about the bishop.

'And how did you find him?' Dom put down the iron, folded the pillow case and laid it on the sofa. He picked up the next one.

'He found me, actually.' Which wasn't exactly a lie, not quite anyway. 'I suppose he just felt bad about my father and all that.'

'So, a coincidence, then.' Dom was concentrating hard folding the pillow case.

'Well I suppose, I don't know, the fact that the judge had been killed, I'm not sure,' McLoughlin shifted awkwardly, 'he'd heard I was the person who found his body. He phoned me, said he'd something he wanted to give me, so I went to see him and there you have it.' He picked up the pages and the envelope. 'So the big question is. What can I do with it? Would any of it constitute real evidence? Or is it just hearsay, more talk, more gossip.' He got to his feet and walked over to the glass doors. Then turned and looked back towards Dom. 'What do you think?'

Dom shrugged and pulled another handful of clothes from the basket. Joanne's clothes. Pretty blouses and tops, skirts and trousers, all brightly coloured. 'About the confession. I think it's damning. I think it's embarrassing. But whether, in a court of law, it would be enough to convict, I doubt it. It wouldn't stand up as a dying declaration, unfortunately. The hearsay rules would still apply. He says this. He says that, but without corroborating evidence, well,' steam hissed. The room was filled with a smell that reminded McLoughlin of something. Home, he supposed, it was home.

Dom was concentrating on the job in hand. 'But, it's the way you use it. Maybe you won't get your guilty verdict, your man locked up. But maybe you don't need that.' He put the iron back into its cradle. 'There's more than one way to get justice. There's more than one court. Public opinion is a fairly important one.' He paused. 'If I were you, I'd be thinking about that. And now,' he pointed towards the fridge, 'this is thirsty work. There's a bottle of Austrian white in there. You'll like it.'

They polished off the wine. Dom finished his ironing and sat down beside him. He surveyed the neat pile with a grin of satisfaction.

'Funny isn't it? I'd never have thought I'd get so much pleasure out of something like this. I don't know,' he stretched. 'Don't know why all these women are so keen to work outside the home. I think housework is fantastic. Dead simple and makes you feel good.'

McLoughlin smiled at him. 'Here's to it then. To housework,' and he reached over and they clinked their glasses together. As the doorbell rang. Dom sighed.

'I'd better go,' McLoughlin got to his feet.

'Yeah, probably just as well.' Dom stood too. 'She hasn't been so good the last few days, since she came back from the nursing home. I don't know what it is. She used to be really happy, at ease. But I'm finding it tougher, much more difficult.' He began to move slowly, reluctantly towards the door. He looked back over his shoulder. 'Leave Ryan's statement with me, will you?'

'Yeah?'

'Yeah, I'd like to go through it again. Sometimes it just takes a bit of time.' Dom tucked his shirt into his trousers.

'Yeah,' McLoughlin nodded, 'sometimes just a bit of time.'

They walked together to the lift. Together they travelled down to the ground floor. The nurse from the Alzheimer's Society was wheeling

Joanne in through the heavy glass doors. McLoughlin stood back to let them pass. Dom squatted down.

'How you doing sweetheart?' His voice was gentle, tender.

'She's not so good,' the nurse handed him a plastic bag, 'we had to change her clothes. She had another accident.'

'OK,' Dom stood and took hold of the wheelchair's handles. 'I'll look after her now. Thanks.'

He turned away towards the lift. McLoughlin closed the outside door. He stood for a moment in the sunshine. The nurse looked after them. She smiled.

'He's a lovely man. His wife is very lucky. They're not all like him you know.' She moved towards the minibus.

McLoughlin walked across the road and stood in front of what had once been the railway station. A low stone building, elegant and neat. Wide steps up to the double doors which were standing open. He walked in. A large bright room, pale wooden floor, tables laid with white cloths, cutlery and glasses shining. A waiter, a young man with a long apron wrapped around his waist, approached him.

'Good afternoon, sir, I can help?' He smiled.

'A booking, I'd like to make a booking.' McLoughlin could smell fresh bread.

'Of course,' the waiter moved to a small desk by the door. He picked up a large black diary. 'For when? For how many?'

'Saturday night, for two. Eight o'clock.'

'Of course, sir,' the waiter lifted his pen. 'Your name?'

'McLoughlin, Michael McLoughlin.' He spelt out his surname. He watched as the waiter wrote it down carefully, then closed the diary with a loud snap. He bowed and smiled. 'We'll see you then, sir. We look forward to it.'

Home slowly, the sun hot on his head, the tar on the road beginning to melt, softening, sticky. He turned into the square. And saw outside his house a man lounging against the railings. Recognised him immediately. The suit, even on such a hot day, the glasses, the long nose.

'Mr McLoughlin,' Liam Hegarty turned towards him, his phone in his hand. He held it up. 'You don't answer these days.'

McLoughlin pulled out his keys.

'You saw the bishop.' Hegarty moved towards him. 'You talked. He told me.'

McLoughlin kept on walking.

'He gave you the statement.'

McLoughlin didn't reply.

'We had an agreement, did we not?' Hegarty moved and barred his way.

'An agreement, yes, however, I'm not sure your side stands up to scrutiny.' McLoughlin side stepped him. He began to walk up the steps.

'You're fucking kidding, aren't you? I know what Eamon Ryan told Declan. I know what it's worth.'

'Well you may think you know, but I'm not convinced and until I am you'll just have to wait.' McLoughlin looked back, over Hegarty's head. The square was empty. No one around. There was silence for a moment. 'One more thing, Liam, a question.'

'A question, what?' His voice impatient, angry.

'We've both seen the photos. We both know what the judge did. But what I want to know is why? Why did he do that?'

Hegarty's face reddened. 'That has nothing to do with you. My brother, his life, the choices he made, that's not part of our agreement. Now,' a pause, an intake of breath, 'I've honoured my side. You owe me. I want those photographs and I want them now.'

'Well, tough.' McLoughlin had his key in the lock. He turned it and pushed. The door swung back. He stepped forward. 'I'm afraid you're just going to have to wait.' He walked inside and slammed the door behind him. As behind him he heard Hegarty shout, his fist on the wood. McLoughlin walked upstairs. He looked down from the first-floor window. For a moment Hegarty looked pathetic. And McLoughlin could see he knew it too. He moved away from the door, straightened his jacket, smoothed down his hair. Got into his car and drove away.

Quiet today inside. Just the occasional high-pitched
whine of a saw, and the radio, a football match by the sound of the
commentary. Ian had said they would be finished soon. He could start
arranging to get his furniture out of storage and move in. It would be
good to sleep in a proper bed again. He felt exhausted now, shaken by
the encounter with Hegarty. He lay down on the mattress and closed
his eyes. The boys in the photographs filled his mind's eye. Was he
doing the right thing? He wasn't sure any longer. He turned over,
hugging his arms around his body. He could see Sorcha Hegarty, hear
the pain in her voice. He wished he'd been able to help her. He rolled
over, sighed, and slept. Until his phone rang. He pulled himself up,
and looked at the screen.

'Dom, hi, how you doing?'

'Mick, listen,' Dom's voice was insistent.

'OK I'm listening.'

'The evidence. I've found it.'

'What?'

'Something new. Can you come over? I'll show you.' Dom laughed.
'It's fucking brilliant.'

The papers were strewn across the table. Dom was sitting on the sofa
holding a plate of pasta with some kind of tomato sauce. Joanne was
on a beanbag, close to the TV. She turned when he came in. She smiled
and waved. Her face was covered with food, and so was the large bib
she was wearing. But as the dog scooted past McLoughlin's legs into the
room, her expression changed. She cried out, and cowered away.

'Sorry,' McLoughlin grabbed hold of Ferdie's collar. 'Didn't think. What'll I do with him?'

'Here.' Dom got up and quickly moved to the glass doors. He slid them back and pointed. 'Put him out here. It's not too hot at the moment.'

Joanne had risen, uncertainly. She moved back and away, swaying from side to side and humming loudly.

'It's all right, love, doggie all gone,' Dom stood between her and the sight of Ferdie who, in a disgruntled way, was inspecting the limits of the balcony. Dom took her hand. 'Tell you what, would you like some ice cream? In your room? Strawberry ice cream and I'll put your TV on. Would you like that?'

She smiled. Dom nodded to McLoughlin. 'Sit yourself down, won't be a minute. There's beer in the fridge if you fancy.'

McLoughlin stood by the table and looked through the papers. He noticed where Dom had made marks, comments. Eamon Ryan's statement was detailed. It began with his early enthrallment with republicanism. His family had it in their blood. Grandfathers and granduncles who had fought in the War of Independence and the Civil War. A proud tradition of resistance. They lived in Monaghan, a border county. Always conscious of the British presence across the fields. He spoke of his loathing for the Union flag and all it stood for. He watched the helicopters in the sky, heard the sound of guns, saw the volunteers who came south to have their wounds treated. And he wanted to be part of it. Bloody Sunday was the last straw. He'd do anything now.

'Having fun?' Dom sat down beside him.

'Is she OK? Sorry about the dog. I should have left him at home.' McLoughlin lifted his bottle and took a swallow.

'It's fine. You'd be amazed the effect strawberry ice cream has.' Dom hefted the bottle opener in his large hand. 'You OK? Want another?'

McLoughlin shook his head. 'Not at the moment, thanks,' he pulled the piece of paper towards him. 'I've had a look. A lot of self-serving rubbish really. Shoring up his place in history.'

Dom flicked the bottle top away and took a long swallow. 'Yeah, most of it. Standard stuff you'd read in any online blog. But he gets more interesting when he starts talking about Reynolds. Very critical of what he did.'

'Yeah, I read that part. Guilty conscience, remorse, I reckon.' McLoughlin wiped his mouth with the back of his hand.

Dom looked at him. 'I think it's a bit more than that. I think he was genuine in his feelings. And I'll show you why. Look.' He riffled through the pages and pulled out one. 'I'm going to read this to you.' He cleared his throat. He began.

We left our safe house in Finglas early around six. There was me, Mac, Conor and Jim. We separated. Mac went direct to Dundrum. I went by myself and Conor with Jim. We each got the bus, separately. The car was parked, waiting, in Ringsend. Jim had the key. It was a yellow Vauxhall Cavalier. There was a sawn-off shotgun in the boot. Jim got it out and put it down by his feet. Mac didn't come with us. The look-out needed to be in place by the time we got there. We sat around for a bit. We were all nervous. This was the biggest thing any of us had ever done. Around eight-fifteen Jim drove to Dundrum. We knew the van would get there around nine. We wanted to be in place beforehand. We parked up the side street next to the post office. I could see Mac at the bus stop outside. There were a couple of other people there, a woman and a young guy. A few people walking past, but it was early, quiet. Mac signalled that the van was arriving. We knew there'd be security on the transfer of the money so we waited until the bags were inside and the van had gone. Mac signalled the all clear. Conor and I got out of the car. I was sweating, my heart was pumping. We went inside. There were a couple of old ladies in the queue. Couldn't be helped. Conor stood at the front. I shouted, kicked in the door to the back room, waved my gun at the postwoman. She turned milk white. I always remember. Put her hands up. It was weird. For a moment I couldn't figure out why she was doing that. Then I realised. The gun in my hand. Anyway, the two bags were on the floor. She hadn't opened them. So we grabbed them. It was so easy. Candy and babies come to mind. Too easy. We headed out. But when we got outside Mac was looking pale, scared. And then I saw a garda car had stopped. Jim had moved our car. It was on a double yellow line. As we came out this guard was walking towards Jim. We were behind him. I saw him approaching the car. Then I saw Jim lift up the gun and shoot him. The noise was horrific. I stopped, I couldn't move. The guard fell like a stone. He was covered in blood. Blood everywhere. And I saw then, two more guards coming for us. I grabbed the bags and flung them into the car. Jim took off before I could get in. I turned around. One of the guards had Conor and before I could move the other got me. I looked for Mac. No sign. Mac was good at that, good at disappearing into a crowd. They took us to the local station. We could hear the reports coming in on the car radio. An ambulance had been called for the guard who was shot. Joe McLoughlin. He was probably dead already. No time for a priest. I vomited in the car. I was in bits. When they got us into a cell they laid into us. There was no holding back. They beat us to a pulp. But you know, even then I pretty much felt we deserved it. Jim didn't need to shoot the guard. I don't know why he did it. But it was wrong. And I've never stopped feeling like that.'

'So, one thing.'

'Yeah,' Dom grinned at him. 'What's that?'

'Mac, who the fuck is Mac?'

McLoughlin thought back over everything he'd read about that day outside the post office. The two old ladies inside. The people at the bus stop. But he'd never heard the name Mac mentioned before.

'Yeah, that's what I noticed too. Who the fuck is Mac? The one that got away?'

'No one ever mentioned a look-out either. It was always just the gang of three, Conor, Eamon and Jim.'

'That's what I thought. But look, here,' Dom pointed to the last page, the signatures. McLoughlin looked down. He read out loud. *'Signed by Eamon Ryan, witnessed by Theresa Ryan, Padraig Ryan.* Theresa Ryan née MacFeeley. Family, died-in-the-wool Republicans from Derry. In those days she was always known as 'Mac'. Dom raised his glass triumphantly. 'Got married to Eamon Ryan after he was released. They had a son, Padraig. She nursed Eamon through his cancer. Still living in Waterford.'

'So,' McLoughlin let out a whistle. The dog scratched at the glass doors and whined. Dom made as if to get up. 'Leave him,' McLoughlin waved his hand, 'he's grand.'

'So, I reckon, Mick. I reckon if you paid a visit to Theresa Ryan you might find her amenable to making a statement. New and credible evidence. The kind of thing that at the very least could occasion a trial. And not only a trial but a conviction.'

McLoughlin shook his head. 'Just one problem. She'd be implicating herself. Putting herself in the frame too.'

'Yeah, maybe,' Dom shrugged, 'but you don't know what's been going on in her life. Not everyone likes the way the war ended, the way the spoils were divided, the way the power shifted. I'd go and see her. You've nothing to lose.'

They sat at the table. Dom produced bread and cheese and some beer. He'd put Joanne to bed. She'd fallen asleep, he said, watching TV.

'I don't know what happens with her. But she'll probably wake around one or two.' Dom cut himself a slice of cheddar.

McLoughlin spread butter liberally on a crust of bread. 'And will you have to get up?'

Dom shook his head. McLoughlin could see the grooves of tiredness beneath his eyes. The slump of his broad shoulders. 'I'll hear her and I'll get up too. Sometimes I can settle her down with a DVD but often at night she'll just wander around the room. Sometimes she cries. Sometimes you can see she's frightened.' He sighed, grabbed his bottle. 'Here, news time. Let's see what's happening in the world.' He picked up the remote and moved towards the sofa as the TV came on. The weather was the top story. Shots of beaches, children paddling, sand castles, girls in bikinis, queues for ice creams.

Then the picture changed. Walls, barbed wire, guard dogs on patrol. The newsreader's expression was serious, solemn as she read. 'Police in riot gear were called to the Midlands prison today...'

'What's she saying? What's happened?' McLoughlin got up from the table and joined Dom.

'Shh,' Dom pushed him back. 'Listen.'

'A routine search of the cells was taking place. A large number of mobile phones and other contraband had been seized, when fighting broke out. Our crime correspondent has sent us this report.'

The reporter was standing outside the prison. Behind him police vans were coming and going, and gardaí wearing helmets with visors, carrying shields and batons were lining up. The reporter described what had happened. A search of the blocks. Resistance from the prisoners. A pitched battle took place. The canteen was wrecked. A number of injuries, some serious. Ambulances were called.

'Among the casualties was the notorious career criminal, Brian O'Leary, imprisoned for multiple drug offences and crimes of violence. Mr O'Leary is understood to have been transferred to St Vincent's hospital for treatment for a head injury. Mr O'Leary's solicitor made this statement.' The reporter looked down at his notes. He began to read. '"We are extremely concerned at the state's failure to protect our client Mr Brian O'Leary. Mr O'Leary's injuries are consistent with a beating by a rubber truncheon. He also has extensive burns to his face and his eyes which appear to have come from prolonged exposure to teargas. A complaint has been made to the Department of Justice."'

'So, poor old O'Leary.' Dom took a swallow of beer. 'Must be losing it. Not like him to be on the receiving end.'

McLoughlin stretched out his legs. 'Usually too cute for that. Still, he'll be finished without the phone. Won't be able to keep a grip on the boys outside.' He drained his bottle.

'Want another?' Dom made as if to get up. 'I'll get them,' McLoughlin stood. 'You look as if you could do with a rest.'

He moved towards the fridge, pulling out a couple more bottles and the opener.

'The boys outside,' McLoughlin sat down. He yanked off the caps and handed a bottle to Dom. 'Who would be his main man, would you think?'

Dom drank, wiped his mouth with the back of his hand. 'Well, there's Stevie, the little brother. But he's a bit light upstairs.'

'Is he the gormless-looking one? Red hair and freckles and a bit of a squint?'

'You got him. You'd almost feel sorry for him.' He paused. 'The name on everyone's lips. Martin Millar, do you remember him?'

McLoughlin tried to think. He used to know them all. Used to know everything about them. Now he wasn't sure.

'Martin Millar, give me a few clues.'

'Millar was an orphan. Drugs got the parents. There was a granny who did her best.' Dom closed his eyes.

'Grannies, they're great. Always a granny to step in.' Like Mags Maguire, McLoughlin thought.

'Yeah, but in this case Millar's granny wasn't up to much. Couldn't cope with the boy, so O'Leary's mammy took over. She was good at that. She ran a bit of a boy's town out in their house.'

'I remember. Not so much a boy's town, more like Fagin in Oliver Twist.' Calling there, looking for Brian. Kids everywhere. A big pot of stew on the cooker. Clothes drying over the fireplace. Tripping over dogs and cats.

'Yeah, you have it,' Dom sat up straight and stretched. 'Martin Millar was almost a son to her. I knew one of the social workers who tried to step in and get him taken away, sent to a more suitable foster family. Problem was he was mad about Mammy O'Leary. And in spite of everything she was good for him. Got him to go to school. At least until he was fifteen.' Dom yawned. He looked exhausted. 'My friend, the social worker, told me his parents had pimped him out when he was little. You'd almost feel sorry for him, and you might understand how he turned out the way he did. You might, or then again you might not.'

'Ah, yes.' McLoughlin could see the kid. Small for his age, but already aggressive, angry. Throwing stones at the police car when they came to arrest Brian that last time. 'He's the one they call Lennon, isn't he? The glasses?'

Dom nodded. 'That's him. So when Brian went to prison he left school. Took over where Brian had left off.' Dom leaned back into his seat and crossed his legs. 'Now he'd be O'Leary's representative on earth. All the time O'Leary's been in Portlaoise, Martin is collecting his debts, keeping the stuff coming in, making the deliveries and distribution, generally being his master's voice. And,' he picked up his bottle, drained it, and wiped his mouth, 'expanding O'Leary's sphere of influence.'

'Oh?' McLoughlin looked at him.

'Yeah, O'Leary had never been into girls or anything, how would you put it, messy.' Dom grinned. 'He was doing just fine with the drugs.' He paused. 'So,' Dom put his beer down on the table, 'girls and all that stuff. Brothels in every small town from here to Belmullet. A steady supply of young ones from here to the Black Sea. Most of them only too delighted to get away from whatever muddy little dump they've grown up in. History hanging heavily. Fascism, communism, borderlands, the armies of Europe tramping backwards and forwards. So, great idea, come to Ireland,' he waved his arms, 'gateway to the future.'

'And Martin Millar just waiting to get them in his clutches,' McLoughlin looked towards the TV. The weather forecast, a blocking high coming up from the Azores. The temperatures in the high twenties. 'What'll happen now? O'Leary in hospital. No phone. No contact.'

'Well,' Dom leaned back and crossed his legs again, 'a temporary blip I'd say. Watch this space. Normal service will be resumed soonest.'

'So, what should I do about the other?' McLoughlin gestured to the pages of Eamon Ryan's statement. Dom reached for his laptop. He opened it up. His two index fingers moved slowly over the keyboard and stroked the touchpad. He turned the screen towards McLoughlin.

'Here you go,' he nodded towards the brightness. McLoughlin leaned forward, putting on his glasses to read. An article in a regional newspaper. Theresa Ryan, active in the local community. Involved in raising money for a new hospice. A photograph. A woman, hair dyed bright red, face thin to the point of gauntness, standing in a garden. Open to the public to raise money for a new hospice. An address. And a photograph taken at Ryan's funeral, holding a red rose.

McLoughlin scrolled back. A long list of archive material. How she came from a Republican family, spent time in prison for possession of firearms. Took part in the dirty protests in the early 1980s.

'If I was you I'd go and see her. Just turn up. Don't give any warning.' Dom closed the computer and took off his glasses. 'Don't give her the chance to say no.'

It was still warm when McLoughlin left the apartment. Joanne had woken. Out of a nightmare it seemed. Loud screams from the bedroom and Dom rushing to her. McLoughlin put the empties in the bin, washed the dishes and glasses, picked up the pieces of paper with Dom's handwriting scrawled across them, then opened the glass doors and let in the dog. He grabbed him by his collar and half dragged him towards the lift, waving a quick goodbye to Dom, who was now holding Joanne on his knee as she sobbed. Outside on the street he let Ferdie go. The dog ran around in circles for a bit, then settled down and trotted at his heel.

It was almost dark by the time they reached the square. Lights shining from the houses' long front windows. Sounds from the gardens, music, voices and the breeze blowing the smell of a barbecue. The skip had gone from outside his gate and one of the men had tidied up the small front patch. He leaned on the railings for a moment. He could smell sweetness. Night-scented stock trailing through the grass. Ferdie ran down the small front path to the basement, and stood up, scratching on the door. It opened.

'Ferdie,' McLoughlin followed him. The small hall was lit by the lamp on the table, and Ferdie scurried past it towards the closed door at the end.

'Ferdie,' McLoughlin hissed at him, hurrying to grab him just as he made a jump for the handle. He hooked his fingers inside the dog's collar. He heard voices. Elizabeth's, tuneful, gentle, and the sound of a man. A deep voice. A rumble in his throat.

He half pulled the dog away, and heard movement inside. Elizabeth's voice louder, as he backed off, looking around, pulling the dog with him, into the room at the front of the house, boxes piled high, holding Ferdie tightly as he heard Elizabeth, in the hall now. Saying goodbye, pleasantries exchanged.

'Careful going home. It's dark outside. Can you manage? Let me know if you're not OK. If you want to come and see me tomorrow, phone me. All right?'

The man's voice barely audible as he moved away, mumbling.

The squeak as the door closed. The click as the lock engaged. Elizabeth's footsteps and Ferdie now, pulling away, scratching to be let free. As McLoughlin stepped out into the light. And Elizabeth's face, white, her mouth opening as if to scream.

'God, what a fright,' laughing, nervously, her hands clutching her throat. 'How long have you been there?'

'Sorry, really sorry, didn't mean to scare you.' He put out his hand and touched her arm. 'The front door was open. Ferdie came in. He made a beeline for your door. I had to stop him from barging in on you. He's got this great trick. He jumps up and hits the door handle just so. And bingo. He ran in here,' he gestured behind him.

'Oh, that's OK,' she giggled, relief. 'The front door, open, was it?' She moved towards it. 'I think I need to get someone to look at the lock. I've noticed, you have to give it quite a thump to make it stick.' She yawned. 'Oh, sorry. It's been a long day. I'd better get myself off home.' She moved towards the lamp and he could see. The lines around her mouth, the shadows under her eyes.

'You go.' McLoughlin smiled at her. 'I'll look after everything here.'

'Are you sure?' She looked around at him.

'Of course. Go on,' he gestured with his head.

She smiled and nodded. 'OK, my bag, I'll just get it.'

He followed her into her room. 'I'll lock up. There's a couple of things I want to get out of my boxes.' He smiled at her.

'Thanks Michael, that's nice of you. It's been a long week, this week, for some reason.' She pulled a large basket from beneath her desk. Her shoulders were slumped.

'Before you go. I just wanted to check. You're still on for dinner on Saturday night?'

'Dinner?' she straightened. 'Oh, yeah, lovely. You found somewhere you'd like?'

'The restaurant down there on the front, in the old station building. Menu looks good. I've booked for eight. Is that OK?' He wondered suddenly. Had he done the right thing?

'Yes, fantastic.' She slung her basket over her shoulder. 'Why don't you come by my house, say around seven. We'll have a drink in the garden. It's really nice at this time of the year.'

He walked her to the front door. He watched as she disappeared from sight. He moved back inside, back into the light. Ferdie had run ahead and was lying curled up on Elizabeth's couch. McLoughlin sat down at the desk. Her diary was open. He pulled it towards him. He ran his eye down the list of appointments. '9 p.m. Dudgeon' was printed. He swung back in the chair. Then pulled himself forward again. A ring binder was on the desk next to the diary. He opened it up, flicking to the last few pages. Elizabeth's writing was neat, precise, tidy. The page was headed Samuel Dudgeon, the date, 26th July 2013. He sighed. Wouldn't do to read on. Breach of trust. He closed it over, then looked around. Ferdie was asleep, his eyes closed, his head relaxed. McLoughlin got up. He walked to the windows and looked out. No lights in his garden. No sounds either. He reached up and pulled down the sash window, locking it tightly.

'Come on Ferdie, time to go home.' He nudged the dog with his foot. Ferdie stirred, yawned, stood. And together they walked out.

It was a while since he'd driven south. Motorway nearly all the way now. Cutting a swathe through Wicklow, Wexford and Waterford. Carving a dark smear across the green of the lush farmland. Plenty of traffic. Cars filled with families going on holidays. People carriers stuffed with children, roof racks laden with bags, boxes, bicycles. Trailers pulling boats of all shapes and sizes.

He leaned back in his seat and put his foot down. Another seventy miles or so. Skirting around Waterford and out along the coast, past Dungarvan, the R674 along the clifftop. He'd used Google maps, found the house. Set back from the road, a couple of miles outside the town. Drove slowly past a high wooden gate in the middle of a thick conifer hedge. He turned right, off the road into a narrow lane and parked the car. He got out. Quiet, birdsong, the faint clatter of a tractor in the distance. Fields all around, cattle grazing. He could see what must be the Ryans' house behind a stand of sycamores. A modern building, or rather a modern extension tacked onto a single-story cottage. All painted white. A couple of sheds too.

He pushed through a gate and into the field, the grass long, clinging to his legs. As he got closer he could see a large vegetable garden. Peas and beans climbing up wigwams of bamboo, sweet corn, as high as the elephant's eye, courgettes, large sprawling leaves with yellow trumpet-shaped flowers, lettuces, bright green and glossy dark red, and other plants. Carrots and cabbages, their hearts beginning to bulk up. A circular washing line, shirts, towels, sheets, underwear, all lifting in the breeze from the sea. A Land Rover parked in front of a garage. And at the back of the house a conservatory stretching its length.

A wooden fence separated the garden from the field. He began to pull himself up and over. As he paused to take a deep breath, one leg on either side, he could see a woman, bright red hair cut short, sitting at a table, a mug and a newspaper in front of her. A black cat asleep on her knee.

He dropped down, stifling a cry as his ankle twisted beneath him. He crouched for a moment and looked around. He could hear the sound of a radio coming from the house. The lunchtime news. He stood up slowly. And heard a voice shouting.

'Who the fuck are you? What the fuck do you think you're doing?'

He turned around. A young man was standing a few yards away, a large shovel in his hand. Wearing shorts, stripped to the waist, barefoot. Muscled, his skin tanned. Shoulder-length black hair, parted in the middle and tucked back behind each ear. Heavy black eyebrows, deep-set brown eyes.

The conservatory door opened. The cat ran out and behind him came the red-haired woman. Barefoot too, jeans rolled up to the knees and a loose white T-shirt. A cigarette in her hand, long nails painted red like her hair. She put up her hand as the young man advanced towards McLoughlin, shaking the shovel so McLoughlin backed away, treading carefully, conscious of the pain in his ankle.

'Sorry, sorry.' McLoughlin stopped. 'I wasn't sure if this was right place. I'm looking for Theresa Ryan.' He turned towards the woman, 'Would that be you?'

'And who might you be?' Her accent was northern.

'I'm Michael McLoughlin. You might know the name.'

They sat in the conservatory. It was hot. McLoughlin was sweating. The young man, Padraig, served coffee, brought water too. Theresa, McLoughlin noticed, was extremely thin. Her cheekbones cut through her face. The skin on her neck was stretched tight. Tendons, knotted, so McLoughlin could barely bring himself to look. Her arms were like twigs, the flesh loose around the bones. Her hands and feet were constantly on the move, fiddling, twitching, her fingers nicotine stained. Deep grooves around her mouth, dark circles under her eyes.

No one spoke. McLoughlin sipped his coffee, added milk from a small white jug.

'You've a nice set up here.' He looked around. Bright pink geraniums grew in terracotta pots and there was a vine twining up in one corner. Passion flowers, purple and cream, peeped through the glossy green foliage. 'You've been here for a while?'

She shrugged. Pulled a wad of tobacco from the plastic pouch on the table, and began to fashion a cigarette. 'The old cottage was Eamon's mother's house. She died when he was in prison, left it to him. I couldn't afford to do much with it, but when Eamon came out...' She licked the edges of the paper and rolled it expertly. She put it to her lips. McLoughlin picked up the box of matches. He struck one and held it out. She angled the cigarette into the flame and sucked hard. The paper turned red and caught. She opened her mouth and let out the smoke in a long grey plume. McLoughlin recognised the smell.

'Did you get compensation?' Golden Virginia. He'd smoked it once himself.

She shrugged again, narrowing her eyes against the smoke and picking small strands of tobacco from her bottom lip. 'There's a fund, for prisoners' families. Our friends in the New World if you know what I mean.'

He knew what she meant.

'Eamon was very sick when he was released. We didn't think he'd live for more than a few months, but in fact,' she drew on the cigarette, 'his cancer went into some kind of remission and we had a good few years together. Long enough for him to see Padraig growing up.'

'Treatment, these days,' McLoughlin fiddled with a teaspoon, 'it's great really. I heard a doctor on the radio the other day. He was saying that cancer will become a chronic illness. People will live with it, rather than dying from it. A bit like diabetes or I suppose HIV.'

'Well,' her mouth turned down, 'it wasn't quite like that for Eamon, but...' her voice trailed away. There was an uneasy silence. She put her cigarette down on an ashtray. McLoughlin noticed. It was emblazoned with a shamrock and a Celtic cross. Again the silence.

'Look,' she raised her eyes. They were green, speckled with yellowish flecks. They reminded him of the markings on a trout. Freshly caught from a river. 'Get on with it. What do you want?'

He sipped his coffee, then put the mug down on the table.

'You know who I am.'

She nodded.

'Your husband's statement, the one he gave to Bishop Hegarty.'

'Ah,' she shifted on her seat, 'that. I was wondering when it would surface.'

'I was surprised,' he looked over her head. A couple of magpies had landed on the grass. One of them had found a worm. Pulling it out, inch by inch.

'I was surprised,' he repeated the words, 'that your husband wrote it all down. Why did he do that?'

She shrugged and looked away. The cigarette had gone out. She took it from her mouth and scrutinised it. 'He wanted to put the record straight. He wanted to say what he had done, what he had seen. He wanted people to know why he did the things he did.' She fiddled with the cigarette, then put it back in her mouth. She picked up the box of matches. Then began to cough. She put the cigarette down. She picked up the glass of water and drank from it.

'And you,' McLoughlin watched her. Sweat beaded on her forehead. 'You are the Mac he refers to, aren't you?'

She picked up the cigarette again, and placed it again between her lips. She lifted the box of matches. McLoughlin took it from her. He pulled out a match. He struck it and leaned forward. Again the end of the cigarette in the flame. Again she sucked hard so the tip glowed red. She took it from her mouth, and blew out the smoke.

'Mac, ay, that's me. When I was at school there were two other Theresas in my class. So I was called Mac. It stuck for years, but I never liked it.' She tapped the cigarette on the edge of the ash tray.

'So you were there, that day outside the post office. You saw who killed my father?' His heart had begun to pound.

'I did,' she looked away. 'I did for sure.'

239

'So?'

She said nothing for a moment. She looked down at the floor. She moved her feet. When she spoke her voice was so low he had to lean forward to catch her words.

'Blood on the ground, so much blood.' She looked up and closed her eyes, the lids shutting over those speckles of gold. 'I left as quickly as I could. I got away. I heard the screech of the car as Jim Reynolds drove off. I heard the shouts and screams. I heard Eamon shouting. I couldn't hear what he was saying. I got away as quickly as I could. Got the bus back into town. Got the train to Belfast. Got out of there. Knew what I had to do.' She opened her eyes. She gestured to her son. He got up, walked through the door into the kitchen. McLoughlin could hear cupboards opening and closing.

'But you saw James Reynolds kill my father?' He wanted to hear her say it.

'I saw James Reynolds kill the guard. I saw him do it.' Her son was by her side. There was a glass in his hand. A colourless liquid. She took it from him. She took a deep swallow. And coughed. She put the glass on the table. She looked down again.

'And what do you feel about it? Do you feel the same as your husband?' McLoughlin leaned closer. Her cheeks were beginning to colour up. The alcohol was doing its job. She nodded.

'I do. It was an unnecessary killing. Eamon and Conor could have got away in the car with Jimmy. They could have got away with the money. Instead,' she picked up the glass and took another swallow, 'instead the guard died, Eamon and Conor went to prison. But Jimmy Reynolds, well...' she smiled, a tight bitter grimace.

'You didn't like him?'

'Jimmy, like Jimmy?' She shook her head. 'I didn't trust him. Different from us. His family, they had money. Big house on the south side of Dublin somewhere. He'd gone to a private school.' She paused, lifted the glass and drank. 'The one thing you knew about Jimmy. He'd always do OK. He'd always be looked after. One way or another. Plenty of people keeping an eye on Jimmy.'

'And the money? I always wondered what happened to the money.' McLoughlin leaned back in his chair.

'Whatever happened to the money?' She crossed her legs. Her shoulders had relaxed. She lifted her hand to push back her hair. He could see scars running vertically down her arm.

'So, what I want to know,' McLoughlin took a deep breath. He could feel his mother at his shoulder. 'I want to know, would you?'

'Would I go to the gardaí? Would I make a statement? Is that what you want to know?' She picked up the glass. 'I would, surely. I would.' She drained the glass, and held it out to her son. 'Same again, Padraig, same again.' He got up. His bare feet slapped on the tiled floor. Again the sounds from the kitchen next door.

'But tell me this,' McLoughlin leaned forward. He could smell lavender on a gentle breeze from outside. 'Why would you do that? Why would you betray your, what will I call him, your comrade?'

'Now,' she paused, 'that's a good question.' Her son appeared, the glass in his hand. And another large glass of what looked like orange juice. She touched him gently on the leg. She smiled and for a moment McLoughlin could see. The young woman, her expression warm and loving, her eyes bright with affection, her mouth generous. 'Padraig, the man's asking a question. An important question. Why don't you answer him? You're the next generation. Your generation are the ones who have to live in the world we created.' She took the glass from him and took a sip, this time a small sip. She put the glass down on the table and drank some juice. She wiped her mouth with a tissue pulled from her jeans pocket.

Padraig sat down beside her. He put his arm around her thin shoulders. He pulled her head towards him and kissed her. She rested on his chest

'My mammy is a brave woman. She grew up in a society which was unjust, prejudiced. Bigoted. Full of hate. For her and her kind. Because of their religion, their beliefs.' He paused and sipped some juice, his lips fitting over the lipstick smear on the tall glass. He continued. 'Those people were a majority. But it was an artificial majority. Created when our land was divided. So my mammy and my daddy rose up against those people, to fight for their rights, for their beliefs, for their culture and their language.'

Theresa sat up straight. She took his hand, turned it over and kissed his palm.

'Many people died,' his voice was strong, 'many of their friends died. They suffered. They starved themselves to death for their beliefs. My mam, she suffered. She went to prison. She starved. She was force-fed. She wouldn't give in because she believed.' He paused. He looked down at the floor. His bare feet shuffled on the tiles.

'Yes,' Theresa lifted her head, and reached for her glass, 'I suffered. But I believed. Terrible things were done. On all sides. People were killed, blown apart, a sacrifice to make life better for our children.' She ran her hand over Padraig's glossy black hair. 'We believed. Our violence, our acts weren't gratuitous. We had to do them.' She sipped from the juice glass. 'And then, and then what happened, son? Tell the man what happened.'

'We were betrayed, we were sold out.' He picked up her cigarette from the ashtray.

'Yes, we were sold out. Our birthright sold for what the Bible calls a mess of potage.' She pulled out a match and struck it, then held the flame to the cigarette end. He sucked on it, narrowing his eyes against the smoke. 'A few baubles were flung to us. A bit of power here, a bit of power there. But what did it add up to?' Theresa picked up the glass and drank. 'Not what we fought for, not what we died for.' She banged the glass on the table. 'And not what we killed for.'

Silence, suddenly. Even the birds outside were quiet.

'So,' she stood up, 'so, Mr McLoughlin. You ask me why I will betray my comrade, James Reynolds. A simple answer to your question. Because he and those like him betrayed me, my husband, my son and all we stood for.' She moved towards the door. 'And I realise what it would mean for me. The confession I would make would cost me.'

'You could go to prison.'

She nodded. 'I've been before. It's not the worst in the world. And it would cost them more. Now,' she took his arm. 'My garden, you'd like to see my garden, wouldn't you?'

He left the house through the high wooden gate. As it slid open onto the road he turned and looked back. She was standing amongst the vegetables. For a moment, as she turned away, she had the look of a scarecrow, rags hanging on a broomstick. A straw hat on her head. And the black cat rubbing itself against her long bony legs.

The drive home. The evening sun turning the fields of wheat and barley to burnished yellow. Every now and then, as the road rose he could see the sea. A dark Mediterranean blue. Not a hint of the usual grey or green.

She'd walked him through the vegetable garden. Bending down from time to time to pull up a weed. A tall spire of rosebay willowherb, or an occasional buttercup or dandelion, trying to sneak in under the cover of a courgette plant. She left the nettles though.

'Have to leave the nettles,' she said, 'otherwise we'll have no butterflies. Their eggs, you know, the Peacock and the Red Admiral and the Tortoiseshell, they all lay their eggs on the nettles. So,' she smiled at him as she brushed her hand over the leaves, and winced, 'we have to have some little bit of pain, don't we?'

She'd taken him to the wigwams of peas and beans. The peapods were full.

'Here,' she pointed, 'have a few. They're gorgeous.' He split them down the centre line. The peas lay, almost identical, plump and sweet. He tipped them into his mouth. He chewed and swallowed and looked around. The tall, dark conifers to the front and side of the property. The wooden fence at the back.

'You know you should do something about that,' he jerked his head towards it. 'If I could get in.'

She smiled at him. 'You're right. But we don't frighten easily. And besides we can't hide. Everyone knows us. Everyone knows who we are.' She leaned down and pulled off a couple of courgettes, smooth and green. 'Here, take these home with you. They're lovely when they're so small.'

She bent down and dug in the soil, a trowel in her hand.

'Eamon made this garden.' She held up the spade, a pile of earth balanced on it. 'When he came home from prison this was his salvation. He worked on it every year until he was too weak. Got manure from the farmer next door and we went to the beach after every storm. Seaweed, slimy, I didn't like it, but Eamon, he said it was the best. Said most of Ireland was made of seaweed.' She stood up. Her face was pale. 'I saw the news the other day. The bodies in the bogs. They're digging them up. At last.' She wiped her hands on her jeans. Smears of soil, clinging to her fingers.

She'd told him before he left. She'd speak to whoever he wanted. She was clear about it. The time had come, she said.

'And your son? Does he agree?'

She nodded. 'He agrees. He wants it over. It will be over.'

He sat back in his seat. He turned on the radio. The news headlines. 'A man has been arrested in connection with the murder of retired Supreme Court Judge John Hegarty. He can be held initially for twenty-four hours, then he must be either charged, released or the gardaí must apply to the courts for an extension of his detention. It is believed that the man is in his mid thirties and is known to the gardaí. He's a member of a high-profile gangland family based in the west of the city.'

So, McLoughlin stretched, makes sense. One of the O'Learys. He wondered. Firstly, which one? Secondly, could she make it stick? He pulled his phone from his jeans pocket. He found Min's number. Straight to voicemail. 'Hey, Min, well done. I just heard the news. Give me a call if you have a minute.'

Light was beginning to fade from the sky. He'd be home soon. Tomorrow he'd get back onto Tom Donnelly, drag him away from his golf, insist that he visit Theresa Ryan. Insist that he take a statement from her. Insist that he follow it up.

'What do you think Mammy?' he could see his mother's face in the windscreen. 'Are you happy now?'

She smiled at him.

'Well done, son, well done.'

Samuel held the photographs in his left hand. He dealt them out, slowly, carefully. He placed them in two rows, five in each row. Then he sat back and looked at them.

He had found them tucked away, hidden in the oven, in the old stove in the judge's basement. The judge had paid him to look after things. To do little jobs around the place. Just checking, making sure that everything was in order, the way the judge liked it. He had noticed when he went into the basement that the oven door was closed. It hadn't been closed before, he was sure about that. So he opened it up, put his hand in, found something surprising. Took it home with him.

The first time he had seen the photographs had been in Mr Smith's flat. Mr Smith had sat down on the sofa and picked up a magnifying glass.

'I knew it was you. I've looked at the photos so many times over the years and then when I saw you going into your flat. I knew,' he waved the magnifying glass in Samuel's direction, 'just something about you, I mean for God's sake you don't look like that dapper chappy in the pictures, do you?'

Samuel didn't reply. He couldn't deny it.

'So was that a coincidence or what?' Mr Smith twirled the magnifying glass around by its handle. 'You showing up here? Bet the judge got a bit of a fright.'

Did the judge get a fright? Samuel remembered that first day, in the square, the dog running past him trailing his lead and the judge following. And how their eyes had met.

'All those years gone by. And there's the judge and then along comes you, well,' and Mr Smith had laughed. 'And the photos, had you seen them before? Did you know about them?'

Samuel had shook his head.

'So, tell me, Sammy, I can call you Sammy, can't I?' Mr Smith had given him a big wide smile. 'What brought you to our lovely town? Was it the judge?'

Samuel tried to remember. It seemed so long ago. His father had died and Sam had taken over the firm. And then there'd been all the trouble about the client accounts, and he'd gone to prison and when he was away his mother had died too. The old house where he'd grown up, the big square house in its own grounds, had been sold and the money from the sale had gone to pay back some of his debts. There was a box of things, papers and other stuff waiting for him when he got out. Sitting in the hostel, the address the probation service had given him, a miserable dump with the smell of cheap washing powder hanging in the corridors. And when he opened the box, he found all these documents, his original birth certificate, and a photograph. Such a pretty girl and so young. Only fifteen when she gave birth to him. Her name, Cecily Lane and the name and address of the children's home in which she had lived. The Haven, Dun Laoghaire, Co. Dublin, Eire. He hadn't known. He'd never suspected. Dudgeon wasn't his name, not really. It was just a name he'd been lent. Until he could find his own name. William Dudgeon and Son. That wasn't him. He wasn't the son. Not William's son. No wonder William had treated him with a mixture of despair and contempt.

Samuel had gathered together all his strength. He had left the hostel. Walked as far as the tube station. Ealing Broadway it was. Took the central line to Oxford Circus, then changed to the Piccadilly line and got off at Euston. An old man with a plastic shopping bag, a few pounds in his pocket, he stood and stared up at the departures board. Got himself a cup of tea and a ham sandwich and sat and waited until the evening came and it was time to get on the train. Dozing in his seat, as they flew through the countryside. The stations flashing by, Crewe, Chester, Flint, Colwyn Bay, Llandudno Junction, Bangor and finally,

Holyhead. He remembered Nellie, the washerwoman who came every Monday. She had told him about getting the boat home. She called it the mail boat. It went from somewhere called Holly Head to somewhere called Done Leery. She would always meet people she knew on the boat. And they'd go into the bar and have a drink or two and everyone would sing, they'd be so happy to be going home.

'I know what you'll sing,' he'd say, 'you'll sing the song about the mountains, won't you?'

'The Mountains of Mourne?'

'Yes you'll sing that one, won't you, Nellie?'

And she'd give him a sweet then, a bulls eye maybe. And a hug too.

It was close to midnight when he got on the boat. He was so tired. He found himself a chair and he put his head on his plastic bag and he slept and didn't wake until someone shook him by the shoulder and said they were nearly there and he should get up. And he looked out the window and all he could see was grey sea and grey sky and the grey walls of the harbour and behind them a line of houses painted yellow and blue. Grey church spires too.

Not sure where to go when he struggled ashore. Cold outside, a soft drizzle and a policeman watching the crowd disperse. A polite smile on his face as Samuel approached him, the piece of paper in his hand. Asking him, 'Can you help me sir? Do you know where this is?'

And the policeman taking it, reading it slowly then saying, his accent unlike any that Samuel had ever heard before, so Samuel had to listen carefully to understand, 'The Haven? That's long gone, long gone. Closed down years ago. It's flats now, flats and offices. Nice old building, but not a children's home.'

Then looking at Samuel, noticing the way his face was crumpling, and with the exhaustion from the journey and the disappointment, a tear was sliding down his cheek, he said, 'Listen, I'll tell you what to do. I'll give you a lift. There's a Protestant church near here. The rector, he's a nice guy. Here,' and he pointed to the car parked behind him, 'get in now and I'll drop you round.'

Samuel had sat beside Mr Smith on the sofa and Mr Smith had explained. His son, Ed, was in trouble. He owed lots of money. He'd got mixed up with a crowd who were dangerous.

'Lucky I have the photos,' Mr Smith said. 'I knew they'd come in handy.'

Samuel had seen the man who came to visit. He was young and tall and thin, his glasses round and gold-rimmed. His shoes were always very shiny. Mr Smith was scared of him. He tried not to show it, but Samuel could smell his sweat, smell the way his little sitting room stank after the man had been to visit. After Mr Smith had handed over the cash.

And there was a problem.

'Not sure what I'm going to do, Sammy.' Mr Smith lit a cigarette. Samuel felt sick, the smell of sweat and cigarettes mixed together. 'That bastard Martin Millar. Ed should never have got involved with him. He's a madman. He wants me to give him the photos. He wants to be able to deal directly with the judge. I've told him no, I won't have it. But...' he got up and went into the kitchen. He came back with a large glass of whiskey in his hand. 'I'm not sure how long I can hang on. A mad bastard, you wouldn't know what he'd do next.'

And now Mr Smith had gone. Taken away by the ambulance. Samuel had thought he'd never see the photographs again. But here they were. He picked them up, gathered them together in his hand, shuffled and dealt them out. Vertical rows this time. The picture of the judge with the boy, the boy who had died, was at the top. He looked like a frightened rabbit. His body was thin and white. His eyes were big and round. The judge's hand on his shoulder looked huge. Samuel wondered. What was the boy's name? Was he a Joe or a Pete or a Jack or a Bob? When Samuel looked at him he wanted to scream and cry out, the way the judge screamed and cried out when the flagellant's whip dug into his skin. The judge screamed and cried out. The judge turned his face away from his God. He turned his face to the wall. Samuel didn't have a God to turn from. He had turned away from himself. He closed his eyes and dug his fingernails into his palms. He had made the boy to disappear. He existed now only in

Samuel's memory and only in the photograph. Samuel picked it up. He stroked the boy's thin face.

'I'm sorry boy, poor nameless boy,' he muttered. He piled all the photographs together into a neat pile. He put them back into their snug envelope. He stood up. He walked into the hall. He pulled open the small cupboard. He got down onto his knees and lifted the loose board. He pulled out the shopping bag. Inside were his most treasured possessions. The picture of Cecily Lane and his original birth certificate. His favourite chisel, the wooden handle worn smooth. And the judge's computer. He had opened it up. He had found more photos. In colour this time. More boys. Poor, poor boys. Then the battery had gone flat

Now he carefully placed the envelope in the bag, then he pushed it back and away. He replaced the board. They were all safe now. Safe and sound and out of sight.

Sun pouring around the edges of the shutters as he stirred and stretched. And looked into Ferdie's brown eyes. The little dog pawing at the duvet, as he turned away towards the door. Not happy that he'd been left in the house all day yesterday.

'OK fella, you want out?'

McLoughlin pushed back the duvet and scrambled upright. He picked up his phone. It was nearly nine. Ian would be here soon. And today they were to walk through the house, look at the progress, see what else needed to be done.

He held up his phone, scrolled down through his contacts. Donnelly, Tom. He pressed the call button. Straight to voicemail. Saturday morning, Donnelly was probably on the golf course or maybe he was doing the supermarket shop with the missus.

'Hi Tom, Michael McLoughlin here. Listen, I've got something for you. A witness to my father's shooting. She'll make a statement. She'll go to court. Give me a call. I'd like you to go and see her, sooner, rather than later. Thanks.'

Ferdie was scratching at the front door. McLoughlin opened it for him and together they walked out onto the front step. Already it was hot. Dom would want to know what happened. He was surprised he hadn't phoned already. He tried his number. Again straight to voicemail. What was it, he wondered, about Saturdays? No point in leaving a message. He knew Dom never listened to them. He texted. *Call me. Got on great in Waterford. Thanks for all the help.*

He sat down and watched Ferdie as he ran from tree to tree. A small group of children on the green this morning. One of the girls spotted the dog.

'Yippee,' she shouted, so Ferdie backed away and headed for the safety of the house again, scooting up the steps and rushing past McLoughlin.

'Had enough, have you?' McLoughlin bent down and patted him, then walked into the kitchen. He stopped, amazed. He hadn't realised how much Ian had done. It had been dark last night when he got in and he was so tired he'd gone straight to bed. But now, seeing it in daylight he was delighted. Sun shining in through the window. The double sink, its silky stainless steel, reflecting back the light. The five-burner gas hob and eye level oven in place. And the kitchen units, a mix of stainless steel and wood.

A loud knock and Ian's voice calling out as McLoughlin heard his key in the lock and the front door banging open.

'I'm in here, I'll just be a minute.' He tucked his shirt into his trousers, put his phone in his pocket and shoved his feet into his sandals. Picked up his phone. Smoothed back his hair. Cleared his throat.

'Hi, Ian, good to see you. The kitchen is fantastic. I'm really pleased.'

They walked up the stairs. Everywhere was clean, ready for the painters, just about finished. A loud squeak from one of the floorboards on the landing. McLoughlin shifted from foot to foot. He looked at Ian.

'Yeah, sorry about that. Sometimes they take a while to settle in. But if it doesn't, I'll get it seen to.' Ian smiled nervously. They continued on up. The bathroom was particularly good. McLoughlin was delighted with the tiling, the shower with its big round head, the deep bath, the nicely oval basin. And of course the toilet with the self-closing lid.

'I like that,' McLoughlin chuckled. 'It's cool.'

'Yeah,' Ian nodded and smiled. 'We'll put one in downstairs too.' He broke off as his phone burbled. He gestured apologies and stepped outside. McLoughlin could hear him. He was lining up his next job or maybe his job after that. A hard life being a builder. Always juggling what he was doing now with what was coming down the tracks.

He walked up the small flight of stairs, up to the room at the top of the house. It was no longer small and cramped like the judge's next door. The big window gave him a panoramic view out over the roofs towards Scotsman's Bay. And as he leaned closer, he could get a bright blue wedge of sea. And a white sail. His desk was where he wanted it, a slab of wood, sanded and oiled. He'd need to get a chair. And bookshelves along the walls. But that could all wait. Later today, he thought, he'd go down to the basement and start to shift some of the boxes.

'Mick, you there?' He heard Ian taking the stairs two at a time. He ducked into the room. 'What do you think? The desk, is it OK?'

'Yeah it's great. I really like it.' McLoughlin grinned at him. 'It's just what I wanted. Now all that's missing are the bookshelves. When are they going in?'

Ian grimaced. 'Well, not sure. I'm hoping to be out of here by the end of the week. I've another job waiting.'

'Oh, that's a pity. I really need them. All my books, the boxes in the basement,' McLoughlin hoped he was looking suitably disappointed. So disappointed he might hold off on his last couple of payments. 'I did mention them, a good few times, I'm sure you remember.'

Again the grimace. 'Yeah, well,' Ian shifted awkwardly, 'didn't really budget for the extra time, you know?'

McLoughlin said nothing. He stared fixedly at the floor. A beautiful floor, it had to be said. The same dark Iroko which was laid in all the other rooms. No sign now of where the iron bedstead had once stood.

'Look, tell you what,' Ian was shifting anxiously. 'One of my guys, Maciek, you know him? The demon with the sledgehammer.'

McLoughlin knew him all right.

'He's always looking for nixers, extra money to send home to the wife. I'll tell him to talk to you. He'll see you right.' Ian winked in an exaggerated way. 'OK?'

They walked down through the house. Ian shoved his hand in his pocket and produced an invoice.

'If you could pay me, that'd be great.' He smiled, a charming smile. 'Then we'll only have the painting and the downstairs toilet to deal with.'

They walked into the kitchen. McLoughlin pulled out his chequebook. Ian handed him a pen. He watched as McLoughlin began to write.

'I'll miss this old place. It's been a nice job.' Ian looked around. 'Exciting too, not everywhere you work where there's a murder next door. And you start helping the guards with their enquiries.'

McLoughlin looked at him over his glasses.

'Yeah, the lady cop was around the other day,' Ian folded his arms.

'Yeah?'

'Yeah, she was asking about cars we might have seen and she'd a few photographs, mugshots, you could say.'

McLoughlin nodded, signed his name and handed it to him. 'So, were you able to tell her anything?'

'Nah,' Ian glanced down at the cheque, folded it and put it carefully in his top pocket. 'Not much. One of the guys looked kind of familiar, chubby, red hair and freckles. And I definitely recognised one of the cars. A silver Toyota SUV. We had a bit of a run in, a few weeks ago, when you were in Italy.'

'Yeah?'

'Yeah, we were expecting a skip one afternoon. Someone had parked in the space. Maciek went out to ask the driver to move. But he wasn't there, so we'd all kinds of hassle.' He turned to leave. McLoughlin followed him.

'So, she got him from the car? Did you have the licence plate?'

Ian shook his head. 'Nah, we weren't that organised. And after he left we were able to get the skip driver to come back. And that,' Ian smiled, 'was all we were worrying about.'

She'd need more than a vehicle identification, McLoughlin thought as he waved good bye to Ian who sauntered away, whistling. He hoped for her sake she could stand up her evidence. He knew from bitter experience how bad it was to be found wanting. The case of Mary Mitchell, all those years ago. He'd made a mess of the investigation. Never fogotten it.

He opened the front door and walked down the steps into the front garden and pulled out his keys to unlock the basement. Better get on with starting to move. All that stuff. He'd lived without it for months. He was beginning to wonder; did he need it any of it now?

The front room was filled with boxes. He picked up one marked 'kitchen stuff'. Half opened it. Saw inside a packet of coffee. He could hear Ferdie barking loudly. McLoughlin grabbed the coffee and pulled back the door. He stepped out into the sun. The old lady from across the square was standing by the gate. She was dressed for a cold day, with a heavy paisley shawl around her shoulders. McLoughlin noticed that her right hand, as she rested on the railings, was shaking badly, and her face looked even more pale than usual. She smiled as she saw him.

'I'm feeling a little light-headed. Could I sit on your steps for a moment?' Her voice was tremulous.

He took her arm. 'Why don't you come in? You can be my first official visitor.'

'Oh,' she looked up at the house. 'Is it finished?'

'Just about. I've no proper furniture, but I do have some nice garden chairs.' He picked up the box. 'Take my arm and we'll go up and have, what would you like? Tea or coffee?'

'Thank you, coffee would be lovely,' she smiled. 'I don't think we've met properly. My name is Gwen Gibbon. And you are Michael McLoughlin, aren't you?'

'Well done, you're right.'

They walked together through the kitchen. He opened the door to the deck and sat her down at the small table. She held onto his hand.

He went back into kitchen and busied himself with kettle. His phone beeped. A text from Dom. *In Vincent's A&E with Joanne. She fell. Possible skull fracture. Good news re Waterford. Something else to tell you. Can't talk now. I'll try you later.*

'Now,' McLoughlin spooned coffee into the glass jug, poured boiling water onto it and carried the jug, and mugs out onto the small table. 'Sorry to take so long.' He smiled down at her.

'That's fine. No need to apologise. I'm enjoying being here. I haven't been in this house for many, many years.'

He sat beside her. He poured coffee.

'No milk I'm afraid.'

She smiled. 'I like it black. It makes me feel young. Sugar?' she looked over at him.

'Oh, sugar,' he stood, 'now, I think the builders may have a stash somewhere. Hold on while I go and look.'

They sat on the garden chairs in the sun. Gwen had added two heaped spoons to her mug of coffee. She stirred it vigorously.

'I know nowadays sugar's considered to be some kind of poison, but,' she delicately licked the corners of her lips, 'I love it. When we were children most of our sweet things were homemade. My mother made fudge and toffee and as a special treat we were allowed to buy, can you imagine, buy, a piece of honeycomb.'

'You've lived here for a long time, I take it?'

She nodded. 'Forever really. Forever and a day as the song says.' She sipped her coffee. 'Shopping in the town when I was young, it was wonderful. I remember, Saturday mornings, mornings like this, the sun shining, not a care in the world and going with my mother,' she paused for a moment and wiped her lips with a small white handkerchief. 'It really was the butcher, the baker, the candlestick maker. You know, in those days they'd deliver. I remember a boy on a bicycle coming with a tin of pepper. '

'Yes,' McLoughlin stretched out his legs. 'My father was from near here. He'd talk about all the old shops. And I remember my Aunt Bea, there was a hat shop she worked in. Not sure where that was.'

'When I was at school, my best friend, Pam and I, we used to love trying on hats,' Gwen pursed her lips, 'but the shop here, the hat shop, it was owned by a Protestant family,' she paused and fiddled with the sugar spoon, 'and they didn't employ Roman Catholics. They'd have nice Church of Ireland girls up from the country. They'd live in. Actually, to be honest, many of them weren't treated well. They went to our church on Sundays, and they all looked miserable. Half starved, pale and thin.'

'Really?' McLoughlin looked at her. 'You mean my lot didn't have a monopoly on abuse?'

She smiled. 'Human nature I'm afraid.' She picked up her mug. 'Any more? I'm feeling much better.'

McLoughlin lifted the jug and poured.

'Actually,' she took the spoon and stirred again, 'I remember one of those girls running away. She was going out with a Roman Catholic boy. It was a bit of a scandal. She was friends with the Lane girls.'

'The Lane girls?'

'Yes, the people who lived in this house. I knew them well. The Lanes. Richard Lane, their father, he was a junior manager in Lees, which was the big drapery shop, on the corner.'

The big shop on the corner. Solid, red brick, wooden floor which bounced when you walked on it. Wide mahogany counters, polished. Drawers filled with socks and underwear. Shop assistants, clean white shirts, dark ties, suits, hair slicked back. Bolts of cloth and rolls of ribbon. Shoes, brown and black in neat rows.

'Actually I don't remember Mr Lane. He died before I was born.' Gwen leaned back in the chair which wobbled dangerously. McLoughlin watched her anxiously.

Works in Lees. Every morning at 8.30 he walks along the Square, good morning, good morning, good morning, down to the main street, the town spick and span. The post boxes painted red. He lifts his hat to the ladies as he passes. His suit is pressed. His shoes are shined. He has a white handkerchief in his top pocket. He stops to buy a paper, The Irish Times at the newsagents on the corner. Buys a packet of cigarettes, Craven A with the black cat. Scans the front page. The news isn't good. IRA attacks, army responses. But safe here, in the Pale. The town supports the King. Still.

'Yes, he died before I was born. 1921. His poor wife was pregnant with Cecily. Cecily, now, she'd have been about the same age as me.' Gwen swirled the coffee in her mug.

He walks along the main street. It is July, high summer, warm, so he feels hot in his starched collar, his tie, his jacket, his trousers. He doffs his hat, hallo, good morning, good morning. The children are on holidays. Harry who is ten, Bobby who is eight, Jean who is five, Marjorie who is two and his wife, Elsie, has just told him that she is expecting again. This afternoon she will take the children to the park and then down to Sandycove where they will paddle.

'Well I suppose,' again McLoughlin stretched out his legs and raised his arms above his head. 'Well those days, life expectancy, it wasn't what we're used to. No antibiotics, TB, rheumatic fever.'

She shook her head. 'It wasn't anything like that. He didn't die that way.'

Richard turns into the shop. The morning passes slowly. It's a quiet day. Then just before they close for lunch two men come in. Richard recognises one of them. He comes from the cottages down by the harbour. He approaches them but they brush past. They rush through the shop towards the door that leads to the yard behind. And then two policemen appear at the counter. One of them asks Richard, 'Have you seen a couple of men here?'

'Yes,' Richard replies. He doesn't notice the way some of the assistants and the customers turn their faces away. Pretend to be busy. Pretend they have seen nothing.

'Yes,' he says, 'two men. Paddy Keane was one of them.'

'And where did they go?' The policeman asks.

'They went that way,' says Richard and he points, out into the back. And the policemen run. Richard hears shouting. And the next thing the two policemen come back. They rush around to the side of the building. People stop in the street and watch. More policemen come and eventually everyone sees, the men from the shop, handcuffed.

Richard goes home for lunch. He goes home for lunch every day. Elsie makes soup. Richard has his lunch. He reads the paper. He has a snooze in his chair. He goes back to work.

'No?' McLoughlin looked at her. She turned her face away.

'We don't talk about it much. We're careful who we tell.' Her voice dropped to a hush.

Richard leaves the shop at a quarter to six. He always leaves at a quarter to six. The Angelus bell is ringing as he walks along the main street. He sees people stop, bless themselves. He gets home in time for dinner. Elsie minces the leftovers from Sunday's roast. She makes Shepherd's Pie. For pudding afterwards she stews apples, served with custard. After dinner the children go out to the square to play. Richard helps Elsie with the washing-up. Tomorrow Mrs Hegarty will come and clean the house from top to bottom. Mrs Hegarty is a good worker. Richard isn't sure about her son. He thinks Dan's getting mixed up in all kinds of trouble. He's seen men coming out of the basement next door where the Hegartys live. He saw Paddy Keane from the cottages a few times.

Elsie goes to call the children in from the square. It's so bright outside. They don't want to come. They sit at the kitchen table for their supper. A glass of milk and a piece of bread and dripping. And then, there is a knock at the door. Richard goes to answer it. Elsie hears voices, loud voices in the hall. She puts her head out to look. She sees men. They are dragging Richard away. She sees men she knows.

Richard shouts, 'Don't worry, dearie, I'll be back soon.'

'Yes?' McLoughlin looked at her. Her face was pale again.

'You see, it was the IRA, they took him.'

They take Richard out into the square. It's quiet now. All the children are inside. A horse-drawn cab is waiting. They push him into it. He tries to resist and one of the men hits him on the head with a heavy stick. Blood drips down his face. He slumps forward. The cab drives off.

'Took him?'

'Yes,' she nodded. 'Took him.'

Elsie waits up. She falls asleep in Richard's chair in the parlour. She wakes in the cold light of dawn.

'Richard,' she calls his name.

There is silence. Silence for four days and then a boy walking his dog on Killiney Hill finds the body of a man. His hands are tied. There is a jagged wound in his face and the marks of a beating on his body. A policeman comes to tell Elsie.

'Why,' she screams as the children crowd around and begin to cry, 'why?'

'Why?' McLoughlin sat up straight and looked at her. Gwen shrugged. She gazed out at the garden.

'The word in the town was that he was an informer. Because he had told the policemen about the men in the shop. They said he was being paid by the Castle. That he was keeping information on people.' She shifted in her seat.

People from the town stood outside the house. They shouted nasty things. Someone put a rat through the letter box. Some of the neighbours decided to go. They were frightened. The relations in Belfast would help. There was a cousin in London. A cousin in Bristol. An aunt and uncle in Londonderry. They would go.

'So the family, what became of them?'

Gwen got to her feet. 'I've said enough. I'm tired. I think it's time to go home.'

'Of course,' he stood too. 'Here,' he held out his arm. She took it. He folded her hand over his forearm and guided her back into the house. They walked through the hall. He opened the door. He looked over his shoulder. A woman's face. He could see her. Pale, frightened, a child at her skirts. His hand on the lock. The old lock, heavy brass. As he closed the door behind him he looked back. At the heavy brass knocker. Beneath his feet the granite front step. The boot scraper still intact. The men had stood here. They had knocked on the door. Bang, bang, bang. The door had opened. Richard Lane, aged thirty-five, junior manager in Lee's drapery, married with four children and another on the way. Dragged down the steps, these steps, where McLoughlin walked now, Gwen Gibbon clinging onto him. Stood at the bottom, over the metal cover to the coal hole, where the coal man dumped his sacks, down into the space beneath the steps. Dragged him through the metal gate, the gate which now he pushed open, which squeaked loudly, which squeaked then and Richard thought as McLoughlin thought now, I must get out the Three in One and oil it. Dragged him to the horse-drawn cab, standing where now his car was parked. Hit him when he resisted, a thump on the head. McLoughlin looked down at the ground. There would have been blood, here on the footpath, the same stone slabs now as then. The police would have come. Now they'd have taken samples, got DNA; then, he didn't know.

They crossed the road and walked beneath the trees, Ferdie running ahead.

'You know,' she stopped and looked back. 'Being called an informer. It was then and it is now a terrible slur. It made me think, when,' she paused.

'When,' he looked down. The pink of her scalp showed through her white hair, pulled back into a neat bun, held in place with long pins.

'That nice policewoman came to see me. Isn't it wonderful,' she looked up at him, a sudden smile lighting up her thin face. 'Wonderful that women can do the same jobs as men now, really wonderful.'

'Yes,' he nodded, 'and some do them better than men. You know, thorough, careful, great attention to detail.'

'Yes, she was very thorough, very well prepared. She had her computer. She put it on my table. I didn't think it would work but she knew what to do.' She started walking again, slowly, watching where she was putting her feet.

'And what did she want?'

'She showed me photographs. Said there was someone who they needed to identify. Asked me to look at the pictures and see if I could recognise anyone. And do you know,' she looked up at him, an expression of surprise on her face, 'I did. I saw someone whose face I'd seen before. And I was just about to point him out. And then I thought. Hold on a minute. What are you doing?'

'Yes,' McLoughlin nodded, 'it's a big responsibility, but it's your duty to help the guards if you can.'

'That's what she said,' Gwen nodded. 'And then she told me that they thought they might have a suspect for the murder of poor John Hegarty. So...' they had reached her gate. She reached out and grasped it and hung on tightly.

'So?'

'So, I told her yes, I recognised him.' She turned towards him. 'I was supposed to visit the judge the day he was killed. I was invited for six o'clock, but I fell, ended up in hospital. If I hadn't fallen that day, what do you think? Do you think the judge would have been killed if I'd been there?'

He took her hand and helped her along the path to her front door. 'I tell you what I think Gwen, if I may call you Gwen?' She smiled and inclined her head. 'I think it was lucky you weren't there. I think whoever shot the judge was determined to do it. Here,' he took the keys from her hand, 'it was nothing to do with you, so don't feel bad about it.' He opened the door. 'Now, are you OK? Can I do anything for you?'

She turned to him and smiled. 'I'm fine, thank you Michael for coming with me. I think I'll lie down for a little bit.'

He sat her on the sofa, found her a blanket, kissed her cheek. He left his phone number, scribbled on the margin of the phone book. He'd check on her later. Later, before he went to meet Elizabeth, to sit in her garden and have a drink. Sit in the sunshine and enjoy her company.

He walked across the square, Ferdie at his heels. As he reached the trees his phone rang. He pulled it from his pocket. He pressed the answer button.

'Hi Tom, thanks for getting back to me. You got my message. Let me explain.'

It was just after six when McLoughlin left the house for his dinner date with Elizabeth. The square was filled with children. A birthday party had spilled over from a nearby garden. He could hear Ferdie barking, faintly, and see him pressed against the front window. He was leaving him behind.

He hurried down the front steps, then stopped for a moment and looked around. Sunshine dappled through the trees, children playing, everything bright and gay. And for a moment he saw the square, all those years ago, 1921 Gwen had said, a horse-drawn cab in front of his house and the men, pushing, shoving, beating Richard Lane as they drove him to his death. He shivered and for a moment it was dark as a cloud drifted across the sun. He turned away, turned his back on it and moved into the noise and bustle of the town.

First stop, the wine bar. This evening it was full, the noise level high. Anthony greeting him with a smile, then looked around.

'No Ferdie?'

'No,' McLoughlin shook his head, 'not tonight.'

'Ah,' Anthony smiled and put his index finger to his lips, 'hot date, is that it?'

'Perhaps,' McLoughlin smiled in return. He scrutinised the shelves. 'Now, something a bit special, I think. Something cold and sparkling.'

'Now,' Anthony cocked his head to one side, 'I have just the thing.' He reached out and pulled a bottle from the chill cabinet. He wrapped it in red tissue paper. McLoughlin took the bottle, nodded his thanks, handed over his credit card. Then stepped out into the sunshine again, stopping outside the florist next door and scanning the flowers in their metal buckets. Irises, he thought. Tall, purple blooms. They reminded him of Elizabeth.

He walked back through the town, looking for the turn to Elizabeth's street. And saw how he was outside the shop where Richard Lane had once worked. He could see himself in the plate glass windows. Bottle in one hand, flowers in the other. He straightened. He didn't look too bad. He'd found the iron and the ironing board and pressed his linen jacket. He'd put on his navy blue linen trousers and polished his shoes. But as he stood and looked at himself, a shadow crossed over his reflection. A man, younger than him, smaller, thinner. Short dark hair slicked back from his forehead. Neat and tidy in his dark suit, a white handkerchief in his breast pocket. And the vinyl and plastic of the new shop giving way to the chrome and wood of the old one. The ring of the till and the click of shoes on the hard floor. The men rushing in from the street.

McLoughlin walked around the corner. He could see where the building ended. Where the small yard began. No way out. Trapped, they would have been. The wall high, well over ten feet. As he stood and looked he could imagine their shouts, see the men of the Dublin Metropolitan Police with their caps and their whistles and their truncheons. And a crowd gathering to watch.

It wasn't far to Elizabeth's house. Tucked in beside the Mariners' Church. Pots with nasturtiums trailing over the front steps, scarlet, orange and yellow. And the door painted a glossy black, with a brass knocker, letterbox and around the doorknob a beautiful brass sunburst. As he leaned forward to inspect it, the door opened.

'You're here,' Elizabeth put out her hand and drew him in. 'We're in the garden.'

He held out the bottle.

'Thanks,' she took it and ran her fingers over the tissue paper. 'Great, it's cold. I'll get glasses.'

'Take these too, they probably need water.' He held out the irises. She smiled, then leaned forward and kissed his cheek. Her touch was gentle.

It was warm in the garden, the limestone paving giving back the sun. The beds were filled with flowers, Elizabeth's colours, he thought. Oranges, reds, crimsons, purples, dark blues. He recognised the same poppies as the ones in the judge's garden, with the black splodge in the centre. There was a scent in the evening air. Strong and sweet. He sniffed appreciatively.

'It's lovely, isn't it?' The young woman sprawled on a deck chair looked up. 'It's from the Nicotiana.' She pointed towards the tall plant, whose white, trumpet-shaped flowers drooped down. A small figure, with bouncing curls, appeared from behind the flowerbed.

'Hallo Michael,' she held out her chubby hand and he took it and bowed.

'Leah, how do you do?'

She smiled and curtseyed, wobbling as her little legs bent. 'I do fine, Michael.' She pulled him towards the chair. 'This is my mummy. And my baby brother's in her tummy. Come and say hallo.'

The young woman sat up and reached out to shake his hand. She too had curls, dark and exuberant.

'I'm Jess, I'm Elizabeth's daughter and Leah's mother.' She smiled, her mouth curving upwards, but her eyes were covered by large sunglasses. She was, as Leah had said, heavily pregnant. She fanned herself with a newspaper. 'Sit down. Do.' She pointed to a wooden bench.

They sat in the sun. Elizabeth came out from the house with a tray, the wine poured into tall glasses. McLoughlin sipped. The child played at their feet, singing to herself as she hopped and skipped and jumped.

'The baby,' McLoughlin nodded towards Jess. 'Any day now?'

'Yes,' Jess shifted uncomfortably. 'Any day now. Can't come soon enough.'

Elizabeth picked up a large envelope which was on the tray with the bottle and glasses.

'Here,' she handed it to him, 'this is from Jess.'

'Oh,' he put down his glass. 'Thanks. What is it?'

Jess sat up. 'Mum was telling me, you were curious about the history of your house. So,' she paused, 'I work in the National Archives, so I had a rummage around, found the 1901 and 1911 censuses. They're online now, but my mother said you had no Internet. There's lots of other stuff too. Quite a number of archives are available. It's fun when you start piecing lives together.'

'Thanks,' he began to pull out the pages. The usual spidery hand writing. 'My glasses,' he patted his jacket pocket.

'Oh,' she flapped her hands. 'You don't need to look at them now. Take them home, save them for later.'

'Thanks,' he said again. There was a silence, suddenly awkward. 'Your mother,' he rushed to fill it, 'she's told me about her time there, in the house, the therapists and all that.'

'Yes,' Jess clambered awkwardly to her feet. 'She would.'

McLoughlin got up to help her, but she brushed him away. As she stood her pregnancy was very apparent.

'Are you all right, love?' Elizabeth stood too.

'I'm fine,' Jess's tone was cool. 'We'll go now.' She took Leah by the hand. 'Nice to meet you, Michael. Enjoy your dinner.' They moved towards the house. Elizabeth made as if to follow. 'It's all right, Mum, you stay here,' she called over her shoulder.

'I'll phone you tomorrow, and if you need anything this evening...' Elizabeth's voice trailed away.

'Don't fuss, I'm fine.' Jess didn't look back.

'Bye bye Biddy,' Leah waved her little hand as she trailed in her mother's wake. They disappeared from sight into the darkness of the house. Elizabeth lifted the bottle.

'You'll have another,' she poured. McLoughlin could see a shadow across her face.

'Are you all right? Was it something I said?' He looked at her closely. She was dressed this evening in black. A long tunic made of some kind of stretchy material which clung to her body. A thick rope of turquoise was around her neck. Gold bracelets clinked at her wrists. She was wearing sandals which reminded him of gladiators. Straps around her ankles and across her instep. She looked beautiful, exotic, unusual, and suddenly very sad.

'No, it's not you. It's just that Jess and I have a difficult history. She blames me for, well…' A tear dripped down her cheek. He reached over and brushed it away with his thumb.

'But you're so good to her, the way you look after Leah,' he sipped his wine. The bubbles fizzed in his mouth.

She shrugged. 'I try, but there are some things, you know,' she raised her glass, 'anyway, to tonight.'

He reached over and clinked his glass against hers.

'Tonight.'

They sat at a table by the window. The restaurant was full but not crowded. McLoughlin watched Elizabeth. She was sitting back in her chair. All the earlier tension and sadness gone from her face. She twirled her wine glass in her fingers, then drank.

'This is lovely. You are clever. I'm useless at choosing from a wine list,' she took another swallow, 'this is truly delicious. What is it?'

'It's an Alto Adige from the north of Italy.'

'Where you saw,' she paused, 'him, James Reynolds?'

'Yes, not far from there,' he sipped. 'Now, here come our starters. Fantastic.'

The waiter leaned down, a large platter in his hands. McLoughlin had ordered sardines. Grilled black, garnished with nothing but a wedge of lemon. He bent over them and sniffed.

'Mmm, love that smell. Problem is they're hard to cook at home. The smell clings to everything.'

Elizabeth moved her napkin. The waiter laid a dish with half a dozen oysters in front of her. 'Lovely. This is wonderful.' She smiled at him, picked up the first one. He watched as she swallowed it down. He watched her throat.

'Good?' He cut into the fish.

'Very good.'

He picked a bone from his mouth.

'If you don't want to cook the sardines inside you should get a barbecue. If the weather stays like this, you'll want to eat outside.' She swallowed another oyster. 'I have one. I don't use it that often. I'm not much of a cook. You can have it.'

'Really? That's nice of you. But only,' he paused, a forkful of fish suspended in front of him.

'Only?' She held out her glass for more.

'Only if you'll come and eat with me. It's no fun on your own.'

'On your own?' She sat back and looked at him. 'You must have lots of friends.'

He shook his head. 'Not really. Guards, you know, they've plenty of acquaintances, people they've worked with, spent time with, in all kinds of difficult situations. But,' he put down his knife and fork, 'when you leave that world, you walk away. And if you look back over your shoulder, it's gone.' He lifted the bottle. 'So it would be good to cook for you. And I promise, I'll lay down, isn't that what they call it? I'll lay down a supply of this.'

'Done,' she clinked her glass against his. 'Again, lovely, thank you.'

McLoughlin sat back in his chair. The room had a high ceiling and long windows which looked out now towards the harbour. And he saw, as he sat, the glass in his hand, the way it had been all those years ago. When it was the railway station. Throngs of people coming up the wide granite steps, through the open doors, queuing for tickets at the counter which was now the bar. And a woman, dressed in black, her face pinched and drawn, her belly swollen with pregnancy and a cluster of children at her side.

It was dark by the time they left the restaurant. They'd both had steak, with skinny French fries and a salad. McLoughlin had skipped dessert. Elizabeth chose the lemon tart with vanilla ice cream. He watched her eat. The methodical way she cut it in pieces with the edge of her fork, then picked up the few crumbs left over with the tip of her index finger. She looked happy, relaxed, at ease.

They walked across the road, towards the row of bars along the seafront, lights strung in a bright ribbon above the tables.

'Here,' McLoughlin gestured. 'We'll have a nightcap, what do you say?'

She smiled and nodded. They sat down. McLoughlin ordered, coffee and brandy.

'I shouldn't,' she smiled at him, 'but you know what? I will.'

McLoughlin felt in his inside pocket for his wallet. He pulled out the envelope Jess had given him. He laid it on the table. He tapped it with his hand.

'Nice of your daughter to do this for me.'

Elizabeth nodded. 'You can get a lot of that information online, but I told her how you were in the middle of renovations.' She picked up her coffee cup. 'That house, it means a lot to so many people. It has quite a history.' She sipped.

'Yes, I was talking to the old lady who lives across the square today.'

'Gwen Gibbon?'

'Yes, we had quite a chat. She told me an extraordinary story. About the man who was murdered by the IRA, back in 1921.' He looked around. It was busy here still, even though it was nearly midnight. All the tables were crammed with people. A jazz quartet had set up under an umbrella. The music drifted towards them.

'Richard Lane? She told you the story of Richard Lane?' Elizabeth crossed her legs, jiggling her feet to the rhythm.

'Yes, I didn't know about him.' He leaned towards her. He slipped one arm across the back of her chair. 'But now, it's as if when I'm in the house or wandering around,' he gestured, 'through the town, I feel as if I can see him and his wife and children.'

She took his hand. 'I'm sure you don't believe in ghosts, but there are many ways of being haunted.' Her touch was warm.

He smiled. 'It's an odd kind of coincidence. My father murdered by the IRA, and the family from my house, the same kind of tragedy visited on them too.'

She put down the glass. 'Our history, you'd wonder if we'll ever really move on.' She squeezed his hand. He moved closer and his lips brushed her cheek. As he heard his name being called, and a shadow falling over their table. He looked up. Liam Hegarty was standing beside them.

'I thought it was you,' Hegarty's voice was suddenly loud. 'I've called you a number of times today.'

Elizabeth pulled away. McLoughlin sat back in his chair.

'Ms Fannin,' Hegarty made a formal bow. 'I see you've met our new neighbour.'

She nodded.

'You're a good judge of character. Used to peeling back the layers and seeing the essence of a man. So, what do you make of him?' Hegarty swayed gently. And the woman at his side, not his wife, McLoughlin noted, grabbed hold of him.

'Liam, we should go.' Her voice slurred, just enough to be noticed.

'Yes,' McLoughlin stood up. 'You should go. I've told you. I'll be in touch when I'm ready.'

'Ready? When you're ready? What about me and what I need?' Hegarty was beginning to shout.

'Liam,' the woman took his arm. She was young enough, McLoughlin noticed, to be Hegarty's daughter. 'Not here, not now.' She looked around.

'Not here, Mr Hegarty, not now. Your friend is right. I'll be in touch.' McLoughlin held out his hand and took Elizabeth's. She stood and turned away. She pulled her hand free and began to walk. McLoughlin noticed faces, greedy under the lights, watching, listening. He moved after her. Then looked back. Hegarty and the woman had gone.

'What was all that about?' She stopped and turned to face him

McLoughlin shrugged. 'Just, something, just, I can't really,' he paused.

'I think it's time I was going home.' Her voice was cool.

'I'll come with you.' He felt sick, lost.

'No, really, there's no need. It's not far.'

'Please,' he didn't want to sound desperate. 'I'd like to.'

They stood at Elizabeth's front door. She had opened it and stepped inside. He wasn't sure whether to follow. He felt awkward, adolescent. He moved into the hall. He leaned forward and kissed her, first on her cheek, and then on her mouth. She pulled back. She put her hands against his chest.

'I've had a bit too much to drink.'

'Really?' He smiled. 'I have too, it's great.'

'Not for me. Not now. I'd like to ask you in, but,' she moved away, 'I've had a wonderful time. A really lovely time with you—'

'Look, I'm sorry, that business with Liam Hegarty, it's just,' he interrupted.

'It's just,' she shrugged and looked down, 'don't misconstrue what I'm saying. I like you very much, but.'

'It's OK Elizabeth, I know what you mean,' he was trying not to show his disappointment. 'I'll go.'

He turned away. And noticed. A small drawing. Framed. A child with curly hair.

'Leah, I presume?' He reached out to touch it. 'Or is it her mother? Those curls are unmistakeable.'

'Actually,' Elizabeth's face was unreadable, 'it's neither. It's a drawing of Ben Bradish, when he was a child. He gave it to me many years ago.'

'Oh,' his hand dropped to his side. 'I see.'

'Yes, I think perhaps you do.' She looked as if she was going to cry. He took her hand. It was cold. He squeezed it gently.

'I'll go, but I haven't forgotten. Your offer of the barbecue. I'll take you up on that.' He needed another drink. As he walked down the front steps his phone began to vibrate in his pocket. He pulled it out and scanned the screen. Four missed calls from Dom Hayes. And Hayes calling him now.

They sat as usual on Dom's big leather sofa. Dom had poured him a beer. He drank as he watched the news. The RTÉ digital channel, which played and replayed over and over again.

'I called you as soon as I saw it,' Dom looked exhausted. His face was pale, his eyes bloodshot, dark circles beneath them. He picked up the remote and raised the volume. McLoughlin recognised the road, the high wooden gate, the house, the garden. Now it was filled with police, their white overalls gleaming in the afternoon sunshine.

'How did they die? Did it say?' He put down his glass. He felt sick.

'Not on the news, but I got in touch with a mate in the area. Single shots to the back of the head. One thing though,' Dom put down his glass and rubbed his face.

'Yeah?'

'They found a dead cat beside their bodies. Someone had disembowelled the poor creature.'

McLoughlin could see the cat and the woman. Standing among the courgette plants. Silhouetted against the sun. The woman, like a scarecrow, the hat, the clothes hanging from her body, the cat rubbing itself against her legs.

He listened to the voiceover. There was a description given of the two people who had been killed. And old black and white photographs. Theresa Ryan, MacFeeley as she was then. Young and pretty, long black hair down her back. Footage of her being led from the court in Belfast when she was convicted of terrorist offences. Holding up her handcuffed wrists, giving the black power salute. And photos of her son, a small boy at the beach. A bucket in one hand and a spade in the other. Interviews with her neighbours. A nice woman, they said, we'd see her at Mass and shopping in town. She got involved with fundraising for the local hospice after her husband had died there. Her son was a good worker. Small builder. Played for the local GAA team when he was younger.

The crime reporter stood in front of the gate. The state pathologist, Dr John Harris, was expected soon, he said. He would make a preliminary examination at the scene and a post-mortem would take place at Waterford General Hospital.

'You got in touch with Donnelly, I take it.' Dom drained his glass and got up, heading for the kitchen. He pulled open the fridge, took out a couple more bottles, holding them up and gesturing.

'I told him.' McLoughlin lifted his glass and nodded. 'He said he'd go and see her. He said it sounded good. For the first time he said, maybe they'd be able to proceed against Reynolds. Put together a strong enough case so they could apply for extradition. It'd take a while but, well, patience, a virtue and all that.' He drank.

'I can't fucking believe it,' he put down his glass, 'after all these years.' He covered his face with his hands. He wanted to cry, but no tears would come. There should be tears for Theresa and her son, he thought. He tried to put himself back there, the vegetable garden beautiful in the sunshine, the woman with the red hair and the cigarette between her fingers, the cat sleeping on her knee, and her son, sitting close, protecting his mother, pulling her to him. But unable to shield her from the horrors that lay ahead. McLoughlin couldn't bring himself to imagine what they had suffered, but the pictures came unbidden.

Dom padded slowly back to the sofa. He sat down heavily. He poured. Silence in the room. The sounds of the street audible now. McLoughlin waited for the beer to settle in the glass. Dom shifted beside him.

'It makes sense. I couldn't figure it out before but now it makes sense.'

McLoughlin lifted his glass. 'Make sense? What makes sense? Nothing makes sense to me.'

Dom looked away. 'So much going on with Joanne. I should have told you before, immediately,' he drank

'Immediately?' McLoughlin looked at him.

Dom sighed. 'Get my laptop will you?' He pointed to the table. 'I'm so tired. I can't move.'

McLoughlin stood. He walked over and picked up the computer. He sat down again on the sofa. Dom took it, and opened the lid. His hands moved over the keyboard.

'You told me about the Irish bar in that little town. You described, if my memory serves me right, the woman you met, Reynold's Italian wife. Well,' Dom turned the screen towards McLoughlin, 'this is her, right?'

McLoughlin looked. The website he had seen before. Irish pubs in Italy. The Shamrock Bar, the street, the town. A photograph. The good looking blonde woman, standing outside, a glass of Guinness in her hand. Her name. Monica Di Spina Reynolds. A short statement in English. 'My husband is Irish and I am Italian. We are very happy to welcome everyone to our bar. We offer Irish hospitality with Italian style and service. *Céad míle fáilte agus buon giorno.*'

Dom clicked again. 'And would you say that this is also the same woman?'

McLoughlin looked again. The screen showed a series of articles about the Red Brigades. The scourge of Italy in the 1970s. They kidnapped and murdered the former prime minister, Aldo Moro. They caused havoc. Robberies, gun battles in the streets, anarchy. Eventually it all came to an end in the 1980s. Their top people went to prison, their ideology discredited. There were some photographs too. One of the leaders, Antonio Di Spina and his daughter Monica. Taken when he was released from prison in 1986.

McLoughlin lifted his glass. 'Would you look at that?'

'So?' Dom smiled at him. 'What do you think? Where did she tell you she met Reynolds?'

McLoughlin drank. 'Barcelona she said. She chatted away. Made me a cup of tea. Talked about her husband and his friends from Ireland. Their son, studying in Rome. Very friendly, very open. Not a hint of secrecy.'

'Hiding in plain sight, I'd say. Easier to keep the big secrets when you open up about the little things.' There was silence for a moment. Outside a siren whooped, and there were shouts from night-time revellers in the street.

'So,' McLoughlin tapped the screen, 'how come you found this? What made you have a look?'

'Oh you know. Too much time on my hands. So I idle away clicking here, clicking there, following this link and that. And bingo.' Dom closed the laptop and pushed it aside. 'But what I really wanted to tell you, the really important thing I should have told you, would have told you if all this stuff with Joanne hadn't kicked off,' he pointed towards the balcony, the telescope. 'The other evening, I'm sitting out there, Joanne's watching *Peppa*, the boat's just come in, so I'm scanning the crowd, not paying much attention and suddenly I see her.'

'Her?' McLoughlin sat up straight. 'Her, the wife? When?'

'Let me see, it must have been the day you went to see the Ryans. After we'd had that conversation.' Dom shifted, then stood up and stretched. He began to walk slowly around the room.

'Jesus, do you think?' McLoughlin looked up at him.

'Who knows? I saw her walk away from the terminus. She got into a car, a black SUV. I didn't get a licence plate and I didn't see anything after that.' He picked up his glass and drained it. 'Now. I'm wrecked, more wrecked than you can imagine. I'm away to bed, but you stay if you want.' Dom stood, walked into the kitchen and turned on the tap. 'Oh, and by the way, the arrest, the judge.' He filled a glass with water. 'Did you hear?'

McLoughlin stood too. He shook his head. 'Nothing. I phoned Min but she didn't pick up.'

'Well, I heard that it's Stevie O'Leary, Brian's baby brother.' Dom drank. He wiped his mouth with the back of his hand. 'I hear it's not going well. They got something off Brian's phone, the one they confiscated in Portlaoise. Something which should have been incriminating. But they can't stand it up.' Dom rinsed the glass and put it on the draining board. 'Anyway, I've had it for tonight. Stay if you want. That business about Reynolds' wife. In the light of what happened to the Ryans, well, you should pass it on.'

'Thanks. I will,' McLoughlin pulled his phone from his pocket. 'I'll do it now.'

'Text him, he'll do nothing about it until the morning anyway.' Dom lifted a hand as he turned towards his bedroom. McLoughlin shrugged. Dom was probably right. His fingers clicked the letters. *Tom, something you need to know. James Reynolds' wife has been seen in Dublin. Her name is Monica Di Spina Reynolds. She has terrorist connections. Call me first thing.* He pressed send.

He should go home really, but he couldn't face it. He didn't want to be on his own. He thought of Elizabeth. He'd hoped tonight would be the start of something, but Liam Hegarty's intervention hadn't helped. The woman with him, blonde hair swept up, short skirt, tight skimpy top, young enough to be his daughter. Her hand on his arm, the easy familiarity. It left a sour taste.

He should go home, but he couldn't face the empty house. He could imagine Elizabeth, sitting in her kitchen, warm and comfortable, the door to the garden open and the scent of the flowers hanging in the night air. She had her family to love and care for. Her work, her clients. She was admired and respected. She didn't need him.

'Stop,' he said out loud. 'Stop the self-pity.' He sat down on the sofa and turned on the news channel. He watched the report over and over again. He shouldn't have gone there. He should have left them alone. There was enough pain in their lives already. He had meddled. He had disturbed the equilibrium. And they had paid for it.

The house behind the high evergreen hedge. But open at the back. He'd said to her, if I can get in so can anyone. And she'd said they didn't frighten easily. He tried to think, to remember. He'd driven along the road from Waterford. Hardly any traffic. The clatter of a tractor in the distance. Houses, scattered, big gardens, farmland. We all knew her, the woman in the town had said. We knew her husband and her son. Her habits, her routines, her visitors. Who came to see her. All it took was a slight deviation from the norm. And he had been that deviation.

He looked towards the plate glass windows. He had a sudden desire to break something. Smash something. Hurt someone. Destroy, that was it, he wanted to destroy something. He walked around the room, watching the news report. Then he picked up the remote and turned it off. He sat down and felt in his pocket for the envelope Jess had given him. He began to read. He reached for Dom's laptop. His hands moved over the keyboard. So much information. All there if you knew how to find it. A couple of clicks and he was in.

Once upon a time there was a square in a town. It wasn't a very big town. It wasn't a very big square. The town had a harbour and two piers and a ferry which crossed the Irish Sea. It had many churches. Three were Church of Ireland. One was Roman Catholic. There was a large Presbyterian church and a small Methodist one. The town had shops and schools and a beautiful park with a long herbaceous border, tea rooms, two circular fountains and a playground. The town had the seafront, saltwater swimming baths and the terraces for sunbathing. It was a happy place. Happy and secure. And everyone knew where they belonged.

McLoughlin pored over the 1911 census which Jess had printed out for him. She had given him the entries for all the houses in the square. He flicked through them. It was immediately obvious. The majority of the occupants were Church of Ireland. And scattered through the houses, usually one for each, was a Roman Catholic. Except in one or maybe two cases, they were all servants. Described variously as domestic servant, general servant, cook, house parlour maid. And here and there were a few names he recognised. The Gibbon family, living where Gwen still lived.

He leafed through the pages and found his own house. Recognised the names. Richard Edwin Lane, aged thirty, his occupation shop assistant, draper's. His wife was Elsie Violet, aged twenty-four. They had a son, Henry, three, and a daughter, Marjorie, aged one.

And what of the house next door, the judge's house? Just one family living there. The Chamberlains. George Ashton, aged sixty-seven, was described as City Marshall, Dublin. His wife, Daisy, was thirty-eight. They had four children, Harry, fifteen, Elizabeth, thirteen, Jean, twelve, and Dorothy, six. And also living under the same roof was Mary Bridget Hegarty, aged twenty-seven, Roman Catholic, born in Castlebar, Co. Mayo, her occupation listed as cook, domestic servant. She could read and write. She was a widow. The last name on the list was one with which he was very familiar. Daniel Patrick, aged nine, Roman Catholic, student, could read and write.

So. McLoughlin could imagine: May Hegarty and her son, Dan. Down in the basement. A large house, a large family above. Clothes and bed linen to be washed, ironed and mended. Food to be prepared and cooked. Floors to be scrubbed. Rugs and carpets to be swept and beaten. Silver and brass to be polished. Windows to be washed. Stairs to be climbed. Coal to be carried. Hearths to be cleaned, fires to be lit. Days which began at dawn and ended long after everyone else had gone to bed. And a son to be reared. To be sent to school. To be educated, instructed, taught. To be brought up to better himself. But to stay true to the faith, to the country, to the people.

He got up and went into the kitchen. He stopped for a moment and listened. He could hear the sound of snoring. Poor Dom. He found a bottle of whiskey and brought it and a glass to the sofa. He sat down again, the computer on his knee. He logged onto the *Irish Times* archive. He began to search. Anything to do with the Lane family. A small piece about a prize-giving in the Mariners' School in 1916. A grainy photograph of small children. And Harry Lane's name. He won a medal for the 100 yards sprint. A news report of Richard's death, his body found on Killiney Hill. McLoughlin found his death notice. He was described as a beloved father and husband. Five years later there was a death notice for Elsie Violet Lane. *After a long illness*, it said. *Funeral to Dean's Grange. Safe in the arms of Jesus.*

Another small photograph. A group of girls standing outside a tall forbidding building. He recognised it. The orphanage three streets away, the Haven. The date was 10th June 1930, the occasion, the annual garden fete. A visit from the Archbishop. A row of girls holding bunches of flowers. He read the caption and found among the names, Jean and Cecily Lane. It was hard to distinguish their features but Cecily had long plaits hanging down over her shoulders.

In the sports section of the paper he found Harry's name again. Playing football for Sligo Rovers in 1932. A small paragraph, a news report, the death of Marjorie Anne Lane, found drowned in the Grand Canal. Foul play not suspected. In 1940 a private, Robert 'Bobby' Lane, originally from Dun Laoghaire, died at the retreat from Dunkirk. And then in 1947 another death notice. Cecily Evangeline Lane. Aged twenty-five. *Sadly missed by the Monsell family, Donnybrook.*

He poured himself more whiskey. He picked up a pencil, found a piece of paper. He scribbled some notes. Richard had died. Elsie had died. Cecily and Jean had gone to the Home. Somehow Harry had spent some time playing football in Sligo and Robert, Bobby, had Gwen mentioned him? He must ask her again. Marjorie had drowned in the canal. And then poor Cecily. Died when she was twenty-five. The Monsell family from Donnybrook, whoever they were, had mourned her. Whoever they were. He typed in the name and up came the answers. Herbert Monsell, an obstetrician, Master of the Rotunda, his wife, Isabel, sons Guy and Andrew, daughters Emily and Harriet. A recent article, a review of a book, a history of the lying-in hospitals as they were called. Photographs. Herbert was tall and handsome. A reformer. Known for his compassion to the many young women who came to the hospital, unmarried, penniless. A photograph of the Monsells at home in Ailesbury Road. A formal portrait, posed. Mother and daughters, seated, in the front and behind them father and two sons. And a small figure to the side. Wearing a maid's cap and apron. Something about her. A look he was sure he recognised.

He got up and walked towards the sliding doors. He opened them and stepped outside. And felt rain. The sky dark, a sudden chill, the tiles wet. Rain on his face as he looked towards the sea. He was suddenly exhausted. The clock on the town hall chimed. One, two, three, four. Theresa Ryan and her son would have been moved. They'd be in the morgue, in the local hospital. The air would smell of disinfectant and bleach. No more scent of the sea and the soil. He'd phone Johnny Harris in the morning. He was sure he'd look after them properly. He would treat them with respect. Johnny was like that. A decent man.

He drained his glass and walked inside. He stretched out on the sofa. Sleep would come quickly, he thought. But he lay for a while. Twisting, turning, seeing faces, in his mind's eye. The pen and ink drawing on the wall in Elizabeth's hall. The resemblance to Leah and to Jess. The look on Elizabeth's face as she told him. What exactly had she told him? He tried to remember what she had said about Ben Bradish when they talked that afternoon in the garden.

I admired him. I respected him. He taught me a lot. I still miss him.

And before that when she told him about how Bradish had come to set up the Therapy House. He had a succession of women in his life. He never married. He'd had a number of children, each with different mothers.

He rolled over, tucking his hands beneath his arm pits. So? She had baggage. So? He had baggage. They weren't young. They weren't new to this business. She hadn't told him about her relationship with Ben Bradish. She'd never said who Jess's father was. And why should she? What business was it of his? But he couldn't stop seeing her face as he rolled from side to side. And the face of another woman. Theresa Ryan, sitting at the table in the conservatory. Surrounded by flowers. Her thin hands reaching for the tobacco, reaching for the vodka, reaching for her son.

He sighed, stretched, then slept. And woke, the sun bright in his eyes, and a hangover which got him up. Looking at his watch. Gone nine o'clock and shit, he remembered, the dog, locked in the house since the evening before. He grabbed his jacket, grabbed his phone and wallet. Stuffed the pages from the census and *The Irish Times* in the envelope, scribbled a thank you note to Dom and left the apartment, pushing through the lift doors and out into a wet Sunday morning. Cool still, almost cold, the sky dove grey, layers of cloud like cotton wool. And as he walked quickly along the seafront his phone rang. He pulled it from his pocket.

'Tom, hi, you got my text?'

He sensed scepticism in Donnelly's response. For a start, the murders of the Ryans were being investigated by the local guards. He wasn't involved at all. As for the sighting of Reynold's wife, well.

'Look,' Donnelly's voice was cool, 'in his day Dominic Hayes was the best, but you know, he's been retired for a while. He's very tied up with poor Joanne. I wouldn't be too sure…' His voice died away.

'So,' McLoughlin stopped, 'who can I speak to?'

'Well,' Donnelly paused, 'look I'll check it out, I'll get back to you.' It sounded as if he was drinking something, a cup of tea or coffee maybe. 'Look, I know what this means to you. Just when it seemed we might have something, this happens.'

'Yes,' McLoughlin felt as if he was shouting, 'yes, just when we might have got somewhere this happens. And it's not a fucking coincidence, I know that and you do too. And as far as Dom Hayes is concerned, his wife may have Alzheimer's but his head is as clear as a fucking bell. If he says he saw Monica Reynolds, then he saw her. And I want something done about it. Do I make myself clear.'

Silence, then a sigh. 'OK. Leave it with me. I'll get back to you.'

The dog was waiting just inside the front door. He jumped up, barking loudly, his tail wagging. McLoughlin let him out into the garden. Put on the kettle, made coffee. Made toast. Took his mug and his plate out onto the deck. Then walked down the steps into the garden. Looked up at the height of his house and the houses on either side. Thought of May Hegarty. How she must have worked. Up and down the stairs. Morning to night. And all the other May Hegartys in all the other houses.

He drained his mug, finished his toast. He needed some exercise.

'Come on Ferdie, walkies.' He clicked his fingers and the dog bounded ahead back up the steps, through the house to the front door, his tongue flopping, his tail wagging. He nudged the lead which was lying on the bottom step, then picked it up, holding it carefully in his mouth. Together they hurried out, across the grass towards the main road. And saw, just ahead, the thin, upright figure of Gwen Gibbon, wearing a grey skirt and a white blouse, a large black bag hanging from her forearm. The dog barked, a series of yaps and Gwen turned, a smile on her face. She bent down and patted Ferdie on his head, and he tried to jump up at her.

'Get down, Ferdie, you stupid mutt,' McLoughlin pulled him away. 'Look at him, muck all over your nice skirt.'

'Don't worry,' Gwen smiled at them both, 'this is just an old thing.'

'Well,' McLoughlin handed her his handkerchief, relieved that it was clean, 'old or new, it's very nice. You look very nice today.'

She wiped her skirt, brushing off a few stray blades of grass. 'It's my going to church outfit. Listen.'

The bell tolling slowly, regularly.

'Walk with me,' she held out his handkerchief. 'In fact, why don't you come with me. Sunday morning service, it's always a pleasure. Lots of nice hymns.'

McLoughlin grimaced. 'Not sure it's my cup of tea and anyway there's himself.' He pointed to the dog. 'Don't think he'd be too welcome.'

'Oh, don't worry about that. You've got his lead. You can tie him up to the railings outside. He'll be fine. Look,' she pointed towards the church across the road by the park, 'give it a go,' she took his arm, 'so nice to have a handsome man to escort me.' And she smiled up at him, a winsome smile which brought a shine to her eyes and colour to her cheeks.

The church was half empty, or half full, McLoughlin thought, chiding himself for his immediate negativity. The congregation was spread throughout the oaken pews. They walked slowly up the central aisle. McLoughlin genuflected, sinking reverently down onto one knee. Hadn't been to Mass apart from funerals for years, but it was a habit hard to break. Gwen didn't seem to notice. She drew him into a row, three from the front. An organist was playing quietly.

McLoughlin looked around and noticed what was missing from this church. There were no Stations of the Cross. There were no crucifixes. There were no statues of Christ, Our Lady or any of the saints. The altar was against the back wall under a large stained glass window.

His eyes wandered around and he noticed. The memorial plaques on the walls. He recognised some of the names from the census. Grace, Morton, Chapman. And a large marble tablet dedicated to the men of the parish who had died during the First and Second World Wars. A wreath of faded poppies was still hanging from it and he saw a name he recognised. Robert Lane.

'Gwen,' he whispered and pointed, 'there, Robert Lane, is he one of the Lanes from my house?'

Gwen looked up. 'Yes,' her voice was low so he inclined his head, 'he died at Dunkirk, poor boy. Those children they didn't have happy lives. Cecily in particular, same age as me. I remember seeing her here when we were both little ones. Then I didn't see her for years.'

'No? What happened?'

'Well,' she looked around, 'I shouldn't gossip really, but I know you'll be discreet. She and her sister Jean went into the orphanage, the Haven. All the children there, they became domestic servants. They were sent to respectable Church of Ireland families, when they were fourteen or so.'

The organist was playing more loudly now. McLoughlin recognised the melody. Bach, he thought it was. He put his head closer to Gwen's. He could smell lavender. She continued. 'Cecily went to a family in Donnybrook. Very wealthy. The father was a doctor, the Rotunda I think. Poor Cecily, one of the sons took advantage of her. Terrible thing to do. She became pregnant. She was sent away to England to have the baby. He was adopted.'

'Oh, I see.' McLoughlin sat back in his seat as the organ music began to swell.

'And then a few years ago Sam Dudgeon, you know my friend, who used to play backgammon with the judge?'

'Who was going with you for sherry that evening?'

'Yes. Sam. Well, he's poor Cecily's son. He had discovered he was adopted.' Gwen fidled with her hymn book, smoothing down the soft leather cover. 'That compulsion, to find where you come from, well, it brought him here. '

'To find his family?'

'Yes, but there was no one. Poor Cecily, she died young. They said it was cancer, but I always thought it was a broken heart.'

The organ was loud now, a flourish of chords. There was the clatter of shoes on the wooden floor as the congregation stood. McLoughlin resisted the temptation to turn and stare at the small procession which he could see out of the corner of his eye. It was led, he realised, by a woman. She was tall and slim. Her long brown hair flowed down her back. She was wearing white robes. Her feet peeped out beneath them. Brown feet in sandals, with scarlet painted toe nails.

'That's our new rector,' Gwen hissed, 'isn't she magnificent?'

The choir followed her up the aisle, singing. The congregation joined in. Gwen's voice was high and quavering. He tried to follow, but he could hear how out of tune he was.

The choir took their places. The rector took hers.

'Let us pray.' The rector's voice rang out. The congregation sank to their knees. McLoughlin buried his head in his hands. He heard the words of the prayers. They were, at one and the same time, unfamiliar and similar. The same words perhaps, but their delivery made him listen in a different way. As they finished Gwen grabbed hold of him and together they sat back on the pew. Then stood again. Gwen handed him a battered hymnal and pointed to the page. The organ rang out and the choir and congregation swung in behind it. Again he tried to follow the tune, but again he failed. Sunlight filtered through the windows, reds, blues and greens from the stained glass flickering across the tiles. The church was calm, the atmosphere serene. Members of the congregation came to the lectern and read the lessons. He knew the readings and the Our Father, or the Lord's Prayer as they called it. But its ending was different.

For thine is the kingdom, the power and the glory, for ever and ever Amen.

There was no communion. One more hymn, another stirring tune, played with vigour by the organist. Then the rector got to her feet and climbed up to the pulpit. She cleared her throat. She began to speak.

'Our verse today is from the gospel of John, chapter eight, verse twelve. He that followeth me shall not walk in darkness, but shall have the light of life.'

McLoughlin listened. She spoke of witness, of living according to the tenets of one's belief. Her voice was strong but not strident, powerful but gentle. Her gestures were expressive as was her face. As she finished she reminded everyone that the soup kitchen in the church hall next door, needed volunteers.

The organist began to play again. He recognised the tumbling chords of a Bach chorale as the rector, followed by the church wardens and the choir, walked slowly down the aisle. Gwen was slumped in her seat. He bent over and took her hand.

'Are you all right?'

She looked up. He could see she had been crying.

'What is it?' He pulled her gently to her feet.

She smiled. 'It's nothing really, it's just, it reminds me of my mother.' She straightened herself and picked up her handbag. 'She loved this church and that last hymn we sang,' she gestured to him to move out into the aisle, 'we sang that at her funeral.'

He stood back and let her pass.

'I'd better go,' he whispered, 'the dog, you know?'

'Not yet,' she took him by the arm. 'There's someone here you should meet.'

The man was standing by the baptismal font at the back of the church. The heavy tweed overcoat, the shopping bag at his feet, the hat in his hands, which, even today with the sun beginning to break through the clouds, were gloved.

'Sam,' Gwen waved at him. 'Sam, are you going for tea?'

He looked uncomfortable. He looked away.

'Good,' she touched his shoulder, 'I want you to meet my new friend.' She drew Michael towards him. 'Michael, this is Sam Dudgeon. I've been telling you about him. Sam, say hallo to Michael. Michael's bought the house, you know?'

The man looked at him. He didn't speak. McLoughlin held out his hand. Dudgeon didn't reciprocate. He turned away.

'I'm not staying. I'm not well. I need fresh air,' he pushed through the congregation, out through the large oak door.

'Oh,' Gwen's face fell. 'I am sorry. How rude. He's not usually like that. He's usually very sweet, very kind. Oh dear.'

McLoughlin watched the elderly man, the hat now jammed on his head, the tweed coat pulled tightly around him. McLoughlin moved slightly to get a better view. He could see now the railings where Ferdie was tied. As Sam Dudgeon approached Ferdie stood, his small body tense, alert, his face stuck forward and a sudden deep growl. Sam Dudgeon paused, then hurried through the open gate, onto the footpath, turning towards the seafront and disappearing from view. There was something about him. He remembered the photographs. There was one in particular. A group of men standing around the judge, glasses raised. The boy on the judge's knee, naked and frightened. One of the men looking away. The same beaky profile. McLoughlin put his hand on Gwen's arm.

'Gwen,' he said, pulling at her sleeve to attract her attention, so she turned away from the lady with the tight perm and gold-rimmed glasses with whom she was exchanging recipes for blackberry jam, 'Gwen.'

'Yes Michael, what is it?'

'Gwen, how well did Sam Dudgeon know Judge Hegarty?'

She began to answer, but his phone rang. He looked down at the screen. He held up his hand in apology to Gwen and turned away.

'Hi Min, what's up?'

'Mick,' her voice was sharp, anxious, 'glad I caught you. Listen, I need a favour.'

The End

McLoughlin stood in the doorway and looked into the hospital room. He recognised the man in the bed although he'd changed considerably since McLoughlin's last sight of him. Fifteen years ago, as he was being taken away to the prison van, handcuffed to an officer, his face red with rage, his mouth open, invective spilling from it.

'I'll get you, you fuckers, you think I won't, you think I can't, but you wait. You're all going to pay for this. And you, Hegarty, you smug bastard, your turn will come.'

Now Brian O'Leary lay back against the pillows, his eyes closed. His face was ashen. His freckles stood out against the pallor. There was thick grey stubble on his chin, all that was left of his once red hair. An array of monitors beeped and blinked. A tube fed into his left arm, something dripping from a bag on a stand. McLoughlin moved slowly towards him.

'Stay where you are,' O'Leary's voice was low but strong. His eyes were still shut.

McLoughlin looked around. Inside the room there was no sign that O'Leary was a prisoner. Just the two armed guards in the corridor outside.

'Get on with it.' McLoughlin wasn't going to be intimidated. 'You said you wanted to talk to me, so I'm here. Get on with it.'

He pulled a chair towards the bed and sat down.

He'd asked Gwen to look after the dog, said he'd be back in an hour. Thrust the lead into her hand, then hurried away. Min had said she'd meet him at the hospital entrance. He couldn't see her when he pushed through the swing doors and wiped his hands with the alcohol cleanser from the row of dispensers. He looked around. The large atrium was crowded and noisy. He moved further inside and saw her sitting at a round table, two mugs of coffee and a laptop at her elbow. She was on her own. She looked exhausted.

'So, what's this all about?' He sat down.

She smiled. 'Thanks for coming. Here,' she shoved one of the mugs towards him and opened the computer. She explained. The confiscation of the phones in the prison. It should have been a routine operation. There'd been too much publicity about the amount of access prisoners had to them. The Minister wanted it sorted. It turned into a fiasco. It got completely out of hand. There'd been a full-scale riot. O'Leary was just one of the casualties.

'He got a bang on the head but that wasn't the worst of it. He had a heart attack. He's upstairs here. Waiting for bypass surgery. Lucky, isn't he?' she gestured around, at all the other people, young and old, fat and thin, healthy and unhealthy. There was a loud buzz of conversation. She raised her voice. 'The fucker's going to be fast tracked. Skipping the queue.'

'Typical.' McLoughlin picked up the mug and sipped. It was surprisingly good.

'Anyway, there was a routine scan of all the phones. The usual stuff. Most of it was untraceable. Pay as You Go. But,' she turned the computer screen towards him, 'this was on O'Leary's. You can see why he went mental when the officers tried to take it.'

She pressed the touch pad. McLoughlin leaned forward to get a better look. It showed a room he recognised. The sofa and chairs, the glass cabinet, the pale green carpet, the portrait on the wall, and the judge, on his hands and knees. A dog's lead was around his neck. Min pressed the play symbol. The lead was jerked savagely. The judge fell forward. The lead was pulled tightly and the judge was up now, on his knees, his hands clasped tightly together. His face was red, contorted. He was gasping for breath, his mouth open. A foot kicked him, forcing him to the floor. He rolled over on his back waving his hands and feet in the air, and again the lead was pulled, tightly dragging him up into the begging position.

McLoughlin sat back. 'Incredible.' He sipped his coffee. 'So who's holding the phone? Is it Stevie? Is that who you arrested.'

Min shook her head. 'We don't know who it is. We arrested Stevie before we got this. There'd been sightings of his car in the square. In fact outside your house, and when we showed his photo around there were a few tentative identifications. The old lady who lives across from you, she said she'd seen him. She was taken with his freckles.'

She paused and cleared her throat. 'So we brought him in. But we've got nothing. We won't be able to hold him for much longer.'

McLoughlin pointed at the video. 'Pity, no sound. Is there none at all?' He reached over and pressed play again and fumbled for the volume control.

'Unfortunately no, nothing.' They watched as the scene played again. 'I've been trying to question O'Leary. The doctor won't let me near him for more than a couple of minutes and the last time O'Leary would only speak to me in Irish, and to be honest, mine isn't the best. And then he said, *"ni labhróidh mé ach le Michael McLoughlin."*'

'"I'll only speak to Michael McLoughlin," the slimy little bollocks.' McLoughlin shifted on his chair. 'It's just a delaying tactic. He's no interest in me. He just wants to string it all out.'

'Yeah of course,' she sighed. 'We have the video, but it's not much use. We don't even know if the person who filmed what happened was the same person who shot the judge. It probably was, but,' she shrugged, 'it's not evidence. So we're still up shit creek. And so…' she closed the computer lid.

'You want me to try and work my charm on him, is that it?' He finished his coffee.

She nodded, 'He's upstairs in the special care unit. I've cleared it with the docs. Look,' she picked up her mug, 'anything you can get out of him. Really, anything.'

McLoughlin sat beside the hospital bed. O'Leary hadn't moved. He was lying still, the crisp white sheets tucked neatly around him.

'So,' McLoughlin straightened. 'You told Sweeney you'd only talk to me. Get on with it.'

O'Leary stirred. '*Tá tart orm. Tabhair dom braon uisce.* 'He lifted a hand.

McLoughlin stood. He picked up the plastic drinking cup, and leaned over. O'Leary's eyes flicked open. They were large, bulbous and pale green. They reminded McLoughlin of a goat. O'Leary opened his mouth. McLoughlin held the spout to his lips. There was a gurgling sound as he sucked hard. Then gathered the liquid together in his mouth and spat. It just missed McLoughlin's shirt front.

'OK, I get it.' McLoughlin replaced the cup on the locker. 'I'll just say *slán abhaile* and I'll leave you to it.'

'What's your rush?' O'Leary smiled. 'Don't be so fucking sensitive. Sit down. Let's have a chat.'

'About what precisely?' McLoughlin hesitated, his hand on the back of the chair.

'Oh you know, this and that. And the other.' O'Leary made as if to push himself up on the pillows. His face contorted.

'The other, I'd have thought we'd want to talk about the other,' McLoughlin sat down. 'Namely the murder of Judge John Hegarty. And what that bit of video was doing on your phone. And specifically who was the guy holding the lead. Now,' he crossed his legs, 'if you can shed some light on that I'm sure Inspector Sweeney would be very pleased and possibly even grateful.'

'Grateful, now,' O'Leary stirred and smiled. 'I'd like that. *Is cailín beag álainn í.* A pretty little girl. That blonde hair, is it natural? I like pretty little girls. And I could do with a bit of gratitude. Lying here, all on my own, your thoughts turn to, well I'm sure you can imagine.'

McLoughlin said nothing. He looked at his watch. He'd give him fifteen more minutes.

'Pretty, she is, like your niece, your Constance. Nice name, Constance. After the countess was she?' O'Leary twisted around so he could see McLoughlin's expression.

'Constance, yes you're right,' McLoughlin knew better than to react. 'The countess, Madame Marckievıcz.'

'A clever girl like her namesake. A great interest in the pursuit of justice. Looks after the underdog does your niece Constance. Very helpful.' Again O'Leary smiled, this time drawing his fleshy lips back over his teeth.

'Is that right? And how may I ask did you come by this information?' McLoughlin gripped the edges of the chair tightly.

O'Leary tapped his forehead. A dull hollow sound. He giggled. The monitor beside the bed began to beep more quickly. 'She's a helpful girl, I'll say that much for her. Funny, isn't it? Mustn't have much respect for her old uncle. She's not on your side, that's for sure.'

McLoughlin could feel his jaw tightening. 'OK Brian, this is how it is. The cops have your little brother, little Stevie, and you can be sure they'll squeeze your little Stevie until his pips squeak.'

'Not for much longer. The clock is ticking.' O'Leary held up his arm, the sleeves of the hospital gown falling back so McLoughlin could see his freckles and his watch. 'I reckon he'll be out any time now.'

'You think? Tell me Brian, let me in on the secret. That video. That wasn't Stevie, so who was it? My guess it's more likely to be Martin. It's more his style. A nasty little fucker, your Martin. Wouldn't be enough just to put a bullet in an old man's brain, he'd want to have a bit of fun while he was at it.' McLoughlin's voice rose.

'Fun, you think that was for fun?' Again Brian tried to push himself up and again the monitor's beeping increased. 'You've no idea the things that Martin went through before my Ma rescued him. My Ma, she was a real mother, not like that cunt who brought him into the world. Do you know what she did, she and that useless fucker she lived with?'

'I don't know,' McLoughlin looked at his watch again. 'But you'll tell me I'm sure.'

'You're fucking right I'll tell you. They pimped Martin out. One thing I'll give them, they were fussy. None of your muck, only the best for their poor little boy. Top-notch nonces for Martin. The elites of our rotten world.' He sank back again. 'He's a clever boy, my Martin. He's done great things for the business. The girls now, I'd never have got that together. But Martin, he's always thinking ahead. Watching what's happening in the world, politics, economics, who's winning and who's losing.' Again the monitors beeped. 'He's tough too, I tell you.' Boasting, McLoughlin could hear the pride in his voice. 'You wouldn't want to cross our Martin. Some people try to take him for a ride. Like that stupid bollocks, Ed Smith. Thought he could skim the cream off the top and Martin wouldn't notice.' He began to cough. A harsh rasping sound, sucking air into his lungs.

'Smith, Ed Smith? Anything to Paul Smith?' McLoughlin leaned closer.

'A wonderful thing, paternal love.' O'Leary tried to sit up. 'Lucky his old da had something to save little Ed's miserable skin. If he hadn't they'd have been digging up bits of him all across north County Dublin.' He sank back on the pillows. His eyes closed. 'You think you're so fucking clever, but I'll tell you something and I'll do you a favour. I'll tell it to you for free.' He pulled himself up again, trying to look McLoughlin in the eyes. 'Whatever you think you know, you know fuck all. That stupid cunt of a guard, with her stupid fucking questions. Who does she think I am, that I'd finger one of my own? And as for you. Watch you squirm that's what I want. You put me away. You thought you had me. You thought I was finished, but somehow you got it wrong. Me and my kind, we haven't gone away you know. And your niece, the lovely Constance. We'll have fun with her.'

His face flushed again, beads of sweat standing out on his forehead. 'She's on our side now, Defender of the weak. '

He pulled himself up again, then collapsed back on the pillows. The alarm on the monitor shrieked. Lights flashed and the door burst open, two nurses followed by a young doctor.

'Out, leave. Now,' he shouted at McLoughlin as he bent over O'Leary. McLoughlin backed towards the door and into the corridor. Reaching for his phone. Finding Constance's number. Remembering that day in the street as she was on her way back to court. She got a call. Martin, she said. He wants to appeal, she said. He reached the lift.

'Constance,'

'Yes, Uncle Michael, how are you?' She sounded busy.

'Constance. I have to ask you, your client Martin, is that Martin Millar?'

The lift doors slid open. He stepped inside.

'Why do you want to know?' her voice was wary.

'Just tell me. The parking tickets, were they his? He's a bad guy, Constance, you don't want to get involved with a fucker like him.' He pressed the button for the ground floor.

'I'm not going to discuss my clients with you.' The line was beginning to break up. 'It's none of your business who I represent.'

'Constance, listen to me, the guy is bad, through and through.'

McLoughlin could hardly hear her now.

'Sorry Uncle Michael, but really, it's nothing to do with you.' She sounded very far away, her voice cold, distant. 'I could give you the lecture about entitlement to a defence.'

'I don't want lectures, Constance, I just want you to understand what you're getting yourself into if you take on Martin Millar. He's trouble.'

'Sorry Uncle Michael, can't hear you. Have to go.' The line went dead.

He rushed from the lift. Min was still sitting at the table, her phone to her ear. She looked up and smiled, waving him to the chair.

'Min, listen, get off the phone.' He felt as if he was shouting.

'OK,' she put it down on the table. 'Just arranging dinner for the boys. So?'

'So, I think I have it. Martin Millar.'

'We've gone down that route, Mick,' she looked for a moment as if she was going to cry. 'We did house to house with his picture. No one recognised him. We've no fingerprints, no DNA, sweet fuck all.'

'Check again, check out the parking tickets in the town for the few days before the judge was killed.' He wanted to shake her.

'Why, what did O'Leary say?' She gazed up at him. She still looked like a kid, he thought, with her fair hair scraped back from her face and no makeup. 'Did he tell you something?'

McLoughlin shook his head. 'He wanted to put the boot in, to make me feel shit. And in doing so he mentioned something he shouldn't. Just a chance.' He didn't want to tell her. The alarm going off on the monitor, the medical staff rushing in. He lifted the lid on the computer. 'Let's look at the video again. Quickly, go on.'

Min stroked the touch pad. They could see the room and the judge. She pressed the play symbol.

'Look, two things,' he paused the video. 'See, there,' he pointed towards the painting. 'Look, there's a reflection in the glass. It's faint, but you might be able to get something from it and,' he pressed play again. He could see it now. The lead around the judge's neck. It hadn't been in the house when the Guards searched it. But it was like the lead that Ferdie had found, dumped in the rubbish when they went to Paul Smith's that day. That stupid bollocks, Ed Smith, O'Leary had let it slip. Lucky his old da had something to save his miserable skin. McLoughlin could see the dog. Carrying it in his mouth, dragging it home. 'The dog lead. I have it. I'm pretty sure it's the same one. You might get lucky. There might be prints.'

They drove, in a small convoy, McLoughlin in front, Min behind, back out along the sea road towards the square. He stopped at Gwen Gibbon's flat. He signalled to Min to wait. He knocked on the door and disappeared inside. A few minutes later he was back, the dog jumping up at his side and the lead coiled, wrapped in a plastic bag. Min leaned out of her car window, her phone in her hand.

'O'Leary's dead.' Her expression was bleak. He didn't reply. 'You didn't tell me that bit. The doctor's furious. He says he's going to make a complaint.'

'Let him, I did nothing. O'Leary worked himself up into a rage. I didn't have to do a thing. Here,' he held out the lead, 'it's filthy, I'm afraid. And God knows how many people have handled it. But,' he shrugged, 'you never know. You might get lucky.'

She reached through the window and took it. 'I don't know what to say.'

'Thanks would be a good start,' he clicked his fingers and the dog sat. He clicked them again and the dog held out his paw.

'I've got someone checking the parking tickets.' She smiled at him and pushed a strand of hair back into her ponytail. 'You never know. It's the little things isn't it?' She started the car. 'Listen, I meant to say. I'm really sorry about that business in Dungarvan. I hear she was going to make a statement.'

McLoughlin nodded. 'That's what she said.'

'Do you think she'd have gone through with it? Old loyalties and all that?'

'Well,' McLoughlin could see her, standing in the vegetable garden, the cat winding itself around her legs. 'Someone thought she would. Otherwise they'd have left her alone.'

'And did I hear something about Reynolds' wife?'

'Jesus, news travels, doesn't it?'

She laughed. 'Not news. We call it intelligence.'

He stepped back.

'Look,' Min leaned out again, 'the guys in Waterford, they're circulating her photo. Someone will have spotted her.' She put the car in gear and moved slowly away. He raised a hand and watched her drive off. Beside him Ferdie whined and rubbed himself against his knee. They walked across the green and sat down on the front steps. McLoughlin took out his phone, punched in Johnny Harris's number. Heard his voice, 'Michael dear boy, what can I do for you?'

'Fancy coffee, a nice biscuit or two?'

'Sorry, too busy, a lot on as you probably know.' Silence for a moment.

'Can you tell me, I was wondering,' McLoughlin looked towards the square. Gwen had come out of her basement and was sitting in the sun in her little front garden. 'Theresa Ryan and the boy.'

'Executed, plain and simple. Hands behind their backs, shot in a kneeling position.' Harris's voice had a bleak ring.

McLoughlin swallowed hard. He couldn't speak.

'Other injuries too, consistent with what I would call torture.' Harris was brusque.

McLoughlin's mouth was filling with saliva.

'Both had extensive facial injuries. Black eyes, broken noses, broken teeth. Mrs Ryan also has what look like cigarette burns on her inner arms.'

'The cat?' McLoughlin stood and fumbled for his keys. He could feel something travelling up into his mouth. He hurried down the little path towards the basement door and unlocked it.

'We don't usually do PMs on animals, Michael.' Harris sighed loudly. 'However as a cat lover, I'm afraid I was pretty upset to see what was done to the poor creature.'

McLoughlin pushed open the door to the small toilet under the stairs. He lifted the seat and leaned over.

'Someone slit the poor thing from chin to tail, while it was still alive. Incredible amount of bleeding. Who'd have thought such a small animal could have so much blood.'

McLoughlin braced himself with one hand. He retched, again and again.

'Michael, you all right?' Harris sounded concerned.

McLoughlin coughed and spat, then sat down on the toilet. He wiped his streaming eyes with paper.

'Sorry Johnny, late night last night. Not feeling the best today.' He turned on the tap in the small basin.

'Hope it was worth it.'

McLoughlin bent over and splashed water on his face.

'Not sure to be honest. But at the moment I'm most concerned about the Ryans and what happened there.' He wiped his face again.

'Yeah, there was a lot of talk about you and your visit. The guy in charge, Liam Cassidy, the local sergeant. He's a useful sort. I'm sure he'll do what he can. Now,' Harris's tone changed, 'have to go. Full house here and it's holiday time so we're seriously short-staffed. I'll let you know if there's any more news. OK?'

McLoughlin stepped out into the hall again. The dog was lying curled up on the doormat. McLoughlin opened the door to the front room. He switched on the light. He should do something with the rest of his day. Time to start moving some of the boxes of books upstairs. He thought back over his conversation, if he could call it that, with Constance. All that bullshit about people deserving a defence. She didn't have a clue. He'd have to talk to her. Explain the dangers involved in guys like Millar.

Come on, for God's sake, get a move on Michael. He could hear his mother's voice in his ear. Stop feeling sorry for yourself.

'All right, Ma, you win,' he spoke out loud. He opened the box on the top of the pile. Cookery books. He moved it to the door. Underneath it were his favourite children's books. The William series, the Enid Blytons, the Robert Louis Stevensons. He'd kept them for the child he never had. Underneath again was a box of biographies. He ran his hand over the spines. And found, yes, he'd thought it was here, *Daniel Hegarty, A Life Examined.* The author was a well-known academic and writer. McLoughlin knew him to see. He was tall, pompous, opinionated.

McLoughlin pulled out the book. He leaned against the window, angling it to get the light. He turned to the index, flicking through the entries. And there it was. The name, Richard Lane. He found the page. He read what it said.

Lane lived with his wife, Elsie and family of four children at 10 Victoria Square, Dun Laoghaire. He was a junior manager in Lee's draper's in George's Street. The young Daniel Hegarty who lived next door had evidence that Lane was a very active anti-IRA man. Lane supplied information to the DMP about local IRA volunteers. He was instrumental in the arrest and imprisoning of the volunteers Patrick Keane and Seamus Dillon. A decision was taken that Lane posed a significant threat to the activities of the IRA in that area of south County Dublin. Under Hegarty's command Lane was removed from his house. The unit took him to Killiney Hill. He was questioned vigorously. A cheque for the sum of twenty pounds, made out to Lane, from the British administration was found in his pocket. A court martial was convened and Lane was found guilty of treason and executed. Unfortunately for security reasons it was not possible to return Lane's remains to his family. A subsequent search of Lane's house found a list of names of local members of the IRA.

A subsequent search of Lane's house found a list of names of members of the IRA. What could that mean? He tried to imagine. Perhaps something to do with his work. Bills to be paid. Deliveries to be filled. Or maybe they were right. Maybe Richard Lane was an informer. Or to put it another way, maybe he was a loyal supporter of the Crown, then the lawful authority, intent on helping the forces of law and order. Did it matter then? Did it matter, now? What did matter was that this man was kidnapped in front of his wife and family. Taken away, questioned, tortured and killed. That was what mattered.

He closed the book and put it back into the box. His hands were dusty, dust lodging in his throat, so he coughed. He needed water. He moved into the corridor. Elizabeth must have left the door to her office open. Light from the back windows was angling into the basement's gloom. He walked towards it. He had noticed small bottles of water on her desk. He picked one up and twisted the cap. He sat down in her chair and drank deeply. A file was lying beside a pile of books. The name printed neatly: Samuel Dudgeon. He opened it. There was an address. It was familiar. He lived three doors away from Paul Smith. He flicked through the pages. There was a description written in Elizabeth's clear handwriting. It was headed *Dream? Hallucination?* It described a scene.

A man is lying dead. I look at him. I hate him. I fear him. I want to destroy him. I lift the hammer. I shatter his face. I am filled with guilt. The bad things I have done. I let a boy die. I let a boy's death go unpunished. I need to make amends. I need to tell the truth. I see my mother. She comes to me. She touches my face. She looks like a child. Her hair is long and plaited. She tries to pick me up but I am heavy. I am old. She begins to cry. Tears pour down her face. A river of tears. They swirl around my feet. I see my mother. She is dead. I touch her face. It is cold. My hands are cold, frozen, white. I cannot warm my hands. They are cold now, forever. I hold up my hands. I make fists of them. My mother is dead. I see the man who took away her life. I need to punish him. I will smash his face. I will rip out his eyes, his mouth, his mouth which spoke lies. I will die rather than live with my guilt. The man comes to me. His face is shattered. I lay out the backgammon set. I pick up the dice. I have the black dice. He has the red dice, red like the blood which trickles down his face. I throw the dice. Double sixes. I play. I beat him. I always beat him. I tell him. I have beaten you.

Underneath was written. *Lewy Body dementia? Hallucinations? Delusions? Referral to psychiatrist, possible need for medication?*

The man with the shattered face. McLoughlin tried to remember. What information had been released? He was certain there was no reference to the injuries done to the judge. Certain about that. He closed the file lining it up neatly. He left the room, whistled for Ferdie and together they walked out of the chill of the basement and into the bright warmth of the summer. As his phone rang and he answered.

'Elizabeth, hi, how are you today?'

Gwen Gibbon sat on the bench in her front garden. This was, she decided, her favourite place. She had sat here so many times in the years she had lived in the square. She had seen the comings and goings. Her memory was still clear. Particularly clear about the old days, when she had lived with her mother and father and her big brother upstairs. Sunday had always been her favourite day. It had a routine and rhythm all its own. A big breakfast, bacon and eggs, toast and marmalade and tea. Church after breakfast.

She sat now in the sun. No one paid any attention to her. No one even saw her any longer. That was what happened, she knew, to women when they got old. They gradually disappeared from view. Which didn't mean they stopped noticing what happened around them. The nice policewoman had come to see her. She had shown her some photos. There was one man she had picked out. He was small and plump with red hair and freckles. She had seen him a couple of times, seen him call into the judge. And there was the other man. The handsome one. Black hair cut short. Slender waist. Blue eyes, gold-rimmed glasses, white teeth and a warm, winsome smile. The policewoman had shown her his photo too. Gwen had hesitated.

'Do you know him? Have you seen him?'

Gwen pondered. The man had brought her flowers, a bunch of sweet pea.

'I thought you'd like these,' he said. He buried his face in the blooms. 'Fantastic smell.'

The other one, with red hair and freckles, hawked, spat a lump of phlegm on the path. And the handsome young man turned to him, 'That's disgusting, Stevie, don't do that, not in front of a lady.'

'Have you seen him? Take another look.'

Gwen took off her glasses. Now his face was fuzzy, unclear. She couldn't be sure. She shook her head. She remembered as she lay on the road that Sunday, pain in her knees, tears in her eyes, she had looked up. There was a face at the upstairs window. And a minute or so later the judge's front door had opened, just a crack. A man stood there. He took a step forward and then Elizabeth was beside her. Elizabeth, bending down to help. And the door closing, the man disappearing.

'No,' she replied, 'I don't recall that face. The other one, now, I've seen him.'

She sat in the sun. She watched the people come and go. No one saw her. No one stopped to say hallo. She turned her face upwards. She closed her eyes. Another perfect Sunday.

The dog had growled at Samuel. Today, outside the church the dog had bared his teeth. Samuel had turned towards the seafront, walked as far as the pier and sat on a bench in the sun. His legs felt weak. And he wasn't sure any longer where he was. Or who he was. People passed him by. Why did no one know him? Why did no one greet him, call him by his name? There were hands on his lap, black shiny hands. They frightened him. He wanted to shake them off. He wasn't sure what, if anything, he really was. Was he a shell, a husk, the skin of a snake, shucked off, dropped on the ground, like the shape of the judge's tweed coat?

Once, long ago, he had a family here in this town by the sea. A mother called Cecily. A grandfather called Richard, a grandmother called Elsie. But that family had long gone. They had been destroyed by the man with the gun. The handsome man on the wall in the judge's house. Samuel had looked up at him. Then looked at his handsome son lying on the floor. That man knew all about blood too. And pain. And getting what you wanted no matter who got hurt. Samuel had lifted his hammer and he had destroyed that handsome face.

Now he leaned back and closed his eyes. His hands clutched the shopping bag. He was safe as long as he kept it close. No one could hurt him. He sighed. The sun danced across his eyelids. He saw shapes, squiggles, bright bursts of light. And among them he saw the face of his mother. She looked so young. She held out her arms and he ran towards them. He buried his head in her breast. He sighed and for a moment he felt happy. That Sunday feeling, that perfect Sunday feeling.

McLoughlin opened his front door. He stepped inside, the phone to his ear. Elizabeth was explaining.

'I'm sorry about last night, about the way it ended. I really had a lovely time. It was just, something about…'

'That's OK,' McLoughlin butted in. He didn't want her to ask. He didn't want to have to explain.

'Anyway,' she paused, 'I didn't ask you in last night. I felt bad about it and a bit silly, but actually,' she paused again. He could see her face, the brightness of her expression. 'It turned out to be for the best, because you won't believe what happened.'

'Go on, tell me,' he walked into the kitchen and opened the door to the garden, Ferdie rushing past him down the steps.

'Jess went into labour, just after midnight. I got a call. She asked if I could come over and stay with Leah. So of course, I had to.'

'Of course,' McLoughlin smiled. 'Of course you did.'

'Anyway, the baby was born very quickly. Just a couple of hours and they came home this morning.'

'That was quick. Don't new mothers usually stay in for a couple of days?'

'You're out of date, Michael. These days if the birth was OK they shoo them home as soon as they want to go.' He could hear the excitement in her voice.

'And everything? Everything OK?' McLoughlin moved towards the sink. He turned on the tap and grabbed the kettle.

'Yes, fantastic, a beautiful little boy. They're going to call him Benjamin.' Elizabeth's voice was firm and clear.

'Benjamin, that's a good name. And you like it?' McLoughlin didn't want to say too much.

'Yes, I like it.' She sounded calm, at ease

McLoughlin put the kettle on its stand and flicked the switch. 'And what about the lovely Leah? How is she?'

'Oh, you know. A bit overwhelmed.' Elizabeth paused. 'I offered to take her to the playground, but she didn't want to leave home. I imagine she's very keen to establish her place in the family pecking order. Big sister, and all that.'

'Yeah.' McLoughlin could just about remember what it was like when Clare was born.

'Anyway, I have to drop over to the office in a bit. An appointment with one of my people.'

'On a Sunday?'

'Yes, sometimes, needs must,' she paused, 'so I was wondering if I could call in,' she sounded hesitant, 'I really enjoyed last night.'

He smiled. The day was suddenly brighter. 'Great. I'd love to see you. Tell you what. I'm trying to do a bit of tidying up here. I'll leave the back door open. Just come up when you're ready. OK?'

'Very much OK. See you soon.' Was that a kiss she blew him? He couldn't stop smiling now. He put the phone down on the countertop and spooned coffee into the jug. He lifted the kettle. And heard a loud banging on the front door. Fuck it. He'd a horrible feeling it might be Liam Hegarty. He put down the kettle.

'OK, I'm coming, hold on a minute,' he'd better get his story straight. He hurried into the hall. The banging was loud, insistent. He took hold of the lock and twisted. As someone pushed, hard, rushing in, a gloved hand grabbing him by the throat, the other slamming the door shut. Forcing him back against the wall and before he could do anything, twisting him around, grabbing both wrists and locking them together with a heavy plastic tie. Then turning him back and slamming a fist into his face. Pain, tears filling his eyes and the taste of blood in his mouth. And the man dragging him, pushing and pulling, so he stumbled up the stairs and into the big front room.

'Gotcha,' his legs kicked out from under, a series of kicks to his ribs and his abdomen, and his ankles then, tied together. So he lay, trussed and helpless.

'Now, how does that feel, you murdering bastard? You killed him. The doctor told me. If you hadn't gone to see him he'd still be alive.'

McLoughlin tried to look up. He craned his neck. He could see polished boots. Tight trousers, long legs, a narrow waist, a blue shirt tucked in. He looked further. A thin face, high cheekbones, clean shaven, black hair cut close to the skull, round gold-rimmed glasses and an expression of anger and loathing.

'Don't look at me, you fucker,' another kick this time to the genitals. The pain excruciating, radiating outwards, taking away every other thought, every other sensation. Nothing now but the pain.

'You tormented him. He was helpless. You took advantage. You knew his heart was bad. You knew he was waiting for an operation and instead of staying away, you forced yourself onto him, plaguing him with your questions. I know what you're like.' Martin Millar was screaming now, a mixture of tears and saliva running down his face, spraying out in an arc as he spun around, his right foot held out, like a striker aiming for the goal mouth, except that it was McLoughlin's face he was aiming for and as his boot connected McLoughlin felt his front teeth shatter. More pain, more blood, then sickness, dizziness and darkness.

Light then, slowly seeping through his eyelids. He was lying on the wooden floor. He could feel the hardness beneath his cheek. He lay still. His face throbbed. He wasn't sure if he could move. A loud sound filled the room. He lay still. He listened.

Sobbing, every now and then a cry of desolation. Footsteps. He watched the boots pass him by. Stop, turn, go on. Stop, go on. Stop, turn, go on. Then a face close to his. Millar squatting, one finger poking him, first in one cheek, then taking him by the chin and twisting his face upwards.

'So, you're awake, you've had your beauty sleep. You're back in the land of the living.'

Millar stood up. He stepped over him, his foot hovering above McLoughlin's chest, above where his heart hammered beneath his ribs. He moved away and sat down on one of the old garden chairs.

'Funny furniture you have here Mr McLoughlin. Would have expected more from a man like you. A few dicky old chairs and nothing else. Sleeping on a mattress in the front room.' McLoughlin could hear the scrape of his boots on the floor. 'Reminds me, so it does, of the gaff where I grew up. Filthy hole it was. No beds, nothing to sit on, no table to eat your dinner. Sleeping on a pile of manky blankets. Stinking they were, stinking of piss and God knows what else. An old sofa, falling to pieces, in front of the electric fire, where those cunts who called themselves my ma and da used sleep.' McLoughlin could hear that Millar was on his feet again. He closed his eyes waiting for the kick, the punch. 'Filthy we were, me and my sister. At school, when we went to school, which wasn't often, the other kids would hold their noses and laugh. Hold their noses. Ooh look at them miss,' his voice rose an octave or two, 'they're filthy, dirty, manky, ooh look at them miss, they've lice, crawling all over them miss, ooh look at them, they've sores and boils and cuts and bruises. And they're stupid. Put them at the back of the room. Teach them nothing.'

Millar was crying again, deep racking sobs. McLoughlin remembered. The evidence given at O'Leary's trial. Mitigating evidence designed to show the good side of the thug in the dock. The child Millar, the child of addicts. Starved, beaten, sold for sex whenever they ran out of drugs. Eventually he and his sister were taken into care, fostered out, but Millar ran away. Found himself a haven in the large shed at the bottom of the O'Leary's overgrown garden. Taken in by Mrs O'Leary, Bean Uí Laoghaire, as the defence counsel called her. Washed, fed, nurtured by Brian, Stevie and their mother. The barrister recalled the guardianship hearing. Eleven-year-old Millar was asked where he wanted to live. My lords, the boy was adamant. The O'Leary family were the best in the world. The state will continue to supervise his growth and development. It will ensure that he receives an education but it is apparent to all that Millar is happy where he is.

'I'd never had a room to call my own until I went to live with Brian and his mammy. Never had a place to put my things. And Mammy knew I wasn't stupid. She knew I couldn't see properly. She got me glasses, like these,' he pointed. 'And a case to keep them in so they wouldn't get broken. I never had anything to call my own until Mammy bought me things.' He sat down again. 'Shopping, she took me shopping, everything new. Everything clean and sweet smelling. A big pile of clothes. Now, she said, get something extra, something for yourself, Martin. There was a belt, stripy elastic with a snake for a buckle. I picked it up. She took it from me. She had this big old coat, big deep pockets. She slipped it into the pocket. Special, she said, that'll be your lucky charm, and she winked.'

He stood up and walked over to McLoughlin. He squatted beside him. He took McLoughlin's face between his two hands. He winked.

'She died you know, five years ago. And you know something, you fuckers wouldn't let her son out of prison to go to her funeral. And for that you will be punished.'

McLoughlin tried to close his eyes, but Millar had hold of his eyelids. 'I'd blind you now, you bastard, but I want you to be able to see what I'm going to do to you.' He stood up. He walked slowly away, then he turned. McLoughlin tensed, waiting for the blow. He heard the creak of the chair as Millar sat down again.

'No rush, no rush at all. A nice Sunday like this. A nice place this square. I'd like to live in a nice place like this.' Millar blew his nose. 'Lovely neighbours you have. The old lady across the road. She loves her flowers. She loves her sweet pea. Like my poor old gran. She had lovely sweet pea. The only thing she cared about. She didn't care about me, that's for sure. And as for the judge, well, he took the biscuit, didn't he?'

McLoughlin tried to move. His feet were numb, pins and needles in his legs. Millar stood up, stood over him, and touched his cheek with the toe of his boot. The toe of his boot so close McLoughlin could smell the polish.

'Funny about the judge. I didn't set out to kill him. I just wanted to have a bit of fun, brighten up Brian's day. Sundays are bad in prison. A slow day, a long day, sure you'd go to Mass for the entertainment. Yes, that's it,' he pressed his foot down hard on McLoughlin's cheek, 'that idiot, Eddie fucking Smith, thought he could take me for a ride.'

The pressure increased. The pain spread across McLoughlin's face. He felt as if he was going to vomit.

'Then his daddy came up with the goods. I nearly split my sides laughing when he gave me a peek at the photos.'

'So,' McLoughlin was trying to speak, 'so why did you shoot him?'

'Oh he can speak can he? We'll have to do something about that.' He lifted his foot and aimed it at McLoughlin's throat. 'But maybe not yet. Maybe not until he's done a bit of begging. Like the judge.' He moved away again. 'Begging he was good-o, like that nasty little mutt of his.' He walked around the room, pacing, his stride long and loose. Then he stopped and looked out the window.

'Do you know anything about shame, Mr McLoughlin? Shame is the worst. Worse than grief, worse than loss, worse than hunger and thirst.'

He sat down on one of the garden chairs, balancing carefully. McLoughin tried to twist around.

'Don't,' Millar's voice was a whisper. 'Don't look at me.' Silence. 'There was a man once, when I was a little boy. I never saw him. They'd blindfold me. I only once heard him speak. Usually it was just grunts and groans and sobs. But once he sang a song. He was happy. He'd got his way. And he sang a song.'

McLoughlin tried to move. He felt sick.

'"She Moved through the Fair", that was it. That day, here, with the judge. He sat down at his piano. He was all polite. I told him the money was going up. He wouldn't be dealing with Smith any longer, he'd be dealing with me. And Brian. He said it was too much. He couldn't afford it. I said he could sell something. He could sell his piano. He said he couldn't do that. And he started to play and sing. That song.' He took a deep breath. '*My young love said to me, my mother won't mind, and my father won't slight you for your lack of kine.*' Millar's voice was a high falsetto. 'Singing away, without a care in the world. And the shame came over me and I could feel him and smell him and taste him.'

He got to his feet. Pacing again.

'And then, the uppity fucker started mouthing off about Brian, how he was scum, how back in his father's day people like Brian would have been shot, got rid of. So now it was begging time except it was him who was begging, not me. And then I thought, I'll really get him to shit himself, so I got the gun, the famous gun and I loaded it, one bullet, from the box in the drawer.' He mimed cocking the pistol, his finger curling around the trigger. 'Give him a fright. I thought I'd give him a fright, but boom. And that my friend was that.'

He sat back on the chair, folding his arms. 'Brian always says that those who inflict it have to be able to endure it.' He paused and looked up at the ceiling. 'And then he says: but to be honest I'd rather inflict it than endure it.'

This time the kick was in McLoughlin's back, right up against his kidneys. Again the pain radiated out, spreading like a dark stain up and down, as far as his head, as far as his feet, so he cried out, feeling tears on his cheeks. Sick so he began to retch, a bitterness in his throat, a dribble of foul smelling spit, rolling down his chin. And then darkness again.

Time passing. How much time? He had no idea how long it had been until the light forced itself back into his eyes. He blinked and tried to move. He tried to think. Where was his phone? He seemed to remember leaving it in the kitchen. And Ferdie? In the garden, he thought. Asleep in the long grass, the ball between his front paws.

He couldn't see where Millar was. There was no sound now. It was quiet. He lay still, trying to assess his injuries. He was pretty certain his jaw was broken, maybe his nose too. His right ankle throbbed. Probably fractured. He wouldn't know until he put weight on it. He didn't think the blows to his kidneys were too serious. He didn't know about the kick to his genitals. He was still in pain but it wasn't as excruciating as it had been. He tried to lift his head and look around. He couldn't see Millar. Perhaps he had gone, had his fun, had his fill, done the sensible thing and left. He tried to lift himself up a bit more but this time the blows came hard and fast. A kick from behind and he could feel one rib at least and maybe more breaking. Patrick Brady, the boy in the bog, was this what he went through, was this what he felt?

And then a sound from outside the room, a voice calling.

'Michael are you there?'

And Millar's hand clamped over his mouth.

Footsteps on the stairs and the rattle of the dog's claws.

'Michael, you up there?' The door bursting open. And Millar on his feet. And before Elizabeth could turn and run he had butted her in the face, so she screamed and fell to her knees, blood pouring from her nose. And the dog, barking, snarling, his lips pulled back over his teeth, his legs braced, his coat standing up along the ridge of his spine. The smell, the smell of the man in the room. He snarled and walked stiffly, slowly towards the man as Elizabeth sobbed and McLoughlin tried to push himself up.

'Here, doggie, good doggie,' Millar bent down and held out one hand, the other hand behind his back. Ferdie stood his ground, then took one step and another step and another. And Millar grabbed him by the scruff, a knife held to the dog's neck.

'Noisy little fucker aren't you? I hate noisy, yappy little dogs like you. I like my dogs big and strong and bold with great big teeth. All the better to eat you with, my dear.' And the knife suddenly slicing across Ferdie's throat, a terrible gurgling sound and blood pumping out, as Millar held the dog away from him, then flung him wide, blood spattering, against the far wall.

Silence then. Elizabeth sat, terror in her face, her hands shaking. Until Millar grabbed her, twisting her arms behind her back and fastening her wrists so she cried out again in pain.

'Now, two for the price of one.' He shoved her down on the floor and grabbed her ankles, tying them together too. He sat up on the chair, bracing his feet. 'Isn't this grand now. Quite a gathering.' He looked over at the dog's body. 'Awful mess. A job to clean it up. Make things nice again. Homely. That's what we want isn't it? But,' he buried his face in his hands, 'we have no home now, not since you killed Brian.'

He got up. 'What will I do to her, Mr McLoughlin? What will I do? You decide.' He bent over Elizabeth and took hold of her by the hair. He touched her chin with the toe of his boot. 'A bit old for you, Mr McLoughlin? No spring chicken, is she?'

'Don't,' McLoughlin tried to speak. He could barely move his jaw. 'Don't hurt her. This has nothing to do with her. Let her go.'

Millar got up. He looked down at Elizabeth. 'Not my type I'm afraid. I'm a gentleman, I prefer blondes. Like your niece, Constance. A natural blonde I suspect, from head to toe.' He walked back towards Elizabeth. She was shaking, trembling so much that her teeth were chattering. Millar lay down on the floor beside her. He put his face up close to hers. He stroked her cheeks, gently, then took hold of her chin.

'Look at me. What's your name?'

'Elizabeth,' her voice was a whisper.

'Nice name, I like that. Old fashioned. Constance is a nice name too.' He twisted her face towards his. 'Look at me, open your eyes. There now, that's better, nice brown eyes. I like brown eyes.'

McLoughlin tried to speak again. 'Don't hurt her. Let her go. Please.'

'Please, that's better, that's nicer. I like that. A bit of gratitude goes a long way. Please Mr Millar, don't hurt the nice lady.' He pushed her away. He lay on his back. 'Constance, there's a nice girl, a pretty girl, a helpful girl. You know, Mr McLoughlin,' he rolled over on his side, 'Constance will help me. She's believes in justice. Now,' he sat up. 'Enough of this small talk. Time for a bit of serious punishment.' He stood. He pulled a cigarette lighter from his pocket. He flicked the lid. McLoughlin could smell the burning fuel. 'Who wants to go first? Ladies perhaps? Age before beauty? Dirt before the brush.'

Silence for a moment. McLoughlin could hear Elizabeth stirring and the sound of her teeth chattering. And then footsteps, slow, careful, footsteps on the stairs outside, the squeak of the floorboards. And a figure standing in the doorway. The familiar outline. The wide-brimmed hat, the sagging shoulders, the long tweed coat, the Tesco shopping bag held by the gloved hand.

'Well, well, well, who do we have here?' Millar's voice loud and threatening. McLoughlin saw him move quickly towards the door. He heard the footsteps, Samuel Dudgeon's footsteps as he walked further into the room. He tried to look up so he could see more clearly but the pain in his ribs was intense and he gasped and collapsed back down. He tried to imagine what Samuel was seeing. The dog, gutted, lying in a bloody heap by the wall. Elizabeth bound, blood on her face, shaking with fear. McLoughlin, trussed up, his face a mess, with bruises, black eyes, more blood. And Martin Millar, capering, dancing, blood too on his shirt and on his hands.

'I think I know who you are,' Millar rushed up towards Samuel and stopped arms lengths away from him. 'You're a mate of the old lady, aren't you?'

He took Samuel by the hand and began to pull him into the room. 'Come on in,' his voice was friendly, cajoling. 'Come on in and join our little party. The more the merrier, that's what I say.'

McLoughlin wanted to cry out, wanted to tell Samuel to turn and run, as fast as he possibly could, as fast as his legs would carry him, down the stairs into the kitchen, out onto the deck, down the steps, into the garden, through the wooden gate into the judge's house, or even better, through the front door, out into the square, shouting, calling for help. Help, help, help, help me please.

But Samuel did nothing. He allowed himself to be drawn in. Allowed himself to be placed on the garden chair, holding the bag with both hands. As Millar took out his cigarette lighter again.

'Now,' he stood over Samuel, 'what have we here,' and he reached towards the shopping bag. Samuel pulled away, then pulled out his backgammon set. He held it up.

'Very nice,' Millar took it from him, sinking down on the floor and opening it out. 'Beautiful piece of work. I never learned how to play.' He picked up some of the pieces, handling them gently, and then the large doubling cube. 'This now, this is interesting.' He turned it over in his hand. 'Two, four, eight, sixteen, thirty-two, sixty-four. Now,' he threw it across the board. It landed with the number two upwards.

'Where were we?' He stood and walked past McLoughlin, kicking him, a savage flick into his knee cap. Elizabeth whimpered and shrank away. Millar turned and squatted beside her, holding the lighter close to her face. The smell of hair, burning, and she cried out.

'Once,' he moved the lighter towards her face, 'twice.'

Elizabeth screamed. Millar moved the flame and ran it down her forearm. Elizabeth screamed again and collapsed on the floor.

'Now,' Millar picked up the dice and again he threw it. This time it landed with the number eight showing. And McLoughlin saw, from the corner of his eye, a dark shape standing, his arms raised, the shape of the coat like the shape of a bat. Something in his hand, which shone in the light from the window and suddenly then, coming down, hard, with force, down, down, down. Slicing into Millar's face, slicing through his forehead, his left eyebrow, knocking his glasses out of the way as he sliced across his eye and sinking deep into his cheekbone. So it was Millar now who screamed in agony, standing, turning towards Samuel, who before Millar could reach him had drawn back his arm and with a speed and a force which was unexpected, jammed the chisel deep into Millar's stomach.

'You fucker,' the words bursting from Millar's mouth as he lunged for Samuel, who again with surprising speed and agility, stepped sideways, turned, the chisel in one hand, the shopping bag in the other and began to run, towards the door, towards the landing, towards the stairs. And Millar after him, but slowing now, blood dripping from the gash in his stomach, slowing and as he reached the stairs, falling, falling, falling forward, the sound of his body hitting the floor, a scream and then silence.

Silence, then the sound of footsteps on the stairs. The squeak of the floorboard, the persistent squeak and McLoughlin thinking, before the builders leave I must get them to look at that. It's very irritating. And Samuel in the doorway, the chisel bloody in one hand and the bag in the other. He put them down and walked towards Elizabeth. He knelt beside her. He touched her face, then loosed her wrists and her ankles. He stood and walked to McLoughlin. He knelt behind him. McLoughlin could feel the jerks as he pulled at the ties. He heard Samuel move away. Tried to turn to look after him. Heard him going downstairs. Heard the front door open, then close.

McLoughlin pushed himself to sitting.

Phone, he mouthed to Elizabeth. Phone. She nodded, and felt in her trouser pocket. He watched as she pressed the buttons.

'Please,' her voice was trembling. 'Please come, guards, ambulance. We've been hurt. Attacked. Come quickly.' Spelling out the address.

McLoughlin moved. Pain everywhere, his face, his broken ribs, his ankle, a pain deep inside. He coughed. Blood in his mouth. He crawled towards the door. Slowly, painfully, onto the landing. Millar was lying head first near the bottom of the stairs. McLoughlin couldn't see. Was he alive? Dead? Conscious? Unconscious? He propped himself against the banisters. And saw Millar's face and his eyes, wide open. One a bloody mess where the chisel had sliced through it; the other filled with tears. And as McLoughlin shrank back Millar tried to turn, to push himself up, blood soaking his shirt. And then the bang on the front door, the sound of the lock splintering, and a voice shouting, 'Gardaí.'

Samuel walked slowly along the road. He was tired. He wasn't sure what had happened. He had gone to the door. He had rung the bell. He had waited. He had pushed the door and it opened. He walked in. He knew this place. It smelt right. But Elizabeth wasn't to be seen. And then he heard, something, what was it? Something which drew him out into the garden, up the steps, into the house, one step in front of the other.

He wasn't sure where he was going, but his feet seemed to know the way. One step after the other. He held the photographs in his hand. He dropped one. He counted his paces. When he got to twenty he dropped another. When he got to forty he dropped another. He walked along the road in the sunshine. Everywhere people, eating ice creams, with their children, holding hands, smiling, happy. And the man with the wide-brimmed hat, the heavy tweed coat and the trail of photographs, behind him.

McLoughlin waited for the vaporetto at the San Marco stop on the Grand Canal. Fifteen minutes later he was in the railway station. He scanned the departures screen, bought his ticket, found the *binario*, climbed on board the train, closed his eyes and tried to doze. Unsuccessfully. He watched the flat countryside rolling past. It was December, the fields empty now, the harvest in, the land waiting for the plough. And the sign on the station as they slowed, then stopped: Bassano del Grappa. The mountains above swathed in heavy mist and a chill in the air. He checked his bag into a left luggage locker, buttoned his coat tightly and put on his gloves as he walked through the town. Along the road called Viale dei Martiri, underneath the trees, each one with a photograph of the partisan who once had hung from it. Down through the squares, down to the river which foamed as it rushed through the valley beneath the wooden bridge. Where now he stopped, leaned over the railings and looked down. A long way below the river roiled, the colour changing as it crashed over the rocks. Glassy brown, glossy black, ominous ochre, the crests of the small waves gleaming white. The sound from the river was a low, sullen roar. He leaned over and watched, then straightened and looked around. The bridge was busy today. Saturday, market day. Shoppers, locals, not visitors. A different feel to the place in the middle of winter. A small-town feel, the tourists all gone home, the tourist menus, the lasagne, carbonara, bolognese, put away until spring.

He leaned with his back to the railings and watched the people as they came and went. It was cold, a brisk wind ruffling his hair and making his nose run. He took a handkerchief from his pocket and wiped it. Then he turned and began to walk, slowly, deliberately, across the bridge.

It was afternoon. The light was beginning to slip away. He hunched into his coat. The area on the far side of the bridge was familiar. He could see the café with the museum on one side of the road. But he turned, heading down along the river's embankment. A low stone wall ran beside the footpath. There was a sense of dereliction, abandonment. A few warehouses, old buildings, closed and shuttered. No one around, hardly any traffic. But still the river, the water at this level appearing colder and greener.

He stopped and leaned over the wall. The ground dropped steeply. The summer growth had died back. A few hardy perennials clung to the bank. Something which looked like thyme or sage perhaps. Nothing much else that he could recognise. Nothing that looked substantial enough to grasp. And the wall, crumbling here, the capping stones loose, the mortar dead. As he leaned over a stone became dislodged. It began to roll, slowly at first, down the steep slope, then picking up speed and bouncing from rock to rock towards the water's edge. It disappeared with an inaudible splash. Just the faintest puff of spray as it broke the surface.

McLoughlin moved away. He pulled out his phone. A text message from Elizabeth. She was at a conference in London. Psychotherapy in the twenty-first century. He had insisted she go. He would be fine without her and it would be good for her too. Her hands no longer shook, she had begun to sleep again and the scar on her forearm was fading. He read her message. *All well here. Hope you OK. Lots of love.*

He tapped out his reply. *Love you too. I'll call later. Xxx.* Then he turned from the river and walked quickly back up the road towards the main street. His injuries were improving. His ribs and ankle had healed. His jaw had been wired for weeks and when the wire came off the work had begun on his teeth. They didn't look bad now. Kidneys and other internal organs were fine. Only his head from time to time caused problems. And he missed Ferdie. Sometimes he thought he could hear the rattle of the dog's claws on the floorboards. He still expected him to burst open the sitting room door. His tail wagging, and giving voice to little whines of pleasure.

As he reached the main road he saw the Museo degli Alpini, then just past it, the turn to right and the Shamrock Bar, the same dancing girls, dressed in green, thatched cottages and donkeys and carts decorating the windows. He pushed through the door, his footsteps loud on the wooden floor. The woman was behind the bar, her back to him, and she turned, a professional smile on her attractive face, her makeup immaculate, lips red, teeth white, eye lashes long and luxuriant. As she recognised her customer, her smile died. She reached beneath the counter. He looked above her head and saw the camera. He waved, a broad grin, showing his teeth, then winked, and looked back at her.

'*Buon giorno, signora.*' His voice was loud.

She didn't reply.

'*Come stai?*'

Again no reply.

'Would you prefer it in Irish? How about, *dia dhuit?*' He could hear footsteps. The door behind the bar opened. James Reynolds came in. He didn't look well. He had lost weight. His face was thin and haggard. He needed to shave.

'Well, what do we have here?' McLoughlin shifted from one foot to the other. 'Are you not going to offer me a drink? A cup of tea, or maybe a glass of whiskey? Last time you were so friendly, you couldn't do enough.'

The woman's face was without expression. She took a step towards him. 'Get out. We don't want your kind here.'

'It's all right, Monica, I'll deal with this.' Reynolds put his hand on her arm and pushed her back.

'Monica, of course,' McLoughlin smiled. 'Monica Di Spina, from the famous family. Who'd have thought, the two of you, a marriage made, well,' he moved forward and rested both his hands on the countertop, 'made somewhere.'

'What do you want?' Monica's voice was calm and cool.

'Nothing from you. Although,' McLoughlin remembered what Harris had told him. The injuries inflicted on Theresa Ryan and her son. The cat, slit from chin to tail. 'Well, I'd be interested to know...' his voice trailed away.

'To know?' She moved again, this time closer to her husband.

'The Ryans,' he swallowed hard.

'Look,' Reynolds held out his hands in a gesture of supplication. 'Look,' he repeated the words, 'we've nothing to say about that or anything else.' He lifted the countertop. McLoughlin began to back away, then stopped. He would not allow himself to be intimidated.

'No? I wonder why.' McLoughlin could feel his heart beginning to race. 'You don't want to talk about that, but I want to talk to you about my father.' At last he had said it. 'Come for a walk with me, indulge me. I've been waiting a long time for this. Truth and reconciliation, isn't that what you call it?'

Reynolds looked at his wife. She shook her head. He walked to the coat rack behind the door and took a scarf and leather jacket from it. He put them on. McLoughlin could see the way he patted the pockets.

'I won't be long.' He leaned back over the counter and kissed her on both cheeks.

And together McLoughlin and Reynolds walked out into the cold November afternoon.

He got home to Dublin on Sunday afternoon. Home in time to have a bit of a sleep, then cook dinner for Elizabeth. She'd be arriving around six in the evening. He'd meet her off the air coach in the town. They'd walk to his house together. And together they'd eat in his beautiful new kitchen. She'd got used to his house at last. She still didn't like being there on her own, but time was exorcising the ghosts of that terrible afternoon. He knew that she could still see Martin Millar in the big room upstairs. And the body of the dog, his mouth and eyes open. Even though McLoughlin had ripped up the floorboards, replaced them with clean, unblemished wood. Painted the walls so there wasn't the slightest hint of blood anywhere. Bright colours, yellows and greens. Cheerful colours which banished all thoughts of darkness. But still, she liked to go home to sleep in her own bed, within her own walls. And he didn't mind. As long as she was happy that he would come with her.

He put a chicken in the oven to roast with seasonal root vegetables. Turnips, parsnips, red onions, some butternut squash and a couple of beetroot. He peeled potatoes for mash, made the way his mother had taught him, with an onion chopped through and plenty of salt, butter and milk. It was nearly time to go. He opened a bottle of red wine, the kind that Elizabeth liked, then switched on the TV to get the early evening news. And saw a familiar face. He sat down on the sofa to watch. He listened to the words of the newsreader.

'Italian police are investigating the death of a former IRA member in the town of Bassano del Grappa, in the Veneto region north of Venice.'

The report showed places he recognised. The Viale dei Martiri.

'According to local sources, the man's body was found around midnight last night. He was hanging from a tree. This particular area is known for an atrocity which took place during the Second World War when German troops hanged a number of partisans from these same trees. The man's body was identified by his wife. His identity has not been officially confirmed but local sources have stated that he is James Reynolds, who was suspected to have been involved in the murder of Garda Joe McLoughlin in 1975. Sinn Féin have, so far, made no comment.'

McLoughlin got up. He put on his coat, picked up his scarf, his keys, his phone, his wallet. He let himself out of the house, locking the door. He walked slowly down the steps. It was cold now. The sky was clear, the stars bright. The Plough hung low. It had hung low over Bassano yesterday evening as he and James Reynolds left the Shamrock Bar. They walked up the narrow street and stopped outside the little museum. Reynolds looked through the door, then moved away. 'We'll go somewhere else, I think.'

They crossed the road, heading towards the bridge. Bright lights shone from a modern facade. Reynolds pushed the door open. He gestured, 'Come in, have a drink with me, why don't you?'

Music was playing loudly from a jukebox. The walls were decorated with stills from American movies. Audrey Hepburn in *Breakfast at Tiffany's*, Debbie Reynolds from *Calamity Jane*, James Dean in *Rebel Without a Cause*. They sat a small table covered with a red and white checked cloth. Reynolds ordered grappa. The barman chatted with him. Reynold's Italian was fluent and effortless. They drank.

'I knew you of course, that day. I recognised you immediately.' Reynolds wiped his mouth with the back of his hand. 'When I went back into the bar I checked the CCTV. I could see the look on your face when Monica showed you the photograph.'

'I wasn't sure.' McLoughlin drained his glass and gestured to the barman for a refill.

'I thought there'd be trouble. I didn't think you'd walk away. All the rest of that day I was waiting for you to come back. I went out to look for you. I asked in the railway station. I know most of the guys who work there. They'd seen you arrive and they saw you leave.' Reynolds drummed his fingers on the table top. 'Something about you. One of them asked, friend, enemy which is it?'

The barman cleared away the empty glasses. Reynolds looked up at him and smiled. The man muttered something in Italian. Reynolds shook his head, put his hand on the man's arm.

'What's he saying?' McLoughlin watched the barman, the deliberate way he walked back behind the bar, poured more grappa.

'Nothing much, just asking where you're from. I told him, *in patria*, from home.'

The barman came back to the table. A tray in one hand with the glasses and a couple of dishes of salted almonds and some olives, black and green. He slowly, carefully laid them out on the table. Again a muttered exchange.

Reynolds picked up his glass. He gestured to McLoughlin to help himself. 'I heard about the funeral. I could understand your anger. How you felt about me and what had happened.'

McLoughlin looked at the dish of olives. He felt sick. 'Why didn't you come back then? You say you understand how I feel. Well if you do, then you could do something about it.'

Reynolds sipped then looked towards the bar. 'It's not that easy. Not now. Monica and me, we're in deep. We got ourselves mixed up in all kinds of shit. Dirty money in, clean money out. It's a long, long way from the boys of the old brigade.' He looked away again. 'Monica has a lot of, what you could call, contacts. They're very valuable. To a lot of people. And when you're in, you stay in. You've no choice in the matter.'

'People?'

Reynolds swung back in his chair. He gazed around the room. The barman was polishing glasses. Ostentatiously.

'The kind that haven't gone away.' Reynolds picked up his glass. It jerked slightly and a few drops of liquid fell onto the table. He drank. McLoughlin watched him. He could do it, he was sure he could do it. He had done it to Paul Smith. The element of surprise. He could do it now. Reynolds put down the glass. One hand disappeared beneath the table. He fumbled in his pocket. McLoughlin tensed. A paper napkin. Green with the words The Shamrock Bar in orange printed across it. He wiped his mouth.

'*Adriana, per favore, una birra.*' His voice suddenly loud. 'Beer, would you like a beer?' McLoughlin nodded. '*Due, Adriana, grazie.*' He fiddled with the napkin, pleating it, then smoothing it out. 'Big business, Europe-wide. Making a fortune. Cigarettes, girls, dope, harder stuff too. You name it. They're a talented bunch. Turn their hand to anything.'

'And you, what have you turned your hand to?'

The beers came in tall glasses, white heads which reminded McLoughlin of the ice creams he had eaten with Elizabeth and Leah, that hot day in the square.

'You wouldn't want to know. No one would want to know.'

Reynolds lifted his glass and drank. He wiped his mouth with the back of his hand. He looked away. The music was suddenly loud. Doris Day singing. The Deadwood stage was rolling on over the plains.

'And the Ryans, Theresa and her son?'

Reynolds looked away. He looked down at the napkin. 'I didn't want Monica to go. I told her we could fight it here. Through the courts.' He laughed, a mirthless sound. 'Onto a loser. It'd be lifting a lid you see. Questions would be asked for which there are no answers.' He picked up his glass and took a long swallow. He put it down and wiped his mouth again. 'Not just about your father and what happened that day. It would go deeper. Monica said no. Nip it in the bud. Dead meat, she said. From the moment you walked into the bar last summer. Dead meat, that's what they were.'

The barman was hovering. McLoughlin drank his beer. It was strong, a rich yeasty flavour.

'A risk, surely, for her to go to Ireland like that.'

Reynolds smiled. 'Monica's good at risks. She thrives on them. She grew up in that kind of world. Her father was on the run for years. She knows all about watching your back.' He looked down at the table. He spread out his hands. His fingernails were bitten to the quick.

'And what about doing the right thing? What does she know about that?' McLoughlin fiddled with his glass.

Reynolds looked away. 'Depends, doesn't it? Your definition, what the right thing is.'

'So, we're back to ends and means?'

Reynolds didn't answer. He picked up his glass and drained it. He raised his hand. The barman moved slowly back towards the row of bottles and line of shiny chrome pumps.

McLoughlin drank again. 'Your son, she wasn't worried about what might happen to him?'

'My son?' Reynolds looked at him. 'I don't have a son. We don't have a son.'

'No?' McLoughlin ran his fingers up and down the sides of the tall glass. 'She told me, your son, studying in Rome. She was very clear about him.'

Reynolds smiled. 'Monica can't have children. A car crash when she was a teenager. She had to have her womb removed.'

'Oh, I see.'

'You don't really.' The barman placed a full glass in front of Reynolds. His hand rested on his shoulder for a moment. McLoughlin could see how his fingers squeezed hard. Reynolds shifted awkwardly. The barman moved back, just enough. 'You don't see at all.' Reynolds' voice was high-pitched now. 'It happened when she was on the run with her father. She's never forgiven the state for that. She takes it all very personally, very, very personally.' He paused, looked down. 'This son, sometimes it's a daughter. Sometimes I hear her in the bar, she's chatting away. She has the whole scenario, school, college, boyfriend, girlfriend. Sometimes she even has grandchildren.'

'So,' McLoughlin looked at him, 'I should feel sorry for her now. Sorry that her crazy father and his crazy politics ruined her life, is that it?'

Reynolds didn't answer.

'So easy for you. Always someone else to blame. The state, the police, the politicians, the system. Always someone else.' McLoughlin drank. The beer caught in his throat. He coughed. 'And what about you? Your legacy. The dead. The maimed. The lives wrecked. The hate and bitterness left behind, was it worth it?'

Reynolds picked up his glass. He finished it off with a flourish. He wiped his mouth again.

'Worth it? Worth killing your father? Now there's a question. I see them in Stormont. Doing business with the DUP, that bunch of bigots. I see them in the twenty-six counties, sitting in the Dáil. I hear their speeches. The opinion polls, they're gaining strength all the time. I ask myself, was it worth it? What'll they be in a few years' time? Part of some crappy coalition, shaving cents off the old age pension, bickering over trolleys in A&E and water charges, for fuck's sake. Was it worth it?'

McLoughlin swirled the beer in his glass. Theresa Ryan, sitting in her conservatory, the cat on her knee, the sun hot, the sky blue. Theresa Ryan, dead on the mortuary slab. A bullet through the back of the head, her body marked with the signs of torture. Her son beside her. The cat, slit from chin to tail. What was it she said? A bit of power here, a bit of power there. Not what we fought for. Not what we died for. And not what we killed for.

Reynolds stood. The barman picked up the cloth and began again to polish the gleaming glasses. Reynold pushed his chair towards the table. It grated on the tiled floor. 'I dream about that day, the day I killed your father. He comes closer and closer. He's smiling. He looks happy. In my dream I see that. On the day I didn't. I didn't see anyone. I saw nothing except the uniform. I lifted the gun. I fired. I didn't see anything after that. I didn't care. Now,' he moved towards the door, 'I think it's time.'

They stood in the street side by side. It was quiet, cold, dark. McLoughlin moved towards the bridge. He could hear the river below. He put out his hand and touched the wall. He tensed. The footpath was narrow. He pushed against Reynolds. The river below, the steep drop, rocks beneath. He could do it, he knew he could. Reynolds turned towards him. His face was shadowed.

'Why did you come here?'

'Why do you think?' McLoughlin could feel sweat on his back.

Reynolds stepped into the light. 'You should know, I'm sorry about what I did. I'm sorry about a lot of things.'

'You want forgiveness, is that it?'

Reynolds shook his head. 'There's no forgiveness for people like me. We have to live with our sins.' He closed his eyes. 'I see them all. The people I killed. They share my life. When I wake, when I sleep, when I dream. There's no escape. Monica doesn't understand. She sees nothing. Except her child that never was.'

He turned away. His pace was calm, unhurried. McLoughlin followed him. Together they walked, side by side. Up through the town, towards the station. When they reached the row of trees, Reynolds stopped.

'Look,' he pointed to the photographs attached to the trunks. 'These men were brave. They stood up against tyranny and oppression. They had no choice. There was nothing else they could do.' He walked from tree to tree. He read out the names. 'Puglierin Fiorenzo, 29th

September 1944. Cervellin Giovanni, 29th September 1944, Cocco Pietro, 29th September 1944. And this one, this is sad,' he pointed again, 'Ignoto, unknown. Same date, day, month, year.' He rested his hand for a moment. 'Important, isn't it, to have a memorial. To be remembered. I wonder sometimes,' he moved ahead, then looked back, 'what will I be remembered for? How will I be remembered? Who will remember me?'

McLoughlin walked away, towards the station. He looked over his shoulder. Reynolds was standing still, staring after him. Then he too turned and when McLoughlin looked again he was nowhere to be seen.

Now he waited at the stop for the air coach. He felt empty. As the bus turned into the main street he could see Elizabeth. She was standing up, reaching for her bag. She saw him through the windows and waved. The doors opened with a loud hiss. He moved forward. He held out his arms. She stepped into them. He held her tightly. Her voice was in his ear.

'I heard the news. It's over now. It's all over now.'

Acknowledgements

My thanks to:

Gay Johnson, Kordula Packard, Renate Ahrens-Kramer, Phil MacCarthy, Cecilia McGovern, Sheila Barrett, Harriet Parsons, Sarah Caden, Renée English, Eithne Henson and Simon Parsons who read various versions of the novel and gave me their comments and support.

Paul Bowler and the late David Lane for their extensive knowledge of guns and all that goes with them.

Michael Ryan for his help with the legal aspects of the story.

Cora Newman for her suggestions for music for the judge's funeral.

Paula O'Riordan and Thomond Coogan for their help with the Irish translations.

Dan Bolger and all at New Island Books who have given me the opportunity to bring life to the people of Victoria Square.

My husband, John Caden, who never wavered in his belief in the book and in me.